Danna found he... eyes. It wasn't l... equilibrium, but... strikingly haunting about the way he looked; strong and uncompromising, as powerful as a tiger. She sensed that when he approached a woman, he'd move just as confidently, circling his prey, playing with her emotions until he pounced with a sensual precision that would leave her helpless to resist. He had that power about him, the power to entice—to seduce.

Danna didn't have any misgivings about her ability to represent the League. Diplomatic manners aside, she was a tough-minded lady when it came to doing her job. Unfortunately, that determination didn't neutralize her curiosity—a purely feminine inquisitiveness that had her wondering what it would be like to be held in the Korcian's strong arms. . . .

True Blood

patricia waddell

tor romance

A TOM DOHERTY ASSOCIATES BOOK
NEW YORK

This is a work of fiction. All the characters and events portrayed in this book are either products of the author's imagination or are used fictitiously.

TRUE BLOOD

Edited by Anna Genoese

A Tor Book
Published by Tom Doherty Associates, LLC
175 Fifth Avenue
New York, NY 10010

www.tor.com

Tor® is a registered trademark of Tom Doherty Associates, LLC.

ISBN-13: 978-0-765-35464-8
ISBN-10: 0-765-35464-0

First edition: September 2006

Printed in the United States of America

0 9 8 7 6 5 4 3 2 1

This book is dedicated to
Karen Wilson.
She knows all the reasons why.

True Blood

One

To diplomatically negate a call to arms the mediator needed the cooperation of the parties ready to blast each other to smithereens. All Danna MacFadyen had was a casualty list with 46 names on it.

There had been an *incident* in League territory.

General Tutunjan, Commander of the Korcian Guard, had issued an ultimatum: deliver the perpetrators or else.

It was the "or else" Danna was supposed to prevent. A war between the League of Planets and the Korcian Empire would, by sake of treaties and trade agreements, involve the entire galaxy.

"Tutunjan isn't going to take his teeth out of this one until the execution needles are empty."

The remark came from Earth, out of the experienced mouth of Danna's friend and mentor, Senior Ambassador Matthew Gideon. Both were members of the Diplomatic Corps, but Danna was closer to the hot zone. If the situation went up in flames, her ass would be the one to get burned.

"So when do I get into the game?" Danna asked. It

was the first serious assignment she'd been given since joining Ramora's embassy staff.

"As soon as Ambassador Synon announces the name of the neutral investigator. You know the drill."

The drill was a team of three investigators; one on the offensive, one of the defensive, and one to play referee. This was the first time Danna had been put on the defensive.

"What can you tell me?" she asked.

"Not much," Gideon's voice came again. "It was a routine hop from Ramora to Earth. No distress calls, just a big bang smack in the middle of League space. The interstellar drive could have gone nuts, or someone could have done exactly what Tutunjan is accusing them of doing. It doesn't take a lot of imagination to put a high frequency detonator in a cargo bay."

"Do you think it was sabotage?"

"Terrorism or tragedy? It's too early to say. I've got a team working on all the possibilities. As soon as the evidence seals are removed, get your hands on something. Anything. We need facts, not speculation."

Danna didn't like using her psychometric skills unless it was absolutely necessary. Emotions had no geographical boundaries. The energy created in one person's mind could move across time and space to appear in the mind of another. It could also leave its imprint on an object.

Danna could read that imprint, learn the history of an object by touching it, and sometimes, if the imprint was strong enough, she could venture beyond the object in her hand.

The first time she'd picked up something and found herself stepping into a dreamscape, she'd been terrified. She could still remember the frightening clarity of that moment, still feel the suffocating sense of being locked inside another person's world, inside another person's mind. Now, she knew that every emotion had its own color; red and gold and blue, white and a hundred shades of gray, passion and love, greed and envy, despair and hope.

She'd seen them all. Felt them all.

"I'll do my best." It was all she could say. Diplomacy didn't come with guarantees. Neither did her psychic ability. "What happens if I get a *reading* and it points in the wrong direction?"

"You're there, I'm here. It's your call."

"I love you, too," Danna cooed just before the transmission, boosted by half a dozen satellites between Earth and Ramora, went dead.

She had just enough time to finish the herbal tea she'd brewed in an old-fashioned pot, the only way to do it if you wanted more than steamy water with artificial flavoring, when the commlink buzzed again.

"Officer MacFadyen, Ambassador Synon requests your presence in the conference room."

Show time.

"I'll be right there." Danna returned the empty teacup to the kitchen, disliking the slight trembling of her hand as she put it into the sanitizing unit.

What did she have to be nervous about? Just a galactic confrontation between the two most powerful governments in the universe, which happened to be her first big chance to do more than smile at diplomatic cocktail parties. Nothing major.

Leaving the tiny kitchen, she paused to appraise herself in the decorative mirror on the wall of the main living area. Appearances were as important as words in the negotiation game. You needed to look like you had all the answers, even if you didn't have a clue.

Her attire was in good taste, bringing the overall effect of her physical appearance to an impressive, but not overdone, level. The calf-length flare of the silk jacket she'd matched to a pair of wide-legged slacks was attractive, lessening the severity of its basic dark blue color. The only official designation she wore was a small League badge on her lapel.

Wishing wisdom was something you could download and assimilate in a matter of moments, Danna reminded herself that success came in small steps. The first thing on the agenda was to defuse the situation. That meant pouring coolant on General Tutunjan's militant attitude.

Her embassy quarters faced an inner courtyard. Stepping outside, Danna took a moment to appreciate a near perfect evening. The final shadows of twilight had given way to a pure dark night. Ramora had six moons, three large and glowing like silver coins, another three so small they technically qualified as orbiting asteroids. Whatever the classification, they added a distinct beauty to the night sky.

Despite the urgency of the situation, Danna took a moment to think about home. She smiled at the memory of what she'd left behind when she'd accepted the job on Ramora's embassy staff. She missed the sounds of Earth the most; the roar of the Atlantic Ocean as it rushed onto the beach in front of her family's home, the shriek of hungry gulls circling overhead, the hush that came with twilight. She missed the long lazy evenings on the front porch where she'd sat for hours looking up at the heavens.

Earth's singular moon had always reminded Danna of the human soul. It had phases, like the cycles of a person's life. The sun might have been the god of ancient civilizations, powerful, steady, never-changing, but the moon represented the frailty of the people who spent generation after generation staring up at it.

She'd traveled a good portion of the galaxy since leaving Earth, and had yet to find a race that wasn't plagued by the human condition. Ethnic groups clashed, legal systems rarely agreed, and there were still places in the galaxy where one race considered themselves superior to another.

Technology wasn't perfection, and man's nature had changed little over the millennia. People were still people, no matter what planet they called home. What technology did offer was an expansion of the horizon, both geographically and personally.

Anyone who spent time in space soon realized just how deep the universe really was. Space was just that—space. Empty. Void. Silent. It had no understanding of day or night, time or seasons. No compassion, no love, no hate. It simply existed, unique and unto itself.

Danna loved that distinctiveness and the challenges that came with it. Despite her psychometric skills and the doors they could have opened, she'd chosen a career in diplomacy. Words weren't something you held in the palm of your hand. The art of using them to their best advantage was a constant challenge.

Adrenaline was already pumping through her veins. It was always like this just before she stepped into the arena of motives and hidden agendas that made the diplomatic wheel go round. As vast as the universe was, it was held together by politics. The glue was a combination of trust and distrust, a volatile mixture that could easily explode into disaster if the two largest governments found themselves engaged in war.

At well past the dinner hour, the impressive embassy was, for the most part, dark and silent. Even in the residential wings, quiet ruled. Beyond the embassy's courtyard walls, the background noise of city traffic and people underlay the evening like a pulsing heartbeat.

It only took a few moments for Danna to reach the main pavilion of the embassy with its glassy tile floors, crystal columns, and domed ceiling. The building mimicked those constructed around it. Technically advanced, but not culturally stifled, Ramora had a rich history in art and science. Danna had been with the diplomatic staff for two years and never tired of exploring the capital city, Seramia, when time permitted.

Two security guards stood outside the conference

area. Dressed in embassy uniforms, blue with gold trim, they acknowledged Danna with curt nods before simultaneously reaching out to open the huge double doors. She stepped into the conference room to find Ambassador Synon exchanging words with the other members of the Tribunal.

The neutral investigator was a Japolean dwarf. Thickset, with a ruddy complexion, he had brawny limbs and stubby fingers. Ginger-colored hair framed a leathery face with a bulbous nose and amber eyes. Dressed in a snug brown tunic, he looked more like a barrel with legs than a mediator. His counterpart was just the opposite, and a complete surprise.

Powerfully built with a tawny mane of hair that fell to his shoulders, the Korcian reminded Danna of an exotic cat that had found its way out of the jungle and into civilization, or an ancient Viking who'd stumbled into a time warp. Take your pick. Either way, he was lip-lickingly handsome.

His features were strong and finely chiseled; a full mouth, the lips dangerously sensual, and eyes . . . God, what eyes! Neither brown, nor green, nor gold, but a combination of all three, they held a glint of the savage nature that had never been completely purged from the Korcian race.

"Welcome, Officer MacFadyen," Ambassador Synon said. All three men came to their feet. Behind them, a service droid floated in midair, waiting to distribute refreshments.

Danna liked the droids on Ramora. They weren't outfitted to look like humanoids with glass eyes and fake hair like the ones on Earth. They were machines, not servants, and the Ramorans were a practical people, so their machines looked like machines, and their servants walked and talked because they were alive and got paid for doing a job.

Ambassador Synon stepped forward to greet Danna more personally, leading her to one of the six chairs that circled the meeting table. He was an elderly man with an elegance born of experience. Attired in the standard dress of a Ramoran male, a long, open-faced robe worn over loose-fitting trousers and a high-collared shirt, he stood tall and stately. Synon's wrinkled face had character, and there was honesty in his deepset eyes. Danna was thankful he'd been assigned the task of Chief Mediator.

"Allow me to introduce the rest of the Tribunal," Synon said. "This is Magistrate Gilfo of the Japolean Court. He will act as the neutral investigator, reporting directly to me."

The dwarf bent into a quick bow. "My pleasure, Officer MacFadyen."

Synon then indicated the man to his right. "Commander Cullon Gavriel, the Korcian Empire's liaison."

Danna couldn't keep her gaze from sweeping over the Korcian again. Every inch of his supple body was hard and stripped of excess fat. His high-planed face held a grim determination. A faint scar showed like a white thread against the naturally bronzed skin of his left cheek.

Once refreshments had been served, Ambassador Synon didn't waste any time getting down to business.

"The three of you are here to determine the circumstances, whether fair or foul, that led to the explosion onboard the *Llyndar* and the deaths of its entire crew. The wreckage is currently with the Forensic Bureau. The salvage ship will dock tomorrow morning. The evidence pods will be restricted until all data is entered into the records. Then, and only then, will the seals be removed for your personal inspection. As Chief Mediator, I will oversee the reporting progress to both the League and the Korcian Empire. All information will be shared so that an impartial and equitable determination can be made. In that regard, I will screen all transmissions. Are you in agreement?"

Each member of the Tribunal agreed.

Now seated, Danna found herself staring into a pair of predatory eyes. It wasn't like her to let a man affect her mental equilibrium, but the Korcian did. There was something strikingly haunting about the way he looked; strong and uncompromising, as powerful as a tiger. She sensed that when he approached a woman, he'd move just as confidently, circling his prey, playing with her emotions until he pounced with a sensual precision that would leave her helpless to resist. He had that power about him, the power to entice—to seduce.

Danna didn't have any misgivings about her ability to represent the League. Diplomatic manners aside, she was a tough-minded lady when it came to doing her job. Unfortunately, that determination didn't neutralize her curiosity—a purely feminine inquisitiveness that had her wondering what it would be like to be held in the Korcian's strong arms.

The Korcian chose that precise moment to smile, as if he were the psychic and had just read her mind. Danna realized she was playing right into his hands. When a man knew a woman was nervous around him, he could assume the odds were in his favor.

She countered the supposition by asking him a direction question. "What makes your government think the explosion was anything more than a tragic accident, Commander Gavriel?"

He slumped back, or relaxed, depending on one's point of view. The casual pose didn't fool Danna. This was a man who knew exactly what he was doing. His confidence, sensually brushed with a hint of danger and unpredictability, was as unsettling as it was fascinating.

Another stunning smile appeared just before his answer. "My government is merely taking a precautionary stance."

His reply was curiously dispassionate, but Danna sensed there was something hidden beneath the surface of his words. One look had told her that Commander Gavriel was constantly evaluating and calculating, and that being forced to work with a team of investigators made him even more cautious.

Still, there were times when you had to forsake caution and simply state the facts. This was one of those times.

"Precautionary, Commander? The League received news of the explosion less than six hours before it received General Tutunjan's ultimatum. Don't you think that's a little hasty, considering there's no evidence one way or the other?"

Magistrate Gilfo squirmed in his chair, but he didn't interrupt. Danna gave the Korcian enough time to formulate an answer. When he didn't respond, she tossed out another question.

"The investigation is still in its preliminary stages, Commander. Unfortunately, the explosion didn't leave much to examine. It could have been an accident. Faulty maintenance of the interstellar engines. A fuel leak. We may never know what really happened. Is the Korcian Empire willing to start a galactic war on the assumption that a person, or persons, unknown, deliberately murdered forty-six people?"

This time she got a response.

"The *Llyndar* underwent a full systems check before leaving Ramora. Less than twenty-four hours later, the only thing left was a handful of stardust."

Danna's eyes narrowed until little more than gleaming slits of brown showed between her thick black lashes. She hadn't known what to expect from the Empire's liaison, now she did. As little as possible.

"Interstellar flight, while efficient and economical, can still be unpredictable, Commander. General Tutunjan's reaction is preliminary and reactionary. There's no evidence to support a terrorist theory."

Gold-tinted eyes warmed appreciably. "What makes you think there's no evidence?"

Danna's heart pounded as a new dose of adrenaline leapt into her bloodstream. This was it. The game she knew so well, thrust and parry, questions and just enough of an answer to tease your opponent into lowering his defenses.

"If you had hard facts, Commander, we wouldn't be having this conversation. I'd be on Earth, attending a War Assembly."

The Korcian's expression changed to one that Danna found dangerously reminiscent of a predator that had just found his next meal.

"You're right, Officer MacFadyen. If irrevocable proof existed, our two governments would already be at war."

"Then why slam the League with an ultimatum? Wouldn't cooperation be more efficient?"

"We are cooperating."

Danna took a sip of the wine Ambassador Synon had poured for her. Her instincts were heating up, throbbing with every breath she took. The Korcian knew something. Something he wasn't sharing with the Tribunal.

"Very well, Commander. Let's assume, for the moment, that the destruction of the *Llyndar* served some distorted purpose on a terrorist agenda. What would that purpose be?"

"Military technology," he said succinctly.

"The Korcian Empire certainly has that," Gilfo interjected, drawing everyone's attention. "Of course, the Treaty of Vuldarr would have to be declared null and void. It prohibits the sale or exchange of military technology without mutual consent of the League Assembly and the Korcian High Council."

Danna flinched inwardly at the thought of the technological power of the Korcian Empire being sold on the black market. The commander's people had been exploring the galaxy when the rest of the humanoid races had been huddling in caves for warmth. The first ship to be equipped with an interstellar engine had been a Korcian starjet. No one in the galaxy could match their military technology, or their passion. Fighting wasn't just in a Korcian's blood, it was in his very soul.

Seeing this particular Korcian made a believer out of Danna. General Tutunjan hadn't sent a diplomat to the negotiation table, he'd sent a warrior.

"There are groups that would profit if the Treaty was set aside," Ambassador Synon interjected. "Arms dealers who manipulate the unrest in the outer sectors for personal gain. Powermongers who think the universe and its contents are theirs for the taking. However, an armed conflict between the Korcian Empire and the League would monopolize the very resources the dealers market."

"I agree," Danna said, taking up the ambassador's logic. "The League doesn't support the sale of illegal arms, nor does it harbor terrorists."

"Perhaps not willingly," Cullon replied dryly. The glint in his eyes held the confidence of a brick wall as he added, "The *Llyndar* carried a Korcian registry. The explosion took place in a sector controlled by the League. My government is within its rights to demand an explanation."

The glass tabletop allowed Danna to watch as Cullon stretched out his long legs. His black boots ended up a few inches away from her own shoes. She pulled her feet back in a move of self-preservation that was as old as male versus female.

Cullon met her gaze, his uncanny eyes sharper than ever, seeing things she didn't want him to see. Instead of putting Danna on the defensive, it had the opposite effect. She responded with a sharp observation that brought another squirm from the Japolean dwarf.

"Explanation or revenge, Commander Gavriel?"

"Both, if necessary."

The reply was curt, to the point, and dead serious. If the explosion that had claimed 46 lives demanded retaliation, the Korcian Guard would deliver it—armed to the teeth.

"The League is investigating every possible explanation," Ambassador Synon said, his calm voice filling the volatile silence that followed Cullon's blunt
reply. "Until then, all is speculation. May I suggest
another meeting in the morning. One that will offer
us the opportunity to approach the problem with less
emotion."

Danna knew the ambassador's remark applied to her
more than it did to the other members of the Tribunal.
The realization didn't please her. She was a professional. Her career dictated that she deal with people
from differing cultures and philosophies. So why did
the Korcian make her insides flutter?

Danna didn't like the answer any more than she
liked the obvious reason. In the years that she'd been
working her way up the diplomatic ladder, she'd forgotten how intense physical attraction could be. Actually, she'd made a point of forgetting. Her last
relationship wasn't worth remembering.

The meeting now adjourned, Danna stepped into the
pavilion area to find Magistrate Gilfo waiting for her.
Her Korcian counterpart was nowhere in sight.

"I must say, you aren't afraid to ruffle a few feath-
ers, are you?" the dwarf remarked. "Don't know of
many who'd take a Korcian on the way you just did.
They're an intimidating lot."

"Yes, they are," she agreed. "But the League isn't
going to be intimidated. Whatever happened on the
Llyndar, it wasn't sanctioned by my government."

The dwarf didn't comment. His role was that of a
neutral observer—all eyes, all ears, and no voice until
the final review.

"Synon was right," Danna said, allowing some of
her frustration to show. "This is all speculation until
the evidence pods are unsealed. Hopefully, the wreckage will be able to tell us something."

"I'm sure it will," Gilfo agreed, adding an encouraging smile as he turned to leave her. "Until tomorrow morning."

"I'll see you then," Danna said before taking herself across the lobby. She was on her way back to her quarters when she decided the last thing she needed was the claustrophobia of four walls. She took the closest exit, leaving the embassy behind.

The night was warm and comforting, the largest of Ramora's moons hanging just above the horizon. A meteor thrust its shining spear through the dark dome of the sky. The luminous tail glowed faintly, then died away. It reminded Danna that living beings didn't share the immortality of the heavens.

The 46 people on board the *Llyndar* were a perfect example. Life was fragile even when it was sheltered by the world that created it. Take that life into space, into a desolate environment that lacked air and water and warmth, and you were asking for trouble. Yet nothing fascinated the sentient soul as much as the endless bounty of the stars.

Danna walked along the main boulevard that separated the embassy from the commercial section of the city. At night, Ramora's capital shone like a necklace of bright lights draped around the mouth of the Seramian Inlet.

During the day, the metropolis was a hub of activity. Aesthetically pleasing buildings mixed with small parks and quaint shops that displayed goods from every corner of the galaxy; Palatkian perfume made from the saliva of white spiders, Gasparian incense and meditation orbs that promised sweet dreams, Zaranian silver fashioned into some of the most beautiful jewelry Danna had ever seen.

Seramia's citizenry was just as interesting. Tall and elegantly slender with dark hair and pale eyes, the Ramorans were a beautiful people. The natural energy and curiosity of their race, along with a good dose of common sense, added to the prosperity of their culture.

Even with the stress of the current situation on her shoulders, Danna felt the charm of the city. The streets were wide, the sidewalks smooth and flat and glimmering with the luminous quality unique to Ramoran marble.

She passed a small café where couples were seated, talking in soft voices between sips of wine. Danna's mind was instantly occupied with thoughts of the Korcian warrior with tigerlike eyes. She hadn't allowed herself the luxury of a lover for a very long time.

Knowing she couldn't afford the distraction now, she crossed the street, leaving the quaint café behind. She walked on, turning the corner and heading south toward a small park she favored whenever she needed to be alone.

Danna made herself comfortable on a bench near a bubbling fountain. Around her the lush vegetation lay in shadow. She sat quietly, focusing her thoughts on the investigation that would begin in earnest the next morning.

If the explosion had been deliberate, things were going to get complicated. Terrorists didn't think like other people. They didn't use logic or rational reasoning. They simply destroyed in the name of whatever cause inflamed their hearts and minds.

There were groups, led by zealous individuals, who would love to see the Treaty of Vuldarr go down the tube. The accord had been in effect for only a hundred years. Prior to the agreement, the Korcian Empire had ruled half the galaxy, while the League had promoted democracy in the other. Rather than bump heads, the two governments had been wise enough to join forces. Now, separate but equal, they were the stabilizing force in the outer regions.

Her time in the Corps had taught her that the political landscape of the galaxy was a fragile thing, too easily manipulated by everything from bribery to personal razzle-dazzle. She was pondering the possibilities when the Korcian's rich voice came out of the darkness.

"Officer MacFadyen."

She looked up to find him standing over her. Several inches over six feet, broad-shouldered and well muscled; he looked menacing standing there in the dark. Danna came to her feet, disliking the fact that her five feet seven inches of height wasn't enough to meet him eye to eye.

"I followed you," he said, his tone unapologetic. "We need to talk."

"We did talk, Commander, but I wasn't saying anything you wanted to hear."

His eyes gleamed with amusement. "And what do you think I want to hear, Danna."

The use of her first name breached protocol at the same time it made Danna feel oddly vulnerable, as if she was about to do something totally out of character. Unnerved, but not undone, she responded. "Cry 'Havoc,' and let slip the dogs of war."

"Is that what you think? That I can't wait to wrap my hands around a laser rifle?"

"You're a soldier, aren't you?"

"No."

"If you're not military, what are you?"

"Enforcement."

Danna drew in a breath of dewy night air, feeling the surprise as much as hearing it. Enforcement was the security branch of the Korcian government, internally and externally. The men who filled its ranks were the best trained, deadliest fighters in the galaxy. They employed their skills under the umbrella of one simple rule—win at any cost.

"The Korcian High Council doesn't send an Enforcer to do a diplomat's job," she said. "Mind telling me what you know that I don't?"

"Not here." Without warning a strong hand closed

around her elbow. She was guided out of the shadowy park and back to the sidewalk.

"Where are we going?" Danna pulled back, but the effort was a waste of time. The Korcian wasn't about to let her go.

"Someplace where we can be alone."

TWO

They walked toward the embassy, passing the little café with its floating droids and canvas canopies over industrial-strength plastic tables. Seramia was a city of food and wine, exotic scents and fascinating sounds. The ambience was even more alluring at night when its people came out to play.

A woman's soft laughter drifted on the evening air, followed by a man's insistence that she not run away. It was an intimate male/female exchange, one that brought a smile to Danna's face without her even realizing it.

Normally, her first reaction to a man was mental, but that didn't hold true with the Korcian. Strikingly male, assured, fluid and graceful, he kept intruding into her thoughts.

"What's wrong?" he asked, instantly alerted by the change in her expression. His voracious eyes probed the darkness, his hand moving to the hilt of the dagger strapped to his right thigh.

"Nothing," she said, looking down at the smooth surface of the sidewalk. She wanted to say that she'd stumbled on something, but the street was too well lit for her to get away with the lie so she said something just as far from the truth. "The smells from the café are making me hungry. I thought about going back and getting something to eat."

"I'll feed you when we get there," he said, surprising her again.

"Where exactly is there?"

"Someplace secure," he said dismissively. He hurried her down a street that led them away from the embassy, toward an exclusive residential area.

The houses were uniquely Ramoran with graceful arches, subtle contours, and lots and lots of glass. Lavish gardens shielded the private residences from the street, but faint bits of conversation still found their way into the night through open windows. Casual family chatter and social conversation; few people knew of the crisis brewing at the embassy.

"You can let go of me now," Danna said. "I'm as curious to hear what you have to say as you are to say it, Commander."

He gave her a deliciously disturbing smile before his hand dropped away. "My name is Cullon."

Danna didn't acknowledge the remark. The very fact that Cullon Gavriel was an Enforcer provoked caution. His existence was in direct contrast to her own. Diplomacy mirrored compromise. Men like Cullon Gavriel lived in a world without concession.

She didn't realize he'd taken quarters outside the embassy until they turned onto another street. Until then, she'd assumed he was simply taking a shortcut through the residential area to a café or tavern of his own choosing.

A swipe of his index finger over a bio-sensor opened the outer gate. He put his hand on her lower back, a light pressure that guided Danna down a path made of flat, luminous marble stones. At the end of the path, he satisfied another bio-sensor to open the main door of the house.

Danna stepped into the front room. Its glass ceiling, built in triangular sections that formed a crystal pyramid, had been designed to impress. In typical Ramoran style, the room opened onto a luxurious courtyard. A fountain sculpted from opaque crystal served as the focal point around which a small private jungle bloomed. Enormous fan-shaped ferns and feathery palms swayed lazily in the night breeze. Exotic clusters of Ramoran roses and white-tipped spider plants added color and scent.

Unlike Earth, where houses were sectioned off into living and eating, sleeping and bathing rooms, a Ramoran home was open and revealing. Tall panels of stained glass separated one area from another, offering privacy without doors. The architecture allowed nothing to hinder the fluid design that swelled gracefully from carpeted floor to domed ceiling.

Cullon motioned her around one of the glass panels. "What do you want to eat?"

The question shook Danna out of her private reverie. "Eat?"

"You said you were hungry. I'm not much of a cook, but I can keep you from starvation."

"I didn't think Enforcers took culinary training."

"Eating is part of surviving," he said matter-of-factly.

Danna absorbed the remark as she studied the Korcian one more time. The controlled way he moved, the stark clarity of his eyes, the alertness that oozed from every pore, all of it spoke volumes about the training he'd undergone to reach the highest level of Korcian security.

"Whatever you eat, I'll eat," she said, hoping his diet wasn't too bizarre.

"What do you know about Korcian history?" he asked as he began rummaging in one of the cabinets.

Danna sat down at the counter, taking a moment to appreciate the skill that had gone into producing the tiny polyglas tiles that formed its surface. The design was an arabesque motif with intersecting semicircular shapes.

She switched her attention from the counter's design to the ruby depths of the wine that appeared in front of her, before lifting her gaze to meet that of the man. "The Korcian Empire has more history than the rest of the galaxy put together. What should I know?"

"Do you know what a True Blood is?"

Danna took a sip of tangy wine before answering him. "The Korcian Empire began as a group of related families," she recited, drawing from her classroom experiences at the University of Galactic Studies. "Each family leader was responsible for his own territory, not unlike the medieval clans of ancient Earth. Centuries later, the term True Blood was given to the males who could trace their DNA back to the original eight families, thus the eight original kings."

"It's a little more complicated than that."

"I gave you a short synopsis." Another sip of wine, a deep breath, and more history. "The families had set-in-concrete hierarchies. The eldest son of the eldest son sort of thing. A law against marriage between the major families helped to maintain stability, but it didn't stop private alliances from forming. Dynastic marriages were commonplace."

A platter of sandwiches appeared on the counter. Danna helped herself to one, chewing thoughtfully as her host added a smaller plate piled high with chunks of fresh fruit.

"Do you know what caused our last civil war?" Cullon asked, after devouring one sandwich and reaching for another.

"Fundamentalism," Dana answered quickly. "After interstellar flight, the Empire began expanding beyond the Korcian solar system. It was inevitable that interracial marriages would happen, that Korcian blood would be thinned by the assimilation of other races. The family leaders didn't like it. They did an about-face. Instead of conquering other worlds, they withdrew, isolating themselves from the rest of the galaxy. Protecting their pedigree."

"Pedigree," he chuckled. "Only a Terran would use that term."

"It fits," Danna said. "The majority of Korcians are a result of well-planned breeding."

In the span of several seconds, the Korcian's expression registered irritation, surprise, then another devastating smile, the kind Danna was beginning to classify as "enigmatic." She continued with the history lesson.

"Unfortunately, your forefathers didn't stop to think that isolating themselves would bring out the worst traits along with the best ones. Rather than allow an infusion of fresh genes and fresh ideas, the old monarchs plunged their heads deeper into the sand. Utopia turned into hell. Then again, narrow-minded philosophies usually do."

Danna picked up the empty sandwich platter, but left the wine glasses. Once the platter disappeared into the sanitizing unit, along with the utensils Cullon had used to prepare the tasty meal, she turned back to him.

"After the war, fundamentalism gave way to military feudalism," she said, continuing the historical review. "The current empire still reflects that philosophy. The higher the military rank, the greater respect a man receives."

Instead of a debate, Cullon gave her a quick smile. "The League may not like our style of government, but the military has kept the Empire intact for over a thousand years."

"Are you a True Blood?"

"From the marrow of my bones to the tips of my toes," he said proudly.

"Why doesn't that surprise me?"

"There aren't many of us left," he said as he picked up his glass and headed for the main area of the house.

Danna did the same. She sat down on a cushy chair, tucking her feet under her. "So what does a Korcian history test have to do with the explosion on board the *Llyndar*?"

"Everything." He sat down and stretched out his legs, intruding on her space the same way he'd done earlier in the conference room. "One of the *Llyndar*'s crew was a True Blood."

"I don't recall any mention of a True Blood on the fatality report."

"There wasn't one. He was traveling under an assumed identify. The name listed on the ship's manifest is Vosca Komarr. His real name was Chimera Namid. He worked for the Korcian Trade Bureau."

Danna settled deeper into the chair. "Why was Namid traveling under an alias?"

The Korcian raised an eyebrow, but the predatory glint in his eyes didn't ease one iota. "Good question. As soon as I find the answer, I'll share it with you."

The little Danna had been told didn't explain why Cullon had rousted her out of the park and insisted that they speak in private. She put the facts together the best way she could and came up with her own possibility. One she didn't much like.

"The Korcian Empire knows terrorists didn't blow up the *Llyndar*. Putting the fleet on alert is a smoke screen. You're using the Tribunal to mask your real mission. Someone's killing off True Bloods and the High Council is getting nervous."

Danna left her chair to pace the room. She was frowning by step two. Any organization, even one as strong as the Korcian Empire, could be rendered impotent by a few carefully planned "accidents." With eight years in the Diplomatic Corps under her belt, Danna had become quite good at sifting through lies and half-truths. Her psychometric skills didn't make her clairvoyant, but she did have a strong sixth sense. She'd allowed an impasse to exist most of the evening, but no longer. It was time to get to the truth of the matter.

"Murder implies personal motives, not political ones," she said thoughtfully. "An assassination disguised as an accident serves a private agenda. Public assassinations are staged for maximum effect—eliminate the opposition and send a warning. Which one applies to your Mr. Namid? Murder or assassination?"

"There's a new fundamentalism movement inside the Empire," he told her. "It centers around True Bloods. And like the old one, it could prove disastrous."

Danna's dark gaze grew more direct. "Did Namid's pedigree make him a member of the movement?"

"Not necessarily. I'm a True Blood, but I'm not a fundamentalist." He shrugged his shoulders, indicating that there was no clear-cut way to make the distinction.

"Why was Namid on his way to Earth?"

"No one knows."

"Do you think his position at the Trade Bureau had anything to do with it?"

"Namid's job didn't allow him access to military weapons or classified technology. He was a clerk. One of thousands."

"Maybe he was working with someone who does have access. Laser rifles are selling for five thousand credits on the black market."

Another shrug. "It's a possibility. But I don't think so. My instincts tell me it was something else. Something personal."

"And you trust your instincts?"

His eyes turned a darker, more menacing gold. "They're the only thing I do trust."

The answer didn't surprise Danna. She was accustomed to reading tones, expressions, and body language. Men like Cullon were loners, isolated by the profession that kept them on the dark side of life. Like the Korcian, Danna had learned to trust her instincts. Cullon Gavriel was a man with a past he didn't talk about and a future that rode the winds. He lived in a world of codes and ethics that had nothing to do with diplomacy and everything to do with getting the job done.

The distant rumble of thunder warned of a storm blowing inland from the Seramian Sea. Short on time, Danna tossed another question into the ring.

"Why do you think Namid was using an alias and sleeping in a lumpy bunk on board a freighter when he could have been traveling first-class on a commercial transport?"

"That's what I came to Ramora to find out."

Danna looked at Cullon with unveiled impatience. As expected, her scrutiny bounced off the Korcian's wide chest like sunlight hitting a mirror, but his attitude didn't keep her from saying what was on her mind. "You said your instincts are telling you that Namid's death had something to do with his personal life. That brings us back to murder."

The amber depths of his eyes changed again, becoming as intense as a flame against the backdrop of a moonless night.

"That's where you come in. I can waste time interviewing the people who knew Namid, sorting through gossip and his personal belongings for a clue, or I can put something he owned in the palm of your hand and follow your lead."

Again, Danna wasn't surprised. She'd been expecting this very thing ever since Cullon had waylaid her in the park.

"So that's why I was assigned to the Tribunal. Someone in the League uppity-ups owes the Korcian Council a favor."

"You were already here, working on Ambassador Synon's staff," Cullon said, offering no apologies. "Sometimes fate works with us instead of against us."

"Does Ambassador Synon know the Tribunal is a sham?"

"No."

"What about General Tutunjan?"

"No. The order to alert the fleet came from the High Council. That's all the general needs to know for the time being."

"What about my government? If all you wanted was a loan of my skills, why not just come and ask for them?"

"I wish it was that simple."

"That's not an answer."

"It's the only one I can give you."

Danna looked toward the door. She could walk out of the house, then march into Synon's office first thing in the morning and end the charade. It wasn't nice to fool the League into thinking they were on the verge of war. Instead, she thought of 46 dead men.

Murder, assassination, or tragic accident?

The question demanded an answer.

"I need your help," Cullon said.

The words seemed forced from him, as if he hadn't wanted to say them. Danna suspected it was because he didn't like admitting that a big, bad Korcian Enforcer couldn't get the job done alone.

She looked down at her hands. Their average appearance belied the power they concealed. Cullon was right. Her skills could point him in the right direction.

Putting the decision on hold, Danna crossed the room and stepped through the archway that separated the house from the outer courtyard. Wind, heavy with the scent of the nearing storm, skipped and whistled through the trees.

Only one of the moons that had illuminated the summer sky earlier in the evening could be seen now. The other two were covered by thick clouds with dark charcoal bellies.

Cullon join her. He remained silent for several minutes, waiting for Danna to make the first overture.

She let him wait.

It was just a flicker of fear, compared to what she'd felt in past years, but it had to be dealt with before she could agree to do what the Enforcer wanted. Until now, she'd honestly believed that the explosion had been an accident.

"What is it?" he asked, seeing her reluctance.

A moment more and Danna turned to him. "I have to know everything you know. It's the only way I can read Namid's imprint properly."

"I didn't know there was a right way or a wrong way," he said.

Breaking eye contact, Danna looked up at the night sky again. Most of the stars were blocked from view by the growing storm clouds, but not all of them. One yellow star stood out brighter than all the rest. Nearby, almost lost in its glare, a dimmer star blinked. Danna knew the name of both, but she couldn't bring them to mind.

The touch of Cullon's hand took her by surprise. He reached for her chin and turned her face toward him. His fingertips brushed as lightly as a butterfly across her bottom lip. The slight touch heightened the anticipation she'd been feeling all evening.

"What's it like?" he repeated.

"Like stepping into a rainbow," she said softly.

His hand dropped away. "Do you go into a trance?"

Danna shook her head. "Not exactly." She paused, searching for the right words. "It's more than a dream, but less than reality. I feel things as much as I see them or sense them."

"And it bothers you."

"Sometimes." She shrugged. "Most people are a mixture of emotions. They leave a muted imprint, one color fading into another. Other people are more intense, more focused."

"And the colors change?"

"Yes, they change."

Danna's hesitation showed on her face. She didn't want to tell Cullon about the darker colors, the ones created by hate and greed and perverted lust.

"Talk to me."

Danna glanced at him, then away, up to where storm clouds blocked the light of distant stars. "People think hate is dark and brooding. If they were asked to label it with a color, the color would be black. But it isn't black. It's red. Blood red."

Wordlessly, Cullon waited for her to finish what she'd started.

"I helped one of the law enforcement agencies on Earth solve a murder." There was no anger in her voice, no bitterness. Just acceptance. The acceptance that something terrible had once happened and she'd been a part of it—even if that part had taken place in a dreamscape. "The only items the police had belonged to the victims."

Breath eased from her lungs in a low, long sigh before she continued. "He killed four people before the authorities came to me. I tried to sort through the images, but nothing made sense. The dreamscapes were jumbled. The people hadn't known each other. None of the colors matched. I couldn't find a pattern."

"So he kept on killing."

"Yes," she admitted in a whisper as ghostly as the images invading her mind. "His last victim was a little girl."

The world fell silent as pressure mounted inside Danna. She felt pins and needles prickling her arms. It had been years since the crime, but time hadn't weakened the knife-sharp intensity of the memory.

"His name was Deighan. Leonard Deighan. The little girl's name was Lucy. She ripped at the medallion hanging around his neck before he crushed her windpipe. The police found it in her hand."

Danna didn't have to tell him what had happened when the police had placed the medallion in her hand. She knew it showed on her face. She'd been able to identify the murderer because she'd relived the crime. She'd watched and listened and *felt* the twisted emotions that had driven a maniac to strangle the life from an innocent child.

"We don't know for sure that Namid was murdered."

Danna looked at him then, the bleakness fading from her gaze as she confronted the present instead of the past. The memories weren't easily extinguished but she forced them aside. "You wouldn't be here if you thought the explosion was an accident."

Cullon didn't disagree. He couldn't.

Instead, he tugged at the hand she had only just realized he was holding. "It's getting late. I'll walk you back to the embassy. We'll check out Namid's apartment tomorrow, after we've examined the wreckage."

They left the house. The wind was blowing more fiercely now, bending the fragile palms that lined the residential street. The moonlight was almost non-existent, more shadow than light as the clouds continued to thicken. Danna glanced at the digital display on her watch. It was after midnight.

As they walked, she sorted through the information Cullon had given her. There were still pieces missing.

They were inside the embassy gates when she asked, "How did you find out that Vosca Komarr was really Chimera Namid?"

"That was the easy part," he told her. "There were only six Korcians males listed on Ramora's entry logs. One of them booked passage on the *Llyndar*. It was a simple matter of elimination. Komarr was the only one missing."

She gave him an impatient glance. "If the Ramoran authorities cleared his travel pass, then he was Komarr when he arrived and Komarr when he left."

"Namid was Komarr until my government was officially notified of his death. The Central Registry rejected the information as fraudulent. The travel pass had been forged. The Registry asked the Ramoran authorities for a DNA sample. They got it from the apartment he'd rented."

"It confirmed what the Registry suspected and Enforcement was notified," Danna said. "That makes sense. What doesn't make sense is the High Council allowing General Tutunjan to issue an ultimatum to the League. An investigation could have been conducted without churning up political waters."

"Everything's political," he said. His hand was pressing against the small of her back again, gently guiding her toward the exterior staircase that would take her to the second floor and her quarters. "Remember that history lesson?"

"Okay, what's the bottom line? Why Namid?"

The storm chose that exact moment to strike. Water came pouring down as if the clouds hovering over the city had had their bellies split open with a knife. Cullon took her by the arm, propelling her up the steps.

"Which door?" he called over his shoulder as another slashing sheet of rain attacked the building.

"This one," Danna said, pulling back when he would have rushed her past it. A quick press of her index finger over the bio-sensor and the door wheezed open.

She stepped into the room, then immediately turned around to face her escort. "I'd like that answer now," she said, determined to collect as many pieces of the puzzle as possible.

He stepped closer, then leaned down, so his voice could be heard over the clash of thunder competing against thunder. The heat of his breath whispered across Danna's ear, along with the words, "Chimera Namid was the heir to the Korcian throne."

Three

"Come in out of the rain, old friend."

Cullon stepped into a room that was located in the visitors' section of the embassy. The man who opened the door was dressed in a flamboyantly colored robe, a noticeable contrast to the rain-drenched black tunic worn by his guest.

"Let me pour you a glass of warm wine," Gilfo said, turning toward the serving table. The embroidered hem of his garment followed him across the polished wooden floor. "Even a summer storm can bring on a chill."

"Thanks," Cullon said.

The elegant room was a long way from the sultry green jungles of Korcia or the cold, mountainous topography of Japola, yet both men seemed at ease with their surroundings as they settled into chairs near a window that allowed them a rainy view of Ramora's capital city. The only difference was that Gilfo used a stool to get into the chair, while Cullon slumped into his with an agility that hinted he could make himself at home almost anywhere.

"So, is the lovely Terran going to help you?" Gilfo asked. There was no such thing as neutrality when it came to a war between the Korcian Empire and the League. You either wanted normalcy to your life, or you wanted chaos. Japoleans preferred the status quo that had existed since the Treaty of Vuldarr.

The new fundamentalism that was sweeping through the Empire could undo that treaty, along with a lot of other things. The question was, who was killing off the players, a Korcian who disliked the idea of returning to the old ways, or a League citizen who wanted to disrupt the fine-tuned balance of the galaxy? Or a yet unidentified third party?

"I think so," Cullon answered with a sly smile. "I peaked her curiosity when I mentioned that Namid was the heir to the throne."

"I don't suppose you mentioned the others," the dwarf said. His gaze settled on the man seated quietly on the other side of a glass inlaid table. The smile on Cullon's face hinted at something more than simple satisfaction at having enticed Officer Danna Mac-Fadyen into using her skills. Being a wise man, Gilfo formed an opinion and kept quiet about it. The Enforcer made a better friend than he did an enemy.

"No reason to tell her more than she needs to know for now."

"Then you're convinced there's a conspiracy underfoot."

Cullon gave a non-committal shrug. "I'm here for the man who killed Namid. If I end up solving three murders instead of one, so be it."

Gilfo's bushy brows lifted quizzically. "It does seem a mystery. Three dead True Bloods, each the surviving heir of their clan. If memory serves, there were only eight original families."

"Three down, five to go."

"What of you? Are you not the eldest son of the Gavriel clan?"

The remark earned the dwarf a cryptic smile. "If they had started with me, we wouldn't have three corpses on our hands."

Gilfo didn't doubt it. His lethal young friend was an expert at doing what Enforcers did best—protecting and preserving the heritage and sovereignty of the Empire.

Nothing more was said as the two men relaxed, each comfortable with the silence that seemed fitting for a dark, damp night.

Cullon stared out the rain-splashed window, his thoughts returning to the appealing female he had left standing in the doorway of her quarters. A female whose soulful dark eyes didn't belong to a woman with a dossier that read all work and no play.

Cullon didn't have any illusions about the life he led. He was as much a space gypsy as his ancestors had been, always moving, always searching out the next star, the next assignment. He liked his life, like the unpredictability of never knowing from one day to the next what he'd be doing, where he'd be going.

Most of all, he liked the thrill of the hunt.

Danger was a stimulant. The people he came into contact with were the scum of the galaxy; gun runners and drug dealers, thieves and psychotic killers who thrived on blood. For his part, Cullon delivered what Danna MacFadyen and her fellow Terrans would call Biblical justice. To Cullon's way of thinking, it was justice well deserved.

Protect and preserve the Empire. The panegyric phrase drifted through his mind. The oath was a part of Cullon's every action and reaction—a justification for his existence, a moral and legal sword and a shield for the work he performed in service to the Empire.

But that didn't mean he couldn't appreciate a beautiful woman between assignments. Unfortunately, Danna MacFadyen *was* his assignment. Or at least too much a part of it for Cullon to lose his objectivity and do what he wanted to do—strip her down to her lovely pale skin and make slow love to her. The kind of slow, hot sex that would keep them on a pleasure couch all day and all night.

His work wasn't conducive to long-term relationships, even if he did want one, which he didn't. He enjoyed sex, but he avoided emotional entanglements. Time had taught him not to second guess the choices he had to make. His life belonged to the Empire, and if he ever took a mate, tradition demanded that it be one of his own kind.

Yet, several times during the last few hours he'd stared into Danna MacFadyen's bottomless eyes and imagined her on his homeworld, standing naked among the lush green leaves and exotic flowers that made Korcia one of the most beautiful planets in the galaxy.

"Do you think she'll be able to learn anything from the evidence pods?" Gilfo asked, breaking the silence as he refilled his wine glass from a crystal container that caught the light like a prism and cast it back into the room in long, sparkling fingers that caressed the blue carpet and white walls.

"I don't know," Cullon said, putting his personal fantasy on hold. "I've read her file. She's worked on a murder case before. And found the killer. The agency she worked for wanted to hire her on as a consultant, but she turned them down."

He paused to think about the way she'd described it. *"I feel things as much as I see them or sense them."*

Cullon didn't like the idea of exposing Danna to the *feelings* of another murder, but what choice did he have? He needed a direction. All he'd done so far was wander around in circles. Whoever was doing away with True Bloods wasn't leaving any tangible tracks. But Danna wasn't limited to the physical world. If she could read whatever imprint Namid had left behind on his belongings, Cullon might be able to figure out why a man with nothing to hide had gone into hiding.

"An explosion doesn't leave the kind of evidence Officer MacFadyen's used to handling," Gilfo pointed out. "You can't fit what's left of the freighter into the palm of her hand."

"You've seen it?" Cullon gave him a shrewd look.

"I've seen the preliminary report—courtesy of another old friend," the dwarf told him. He stretched out his short legs, then leaned back, wine glass in hand. "All we're going to have to inspect tomorrow morning is a heap of space junk. The explosion gutted the ship."

"Then we'll inspect space junk. I wasn't expecting to get anything from the *Llyndar*. Namid had an apartment in the inner city. I'm going to take Danna there tomorrow afternoon."

The dwarf didn't comment on the use of Officer MacFadyen's first name. Instead, he suggested that Cullon get a good night's sleep. "Once you get a lead, you'll be on the hunt. Rest while you can."

Cullon agreed, exchanging the chair and the dwarf's company for a damp trek to a small, seedy tavern he'd found the previous night. He didn't want to go back to the house yet, didn't feel tired enough, despite the long day.

Ramoran ale in hand, he made his way to the back of the bar, not bothering to look at himself in the cracked mirror above the table he selected. Cullon knew what he'd see. A face that was too lean and sharply angled to be friendly, and two strangely colored eyes that shouted his bloodlines to anyone who looked his way. He'd see the kind of man people gave a wide berth unless they were looking for trouble.

He sipped the ale, not particularly interested in its taste, while life went on around him. The couple seated at a nearby table whispered in low, sincere voices while another customer rambled on about the music that filled the room in loud, ubiquitous notes. The tavern was dimly lit, the air tinged with the odor of spilt alcohol and perfumed female bodies. The service droids glided unhurriedly above the floor, stopping occasionally to refill glasses.

Cullon wondered if he shouldn't do another search of Namid's apartment before he took Danna there. Underneath his meticulous attention to detail, he knew he was only looking for an excuse not to find a willing partner among the crowd.

He scanned the room, noting several solicitous glances. If he kept drinking, he might take one of the women up on their offer. As it was, Danna MacFadyen had aroused him, and only Danna MacFadyen could satisfy him.

And so he found himself sitting alone, thinking about what had transpired in the last few weeks, how uneasy he felt about it, and what would happen next.

Someone was out for blood—True Blood.

Gilfo had been right. There was a mystery to the killings that went beyond the normal assassination scenario. In Cullon's experience there was no greater danger than an extremist with a heartfelt cause to support. He preferred an adversary motivated by greed or passion to one fueled by idealism.

Ideological egos were almost impossible to deflate.

None of the three victims had had military or political ambitions, none had been employed in positions that allowed them access to high-level information, and none had been involved in anything illegal or unethical, at least nothing Cullon had been able to uncover.

Then there was Chimera Namid himself: the heir to the Korcian throne, if the monarchy was reinstituted. That he was the "average Korcian" was all anyone could say about him, and that was a term that covered a lot of ground. If the throne was offered to him in the future, would he have taken it?

The question would go unanswered. Namid was dead. So were Ackernar and Eyriaki. The first two had died in their sleep, unaware of the poison they'd ingested with their evening meal.

But Namid hadn't been poisoned. He'd had his molecules burnt to a crisp then scattered across deep space.

The difference bothered Cullon.

It bothered him a lot.

Murder had two faces—one passionate, the other coldly meticulous.

Achernar and Eyriaki's murders bore evidence of the second. Namid's hinted at the first. It took a lot of emotion to kill forty-five innocent people to get to the one you really wanted dead. Cold, heartless emotion, but still emotion.

That's what bothered him. Namid had been running away from something. Or someone. What or who were the questions Cullon hoped Danna could help him answer.

Under normal circumstances, he'd be working alone, but the High Council hadn't seen things his way. They'd arranged for a Tribunal to be created, and now he was part of a political investigation that didn't allow him the immunity he usually enjoyed. Even if he could identify Namid's killer, he couldn't go after him and return the favor. He was forced to act within the legal perimeters of the Tribunal.

His hands were tied.

Cullon didn't like it. He was certain that the Council was making a mistake, but an ingrained inability to disobey a direct order was a tough obstacle to overcome.

He wanted to antagonize the killer into making another move, into making a mistake—into coming after him. Instead he accepted the conditions he had to work under, finished off his ale, and exited the tavern for the rented house that would seem even emptier without Danna MacFadyen curled up in a chair.

Danna stared at the twisted remains of the *Llyndar* while Ambassador Synon signed the authorization that would allow the Tribunal team into the docking bay. The floor of the bay was littered with bits and pieces of what once had been a Class Three cargo vessel.

The salvage ship had done its job, vacuuming in as much debris as possible after anchoring its towing cables on the battered hull of the freighter. The few recognizable objects were charred black; chairs from the galley, a command console ripped from its moorings by the blast, hatchway ladders that had offered no escape.

Despite the docking station's environmental controls, Danna shivered, pulling her jacket more snuggly about her shoulders. Like most artificial habitats in space, the air smelled sterile and sound echoed off metallic walls.

Danna looked beyond the pressurized windows into the darkness of space. The docking station lay in low orbit around Ramora. Its lattice framework was crowded with ships waiting to be loaded or unloaded while workers in environmental suits jetted between the dormant vessels, performing maintenance checks.

A short siren blast drew Danna's attention back to the quarantined bay. Warning lights flashed red, then amber, then green as the access doors slid open. The acid scent of scorched metal filled the observation room where the Tribunal team was waiting.

"What a mess," Magistrate Gilfo said sadly. They were the first words anyone had spoken since leaving the shuttle. His next statement was in his native tongue, a benediction for the lost souls the salvage ship hadn't been able to find.

"Let's get this over with," Cullon said.

He was standing behind Danna, but she was strongly aware of his presence. She'd spent half the night at her console, accessing files on Korcian history. The genealogy of the Korcian kings read like the Book of Genesis, only three times longer. After sifting through several thousand "begets" she'd finally located the limb of the family tree she'd been looking for—A'vla Namid.

If Cullon was right, and it would take a Korcian historian to prove him wrong, Chimera Namid did have a claim to the throne. A very strong claim. Of the eight kings who had originally ruled the empire, A'vla Namid had been the strongest. He had also been the last, which would have legitimatized Chimera's claim had he wanted to make one.

Danna had also discovered something else. Something her friendly Korcian Enforcer hadn't mentioned. The Gavriel family tree was among the most prestigious in Korcian history. The Enforcer's ancestors not only included a king, one of his great-great-uncles had held the position General Tutunjan now occupied as Commander of the Korcian Guard. Cullon's father had been an advisor to the High Council after his military retirement. That's where the trail had ended. Other than his birth record, and a certified DNA registry as a True Blood, none of the files Danna had been able to access had contained so much as a byte of information on the man who had asked for her help last night.

"Are you ready?" Cullon asked.

She nodded, then rallied her thoughts before stepping resignedly across the threshold and into the quarantined bay. She wasn't looking forward to submerging herself in the convoluted world of this particular dreamscape.

The forensic team had finished cataloging the debris. The Chief Inspector, standing solemnly in front of the evidence tables, wearing a white coat and looking very official, promised them a complete report by day's end. In the meantime, the members of the Tribunal were welcome to look for themselves.

The feeling of trepidation that had accompanied her into the holding area stayed with Danna as she made her way toward the gouged out hull. Looking into it, she could see shreds of environmental insulation hanging like black flimsy ribbons.

One of the forensic inspectors approached them. He

was a sharp-nosed little man with dark, beetle brows arched over pale, serious eyes. As a member of the forensic team he was used to tragedy, to the incessant destruction that came with an explosion of this kind. His expression said he'd seen so many sights like this that nothing shocked him anymore. There was nothing in his face but a benign curiosity to discover the cause of the explosion so his report could be filed.

"There isn't much to see," he said, looking at Gilfo, then craning his neck to look up at Cullon, who he automatically assumed was leading the investigation. "Be careful where you step. I can't vouch for anything holding together under your weight."

"You've confirmed that the explosion was interior," Cullon said. "The interstellar engines?"

"The main engine blew first. The reserve engine second. As for the cause, that's still under investigation."

"How soon will the lab have a residue analysis for us to view?" the question came from Gilfo. He was seated in a hoverchair, floating four feet off the floor. The hand-controlled jets would allow him to inspect the wreckage from top to bottom a lot faster than his short legs could walk through twisted corridors and fire-blackened cargo slots.

"Another six hours," the technician told them. "We're still running an electromagnetic spectrum on the most stressed areas of the ship. So far, there's nothing in the metallurgy that suggests the injection of any foreign substances."

Danna looked at what had once been a cargo hatch. "The manifest said the freighter was carrying synthesized grain. Did you find evidence of any other cargo?"

The man, who hadn't bothered to introduce himself because his name was in plain sight on his security badge, shook his head. Alexander Amoretti it read. The title, Forensic Technician, was printed below it. "We found lots of grain kernels fused to the cargo bay walls, but nothing out of the ordinary. It appears the *Llyndar* was on a clean run."

That said, the tech went his way, leaving the Tribunal to inspect the freighter's charred skeleton.

"I'll start over here," Gilfo said, triggering the jets on his chair. It lifted slightly, then turned toward the largest intact portion of the freighter's hull. "Let me know if you find anything interesting," he called back to them.

"Let's have a look in the pods," Cullon said, heading toward the evidence boxes that had been labeled and left open for their inspection.

The tubular containers were marked with the exact stellar coordinates where the contents had been found floating in space before being sucked up by the salvage ship's vacuum tubes. Most were fragments of something that had once served a useful purpose. Now, mangled and melted from the blast, they looked like black chunks of nothing.

Reaching into the pod, Danna picked up a small piece of scorched metal. As expected, it felt cold and heavy.

"Can you get a reading?" Cullon asked her.

"No. There's no warmth to it."

The gaze that passed between them spoke volumes, a reminder of the conversation they'd had the previous night.

"There's no life clinging to it," Danna told him. "No memories. Objects that never belonged to anyone don't have an imprint. Whatever it was. It's nothing now but refined metal molded by an assembly droid then reshaped by one hell of an explosion."

"Let's see if we can find something more interesting." He moved between the pods, sifting through the contents. In short order he selected an object. Turning, he held it out to her.

Danna's stomach rolled with the familiar queasiness

that always struck just before she attempted a reading. She looked at the blackened private recorder, the kind used to store images until a sentimental moment came along. This recorder's data chips were heat-welded. There was no chance she'd be able to access its holographic display.

Her hands trembled slightly as she reached for the recorder. Like the small fragment of bulkhead, it felt cold to the touch. Cradling it in the palms of her hands, Danna closed her eyes and concentrated, not on the recorder, but on emptying her mind, slowly bringing her thoughts to zero.

The imprint came in a mist of color, a rainbow without shape or substance. Slowly, the shifting kaleidoscope gave way and she could see the dreamscape.

A dingy room, the corners dark. The cloying scent of warm whiskey mixed with the stale odor of sweat and dirty linens. A man, stripped down to his underwear, sat with the recorder resting on his bulky thighs. He was smiling at the holographic image it displayed—a naked girl sitting cross-legged on a bed. The smile on her face looked forced, but the man didn't care. He was more interested in what she was doing with her hands—rubbing them suggestively over her bare breasts, then pinching her nipples.

Danna returned the recorder to the evidence pod. The image faded from her mind, leaving an empty feeling until she reminded herself that sex was as much a part of life as anything else.

"What did you see?"

"When you said something interesting, you meant it," she answered dryly. "I can't tell you his name, but he liked his women young and animated."

Cullon gave her a quick smile. "Life on board a freighter can get lonely."

Danna moved on, dipping her hand into another evidence pod. The imprint she received from an insu-

lated mug that had somehow escaped the fire was too
vague to create a dreamscape. Probably because the
cup had been used by various members of the crew.

"Nothing," Danna said wearily. They'd just finished
with the last pod. Gilfo had joined them, his exploration of the wreckage complete.

"I may have found something," the dwarf said, guiding his chair around so he could face Danna. "It's in
the aft section, near the observation bubble."

Danna followed the magistrate and his floating chair
with a sense of relief. The sooner they found *something* useful the sooner she could exchange the quarantined bay for the fresh air of Ramora. To say the
charred ruins of the *Llyndar* were depressing was an
understatement.

When they reached the section of the ship that had
aroused Gilfo's curiosity, Danna frowned. The belly of
the *Llyndar* had been torn open in a dozen places. The
explosion had blasted the rear of the ship almost completely away, leaving shreds of metal trailing behind it
like streamers after a wild party. The damage inside
the ship indicated that some of the inner systems had
exploded along with the interstellar engines.

The aft section, or rather what was left of it, lay on
its side, split open like a melon hit with a sledgeham-
mer. The guts of the ship ended in a narrow space that
opened via another hatchway into the maintenance
level beneath the main deck. Inspection lights had
been set as single units, unlike the ubiquitous glare of
the docking bay.

"There." The dwarf pointed a stubby finger. "That
speck of shining metal. It doesn't match the rest."

Danna had to lean forward and turn her neck at an
excruciatingly painful right angle to see what Gilfo
was pointing at. When she did, she had to agree that
the dot of brightness didn't match the rest of the
scorched bulkhead.

"What is it?"

"There's only way to find out," Cullon said. He stepped up and into the split belly of the aft section with the grace of a prowling cat strolling into a dark alley.

Using his dagger, it only took a moment to scrape the small speck of sunshine off the midnight bulkhead. Bounty in hand, he returned to where Danna and Gilfo were waiting.

"I can't say for sure, but it looks like a fragment of Korcian opal," he said, opening his palm.

"I'm surprised the forensic team didn't find it," Danna remarked, looking down at the piece of gemstone lying innocently in the palm of Cullon's large hand.

"Depends on how hard they were looking," he replied, reminding her that most people assumed the explosion had been an accident.

"I've seen Korcian opals before," she said, remembering a particular necklace she'd coveted in one of Seramia's more expensive shops. "They didn't look like that."

The gemstones she had seen had been a play of mystery and shadow, jewels that showed every color of the rainbow depending on which way the light struck them.

"They would if they had been broiled like a piece of raw meat," Cullon told her. "This one was fused to the bulkhead like the grain the technician told us about."

He handed the small sampling to Gilfo before reaching inside the top of his tunic. A second later, Danna was looking at a large Korcian opal dangling from the end of a chain, but unlike the one Cullon had scraped off the wall, this stone was polished and stunningly beautiful. He turned the chain and the gemstone began to sparkle, refracting the light in a warm radiance of condensed shades that simmered as if the stone was alive.

"It's called a *kinita*, a lucky charm," Cullon said, before tucking it back inside his tunic. "A lot of Korcians wear them."

"Let me hold it," she said, reaching out her hand to the dwarf.

The moment the opal touched her palm, Danna felt a frisson of feeling wash over her, like a soothing breeze on a still summer night. The tiny fragment of gemstone felt warm and weightless in her hand. Curiosity licked over her as she closed her fingers around it. Her eyes closed at the same time.

Once again, Danna focused inward, clearing the stage for any imprint the stone might offer. The developing dreamscape brought a peculiar dispassion with it, but she wasn't totally detached. Beneath the rationality of being an observer, her mind filled with questions.

Time hung suspended as images began to form, oscillating between a foggy blur and crystal clarity. Continuous surges of emotion pulsed through her veins as the images wavered, causing the dreamscape to focus, then conceal, suspending Danna between reality and illusion.

When the dreamscape finally came it was as radiant as the opal that dangled from the end of Cullon's chain.

Shades of blue and green simmered like a mirage. As the vision intensified the colors exploded; fiery reds and yellows, jungle greens, and ethereal blues that pulsed and shifted. Then the colors changed, growing more subtle as the pattern altered.

The exotic fairyland teased Danna's mind, making her wonder if she'd ever truly seen color before. Sparkling and mysterious, the differing textures of light and darkness drew her deeper into the illusion, deeper into a world where color was the only reality, the only language.

The ever-changing rainbow remained for a while, imprinted over an intangible blackness, until the darkness prevailed and all light vanished. Danna wanted to call it back, but the words died in her throat.

The bubble of the observation lounge made it seem

*as if there was nothing between him and the stars,
nothing but the immeasurable time that had begun before creation itself.*

*He felt alone, as blank as the starscape. There was
nothing but a vague awareness, an emptiness that had
no end. He shivered in the incipient chill that seeped
through the pressurized glass. The future was on
Earth. A new name, a new life—if he had the courage
to embrace it. He searched the heavens for a sign, a
reference that would connect his old life to the one he
hoped to resurrect.*

*There. Orion's belt, and arcing downward another
group of fainter stars—the hunter's sword. He forced
himself to concentrate on the stars as the ship vibrated, then leaped into interstellar drive. Orion's belt
disappeared, blue-shifting before shrinking into a pinpoint of light.*

*That's when he felt it—heat. Angry and hot and boil-
ing, consuming and thunderous. A mushroom of yellow
flame ate away the bulkheads surrounding him. He was
on fire. Everything burning, melting, dissolving. And
he was dissolving with it.*

*"I'm sorry," he screamed as the flames licked at
him. "I'm so very sorry!"*

Danna didn't hear her own scream, didn't see Cullon reach out for her or the fleeting shimmer of color
that flashed toward the floor as she dropped the opal.
All she could feel was pain—burning, devouring pain.

Four

Danna awoke disoriented, her heart hammering, her body damp with sweat. Slowly, small elements of reality condensed around her. She blinked and Cullon's face came into focus above her.

"Are you all right?" he asked, his voice heavy with concern.

"Yes," she mumbled, forcing aside the inherited fear that had come with the dreamscape. Moving from the past of a dreamscape into the present was always unsettling. "Just a little shaky. Where am I?"

"In one of the offices off the inspection bay," Ambassador Synon answered. He was standing nearby and looking equally concerned. "Commander Gavriel carried you in here after you fainted."

Danna looked around the small room with its cluttered desk and sterile, military style furniture framed by dull gray walls. She was lying on a narrow sofa. The leather was worn, the cushions sagging beneath the weight of her body. She sat up slowly, then accepted the glass of water Gilfo had waiting. The dwarf's face lacked its usual cheerfulness.

"Thank you," she said, sensing the currents of tension coiling through the room. She closed her eyes, then opened them. Even now she could see the explosion, the red and yellow of flesh meeting fire, the result of exploding metal on Namid's body. Danna knew, without knowing how she knew, that Namid's heart and spirit had been broken long before his body had died. The dreamscape had been a tomb, the sepulcher of Namid's empty hopes.

"What did you see?" Cullon asked once she'd emptied the glass. He took it out of her hand, passing it to Gilfo, who then set it on the corner of the desk.

Danna couldn't think for a minute; her mind was too clouded by the residue of everything she'd felt while inside the dreamscape. She was uncomfortable knowing everyone was watching and waiting, but they'd just have to wait. It was going to take a few moments to get her thoughts in order.

"The explosion," she finally answered, her voice unusually husky. She shook her head, then shrugged. "Visions don't usually make me faint, but this one was so vivid. So real."

"Can you tell us about it?" Ambassador Synon asked.

Danna tried to stand up, but Cullon's big hand came to rest on her shoulder, gently pushing her back down into the worn cushions of the sofa. "You're still pale. Sit still."

It was an order, not a suggestion, and Danna accepted it because she knew she was too weak to do anything else.

"I can't tell you what triggered the explosion. The dreamscape began only a few moments before the engines blew."

"Where did the vision take you?" Cullon asked.

"I was on the observation deck. The freighter had just moved to interstellar speed. The stars were bluestreaking, and then . . . it happened. The ship groaned like it was in pain and fire boiled through the corridors and hatchways."

Whatever Cullon was thinking, Danna couldn't read his expression. Gilfo shook his head, and the ambassador released a low sigh before saying, "Your vision supports the forensic team's theory that the ship exploded only seconds after engaging the interstellar drive."

"But it doesn't explain what caused the explosion," Danna said. She noted that Cullon made no comment at all.

"Whatever the reason, you've had enough investigating for one day," Synon told her. "You need to rest."

"I wouldn't mind a cup of tea," she said, liking the idea of putting some distance between herself and the scarred ruins of the *Llyndar*. She'd learned a long time ago that distance was one way of maintaining her sanity. Another was time itself. But it was going to be a very long time before she forgot the sensation of blistering flames partnered by the artic cold of space when the observation bubble burst.

This time when she tried to stand, Cullon helped her. His hand remained on her arm as they exited the office and walked toward the shuttle that had brought them from Seramia. Cullon had acted as their pilot, but this time, instead of assigning Danna to the passenger section, he guided her into the co-pilot seat.

"I can strap myself in," she said, pushing aside his hands when he would have done the job for her. "Just get my feet back on solid ground."

Cullon activated the shuttle's controls. One by one the instrument lights began to blink, coming to life under his skilled hands. While he waited for docking-bay exit clearance, he looked at Danna, seeing and measuring all the small signals her body was giving off. The feminine softness of her features bespoke of compassion, yet a hint of iron resolve was there, too. She was still pale. Still upset. Her mouth was a thin, hard line that said what she'd experienced in the dreamscape was still roiling inside her, still upsetting her. Eyes that had gleamed with curiosity last night looked glazed now, turned inward by the things she hadn't shared with the Tribunal.

Saving his questions for later, Cullon concentrated on granting Danna her wish—getting the shuttle out of the docking bay and back on solid ground.

He liked piloting any kind of stellar vessel, shuttle or starjet, but he liked the ballistic ones best. The high-gee blastoff that always felt as if every bone in your body was breaking, the breathless moments in free fall, then reentry, and that long, long glide that made you feel like a bird. Where could a man have more fun and still keep his clothes on?

As he maneuvered the shuttle from its moorings, Cullon cast a second glance at the woman in the co-pilot seat. He tried to imagine what Danna had experienced. The shock and chaos . . . the destruction . . . the finality of a violent death.

He'd spent his entire life protecting people, whether they knew it or not. The idea of not being able to offer Danna the same protection—the assurance of his physical strength and experience, was enough to make Cullon angry. Good and angry.

Despite his mood, he handled the shuttle with an expertise that disallowed anyone inside from gauging his mood. In the hands of an experienced pilot, the sleek little ship could be made to hover like a hummingbird, up, down, sideways, backward, each movement accomplished swiftly and precisely.

Within minutes the small airship had forsaken the darkness of space for the bright sunlight of a Ramoran day. Dipping down through the clouds, Cullon flew over the capital city, descending slowly toward the tree tops, before circling the landing port in the heart of the planet's capital. The shuttle hovered for a moment, then glided onto the elevated deck, settling as lightly as a bird on a tree branch. A flick of the wrist and the passenger hatch popped open. Cullon felt a rush of warm air along with a heightened awareness of the woman sitting next to him.

Disengaging himself from the safety restraints, he reached over and did the same for his co-pilot. This time Danna didn't protest.

"Up to a short walk, or would you rather I commandeer a city taxi-shuttle and take you back to the embassy?" he asked.

"A walk in fresh air is just what I need," Danna said, looking at the now blank control console as if she'd only just realized they'd landed.

They exited the pilot module together, stepping into the main berth of the shuttle. Another few steps took them outside where Ambassador Synon and Gilfo were waiting. Wordlessly, they entered the tube elevator that would take them to the terminal floor of the landing port.

The short walk to the embassy was a silent one. If the other two men thought it strange that Cullon remained by Danna's side, no comment was made. Ambassador Synon waited until they were inside the embassy's front courtyard before suggesting that they all dine together that evening.

"The final forensic reports will be available by then," he said before looking directly at Danna. "In the meantime, may I suggest a long nap. I dislike the idea of this investigation putting such a strain on you."

"I'm okay," she insisted. "See you at dinner."

Cullon watched until Danna had reached the top of the exterior staircase that led to her quarters, then left the embassy, walking toward the inner city. He'd give her just enough time to have the cup of tea she'd mentioned before paying her another visit. The imprint she'd gotten had to belong to Namid—it wasn't likely that anyone else on board the *Llyndar* would have been wearing a Korcian lucky charm. The average freighter crewman wouldn't have been able to afford the gemstone. Korcian opals were as rare as honor among thieves.

Alert to his surroundings, Cullon took note of the thickening mid-day crowd that was beginning to filter out of the city's office buildings and shops and onto the streets where open-air cafés offered a variety of food and drink.

Trained to be aware of everything around him, Cullon watched the spectacle of anonymous passersby. The sounds of life and commerce were everywhere. A young businessman called out for a taxi-shuttle, waving an arm as one of the conveyances whished toward him. Nearby, a reed-thin woman chattered excitedly to her not-as-old male companion. A delivery man, attired in the distinctive yellow robes of a popular pleasure palace, wove his way through the crowd, obviously late for his next appointment. Just ahead of him, a strikingly beautiful brunette, clutching a shopping bag from one of the city's upscale shops, glanced Cullon's way. She was wearing one of the thin, gauzy dresses Ramoran women preferred in the summer. The garment draped over her body like a second skin, showing the outline of a seductive frame.

Cullon held her interest for several seconds longer than she held his. Disappointed, she turned and entered a stylish boutique to finish her shopping.

Wistfully, Cullon looked at the sky blanketing the city. The high hour of the day was passing, but there was still plenty of time to inspect Namid's apartment before the Tribunal officially gathered for dinner with Ambassador Synon.

Taking a right-hand turn onto one of the city's scenic boulevards put Cullon directly behind the embassy.

From there, it was a small matter to make his way from the tree-lined street, via a narrow alleyway between two buildings, to the rear entrance of the embassy's inner courtyard. A maintenance door with an unreliable lock was his gateway into the rear courtyard itself. From there, he could see the door to Danna's personal quarters.

To her credit, Danna didn't seem surprised to see him.

To Cullon's credit, his expression didn't show how much he liked the silky turquoise robe she was wearing. Bare feet, long brown hair, and eyes so deep and dark they took a man into the unknown. What wasn't there to like?

Wordlessly, Danna retreated a step into the relative dimness of the room. Cullon followed her without waiting for an invitation.

"Feeling better?" he asked once the sensors had reacted and closed the door.

"Somewhat. I was just going to have a cup of tea. Care to join me?"

While she walked to the processing unit in the small kitchenette, Cullon looked around the living quarters Danna MacFadyen had called home for the last two years.

It was obvious that she'd put a great deal of effort into making the place into a very personal residence. Instead of sleek metal and stained glass, preferred by Ramorans, the furniture was thickly cushioned in a variety of bright colors and patterns. A framed print of an Earth sunset hung on one wall. Other unmistakable paraphernalia sat on tables and shelves: a large white and pink seashell, a slender glass vase holding one long stemmed red rose, an intricately carved wooden box, and a collection of small jadestone figurines.

Cullon looked toward the bedroom, but all the slightly ajar door revealed was a neatly made bed.

He turned his attention back to the painting that consumed a major portion of the apartment's eastern wall. There were no mountains, no hills. Nothing but reaching fingers of shimmering blue water and a forest of palms and low bushes. The gold tinted sky silhouetted the outline of an isolated beach.

"Have you ever been to Earth?"

Cullon looked to where Danna stood, a cup of steaming tea in each hand. He took one of them before answering. "Once. A long time ago."

"Where?" she asked, moving to sit down in a chair covered in a fabric that was several shades darker than the robe she was wearing. When she sat, the robe opened to reveal a portion of her slender legs.

Seeing her in something other than tailored slacks and a diplomatic jacket was having a strong effect on Cullon's libido. The silken robe draped her upper body, not snuggly, but enticingly. The vee created by the lapels drew his attention. The size of her breasts weren't important to him, but he was curious about their sensitivity. Would they bud the moment he touched them?

The casualness of his arousal jolted Cullon's peace of mind, making him acutely aware of how easily this particular female had gotten through his defenses.

Unfortunately, the glimpse of bare flesh didn't last long enough to satisfy his curiosity. Danna tucked the robe back into place before lifting the teacup to her mouth.

Realizing she wasn't going to blurt out what she'd seen in the dreamscape without a few social niceties to pave the way, Cullon sat down on the big sofa across from her.

"I visited the European continent," he told her a moment later. "I spent several months there."

What he didn't say was what he'd been doing on Earth. He didn't follow a lot of rules, but one of them was to never look back. Second guessing your life didn't accomplish anything but inflating regrets. What was done was done.

"Did you visit any of the protected sites?" Danna asked.

"Some of them," he replied. "My favorite was a large religious relic in old Paris."

"Notre Dame is an amazing building," she said.

Silence stretched out between them as Danna sipped her tea. Cullon sensed she'd rather not talk about the dreamscape, but he couldn't let her file its effects away just yet. He needed to know exactly what she'd seen and felt.

"Did you imprint with Namid personally, or was the dreamscape limited to the explosion?"

Danna hesitated a fraction of a second before answering him, confirming the reluctance he'd sensed.

"You were right. The charm belonged to Namid."

Cullon leaned forward, his concentration targeted. "Were you connected long enough to find out what he was doing traveling under an alias?"

Danna shook her head, sending a cloud of dark wavy hair across her shoulders. "Looking for something. Hoping for something. I'm not sure, the link didn't last for more than a few seconds. What I am sure of is that he felt alone. Not lonely. *Alone*. As if everything he loved, everyone he loved, had been taken away from him. I don't think I've ever felt such despair."

"Korcian rivers run deep," Cullon said, trying to imagine turning his back on his heritage. The idea was too bizarre to take hold. "Anything else?"

"Regret. Despondency. A sense of failure."

"What kind of failure?"

Cullon waited while Danna composed the answer. When she spoke, her voice was subdued, as if she were reliving the experience in order to describe it.

"A feeling of nullity, of loss and grief. The colors were vivid and alive before they faded to black," she told him. "I sensed enough to know that Namid was a man who cared deeply. His emotions weren't mediocre.

When he loved, he loved with all his heart. When he cried, he cried from the depths of his soul."

"That's quite an impression."

"Emotions make the imprint, not the other way around," she said, meeting his gaze head on. "If you asked me what Namid was wearing when he died I couldn't tell you. But I do know what he was feeling."

"Because you felt it too?"

"Yes," she said, fighting to keep her voice even. "I felt what Namid was feeling the moment he died."

"Fear."

"Regret. His last words were 'I'm sorry.' He screamed them out when the fire reached the observation deck."

The shiver that went through Danna's body was visible from where Cullon was sitting. He fought the impulse to go to her, to wrap her in his arms and keep her safe. Someone was killing True Bloods. It was his job to find out the who, what, and why of it, not play white knight to a dark-eyed Terran.

That's what the Enforcer in him was saying. The pure male side of his personality was telling him to forget what he'd learned the hard way and give into his protective instincts. Before he could decide which part of himself to listen to, Danna left her chair and returned to the kitchenette to pour more herbal tea into her cup.

"Did you get any indication of what Namid had to regret?" Cullon asked, following her. He held out his empty cup so she could refill it.

Danna didn't answer him until steam was rising from both porcelain mugs. The spicy fragrance mixed with the scent of the woman who was standing so close Cullon could see his own reflection in her eyes.

"No," she said sadly. "But I did sense that it was more than a single action or incident. The emotions went deeper, as if he felt the need to atone for his entire life. If I knew more about him, I might be able to explain what I felt. Right now, all I can do is guess."

"Was he running away from someone?"

"I don't think so. I didn't sense that kind of urgency. He was thinking about the new life he was about to begin on Earth, but there wasn't any enthusiasm in his heart."

"The more questions I ask, the more questions I get. If Namid wasn't running away from someone, and he wasn't excited about going to Earth, what in the hell was he doing traveling under an assumed name on a freighter that would take him where he didn't want to go?"

"I don't know," Danna replied, seconding his frustration. "Didn't you do a background check on him? What does his personal file say?"

"All I can give you are facts and figures. He was twenty-eight. The unmarried, eldest son of a prestigious family with lots of political connections. His job in the Trade Bureau was more show than substance. If you want to know more, we'll have to check out the apartment he rented when he came to Ramora."

Cullon could see that her hands were trembling as she set her cup on the counter. Unable to prevent it, his protective instincts kicked into gear. "We can wait until tomorrow. Ambassador Synon was right. You need to rest."

"No," she insisted. "The dreamscape upset me, but it didn't do any permanent damage. I agree with you. There's more than an explosion to investigate here. I felt it, even if I can't explain it. The sooner I get another imprint, the sooner I'll be able to give you more than vague answers."

Five

The late afternoon air was sweet with the scent of the sea and sunshine as Danna stepped out of the taxi-shuttle that had carried them across the city to the shores of the Seramian Inlet.

"Namid's rooms are on the fourth floor," Cullon said as he inserted a currency card into the scanner on the taxi's console. He keyed in the code that would keep the taxi locked and reserved until they finished their inspection.

Danna looked up, imagining the view offered by the fourth floor balconies. The building faced the inlet. Stretching out of sight on either side of the building they were about to enter were more residential buildings, each with a narrow marble path running down the side. Gates and railings provided the necessary signal that the pathways were private. This was an exclusive part of the old city, one where the cost of living exceeded the average Ramoran income.

The architecture was pleasing to the eye, its design characterized by a rhythmic fluidity that had a majesty of its own. The resident-security consoles flanking the

entry way to the plush apartments supported a cor-
belled loggia that linked the ground and higher floors.
The front windows were supported by intricate metal
framework and armorglass, the plasticized metal used
in most residential structures.

The only ornamentation on the ground floor was a
wide staircase with white marble balustrades running
up from the sidewalk to the solid front doors. A typical
Ramoran greeting was etched into a plaque above the
door, "May prosperity greet all who enter here."

"How long did Namid live here?" Danna asked.

"Six months and three days," Cullon said as he
pulled an electronic key from his pocket and pointed it
at the main door. "The Ramoran authorities secured
the apartment as soon as the Registry told them Vosca
Komarr didn't exist. I'm the only one who's been inside since then."

"Find anything interesting?" Danna asked as they
stepped inside the lobby of the building. As expected,
it reflected the same fluid style as the exterior. Long,
sleek lines of marble and glass.

"Nothing out of the ordinary."

Danna shut the door on her inner thoughts as they
crossed the lobby to where a glass-fronted lift waited
for occupants. The more she thought about being alone
with Cullon Gavriel in an unoccupied apartment the
higher her anxiety level soared.

She was smart enough to know that when a woman
got involved with a man like Cullon she was taking
nothing for granted. She took her chances and hoped
she got what she bargained for—a few undivided hours
of his attention.

A hot, memorable affair.

Still, it was oddly pleasant to be aware of her femi-
ninity again. She'd pushed it aside for a long time now,
concentrating on her job, working her way up the
diplomatic ladder that would eventually, hopefully,
land her an ambassadorship.

Her energy and efficiency had earned her honors from the University of Galactic Studies, and an offer to stay on as a professor, but she'd declined. She liked the challenge of working beyond the boundaries of Earth, of making her way in a profession as diverse as the galaxy it represented.

Once inside the elevator, Cullon gave a voice command for the fourth floor. In response, polyglas doors slid soundlessly shut and the lift began to move. When the elevator's panels glided open, they revealed a long, carpeted corridor.

Like most residential buildings constructed for multiple occupants, the walls were a pale cream. Several paintings, each showing a different view of the Seramian Inlet, decorated the walls.

"This way," Cullon said, taking her arm, although it wasn't necessary. The corridor was as straight as an arrow.

Danna allowed the contact because to remark on it was to draw attention to the attraction she was determined to ignore as long as she and the Korcian were both members of the Tribunal.

She waited until Cullon had disengaged the door's lock with the same electronic override key he'd used to gain entry to the building itself. Once the door was opened, Danna took a deep breath, then stepped inside.

The room immediately appealed to her. The effect of high arched ceilings and colorful rugs spread over smooth tile floors was broken by walls of windows overlooking a sun-kissed inlet.

Without stopping to inspect the furnishings, she walked to where stained glass panels separated the main room from the balcony she'd spied at street level. She stepped outside to gaze upon the Seramian Inlet with its wind-tossed waves and dazzling white sand. The scent of salt and sea was heavy in the air. The slanting sunlight reflecting off the water gave it a deep apricot shade.

"This is a view I'd sacrifice my budget for," she murmured more to herself than to the man who had followed her outside.

"You like water?"

"My family owns a home on the eastern coast of North America. I grew up with the surf at my back door."

"The oceans on Korcia are a deep emerald green," he said. "But not as green as the jungles. Nothing is as green as a Korcian jungle."

Danna smiled. "Somehow I can't imagine you standing in the midst of rain-drenched ferns and flowering flora."

"Why not?"

She dared a look at him then, making sure her expression didn't reveal more than it should. "You said you'd visited Earth. Did you ever study its history?"

"Some of it."

"Way back, when technology could be summed up in a few simple words like fire and basic survival, Vikings ruled the seas."

The smile he gave her was the most devastating to date. "You think I should be wearing animal furs while I sail iceberg-littered oceans."

Danna avoided a direct reply by saying, "Vikings were tall, flaxen-haired warriors. Fierce fighters and avid explorers. Like Korcians, warfare was as natural to them as breathing. They conquered their way into almost every civilization in the northern hemisphere. When they weren't in the conquering mood, they traded, expanding their influence down the Germanic rivers into the very heart of Europe."

"Maybe my people paid Earth a visit in the long forgotten past?"

"Maybe," Danna mused, turning her attention back to the swirling currents of the inlet. It was safer than looking into Cullon's tawny eyes.

"I'd offer you a glass of wine while we wait for the

sun to set, but the kitchen is as empty as the closets," Cullon said.

The hint that they'd come to work, not watch the inlet turn from blue to gold as the sun inched its toward the horizon, was strong enough to make Danna turn around. Unfortunately, a six foot four inch Korcian Enforcer was blocking her path. Her heart skipped, then settled down. The man was really beginning to get on her nerves.

"Where do you suggest we start, Commander?"

"I'll leave that up to you."

Not sure where to begin, Danna let her instincts guide her. She walked around the main room, touching things at random, seeking the subtle warmth that normally indicated an imprint. The room was sparsely furnished, but the pieces had been selected with an eye for texture and color.

She tried to imagine Chimera Namid living in this room, relaxing in one of the plush chairs while he read, his face set in concentration as the story unraveled before his eyes. She wished she had known him. It was painful that where there had once been a vibrant young man there was now a void, no passion, no vitality. Nothing.

Danna reached out and touched one of several carved figurines on a shelf, but there was no warmth in the wood beyond what the open balcony door and the afternoon sunshine had brought into the room.

She moved on to the bedroom, noting the crisp, unwrinkled coverlet that said the bed had been neatly made by someone. Namid? Probably, Danna decided. The short time she'd been linked to him had left the impression that he'd been a conscientious kind of man.

The closet wasn't as completely empty as Cullon had led her to believe. There were a few items of clothing left; a bathrobe and several jumpsuits that had Korcian fashion written all over them. As if a Korcian could hide his ethnic heritage with a quick wardrobe change.

"Do all Korcians have eyes like yours?" she asked, not bothering to actually touch the clothes. She wasn't ready to imprint just yet.

"Most of them. Why?"

"Just wondering. Namid seemed intent on changing his life. I wonder if he planned to have cosmetic injections to change the color of his eyes. It's a common procedure."

Not waiting for a reply, she walked to the dresser and began opening drawers. Again, some items had been left behind. And again nothing out of the ordinary, at least nothing that couldn't have been replaced if Namid had reached Earth.

Danna continued roaming around the room, taking in the arrangement of furniture and the tidiness of what had been a man's bedroom. "Are you certain no one's been here except you?" she asked as Cullon kept pace with her, walking beside her and only slightly behind. "It strikes me as being a little too neat."

"Some men like things neat and clean."

"Agreed, but most of them don't make wrinkle-free beds."

"Maybe he had a lover."

"Maybe," she said, only half agreeing. Her sixth sense told her that Namid had been alone on Ramora.

"Tell me something I don't already know about Namid," she said as she stopped to study a small collection of books. It was difficult to tell without taking an imprint if they had arrived at the apartment with Namid or been left behind by a former tenant.

"The apartment manager said Namid kept to himself. The security monitors backed him up," Cullon told her. "He went out almost every day, but not for long periods of time."

"And his nights? Did he spend them here?"

"Most, but not all."

"So if he had a lover, he didn't bring her back here."

"No."

"Then she couldn't have been the one to make the bed."

"So Namid was a neat-freak," he grumbled. "Is that significant?"

Danna could tell by his brusque voice tone that he thought she was wasting precious time. Not wanting to muddy the waters with personal contention, she explained her remark. "A person's outward behavior often reflects their thinking process. If they're neat, they're usually detailed and methodical in other areas of their lives."

She stepped back to study the bookcase again, silently reading the titles—some classics, some not so classic, and a few that had been banned on the more conservative planets. The bottom shelf held a stack of Ramoran periodicals, the kind that guided people to the premier restaurants and nightspots that lined the inlet.

"Assassins are methodical people," Cullon said, obviously speaking from the voice of experience. "But they don't get personal about their work. Emotions reduce survival probability."

Danna wasn't entirely sure she liked the implications of what Cullon was saying. She should feel relieved that men like him worked behind the scenes, doing what had to be done, but she wasn't comfortable with the idea. She knew this man, or at least she was getting to know him. He was solid, his masculine presence remarkably reassuring even though she didn't need a bodyguard to inspect Namid's now empty quarters.

Disregarding his last remark, mostly because she didn't like it, Danna continued moving slowly around the room, admiring the clean, polished lines of the furniture and the colors that had been blended to make the room suitable for either male or female. A dark beige carpet blanketed the bedroom floor. The bed cover and drapes were a splattered pattern of aqua blue and desert brown with a touch of white. Another book caught her eye.

Since it was on the bedside table and not on the bookshelf, she decided it probably had an imprint attached.

Looking for something else to target, Danna left the bedroom to enter the bath. The space was adequate but tight, with the shower jammed into a corner and shielded by opaque, etched glass. Towels hung on a rack within reach of anyone not wanting to get the floor wet. The counter area was variegated marble, a favorite of Ramoran architectures because it was plentiful and inexpensive as well as being durable and attractive.

Danna looked at a small metal case, sitting harmlessly on the counter. "Could you pick that up for me please," she said. Cullon hadn't followed her into the bathroom, but he was standing in the doorway.

He raised a brow in question, then shrugged and reached a long arm past her to snatch up the personal hygiene kit.

"There's a book on the table by the bed. Could you get that for me too?"

"At your service," he said tightly.

"I don't like touching items before I imprint with them," she said, explaining herself again. "I don't want a momentary impression getting in the way."

"Makes sense," he said, conceding further as he backed away from the door to give her free access to the bedroom again.

She made her way to the middle of the room, midway of the bed and the windows that overlooked the inlet. There was no bedroom balcony. Pity, Danna thought.

She sat down on the floor, her eyes already beginning to narrow in concentration. "The book first, please."

Once the book was in her hand, Danna felt the smooth, subtle texture of the brown leather. She opened it and began leafing through the pages. It was written in Korcian, but she didn't bother to ask Cullon to translate. The style of the text told her it was poetry.

Like the leather binding, the pages showed signs of considerable wear, as if the book had been touched more than it had been read. None of the pages were marked, so she had no way of knowing if Namid had been savoring a favorite verse before leaving the apartment to join the crew of the *Llyndar*.

Eyes closed and fingers splayed wide over the open pages of the book, Danna cleared her mind, opening the pathway for any imprint to flow freely. Gradually her perception changed, time rolled backward like a faulty clock, and she felt her mind surrendering to another person's energy.

Soon she was deep within herself—and outside of herself. Colors began to form, soft blues and gentle greens rimmed by even lighter shades of gold and orange. Within seconds, the dreamscape became as tangible as the volume of poetry.

It unfolded like a sunset on a lazy summer day. The colors shimmered as images began to take shape. The greens became darker and bolder as they gradually took on the shape of a jungle garden. Feather fronds soughed to a breeze whose warmth carried the fragrance of exotic spice. Water ran from a fountain, down slick rocks to pool at the feet of a large statue. The laughter of children added a surprising dimension to the dreamscape. Sounds were rare, and it took a very strong imprint to transmit them.

Danna relaxed and began to enjoy the elemental power of the scene taking shape around her. Never had she felt so unimportant in the grand scheme of things, more like a grain of sand on an endless beach than a

link to what had once been. The image had its own
power. Colors swayed like wind around the perimeter.

*A woman sitting on the bench. She was young and
lovely, with long dark hair and smooth, flawless skin.
Her attire was a belted robe and sandals, and she was
holding a book in her lap. Her mouth moved as if she
were reading aloud, but Danna didn't have to hear the
words to know she was reciting a verse—one she knew
by heart.*

*"Namid, don't tease your sister. Come and sit by me.
It's time for your lesson."*

*The young boy who wandered into the dreamscape
was as dark-haired as the woman. He came reluctantly, looking back over his shoulder at the fun he'd
be missing. His skin was bronzed by the sun and his
dark blue-gray eyes gleamed. He sat down beside the
woman and the book was passed into his hands. He began to read, but the sound of his voice faded.*

The dreamscape began to fade too. Danna concentrated, trying to get it back. There was a secret that lay
within the colors, she could sense it. There were answers to be found. She could feel them, but they kept
eluding her, shrinking into a shimmering rainbow, beyond form, beyond reach. Then they were gone, given
over to nothingness.

The knowledge Danna hadn't been able to grasp
faded to black along with it, but the sense of something to be learned stayed with her. The universe was a
dizzying complexity of differences. Civilizations separated by time and space had evolved with different
philosophies and ethics, yet no matter the distance,
certain rules applied once sentient beings began the
climb from pools of microscopic life to the stars.
Danna had felt that similarity just now—the bonding
love of a family.

"The book belonged to Namid's mother," Danna announced, opening her eyes. "She liked poetry."

"Did her son?" Cullon asked. It was apparent he was hoping the book might be more than a family memento.

"Yes. He liked poetry. And he loved his mother."

Cullon sat down beside her. "What did you see?"

"It isn't what I saw as much as what I felt."

"So what did you feel?" he asked, giving the book she'd put down on the floor a cursory glance. "A boyhood memory?"

"Yes. Namid looked to be five or six. They were sitting in a garden surrounded by jungle. He was reading poetry to his mother."

"A dutiful son."

His tone implied boring as well as compliant, and Danna couldn't help but think that Cullon Gavriel's childhood had been just the opposite. In fact, she doubted any period of his life would qualify as boring. She got the impression that he had been born with the inclination to rush headlong into danger. It went without saying that his private life would be just as high-geared.

"Okay, we've got a loving, dutiful son who reads poetry. Anything else?" he asked, breaking into Danna's private fantasy of what a handsome Enforcer's private life might entail.

"I got the impression that he not only loved his mother, he respected her. As a person."

"I respect my mother."

Danna smiled. "I'm sure you do."

He smiled back at her. "Is there something you're not telling me, or do you just enjoy being vague?"

"I'm not being vague, I'm trying to explain that a psychic imprint isn't a fingerprint or a DNA scan. It isn't science, it's emotion."

"Then what do your emotions tell you?"

The impatience has left his voice, but Danna could tell he was eager to find out something more substantial than she'd been able to tell him so far.

She brushed her fingers over the now closed volume of poetry. "Namid was disciplined. He understood that life wasn't all fun and games. He respected his mother because she taught him that, along with other valuable lessons."

"What about the box?" Cullon asked, pointing toward the small hygienic case he'd taken from the bathroom counter.

"I don't know. Open it."

It contained the normal items one might expect to find in a man's toiletry kit. All but one.

The ring was large and gold and definitely belonged to a man. Cullon put it on the floor in front of her.

Danna immediately associated its style with the signet rings worn by men on Earth. Rings that identified the wearers as graduates of a specific college or members of a particular association. The stone was black, highly polished, and more oval than round. An engraved letter that looked like a Korcian hieroglyph adorned the center of the ring.

"Do you recognize it?" she asked.

"It's the sign of the House of A'vla Namid."

"A royal cartouche."

"Close enough."

"It's doesn't look antique," Danna noted as she studied the ring lying benignly on the carpet in front of her. "Is it a reproduction?"

"Probably. After the civil war, some of the noble families tried to hide their true identities. Anything that linked them to the old kings was discarded or hidden. It wasn't popular to be a True Blood then. Now, it isn't unheard of for a father to give his son a ring like this to remind him of his heritage."

"Do you have a ring like that?"

"My father does. I won't inherit it until his death."

The simple statement told Danna that the Gavriel cartouche wasn't a reproduction. It was a family heirloom passed from eldest son to eldest son.

"Want to try this one on for size?" Cullon asked.

"That's what I'm here for."

Danna put on the ring and immediately felt the power of the dreamscape. It rose around her, flowing in ripples of crimson red that spread and spread until every nook and cranny of her mind was filled before exploding into a gushing borealis. Thready pulses of white gave it a ghostly impression as she suddenly felt as if she was falling headlong into infinity.

Her mind tumbled with the colors in a confusion of speed and distance, a spinning whirlwind of shadows and emotions. Then, just as suddenly as the disorientation had started, it stopped.

Danna took a deep breath and concentrated on the colors vibrating in sharp, jagged flashes, like lightning slashing across a midnight sky. The image came just as fast, moving over her like a tidal wave. She made a startled sound and braced herself for the impact.

It was night, but there were lights all around. And noise. Lots of noise. Drunken laughter and crude conversation. The ring gleamed as Namid raised a glass to his mouth.

He really didn't belong here. It was vulgar and raw and the holograms weren't very good. The computers were out of sync. The naked girl dancing on the bar wasn't moving in rhythm to the music blaring from the sound system. Instead of looking provocative and sexy, she looked like she was having some kind of cerebral fit.

The glass went down on the table as he stood up. He moved through the crowd, ignoring the primarily male audience as he made his way to the exit. Outside the air was almost as stuffy, almost as sour as it had been inside the club. He stopped to look around, settling his gaze on a particularly tall building.

The crowning glory of the skyscraper was a metallic arch with two widespread wings. Like the holographic dancer, it lacked grace and style.

"Where have you been?" he asked of someone who

was approaching from out of the darkness. "*I've been waiting for over an hour.*"

The colors changed as Danna probed the dreamscape for the identity of the second person. Greens shifted and swirled into a deep russet orange, blues deepened to brooding purple, and the rim of gold dulled until it became nonexistent. She could make out a shape, but it was impossible to tell if it belonged to a male or a female. The colors were moving too swiftly, melting into each other until there was no color at all, only darkness.

Danna released a ragged breath as the dreamscape left her.

"You saw something this time," Cullon said, studying her with intense eyes.

"I'm not sure what I saw." She felt cheated and it showed. She took off the ring and put it back on the floor, next to the book of poetry.

She could see the frustration on Cullon's face. He wasn't used to working with second-hand information, with bits and pieces fed to him through another person's eyes, with impressions that were just that—impressions.

"He was in a nightclub," she told him.

"Where?"

"I didn't see anything that would identify it."

"What was it like? Plush or seedy?"

"Definitely seedy."

"Was he with someone?"

"Not inside the club, but there was someone. Outside on the street. Namid wasn't happy that he or she was late."

Cullon came to his feet, then held out his hand to help Danna stand. Both the book of poetry and the ring remained on the carpet. "He or she? Couldn't you tell?"

"I couldn't see them clearly enough to make a distinction," Danna admitted. "Then the dreamscape faded."

"What *did* you see clearly?"

"A building. A skyscraper with a huge arch on the very top. An arch with wings. It made it look as if the building were about to fly away."

Cullon collected the book and the ring from the floor. He tossed both of them onto the bed before turning to give Danna his most piercing glare to date. "The Imperium."

Six

"The Imperium is part of the Conglomerate."

Cullon didn't answer the implied question in Danna's tone. He'd watched her during the imprint process for any sign that the dreamscapes she'd entered might be as traumatic as the one she'd experienced earlier in the day. He'd continued watching her because he liked what he saw. But now, duty forced him to concentrate on what had brought him to Ramora—murder.

Having the Conglomerate colony of Marasona, corporate headquarters for the Imperium Mining Company, added to the equation intensified that duty.

The Conglomerate was a collection of privately funded colonies in the galaxy's outer regions. There, beyond the legal restraints of the League or the Empire, the colonies were free to do business any way they liked. As with most criminal enterprises, much was rumored, but little was actually known about the faceless executives who supervised the nebulous organization.

Having the Imperium associated with the *Llyndar* explosion surprised Cullon. Senseless violence wasn't the Conglomerate's way; normally the governors prided themselves on their strategic genius. The less attention they called to themselves, the better they liked it.

Leaving Danna to follow, Cullon exited the bedroom and headed for the apartment's compact kitchen.

"I thought the cupboards were bare," she said, arriving in time to watch him fill two glasses with a local white wine.

"I didn't want you drinking alcohol before an imprint," he said curtly.

Since the interplanetary scope of the Conglomerate's illegal endeavors were as well known to the League as the Empire, Danna immediately asked, "What would Namid be doing on Marasona?"

The Imperium was in the dregs of the galaxy. If it was sinful or illegal, Marasona was the place to find it.

Cullon put down the wine bottle, picked up both glasses, walked to where Danna was standing, and handed her one. The words Marasona and Imperium irritated him in equal proportions.

"Does the Empire have plans to annex Marasona?" she asked.

"No," Cullon answered. "If we did, it wouldn't be annexation, it would be extermination. The Imperium isn't anything more than a expensive shield for pirates and gunrunners."

"It's hard to destroy something if you can't find the target." Danna sat down in a chair near the open balcony doors. The heat of the day was getting heavier, but there was still a breeze blowing in from the inlet. "You want to destroy the Conglomerate but no ones knows where it actually exists. *Where* is the Imperium? Its headquarters may be on Marasona, but that's not the real target. Like every Conglomerate colony, the Imperium is a secret cartel driven by profit and power."

"You don't have to tell me how the Conglomerate

works." Cullon stared past the balcony railing at the deep blue of the Seramian Inlet, wishing the wind whispering over the coastal city carried at least one of the answers he needed. "I've spent the last ten years trying to unravel its web."

"That's the irony of it, isn't it? We, meaning the League and the Empire, make a better target than the corporate colonies. The Conglomerate has the money and the means to do us more harm than we can do it."

Cullon lifted his glass in a mock salute. "You're a smart lady."

"I've learned a few things along the way."

"You're right," he conceded. "The Conglomerate doesn't have any unionized force; it may not even have agent saboteurs, but it can afford the weapons to supply an army of mercenaries. The League and the Empire aren't going anywhere. We'll still be here, a big fat target, a year from now or a decade. Time is on their side."

Like his diplomatic counterpart, Cullon knew the real threat to galactic civilization lay in the outer regions.

Opportunists moved quickly. Every time the corporate powers sent out an exploration team to settle a new planet or a habitable asteroid the risk increased. Once found, the consortium of mining and manufacturing companies ceded the extra-territoriality for a new spaceport or settlement, slapped a conglomerate name on it . . . and the public wasn't told that the new corporation was owned by the very politicians who built stumbling blocks to keep the outer regions from being annexed. It was a road with a single destination—trouble.

"Do you think Namid was selling technical information to the Imperium?" Danna asked. "He was employed by the Trade Bureau."

"It's a possibility," Cullon admitted.

He looked at her. The sunlight streaming in through the open balcony doors made her hair shine like dark fire. Even though she was fighting it, the bonding between them had begun from the moment they'd met. Cullon knew it was only a matter of time before his patience ran out, and he brought the waiting to a conclusion. In the meantime, he allowed the anticipation to flow through him, savoring it the same way he'd savored any other pleasurable experience.

"I can't stop thinking about how the colors changed," Danna said. Her eyes focused on him in silent speculation. "The poetry imprint was so serene. But the ring imprint was . . . the colors were different."

"People change," Cullon said, retiring his thoughts of personal pleasure and replacing them with suspicions of murder. "Boys stop being boys and start being men."

Danna looked uncertain, and said so, "It's more than that."

"Give me more than feelings and vague impressions, and I'll act on it. Until then, you're guessing as much as I am."

Danna's head came up sharply. Cullon knew she wanted to tell him what he could do with his share of the guesses, but she didn't. Instead she put on her be-nice-diplomatic face and remarked, "Granted, but it usually takes something traumatic to make people change. You said Namid led a normal life, nothing out of the ordinary."

"I ran every file the Registry had on him, but a computer can't tell you what goes on inside a man's head."

"Maybe Namid wasn't what he appeared to be," she said. "Your gut might not like the idea of him being tied to the Conglomerate, but you have to admit it would explain his presence on Marasona. It's not exactly a vacation planet for the elite."

She was right, Cullon didn't like it. His eyes locked with hers for a long moment. "You forget Namid was a True Blood, and heir to the throne. Treason would leave a bitter taste in his mouth."

"The pages of history are populated by treasonous men," she pointed out. "Maybe Namid was more ambitious than he led people to believe. Maybe he saw the wealth of the Conglomerate as his ticket to the throne. It wouldn't be the first time a king's bought a crown."

"Why buy what's already yours?"

Danna wasn't convinced by his logic. "Maybe Namid had insurance on his mind, the kind a corporate colony like the Imperium could deliver. Would the Korcian Guard defend a True Blood's right to reclaim the throne or would its loyalty remain with the generals who rule the High Council?"

"You're talking about a civil war."

"A civil war unseated the last king. Why not play it in reverse?"

Cullon walked to the counter where he'd left the wine bottle and refilled his glass. If Namid had coveted the throne, eliminating the competition made sense. But who had turned the tables on him? The next in line?

That's where the premise fell apart. The House of A'vla Gavriel was the next in the line of ascension, and he sure as hell hadn't blown the *Llyndar* out of the sky.

Danna put her hand over her glass when Cullon offered to refill it. Skepticism filled his eyes as he asked, "So who killed Namid? Another True Blood with designs on the throne or a corporate assassin?"

"I'd put my money on the corporates. If Namid had a change of heart, it stands to reason they'd want him out of the way."

"You don't sound convinced."

"I'm not," she admitted. "Not totally. Call it womanly intuition, but the feelings don't fit. If Namid was running from the Imperium he should have been frightened or angry. But he wasn't. At least not before he died. He was hurt. Deeply hurt, down in his soul.

And filled with regrets. Those aren't the sort of emotions that comes from playing political roulette."

Cullon decided he had enough possibilities to explore for the time being. "Can you get different imprints from the same object?"

"Sometimes. Why?"

"I'll have Namid's personal belongings packed and sent to the embassy. There's no point in coming back here."

"You want me to try the ring again?"

"I want to know who Namid met on Marasona."

It was growing dark by the time Danna finished with the last of Namid's personal belongings. She hadn't tried a second reading on the ring. She'd wanted to see what other imprints might confirm her first impression of Namid. So far, nothing had surfaced to change her opinion. The other imprints had been very much like the one she called "poetry."

Some of the colors had been dark, but not dark enough to make Namid seem sinister or dishonest. Moody, yes, a little uncertain of himself, but nothing that fit with the regret and loneliness she'd felt in the first dreamscape.

And nothing that linked him to the Conglomerate. So what had he been doing on one of their colonies?

People did travel to the outer regions. The raw resources had to be harvested by someone; industrial droids had their limitations. The outer regions were a frontier for the adventurous, a deep well for the greedy, and a marketplace for the unscrupulous traders that kept men like Cullon Gavriel busy.

Danna showered, put on a robe and sat down in the middle of the bed. A voice command dimmed the lights.

The room around her was furnished in the haphazard taste of someone who liked to collect items along each step of her life; a shelf full of books, polished figurines from the rock quarries on Mars Station, a gleaming crystal pyramid from a little shop on Rosatti Nine. On the wall opposite the bed there was a painting of an ancient clipper ship, its sails unfurled as it skipped across the Northern Atlantic Ocean of Earth.

Danna looked around, knowing each of the objects, wondering which ones she'd leave behind if she made a decision to start all over again, exchanging one identity for another. The answer was easy. She'd leave it all behind. Well, maybe not everything. There was the seashell her father had given her when she was six. Namid had taken the *kinita*, his lucky charm, but he'd left behind the ring, the symbol of his true heritage. Why? Did it remind him of something he'd rather forget, or had something made him believe he wasn't worthy of calling himself a True Blood? Was that the regret he'd felt, the sin he'd shouted out to be forgiven for?

And then, there was a question for herself. Did she really want to know the source of Namid's regret? Whatever it was, she was certain it was personal. Very personal.

A chill of trepidation touched her as she thought of the grave robbers of old. She'd learned to live with her skills, but she'd never liked prying into other people's minds, and that's exactly what she'd been doing all day.

Her gaze settled on the cartouche ring. More than one thing about her first imprint bothered her. Leaving it untouched, she tried to call back the elements of the first ring dreamscape, the sharp colors and the intensity of a feeling she couldn't pin a label on, but the only thing she could conjure up was the duplicity of feelings that separated it from the other dreamscapes.

It was impossible to match the ghost of remembered pain and the sting of heartache that had touched her during the explosion dreamscape with the anger she'd felt while imprinting with the ring. It was as if the dreamscapes had come from two different people.

Namid hadn't wanted to be in the club, and he'd been angry at . . . who? Why hadn't she been able to see the other person?

Knowing she could brood about it for hours, Danna took a deep breath to clear the last images from her mind, and reached for the ring.

It took several minutes before the imprint arrived, vague at first, more thought than substance. Shadowy shapes flitted and swam inside her head, moving in jerks and whirls to an unheard music. Colors tumbled over one another in their haste to enter and exit her mind. Like before, she felt personally disembodied, all her feelings and thoughts transferred to the dreamscape unfolding around her.

Then, finally, a shaft of light appeared, gleaming like the hope of a sunrise. Danna caught her breath at the sudden incandescent flames that jumped from the dreamscape's horizon like fiery sunspots.

She grimaced as the angry colors exploded all around her. It was like being in the middle of a volcanic blast with no way out. Color flamed at the center, undulating like a wind-licked bonfire. A cosmos gone wild. Yet, the domain of the dreamscape possessed her as unrecognizable images swirled, mingled, shivered, and flowed. Dancing lights pivoted, arching gracefully before they died in another explosion of color, only to be rekindled in a soundless harmony of blazing motion that conveyed a maelstrom of emotion.

Unconsciously, she transferred the ring from the palm of her hand to her finger. Her hand curled into a fist. She wanted to get closer to the emotions that had caused the eruption. She needed to understand the anger, to find some reason for everything that had happened.

But the dreamscape refused to expand beyond flames of crimson red rimmed by shades of shimmering gold and silver. Whatever the colors were hiding, they did it well.

Danna opened her eyes, then slumped back against the pillows, emotionally exhausted. Fear and a sickening sort of panic churned in her stomach. She didn't want to close her eyes again, didn't want to see the aftermath of the dreamscape, the colors fading to black, the nothingness returning. She took several deep breaths, then stared at the ceiling. Had the anger been Namid's or someone else's?

Questions, questions, and more questions. When was she going to get an answer? Maybe never. Dreamscapes weren't computer files, they weren't bits of data that could be retrieved in a precise order to be analyzed and labeled.

That's enough. You're digging a hole, but you're not getting any deeper.

She left the bed and watched twilight fade into complete darkness over the city. Security lights came on, outlining the embassy's walls and monitored gates. It was time to dress for dinner and another meeting of the Tribunal.

Danna walked into the embassy dining room the way a soldier marched into battle, armed with a desire to win. Diplomacy had a lot in common with war. There was an edge of danger and excitement that went with the words. The fight could be swift and sharp or slow and painstakingly methodical, the struggles powerful, the ambition of adversaries hidden behind masks of politeness or friendship.

She was attending tonight's meeting with more information than she'd had yesterday. The hard part would be presenting what she'd discovered in her dreamscapes as plausible theory, not psychic hysteria. She couldn't lay out evidence and facts, because she didn't have them, but she might be able to persuade

Ambassador Synon to accept her theory if she put her diplomatic skills to work and used the right words in just the right tone of voice.

For tonight, Danna had set aside her politically correct uniform and chosen something more sophisticated. The midnight-blue silk of her gown didn't have any controversy stitched into the swathe of fabric that slashed diagonally over her left shoulder to meet with a neckline that showed just enough cleavage to hold a man's interest. Another swathe of fabric gathered at her left hip, falling free just above the walking slit that displayed what her male colleagues referred to as the best legs in the Corps.

Etiquette demanded that she acknowledge Ambassador Synon first, followed by Magistrate Gilfo, and then Cullon. Danna did so, using all the grace eight years of embassy receptions had taught her. The Korcian's gaze swept up and down the length of her in immediate male appreciation, and with a flash of amusement Danna deliberately addressed him as Commander Gavriel.

One of the few things Danna did know was that the moment she pointed Cullon in the right direction, he'd be gone, and the Tribunal would turn into a one-man show. She wasn't going to let that happen.

During dinner the conversation was diverted from the topic they would be discussing once the service droids removed the dessert plates. Like most diplomatic affairs, the tolerance for differing opinions was as important as the wine selection.

It wasn't until Ambassador Synon folded his napkin and came to his feet that the real evening began. Danna had been seated across from Cullon and had managed, how she wasn't sure, to react to his heated gaze as benignly as she'd once reacted to a sixty-year-old Carnelian senator's sexual proposition.

Beneath the charm and poise she presented at the table, Danna contained the unease that had been with her for the last two days. The subtleties and pitfalls of diplomacy had yet to be fully challenged in dealing with the *Llyndar* deaths. The gauntlet she was about to toss at the Korcian's feet could easily end up biting her in the butt.

They withdrew to the conference room to have the serious discussion which was the purpose of the evening. Again, Danna found herself seated directly across from Cullon. She could see the eagerness in his eyes. He was a doer in a room full of talkers. The Enforcer was growing impatient.

Within seconds of settling into their chairs, Ambassador Synon's firm voice brought a holographic display into action. The first image to hover millimeters above the table was the logo of the Forensic Bureau. The second image was that of a man with prominent features and blank brown eyes. Gray showed at the temples of his short dark hair, as if sprinkled by a diffident hand. His heavy-jawed face was set with seriousness. Ambassador Synon introduced him to the Tribunal as Chief Investigator Tolvostra.

Tolvostra delivered a dry, scientific report that reached the expected conclusion. The forensic team had found no evidence to support the assumption that the explosion of the *Llyndar* had been anything but accidental.

The Chief Investigator ended his remarks with an expression of sympathy for the families of the crew.

"Thank you," Ambassador Synon replied as the three-dimensional image wavered then disappeared into thin air. He then looked to the members of the Tribunal. "As the representative of the grieved party, Commander Gavriel, I ask if you have found any evidence that would prevent this Tribunal from rendering a verdict contrary to that expressed by the Chief Investigator."

"Nothing of substance."

Danna smiled to herself. If that wasn't a diplomatic answer she'd never heard one.

"Then the Korcian Empire would accept such a verdict should the Tribunal agree that the destruction of the *Llyndar* and the death of its crew was accidental."

"Yes."

Ambassador Synon didn't probe further into Cullon's sudden change of heart. He was a seasoned member of the political arena who had long ago learned to accept whatever victories came his way with grace and practicality.

His next question was addressed to Danna as the defending representative. "Officer MacFadyen, do you concur?"

Danna squared her shoulders and looked across the table, directly into the eyes of a tiger. "No, Ambassador, I do not concur. Rather, I cannot concur."

Her counterpart had the audacity to smile, his eyes steady and unreadable. Danna didn't smile back, but turned her full attention on the two men she had to convince, Ambassador Synon and Magistrate Gilfo. If they supported her theory, Cullon would have no choice but to go along.

"As you know, I used my psychometric skills during our examination of the *Llyndar* wreckage. I was unable to imprint on anything that could be considered subversive. In that regard, I am forced to accept the result of the forensic team's investigation. However, I have had several other imprints."

"What sort of imprints?" The question came from Ambassador Synon. The overhead lights, dimmed for the holographic report, caught his concern for any detail that may have been overlooked.

"This afternoon, I visited the apartment of one of the crew members. His name is listed as Vosca Komarr on the *Llyndar*'s crew manifest. In actuality, he was Chimera Namid, a Korcian True Blood."

Magistrate Gilfo looked more surprised by her bravery in bringing the fact to light than he did by the announcement that one of the crewman had been traveling under an alias. Danna stored the tidbit away for later contemplation, then moved on, not wanting to lose her momentum.

"During the course of my dreamscape, I saw a building . . . the Imperium headquarters on Marasona."

Gilfo leaned forward, suddenly very interested. Brave as she might be, Danna didn't have the courage to look across the table at Cullon's reaction. Another of Gideon's lessons came to mind. "You can best a man with words, but be careful about kicking him in the balls. Even literally."

And to Cullon's way of thinking, Danna was sure she'd done just that—hit him below the belt by divulging what he had shared with her in confidence. She had hoped that he would unveil the truth himself, but he hadn't. Which meant he didn't want anyone getting in the way of his own private hunting party.

"Clarify what you are saying, Officer MacFadyen," Synon requested with utmost seriousness. "Marasona is a corporate colony. The *Llyndar* was a commercial freighter registered to Korcia. I reviewed the logs myself. There were no entries indicating the ship had docked at a Conglomerate spaceport."

Danna continued, omitting the fact that Cullon had confessed to the Korcian ultimatum being smoke and mirrors. There was no point in rubbing salt into the wound, and she had another concern—alienating Ambassador Synon. The Tribunal had consumed his time and energy as well as removing a member of his staff from active duty. All in all, what he didn't know wouldn't hurt him or anyone else for the time being.

"You think Namid was consorting with the Imperium?" Gilfo put in quickly. "It's a fragile assumption to claim with no more than a psychic vision to substantiate it."

"I'm not saying my assumption is correct, Lord Magistrate, only that it opens a possibility worthy of investigation. The Korcian Empire's first thought was of terrorism, and terrorism may still be the cause. Not from the League, but from a third party, the Conglomerate, or more specifically, the Imperium."

"I have to agree with Magistrate Gilfo," Ambassador Synon said in a tone that warned Danna now was the time to run for firmer ground or sink with her assumption. "The manifestation of the Imperium headquarters does not mean the Conglomerate has taken up terrorism."

"Perhaps not," she conceded gracefully, "but it does present an interesting hypothesis, though puzzle might be a better word. If Chimera Namid had intentions of claiming the throne, he would need more than political confirmation. He'd need military support. Since the Korcian Guard is the product of those who cast out the previous kings, it's unlikely they would sustain Namid's claim. Who else could he turn to? Certainly not the League. We're bound by the Treaty of Vuldarr."

"But the Conglomerate isn't," Gilfo injected. "How very interesting. Hypothetically speaking, of course."

"I agree it's a far stretch of logic, but it is plausible," Danna said, delivering her last salvo. "The Conglomerate is growing faster than the League or the Korcian Empire, and it isn't above acting clandestinely to get what it wants. If there is a threat in the galaxy, that threat lies within the Conglomerate. The corporate colonies have no allegiance beyond money and power, no sense of loyalty to anyone or anything but themselves. And they know it's only a matter of time before the League or the Empire steps into the outer regions to put a stop to the illegal trafficking of arms and the transgression of sentient rights that many of the colonies practice. What better reason to support Namid? If his claim to the throne became a reality, they'd have the Korcian Empire as an ally instead of an adversary."

"And yet you're insinuating that they assassinated him," Ambassador Synon said, his voice chilled by the very idea of the corporate states mobilizing into a third galactic power.

"If Namid changed his mind, or indicated in some other way that he intended to betray their trust, assassination would be a solution," Danna replied.

"What say you, Commander Gavriel?" Gilfo asked, diverting the conversation to the opposite side of the table.

Cullon's eyes narrowed a fraction, and Danna knew he hadn't expected her to out-maneuver him. He'd underestimated her, not realizing that she'd competed against men like him before. Confident men who always came to the negotiation table thinking they had a trick up their sleeve, something she would accept without question because it "sounded" so good.

Before replying to Ambassador Synon, Cullon smiled at her, arching one golden brow as if to say he liked a little game playing now and again. Danna smiled back, taking her victories wherever she could find them.

"I think that Officer MacFadyen has a creative imagination," Cullon said, directing his gaze and his words to Ambassador Synon. "There's nothing to indicate that Chimera Namid was interested in the Korcian throne. All we know for certain is that he traveled to Ramora under an assumed name for an unknown reason. His motives were probably personal, since he held no political office."

"That may very well be the case, but our duty must prevail. If the Conglomerate is involved, in any capacity, then this Tribunal cannot render a verdict on forensic evidence alone," Synon replied. The manner in which he made the announcement, his entire bearing and tone, made it apparent that he considered himself a man certain in his position and authority and whatever decision he made would be followed by the entire Tribunal.

It was exactly what Danna had hoped for. Cullon wasn't going to be allowed to turn the Tribunal into a one-man show.

The Ambassador turned inquiringly toward the Enforcer, who he still assumed to be a member of the Korcian Guard (Danna hadn't revealed Cullon's true affiliation for security reasons.)

"I will give this new development serious consideration," Synon said. "We will resume this meeting in the morning."

The moment Synon left the room, Danna could feel Cullon's gaze cutting into her like a laser beam. It was time for a graceful retreat. "If you'll excuse me, gentlemen, I have some research to do. I'll see you in the morning."

She'd barely gotten the words out of her mouth before Cullon was standing by her chair, hauling her up by the arm. "Sleep well, Lord Magistrate," he told Gilfo. "Officer MacFadyen and I are going to have a long talk."

The night was a blanket of darkness, the wind a feather of movement over her skin, but Danna didn't have time to appreciate them, or to admire the moonlight silhouetting the garden greenery. Before she could take the calming breath she was going to need to argue with a man few people would dare to argue with, Cullon had her backed up against the embassy wall.

"You have one minute to explain what just went on in there," he said. His voice was as hard as the cold marble pressing against Danna's back, his eyes even colder, the pupils wide and dark, rimmed by flecks of pure anger-sharp gold.

Gideon had been right . . . kicking a man in the balls, even literally, could be dangerous.

With no hope of avoiding an argument, Danna said what had to be said. "What went on in there was me doing my job."

"Going after Namid's killer is *my* job."

"You're a member of the Tribunal," she reminded him. "Namid wasn't alone on the *Llyndar*. Forty-five other men lost their lives. It's *our* job, the Tribunal's job, to find out who did the killing."

"I know my duty."

"Look, I know you're angry, but—"

"Not angry. Disappointed."

Danna was shaken by the emotion conveyed by the simple word. She didn't like the idea of disappointing the Korcian. She'd rather deal with his anger. She also knew Cullon was feeling the same frustrations she was feeling, but that didn't banish the tension between them. His gaze bore through her with a heat that was primitive and very physical. Danna felt her mouth go dry, felt the awareness surge through her. She tried to push the feeling aside, but it only intensified, flowing into her breasts, and lower, impossible to ignore.

She'd told herself that she didn't need the hassle of an affair with a gorgeous hunk of man who probably spent as much time fending off women as he did enjoying them. Sexual affairs might be physically entertaining but they also consumed a lot of emotional energy, energy better spent on solving a murder.

Not that Cullon was asking. At the moment he looked liked he wanted to strangle her. But if he did ask, Danna wasn't entirely certain she'd say yes. At least not until the Tribunal was disbanded, and even then, she might not get the chance. The Enforcer wasn't the type to stick around once the fireworks fizzled out.

Somehow she managed to keep hold of the conversation, saying, "And I know my duty. You used me, Commander. I'm nothing but a compass to you, someone to point you in the right direction. You want the Tribunal adjourned so you can go flying off to Marasona on your own. Well, that isn't going to happen. Not if I can prevent it."

"You got another imprint this afternoon," he said, ignoring the fact that she'd accomplished her goal. Ambassador Synon wasn't going to adjourn the Tribunal. "One you haven't told me about."

"Yes," she admitted. "But the colors were too intense. I couldn't break through to the dreamscape."

"What did you use?"

"The ring. I went through all the things you sent over, but none of them opened up to me, not the way I needed them to. I tried the ring again . . . ," Her voice faded as she tried to find the words to describe what she'd sensed more than seen.

"And . . . ," he prompted, wanting answers.

Danna needed room to pace and think, but the warrior in Cullon had her exactly where he wanted her—penned in a corner.

She took a quick breath and let out a frustrated sigh. "It was like the dreamscape didn't want to be found. As if it was using the colors to keep me out."

The grimness in his face didn't fade as he looked down at her. "Has that ever happened before?"

"No. That's part of the reason I know there's more to this than we realize. Something's wrong, I can feel it."

"So you tossed the Imperium at Ambassador Synon and he took the bait."

"It's the only thing I have that will keep him from disbanding the Tribunal." She looked at the hard lines and angles of Cullon's face and didn't doubt for one moment that he wasn't happy with the turn of events. "Namid was on Marasona for a reason. Maybe it was because of the Imperium, maybe it wasn't. I don't know that any more than you do, but I do know that I'm not going to turn my back and write off forty-six deaths as accidental when my gut tells me it was murder."

"Your gut may be telling you that Namid was murdered, but it isn't telling you the Imperium ordered the hit."

"My gut is sending me all kinds of messages." She raised her eyes with a look of challenge, wondering if he doubted the things she had seen and felt. "One is that whoever Namid was running away from didn't scare him, or intimidate him. He was hurting."

Danna stopped short of describing it as a broken heart, but that's exactly what it felt like, as if someone had crushed all the love out of Namid's soul.

"You realize that this whole investigation is hinged on gut feelings, yours and mine," he said.

Danna noticed that his tone was calmer, as if he'd decided to save his energy for something more worthwhile than arguing with a Terran. She smiled and said, "Since our guts seem to be in sync, I don't see the problem."

"Don't you?"

She knew he wasn't talking about the logistics of a trip to Marasona. The problem wasn't the investigation, it was the investigators. Their eyes met and locked, their sexuality surfacing for a microsecond. But it only took a moment to acknowledge what they were each thinking, each feeling—desire. It hung in the air like a shifting, incandescent shadow.

"What do you know about the Conglomerate?" he asked. His tone had softened, but he had yet to give Danna the breathing room she needed. She was still pinned between his body and the embassy wall.

"Less than you, I'm sure. You said you'd spent the last ten years trying to unravel their web. Since the corporate colonies are flourishing, I assume you haven't been very successful."

"Who has?" he grunted, showing the frustration that had come outside with them. "The Imperium is one of the most powerful consortiums, but no one knows who pulls the strings. If you run the owners of the industrial enclaves through the computer, all you get is another group of enclaves, and another and another. It's like calculating the square root of π, you never get a final answer."

"But every piece is an increment of the answer we're looking for," Danna said. "Given enough clues, we might be able to solve the mystery of Namid's death."

Cullon didn't argue. Instead he asked, "Have you ever been to Marasona?"

"No. I've never traveled outside League territory."

"The outer regions aren't safe. The colonies are lawless." He changed tone and topic without taking a breath. "You should have told me that you were going to involve Ambassador Synon. I don't like surprises."

"And I don't like being used, then set aside. As long as I'm part of the Tribunal, I'm going where it goes."

He took a step closer, close enough for Danna to smell him, to feel the heat coming off his body. She felt a rush of adrenaline spread through her body, but she refused to be intimidated.

"No one holds the monopoly on murder. Or justice," she said angrily. "If there is a connection to the Imperium, then the League has as much to loose as the Empire."

"You won't like Marasona."

"I don't expect to. But that isn't going to stop me from going. Every society has its rite of passage, the one that teaches us to suffer the consequences of our own actions. I'm not caught up in the excitement of the moment, Commander, and I'm not naïve enough to think any of this is going to be easy. You're a big boy and I'm a big girl. We both know the risk of poking our noses where the Imperium doesn't want them."

He continued staring at her.

"I'm serious. If you think I'm going to be satisfied with commlink downloads of your progress, think again."

"I don't doubt your enthusiasm."

"On Earth, the enthusiasm you're referring to is called stubbornness."

He smiled, then laughed. The deep resonant sound took Danna completely by surprise. She looked from his handsome, roughly elegant face to where moonlight danced on exotic night-blooming flowers. When she looked back, into eyes that had changed once again, taking on the deep hues of a jungle forest, Danna sensed an intensity in Cullon that hadn't been there a moment ago.

Without warning, he threaded his fingers through her hair. They lingered on her scalp for a moment, as if he wanted her to know that he planned to take possession of her. Cradling her head in his hands, he joined their mouths. The kiss was slow at first. Just a brush of breath and lips. A tantalizing sample of his taste and scent.

Sensation swirled through Danna's body and her muscles clenched in response, in anticipation of what was to come.

Cullon pulled back just enough to stroke his thumb across her lower lip, and Danna's held breath escaped. Without realizing it, she moved instinctively closer. Their bodies brushed, eased away as she drew in another breath, then touched again.

Their second kiss took on the wild, hot rush of a mating ritual. Cullon hooked his hand under the swatch of fabric that covered Danna's shoulder and drew it aside, availing himself of the skin underneath. When he nibbled at her throat, Danna felt the cool night air, the searing heat of his mouth, and the erotic pressure of his teeth. She could feel his fingertips along her spine, gentle yet masterful, mapping the depth and heat of her response.

Her senses were overpowered. For a panicked moment she thought she might short-circuit before she had her fill of the wild, thrilling passion of this man—this warrior from another world.

Cullon kissed her again, an impassioned brush of lips to her forehead. "It's time for you to return to your quarters."

Danna looked into his eyes and saw that they'd changed again. The deep green of Paradise had been replaced by golden, hard-edged reality. He'd kissed her and proven that she may have bested him with words, but he'd won in the end. She was his for the taking when the time came—but that time wasn't now. He was sending her to her room like a disobedient child.

Danna could taste the anger on her tongue, mixed with a hefty dose of humiliation, but she swallowed it back. She'd stepped into the Korcian's embrace willingly. He'd won this round fair and square.

He put his hand under her upper arm and led her toward the walkway that would take them across the courtyard to the exterior staircase and the second floor of the embassy.

Though his touch was a little too firm to be casual, Danna didn't complain. She'd surprised him by confessing almost all to Ambassador Synon; he'd surprised her with the sexiest kiss of her life, and taught her something in the process. Korcians didn't get mad—they got even.

Seven

At first the sounds of the nightclub seemed like a horribly disorganized thing . . . people laughing, music blaring, gambling chips rattling against each other as they were tossed onto glass tables, mechanical droids floating through the air.

Cullon had left Danna at the door to her quarters. Neither had said a word to each other after the kiss. There hadn't been anything to say. She knew as well as he did that he needed her skills to sort out what was fast becoming more and more of a mystery. But her refusal to step down and let him take charge had left him with only two choices. He could pull rank, toss her back to Ambassador Synon, and go solo, or he could vent his frustrations with a kiss.

He'd chosen the kiss.

The choice might not have been the right one, but it had certainly been the more satisfying of the two options.

A loud cheer at one of the gambling tables, alerting the crowd that someone had been lucky enough to beat the odds, forced Cullon to concentrate on his surroundings. The pleasure club was a five minute walk from Namid's apartment, so he'd decided to start here, then work his way up the boulevard that followed the curve of the inlet.

As a rule, Korcian males were a lusty lot. It stood to reason that Namid hadn't practiced celibacy for six months. If Cullon was lucky, he might be able to find one of Namid's sex partners. The more he knew about the young man, the closer he'd be to the reason why someone wanted him dead.

"Hello," the female said, "and welcome."

Cullon appraised the club's hostess with a quick glance. She was tall and slender with the blue-black hair normal to Ramorans. Her eyes were a pale blue, the lids dyed pink under dark arching brows. The beaded loincloth she wore reflected the light, calling attention to the parts of her body that weren't covered. Her nipples were rouged a deep, berry red.

"Hello," he said, keeping the introduction short.

"Is your pleasure public or private?" she asked in a purring voice. Like most clubs, the customers could mix and mingle or select confidential entertainment.

"Private."

The hostess smiled. The vices of personal enjoyment were her trade. "We have fantasy suites or pleasure suites. Both come with a companion."

"A friend recommended your fantasy suites," Cullon said, guessing Namid might have preferred that sort of entertainment. There was only one way to find out.

"We have the best in Seramia," she assured him as one of the droids floated their way. She took two glasses off the extended tray, handing one to Cullon. "Did you have something specific in mind?"

"Do you have someone who understands a Korcian's tastes?" he asked, limiting the possibilities in hopes that Namid had indeed visited this particular club.

She gave him an appraising look, measuring his virility from head to foot, then smiled. "We have a companion who specializes in pleasing men like yourself. Follow me."

"If she's pleased other Korcians, I'm sure I won't have a problem," Cullon said.

The hostess glanced over her shoulder as she made her way through the crowd, guiding Cullon toward a spiral staircase that led to the mezzanine level. "No one has ever logged a complaint," she assured him.

Since Korcians were rare on Ramora, Cullon hoped Namid had been one of the girl's customers.

The fantasy suites occupied half the mezzanine level, the other half was taken up by small pleasure suites that were rented by the hour. Cullon paid the required fee—the multi-dimensional reality of a fantasy suite didn't come cheap—then entered, leaving the hostess to snag her next customer.

The cubicle contained a seamless layer of receivers and transmitters embedded in the ceiling. Holographic screening covered all four walls. The companion that came with the suite was waiting.

She was standing beside one of the two body-conforming chairs. Completely naked, except for a gemstone in her navel and rouged nipples, she waited for the door to seal before enquiring into Cullon's personal preferences.

"What did your last Korcian customer like?" he asked as he climbed into the sensory chair that was the mainstay of any good fantasy suite. The chair automatically reclined for maximum comfort.

Smiling, the young woman walked to the small console that controlled a matrix of sensory programs. "Would you like some help undressing?"

"Not yet," Cullon told her.

Accepting his decision, she keyed in the selection, then took her place beside Cullon in the companion chair. Nothing was said as they fitted the half-crown receptor helmets onto their heads. Once they were set up to begin receiving impulses, she gave him a bright smile, closed her sequined eyelids, and let out a long breath.

The moment the matrix took over, impressions began to unfold inside Cullon's brain. A feathery touch of energy ran through his body, as if he were riding on a wave of static electricity. He held himself curiously detached, and felt a faint, ironic smile tugging at the corners of his mouth. How much of this is my thinking? How much is being imposed by the matrix? Then, he found himself wondering if this was how Danna felt when she stepped into a dreamscape.

Cullon knew the changes being imposed on his mind were the result of sophisticated software synchronization, but the imagery forming around him came with an odd emotional jolt. His brain was working through an electronic connection, but the depth and complexity of the imposed imagery was coming from his own mind.

A black sky formed from a microdot, swelling to fit his field of vision, then filling with stars. A small disc appeared, forming its own dimensionality, before rushing toward him. He fell through a bright blue sky, toward an integrating overlay scene.

A garish, angular landscape broke out below him, sunrise, dark red stone and sand, overtopped by a peach-colored sky. There were ruddy hills near the edge of the simulated world. He continued free-falling, his velocity controlled by the fantasy machine. When his companion joined him, free-falling as gently as a feather, he realized they were both naked. He took her outstretched hand and pulled her to his side.

They drew closer to the scene, now only a hundred meters or so above the ground. They floated to the east, toward the rising sun, a fat, orange ball that grew brighter. The color of the desert floor changed with it, growing more intense as if the program's saturation point had been reached.

Mountains came up at them, low here, higher in the

distance, the sun rising over them, and the colors changed again. They floated over a road, rutted deep into yellow soil, then over a turbulent greenish-brown river before reaching the canyon lands, where desert lay on the surface, but deep gorges were filled with water.

"Not yet, but soon," a soft voice sounded in his head, deep and sensual. Cullon knew it was the matrix trying to heighten his sexual awareness. Several intimate suggestions were made before the whispering voice faded away and they floated to the ground.

Cullon and his companion stood alone in the midst of a tangled maze of colors and textures as the fantasy continued to unveil itself. A light breeze ruffled the leaves of towering trees; they were in a glen of some kind, mountains rising up behind them. Cullon raised his hand, motioning his companion to be silent. He could hear them! But who?

He moved, staying silent, stepping lightly until he could see through the bushes into an airy clearing ahead. They were there, not three meters away. . . . The man was young and dark-haired, with a slim, muscular body. The girl was pretty, a year or two younger, and blond. Her breasts were small and high, her pubic hair so light as to be almost invisible.

Cullon watched as the female moved to her hands and knees. Her silvery hair hung loose, falling over her shoulders to brush the blanket. He could see a shining dampness between her legs and knew the man had already prepared her for penetration.

Her lover joined her, taking a place behind her, then reaching forward to fill his hands with her breasts. He massaged them, then moved lower, his hands skimming over her body. He stopped at her hips, and held her in place as he entered her in a single hard thrust, impaling her completely. The female responded with a needy moan. They coupled; the man easing himself out then thrusting forward again, plunging faster and deeper with each movement of his hips.

If Cullon chose, the fantasy would go on from here. He and his companion could join the couple in the clearing, mentally acting out their secret desires. But he didn't want this fantasy, or either of the two women. He wanted Danna MacFadyen and the fantasies that had been building inside his own mind for the last two days.

Pressing his index finger against the control sensor embedded in the arm of the chair, Cullon disengaged the matrix. The image of the two lovers quickly faded to black.

By the time he removed the receptor helmet his companion was standing by her chair and looking surprised that he had stopped the matrix before it had moved on to the next segment.

She walked to the console and punched in a command. The far wall of the cubicle moved to reveal a pleasure suite, the second half of the evening's expensive entertainment.

Cullon left the chair and followed her into the room.

The lighting was dim, recessed in the outer corners of the room and again on the dais that elevated the bed a good three feet off the floor. A small serving bar was built into the wall. Soft, nondescript music drifted from hidden speakers.

The companion moved to the bed and immediately assumed the position of the girl in the fantasy. Cullon had to smile. Mounting a woman from behind was a traditional Korcian position, one most males favored. He wondered if it was the reason she'd selected the desert fantasy.

He was aroused enough to take the female, but instead of shedding his clothes, Cullon poured himself a drink.

"I'm not here to satisfy any sexual desires," he said,

moving to where she could see him through a curtain of dark straight hair. "I'd rather talk."

"Talk?"

"What's your name?" Cullon asked.

"Marvia."

"How many Korcians have you entertained, Marvia?"

"Only two. Have I displeased you?" she asked, concerned that a complaint could cost her a job that paid four times what she'd make in one of the capital's offices.

"No. You haven't displeased me. Sit down."

She sat, folding her legs and giving Cullon a clear view of what he was missing. He handed her the drink he'd sipped, then poured himself another.

"Tell me about the Korcians that come to the club."

She hesitated, knowing she'd be breaking a major rule. Cullon tossed a handful of platinum coins onto the bed next to her. The hesitation didn't last.

"The first one was over a year ago." Sequins glittered as she closed her eyes for a moment. "He was older than you. He liked the fantasy. Sometimes he'd sit through it twice before we came in here."

"He liked the fantasy you just selected?"

"Yes."

"What about the other?"

"Younger than you, and darker. His hair was brown, and his eyes were different. They were blue and silver."

"Did you select the same fantasy for him?"

"Yes, but only the first time. He didn't like the desert."

"How many times did he visit you?"

"Half a dozen," she said, then sipped more of the sweet ale he'd given her. "He liked the tropical fantasy. He said it reminded him of Korcia."

"Are there other couples in the tropical fantasy?" Cullon asked at the same time he noticed the tiny phallus tattooed on the girl's inner thigh. It was a common enough mark, considering her profession, and amusingly stimulating, pointing the way toward satisfaction.

"Most of the segments have multiple partners."

"Did he participate or watch?"

"He liked to watch."

"What about afterwards, did you have sex?"

She looked down at the empty space between her legs before giving him a slight shrug. "Once, but it wasn't very good. I offered him a stimulant, but he wouldn't take it." She frowned then, looking like a confused girl instead of a licensed partner. "Most of the time, he'd just stretch out on the bed and hold me. I fell asleep the last time, but he didn't seem to mind. There weren't any credits taken off my account the next day so he didn't file a complaint. We're not paid to sleep."

"Don't worry, I'm not going to complain about not getting my money's worth."

She gave him an enticing glance. "Are you sure? You paid for a full session. There's plenty of time."

Cullon reached into the pocket of his tunic. A second later, a mini-unit projected Namid's image onto the holographic wall opposite the bed. "Is this the man?"

"Yes." She came up on her knees and stared at the image for a long moment before adding, "I think he was lonely. His eyes were always so sad."

Namid had been in his sexual prime. Not taking a female, especially after going through a stimulating fantasy session, didn't speak to his virility. Then again, Cullon wasn't having sex with Marvia either. She wasn't the female he wanted. Maybe Namid had had the same problem.

"Do you know if he visited other clubs?"

"I can't say. We're not supposed to get too familiar with the clients."

The ambiguous answer made Cullon smile. He finished his drink, gave Marvia a benign pat on her bare bottom, and left the suite. He had more clubs to visit.

* * *

Danna sat on the floor watching data scroll down her
view screen. She'd been plugged into the League network for hours, researching the Conglomerate in general, and the Imperium in particular. The information
was lineal, facts and figures detailing the mining operations on Marasona. She moved on to the next download, trying to find something that would link Namid
to the Imperium, anything that would spark a connection between the heir to the Korcian throne and the
hidden powers behind the Conglomerate veil.

Nothing.

As she stared at the screen, her mind drifted to what
she'd been trying to forget all night.

She'd screwed up big time.

Everything she'd ever been taught, everything she'd
absorbed by osmosis from Matthew Gideon and half a
dozen other top diplomats in the Corps, had taught her
to keep her personal feelings to herself. "Never let
your emotions control your intellect," Gideon had
drilled into her. "And never make assumptions about
anyone else's personal motivations. You'll get kicked
in the teeth every time."

Instead of being kicked, she'd been kissed.

Thoroughly kissed. Kissed better than she'd ever
been kissed in her entire life. Kissed and aroused . . .
and . . . that was the problem. There hadn't been anything after the kiss.

"Computer, cross reference names Chimera Namid,
Vosca Komarr, and Imperium," she said, slamming the
top on the box of chocolates she'd been raiding since
2 A.M.

"No common reference cataloged," the computer
came back in its standard monotone.

Disgusted because nothing made sense, Danna
came to her feet, arched her back until she could see
the light fixture embedded in the ceiling, then decided

she'd wasted time looking for something she knew she wasn't going to find in the first place. Namid hadn't been assassinated for political or social-economical reasons. He'd been murdered.

Personal motivation. That was the key.

And not only for Namid. Personal motivation had kept Danna dislocated between rational thought and emotional upheaval most of the night.

She'd intended to continue her research on the corporate colonies, but she hadn't intended to sit cross-legged on the floor all night, sipping tea and eating sweets. So why was she still here, instead of luxuriating in her bed?

Why? The answer was as plain as the frown on her face—one gorgeous Korcian Enforcer who had booted her intellect out the window with a simple kiss.

Was Cullon her motivation for wanting to go to Marasona or was it finding Namid's killer? Honesty demanded both choices. Justice came first and foremost, followed by her need to get past being an assistant in someone else's embassy. She wanted an ambassadorship. Settling a tense situation between the League and the Korcian Empire would push her appointment up the line.

And she wanted Cullon Gavriel.

The romanticism of the idea made her laugh out loud at the same time as it triggered an alarm inside her head. She was losing her objectivity. It was one thing to be attracted to a man, but letting things move beyond that point at this stage of the game was pure stupidity.

"Okay, Officer MacFadyen, time to put away the chocolate and hit the shower." She disengaged the computer screen. "You're on stage at 900 hours, Earth Time."

The message had shown up on her console shortly after midnight, when she'd given up trying to sleep. Ambassador Synon had finished thinking the situation over. The Tribunal had been instructed to meet for his decision.

Danna showered, setting the bath unit to full massage. When she felt as if a six-handed masseuse had hammered away at her muscles, she shut down the unit and walked to her closet, dripping all the way.

Black on black suited her mood, but she pulled out a standard Corps uniform instead. Dark blue. It was the next best thing. She softened the look by adding a silver-blue blouse, then spent another half hour doctoring the circles under her eyes. The cosmetic mask wasn't her specialty, so it took several tries before the unit created the fresh, glowing appearance of a woman who had had a peaceful night's sleep.

Whatever her motivation, she wasn't going to give Cullon the satisfaction of knowing he'd left a lasting impression.

When she entered the meeting room, Danna found Magistrate Gilfo studying the assortment of fruit on the breakfast buffet. Neither Ambassador Synon nor Cullon had made their appearance.

"Good morning," the dwarf said, waving her inside to join him. "Coffee's hot and the fruit looks delicious. I always enjoy myself when I visit Ramora. Great melons. The sweetest in the galaxy. May I recommend the spiced bread. It's excellent."

Danna selected coffee, scrambled eggs, and fruit. She sat down across the table from the dwarf. "You've met Commander Gavriel before," she said conversationally.

"I made his acquaintance a few years ago. On Iris Five."

Danna managed to swallow her second sip of coffee without choking. "Iris Five is a penal colony!"

A fork stopped midway between the plate and Gilfo's mouth. "So it is." He smiled before popping a chunk of melon into his mouth. After a few chews and a deep swallow, he smiled. "You could say I was born on the wrong side of the Japolean political blanket. Not agreeing with the status quo, I made some waves."

"Iris is a maximum security facility. Your waves must have drowned someone."

The dwarf angled his empty fork at her. "Never underestimate the power of political connections, Officer MacFadyen. They can make or break a man."

"So where did you meet Cullon? In the exercise yard?"

"No. In the dark. He stumbled over me."

Danna had to laugh. "I can't imagine him stumbling over anything. He's as graceful as a tiger."

"And just as lethal."

"I figured that out two seconds after I met him. So what was he doing stumbling around on Iris Five?"

"I can't say, not without stepping on classified toes, but I can tell you that Cullon saved my life. If he hadn't tucked me under his arm, I would have died on Iris."

Danna mulled the remark over as she scooped up a fork of scrambled eggs. Knowing she couldn't last the morning on a night-induced sugar high, she finished half the breakfast on her plate before continuing her mild-mannered interrogation of the Japolean magistrate. "So the big guy saved your life. Just like that? No questions, no "are you guilty and do you deserve to be here conversation," just a quick snatch and go?"

Another piece of fruit disappeared before Danna got her answer.

"It was slightly more complicated than snatch and go, but the end result was the same," Gilfo said. "I returned to Japola, kept my mouth shut and my miniature butt out of trouble until the right set of circumstances came along, then ran for office."

"Changing the aforementioned status quo."

"I'm doing my best."

"Owing your life to a fellow member of the Tribunal puts a dent in your neutrality, doesn't it?"

Before the magistrate could swallow the melon in his mouth and answer Danna's question, the doors opened and Ambassador Synon joined them. A quick glance told him the Tribunal was a duet. He used the time to serve himself at the buffet.

Danna looked at the time displays that lined one wall of the conference room. Rectangular boxes filled with red digital numbers showed Ramoran Time, Earth Time, Aello Time, Sultana Time, Korcian Time, and time on half a dozen other planets. Cullon had exactly three minutes to get his handsome ass in the room or be counted tardy.

As always, the Korcian was on the mark. He strolled in with exactly one minute to spare. He was dressed in a black spider silk jumpsuit with a deep vee that showed entirely too much of his chest. The fabric, commonly used in military uniforms, allowed for maximum flexibility. It also hugged its wearer like a second skin.

Danna couldn't help but notice the change in Cullon's eye coloring when he looked her way. Sheer sexuality radiated from his gaze like a hot sun. She lifted her coffee cup to her mouth to hide the smile that came with thinking about all that testosterone being focused on her.

The thought didn't fit with her morning resolution to resume her all business/no pleasure attitude, but some things couldn't be helped.

There was no conversation until everyone had finished their morning meal and the droids had cleared away the dishes, refilled the coffee urn, and exited the area. Danna noticed the guards were back on duty to keep anyone from absently wandering in with the thought of using the room for their own purposes.

"I have given the new developments in this investigation serious thought," Ambassador Synon said, officially beginning the meeting. "Taking into consideration the territorial boundaries that will have to be crossed if the Tribunal travels to Marasona, I prefer not to make the decision alone."

His words were followed by a simple voice command to activate the communication monitors. Two large viewing screens eased silently down from the ceiling, framing the ambassador between them. Within seconds the link between Ramora and the concerned governments of the League and the Korcian Empire was made. Danna was relieved to see Gideon's face come into focus on the first screen. When the second screen displayed the Viceroy of the Korcian High Council, relief sagged and apprehension took its place.

Viceroy Surazheia had the look of an old soldier who had no intention of fading away. Silver-white hair was pulled back from his face to drape in a warrior's braid over his left shoulder. His mouth was a hard thin line above a square jaw. His skin was crosshatched with the razor-fine lines of innumerable wrinkles and yet every slash looked to have been scratched in hard stone. It was a face that held no secrets, boldly featured and rigid; it said a lot about the man behind it.

His eyes were the multi-color Danna was gradually getting used to, but instead of glittering amber and exotic green they shone in shades of ice blue, steel gray, and flecks of pure black. They looked into the room from hundreds of light years away and were still able to give the impression of not missing a thing.

Ambassador Synon made the necessary introductions, then motioned for Gideon to speak first.

"Being familiar with Officer MacFadyen's paranormal skills, I believe she has used them professionally. That being the case, I also believe that her impression of a possible connection to the Conglomerate, or more specifically to the Imperium, merits further investigation. How that investigation expands is open for discussion."

Before Synon could ask the Viceroy's opinion, he gave it. "You think a True Blood was conspiring with the Imperium. If it's true, and they didn't kill him, I would have ordered his execution myself. Treason is intolerable."

It took Danna a moment to realize the Viceroy was directing the statement at her. Knowing she was being tested, along with her theory, she focused on the image being projected from the High Council Chambers. She shivered slightly when she realized the Viceroy's eyes held no reflection. It was as if they had been cut from slabs of onyx.

"As I told Ambassador Synon, whatever assumptions I make at this point are preliminary and speculative. However, I do feel very strongly that Namid's death is linked to something that happened on Marasona. I saw both Namid and the Imperium headquarters building. He *was* there."

The Viceroy gave her a doubtful look before addressing the man he had sent to Ramora. "Commander Gavriel, your opinion?"

"I agree, Lord Viceroy. Marasona merits investigation."

"Then do it." A microsecond later the monitor went blank.

"A man of few words," Danna said, looking across the table at Cullon.

"Isn't there an old Terran saying about actions speaking more strongly?"

The reply came with a smile that nearly rocked Danna out of her seat. Cullon wasn't talking about words, he was talking about a kiss—the kiss!

She smiled back, silently promising to get even—the Korcian way.

"Ambassador Gideon?" Synon inquired, reassuming control of the meeting. "Do you concur that the Tribunal's investigation should expand to Marasona?"

Gideon didn't respond as quickly as the Viceroy. His expression told Danna he was thinking about sending her back to Earth. Up to now, the purpose of the Tribunal had been to avert hostilities between the League and the Empire by discovering the cause behind the explosion onboard the *Llyndar*. Tossing a corporate colony into the equation changed everything. Danna hoped Gideon would see the bigger picture, not just the immediate scenario of an unexplained threat aimed at the Korcian Empire.

"Commander Gavriel," Gideon began. "If Ambassador Synon has explained the circumstances properly, then you are assuming that an Empire citizen, one Chimera Namid, a True Blood, was murdered. Am I correct?"

"That's the assumption so far," Cullon replied. "Based on what Officer MacFayden has learned by imprinting with Namid's personal belongings, his death doesn't appear to be accidental."

"If that is the case, then the League's involvement in this investigation loses its direct necessity."

"Ambassador," Danna interrupted. It was as far as she got. Gideon went right on talking, his voice as crystal clear as if he were seated at the table with them.

"While the League and the Korcian Empire are allies, it is not League policy to interfere with interior matters within the Empire," Gideon said. "I hope you understand my dilemma, Commander?"

Danna opened her mouth to defend her position, but Cullon beat her to it.

"I understand your position, Ambassador Gideon. Namid was a Korcian citizen. The investigation of his death lies within our jurisdiction. That being the case, I respectfully request that Ambassador Synon disband the Tribunal. I have High Council authority to continue the investigation on Marasona, that's all I require."

"No!" Danna stood up. "Namid and forty-five other men were killed *in* League space. The Tribunal was established because the Treaty of Vuldarr required it. Those requirements haven't changed."

"I believe Ambassador Gideon is concerned for

your safety, Officer MacFadyen," Cullon said before anyone else could reply. "There's no League Embassy on Marasona. The only law the corporate colonies understand is supply and demand. Expanding this investigation could be dangerous. Even if it proves to be a dead-end—"

"It won't," she cut in.

"Commander Gavriel is right," Ambassador Synon said, doing his best to defuse an explosive situation. "There is no law on Marasona. Not knowing what you may find increases the danger."

"No one is going to find anything unless I go along," Danna insisted. "I'm the one with psychometric skills, I'm the one filling in the missing pieces. Without me, there is no investigation."

For an instant something showed in Cullon's eyes. Danna recognized it for the anger it was. She'd hit him below the belt again. The prognosis didn't look good. Surprisingly, it was Gilfo who broke the silence.

"May I offer a compromise," the magistrate said, drawing everyone's attention.

Danna looked from Cullon's cast-in-stone features to Gideon's concerned face and sensed an intensity of purpose that wasn't going to be set aside easily. "What sort of compromise?" she asked, realizing it may be her only chance of keeping the Tribunal intact and functioning.

"As Ambassador Synon has wisely pointed out, there is no formal law in the outer regions." The dwarf looked toward the viewing screen, addressing his remarks to Danna's superior. "However, if Officer Mac-Fadyen travels to Marasona, she will get there on a Korcian ship. Commander Gavriel's ship. That would put her under Korcian protection."

Danna didn't like it. Being under Cullon's protection sounded too much like being under his thumb. There was no way she was going to take *orders* from the Enforcer.

"Protection is one thing," she said. "Having my integrity as an independent investigator compromised is another. I want it made clear that I do not report to, or take orders from Commander Gavriel."

No one seemed to hear her, least of all Gideon. "If I allow Officer MacFadyen to accompany you to Marasona, Commander, can you give me your personal assurance that she will be safe?"

Cullon gave Danna a look that didn't bode well for her future independence. "You have my word."

Eight

Danna's first glimpse of the *Star Hawk* brought her to a standstill. It was easy to imagine the sleek ship slicing through space, swooping and diving like a ravenous bird of prey. The metallic skin of its outer frame was reflective. Outside the docking bay, the ship would blend into the stars like a mirage blended into the horizon.

She hadn't seen Cullon since he'd left the embassy conference room the previous morning, looking none too happy at having to drag her along on what he considered Enforcer business. The glance he'd given her before walking out of the room had promised retribution—in more ways than one.

Knowing the moment she boarded the *Star Hawk* she'd be officially under his protection, Danna hesitated outside the entry hatch. As expected, launch attendants were scurrying about the bay like mice, running a final diagnostic check on all the ship's systems before unclasping the fuel hoses.

Danna knew it was going to be one of those days

when the Korcian appeared on the entry ramp. She had hoped to avoid his official greeting as captain and commander. He was smiling enigmatically, and his eyes shone like gemstones, a sure sign of amusement—he was going to make her pay for upstaging him.

"Gilfo is already on board," he said. "Here, I'll take those." He took her traveling pack and another smaller case, containing Namid's personal belongings, from her hands. "We launch in ten minutes."

Danna took a moment to give the *Star Hawk* another sweeping gaze. "Very impressive. Is it as fast as it looks?"

"She'll break 20 IS if I coax her."

Twenty Interstellar Speed was more than fast, even for a ship that had been built for velocity and maneuverability.

"What do you coax her with, a whip?"

"Tender, loving care," he said, leaning down so the words were a whisper in her ear.

Danna shivered, because she couldn't help herself, and let the remark pass. Whatever attraction she felt for the sexy Korcian needed to stay on the back burner. She was already standing on a shaky professional limb. If she didn't produce results on Marasona . . .

She followed Cullon up the ramp, refusing to think about failure. It wasn't an option.

Once inside, Danna stopped to admire the military efficiency of the *Star Hawk*. Not an inch of space was wasted. The only thing she didn't see was a crew.

"You're looking at him," Cullon said when asked. "The ship is completely automated."

Danna followed Cullon down the main corridor.

"Gilfo is across the hall," he said as the door to her assigned room opened. "Make yourself comfortable."

The husky invitation in his voice made Danna realize she was going to have to tread very carefully. Expecting him to recite the "rules" of the ship, she was surprised when he simply placed her luggage on the bunk and walked out of the room.

She looked at the environmental controls, thinking she might go zero gravity for a few minutes to help her relax when the pre-launch signal came over the commlink.

Moving to the room's only port hole, she watched as the docking crew emptied out of the bay. Launch personnel scrambled for the airlocks as a warning siren fired out three long blasts. Flashing red lights turned to green as the bay dome opened to reveal countless stars surrounded by a velvet blackness that had no measurable dimensions—space in all its splendor.

"Next stop Marasona," Danna mumbled as she shed her jacket and kicked off her shoes.

The moment her bare feet touched the thickly woven carpet she could feel the vibration of the ship's engines. Cullon wasn't wasting any time putting Ramora behind them. Danna returned to the viewing portal as the *Star Hawk* glided into a long, complex curve around Ramora, then swooped out into space, shedding a good portion of thruster fuel and gaining several thousand kilometers per second of velocity.

The vibrations grew stronger as its pilot pushed the *Star Hawk* toward interstellar speed. Danna felt the exact moment when the ship's thruster engines relinquished control to the more complicated interstellar drive. The sleek starcruiser shivered slightly, then relaxed. Beyond the port hole, the stars began to blue-streak.

Danna sat down, then swiveled the chair around to face the computer terminal. Her attempt to access the ship's database failed. Either Cullon hadn't gotten around to installing a translation program or she was going to be forced to request access. Either way, she wasn't going to be able to busy herself with research until she spoke to the *captain*.

The Korcian's casual welcome hadn't fooled her. Cullon was itching to blast her, and Danna knew it.

Launch had taken priority, but since Ramora had faded into a pinprick of light behind them, she didn't have long to wait. The commlink buzzed as if on cue. Cullon's deep voice followed.

"Officer MacFadyen, join me in the control room."

"How do I get there?" she asked, knowing it was probably at the other end of the main corridor, but not wanting to make a fool of herself by ending up in the engine compartment.

"Follow the red lights on the corridor panels."

Five minutes later Danna stepped into one of the sleekest, most sophisticated control rooms imaginable. Dim lighting emphasized the brightly colored lines and text of half a dozen instrument displays. The data from the *Star Hawk*'s extensive sensory array—visual and thermographic imaging, synthetic-aperture surface scan radar, wide-spectrum EM signal receivers, and a number of other more esoteric systems—all flowed into the command module's analysis screens.

Cullon sat facing the most elaborate panel—navigational control. He ignored her until the last of the manual systems were reverted to automatic. With fluid dexterity, he made the process look deceptively simple.

"You wanted to see me," she said as he swiveled around to face her.

"We need to talk."

"So talk."

"In there," he said, indicating a hatchway.

Like a good guest, Danna followed her host. The room was an office, military neat and as efficient as the one they'd just left. Beyond it, through an open hatchway with its sensor on pause, were personal quarters.

Danna didn't like the setting, but she suspected that was the very reason Cullon had left the door open. He wanted to make damn sure she knew she was on *his* turf now. She waited, thinking he was going to sit down behind the console desk and scold her like a disappointed schoolmaster. Instead, he sat on the edge of the desk and looked at her. When he kept on looking, Danna started to get uncomfortable.

"Go ahead, get it out of your system," she said when the silence and his catlike gaze finally got to her.

"Get what out of my system?"

"Anger. You're still mad because I let Ambassador Synon in on all your little secrets, and you're furious because I didn't bow out and let you take over the investigation. So go ahead, yell at me."

"I don't yell."

"Then what are we going to *talk* about?"

He smiled without humor. "The order of things."

"You mean the orders you're going to give. The ones you expect me to obey without hesitation."

"Something like that."

"I'm not under your authority," she said, inching her chin up to let him know she wasn't going to be intimidated.

"You're under my protection. It's one and the same."

Danna was about to protest when his eyes went from gleaming gold to rock-hard brown in a blink.

"This investigation isn't a routine diplomatic mission," he said flatly. "Murder isn't about socioeconomics or sentient rights, it's about death. I can't protect you, if you don't do what I say when I say it."

"You're taking advantage of the situation," Danna countered, her gaze as intense as his. "The last time I looked we were investigating the murder of a True Blood. I'm not Korcian."

Cullon leaned forward, bracing his hands on the arms of her chair. With his steely body only inches away, he captured her full attention.

"What makes you think the murderer won't kill an interfering Terran as easily as he killed forty-six men?" Cullon asked coldly. "If you think diplomatic immunity is going to save your ass, think again."

"I can take care of my own ass." Her smile didn't hold a hint of warmth. "I don't need your protection. I need your cooperation."

"Cooperation," he said sardonically. "Like the cooperation you gave me when you dropped that little bombshell at the conference table."

He leaned in closer. So close Danna could see the golden specks of color that rimmed the darkening brown of his eyes, but she refused to shift into reverse. She met him stare for stare. His face was set in stone. She was praying hers looked the same. After a moment, she gave him a thin smile. Under the circumstances, it was the best she could do.

"Cooperation as in giving me access to the ship's computer. Before we get to Marasona, I need to know everything you know about the Imperium."

With slow deliberation, Cullon returned to where he'd been leaning against the desk. "Good enough," he said, surprising her. "I'll link the console in your quarters. In return for my generosity, you'll agree to follow my instructions, on this ship, and on Marasona."

"That's blackmail."

"It's reality. Take it or leave it."

"Do I have a choice?"

"No."

Danna rose from the chair, standing within easy reach of Cullon's strong hands. "I don't like ultimatums."

"Neither do I."

Danna accepted defeat. She'd hit the Enforcer below the belt—twice. He was only repaying the favor. Being told to toe the line wasn't as enjoyable as being kissed, but it was a hell of a lot safer.

She was heading for the exit and a quick retreat to her own quarters when Cullon stopped her with a few words.

"Namid was the third True Blood to be murdered, not the first."

"What?" Danna turned around to face him, eyes wide.

"Three True Bloods have been killed in the last four months."

Danna absorbed the severity of the statement as she glared at her so-called partner. Three deaths escalated the complexity of an already over-complicated situation. "Why in the hell didn't you tell me? Does Ambassador Synon know? Of course not. No one knows but you and the High Council. That's the real reason for all the smoke and mirrors, isn't it?"

"Sit down," Cullon said, dismissing her words as if he hadn't heard them.

"Who were the first two?" Danna asked as she slipped back into the chair.

"Ackernar and Eyriaki, both further down on the throne list than Namid. They were poisoned."

"Poisoned?"

"It's the difference in methodology that bothers me the most," he said. "Poison is silent. An explosion makes a lot of noise, even in deep space."

"And yet all three were True Bloods. There has to be a connection."

"That's what I'm trying to find out," Cullon told her.

"You said the first two were poisoned. Where, exactly?" Danna asked, trying to connect two more deaths to the one she'd been concentrating on for the last few days.

"In their homes. The poison was added to their last meal. They died in their sleep."

"What kind of poison?

"A local toxin, one any knowledgeable chemist can make from a pretty little flower that grows in the jungle. It leaves a sweet taste in the mouth, but there was no reason either Ackernar or Eyriaki would have recognized the flavor. From what I've been able to discover, neither had any enemies."

"Except someone who hates True Bloods," Danna pointed out. "What about connections, other than their royal DNA? Did any of the three know each other? Did they have anything in common?"

"No."

"So the High Council is making the assumption that the new fundamentalists are taking out the opposition."

"It's an obvious conclusion," Cullon said. "That's what I don't like about it. It's too obvious."

Danna had to agree. "Do you have anything that belongs to Ackernar or Eyriaki, anything I can use for an imprint?"

"Yes." He walked to a closet and opened the door. The items were in a metal case that he put on the desk.

Danna contained her curiosity. "I'd like to look at their files first. The more I know about them the easier it will be for me to interpret what I see."

"I'll link the console in your quarters."

She got up to leave, but once again Cullon's words stopped her before she reached the door.

"I want to be there when you imprint," he said.

"Give me a couple of hours," Danna replied, knowing she'd need at least that long to study the files on the other two men.

The floor of her quarters was littered with personal items, none of which belonged to her. Danna sat cross-legged in the middle of the floor, taking deep breaths. Her eyes were closed, but her mind refused to shut down. Random thoughts scrambled about inside her head, bumping against each other, then breaking apart. Feelings cartwheeled, changing pattern and focus like chips in an old-fashioned kaleidoscope before coming to rest in another reality—the here and now.

"What did you see?" Cullon asked the moment she opened her eyes.

Since the first dreamscape, Namid's strong personality had melted into her, like a grafted branch became part of the tree. Danna couldn't forget the feelings she'd shared or shake off the vividness of being trapped by licking orange flames. She'd tried to exorcise the memory, and failed. Emotions still stabbed at her, but she pushed them aside, choosing the present over the past, and hoping her objectivity lasted until she could be alone and shake off the coils of other people's emotions with a long shower and a glass of wine before a good night's sleep.

Fortunately, or unfortunately in this case, neither of the other two murder victims had strong enough personalities to leave a lingering effect. They had both been normal men with normal lives.

She gave the two men watching her a concise report of what she'd experienced in the dreamscape, looking at Gilfo because she wasn't up to gazing into the depths of Cullon's keen tigerlike eyes. "Ackernar was an uncomplicated man, if you can say that about a Korcian. I didn't sense any fear or concern. He was a loner, but he liked it that way. No regrets, no heartbreaks. These dreamscapes didn't have the strength of Namid's. The emotions were vague, not strong."

"What about Eyriaki?" he asked. "He was a lot younger than Ackernar."

"Yes, and slightly more complicated. He felt restless about things in his life. Discontent, but not threatened." Danna took a deep breath. "I'm sorry. There isn't anything to link them to Namid. No ambitions for a new life, no quest for power. Nothing I could sense that makes me think either one knew their lives were in danger."

"Where does that leave us?" Gilfo asked. He was sitting cross-legged on Danna's bunk while Cullon stood near the observation window.

"With the only lead we've got," Cullon said as he let his eyes come to rest on Danna. "The Imperium."

Nine

Danna decided it was too early for breakfast and too late for a late night snack. The fact that she didn't want to run into Cullon in the galley finished off what little appetite she had. Since leaving Ramora, images of the Korcian no longer insinuated themselves into Danna's mind during the hazy period between wakefulness and sleep. They'd become permanently imbedded in her gray cells.

So, was she in love or in lust?

It was hard to say. For now, she had to admit lust was getting the most marks. Every time she saw, spoke to, or thought about the sexy Korcian, her body started giving off pheromones.

It had been six Earth days since they'd zoomed away from Ramora. They'd cleared the Sonata system and were headed straight into deep space, the haunt of pirates, unaligned traders, and corporate colonies.

Tired to the bone of facts and figures that didn't jell into anything more substantial than wild speculation, Danna shut down her console and left her quarters.

She'd visited the exercise room only once during her short time onboard the *Star Hawk,* but the kinks in her neck and shoulders were begging for a good workout.

She made her way to the hatchway that would take her down one level and into what would customarily be the cargo area. Cullon had converted one of the bays into a high-tech gym.

The moment the door slid open Danna wanted to do an about-face. Her Korcian host was sitting cross-legged on an exercise mat, stripped to the waist. His hands were resting on his bent knees, and his eyes were closed. They opened at the soft chime of the door sensor.

"Sorry, I didn't mean to intrude on your meditation," Danna said. Her breath caught as he came to his feet in one long, fluid movement. He was in black again, a pair of spider silk leggings that clung to his hips and thighs. With his upper body bare and his flaxen hair hitting his shoulders, he looked more the Viking than ever before. Tautly muscled and totally vital, he exuded a leashed energy that said the cat was on the prowl.

"I've been waiting for you."

The disturbing impact of his words was as frightening to Danna as the sensual promise in his tawny eyes. He seemed to be looking not only at her but into her, as if her clothing had fallen away and she stood naked in body and soul.

"I knew you'd come to me," he said huskily.

His deep voice flowed through her; it caressed, vibrated, and reached inside her. Danna inhaled sharply at the river of sensation that swept through her body.

She wanted him.

It was wrong. Or rather, it was the right thing at the wrong time. Danna knew she should say something to stop him, but suddenly the expert on words had no words—all she could do was stare at him. In the dim light, his eyes looked like molten gold. His body was like a tiger's: lean, graceful, ready to overpower.

Without a word, he drew her into his arms. Danna tried to stand unmoving, her hands at her sides, but the vitality he injected into her wouldn't let her remain that way. Her professional detachment vanished with a heartbeat.

His face hovered above hers. Slowly, he found her mouth. He kissed her, tasted her, luxuriated in the feel of her lips against his. He was eager, but hesitant, not wanting to rush her, wanting to demonstrate a respect for her. His hands stroked her arms and then moved down the sides of her body, feeling the contours beneath the snug blue jumpsuit.

Danna liked the feel of his hands. Inside the dark place that housed the most primitive of responses, she felt a tingling, a kindling. As his hands touched her breasts, mingling flesh and fabric, she gasped.

Her arms slipped around his neck; her mouth opened to receive his kiss, and her heart pounded in her ears. His touch caused something to gather in her body that had never been there before; a heavy, unbearable sweetness, a total loss of self-consciousness that she would never have yielded to until this moment. More than anything else, Danna found herself wanting to melt in boneless surrender.

She flexed her fingers, and placed her hands flat against his bare chest. She could feel his heartbeat, a rapid strong percussion of blood and muscle. Narrowing her mind to a pinpoint of concentration, she surrendered to the moment.

His hands moved seductively over her back and hips in long, slow sweeps that pressed her closer to his body. A soothing warmth spread through her, an indescribable sense of rightness and well-being, as if she'd finally found her destiny. She wanted to go on standing like this forever, in the strong cradle of his arms, to feel his heartbeat close to hers. But he backed away, looking down at her.

"Do you want to be my lover?"

Cullon looked at her while he waited for her answer. She parted her lips but made no sound; her dark eyes, heavily fringed with a tangle of black lashes, were as expressionless as pools of water, as if she were afraid to let her feelings show.

Danna didn't think she'd ever wanted a man as much as she wanted this one. Beneath her jumpsuit her body was tightening in arousal, her nipples growing taut and hard, her breasts flushed.

He took a half step backward, drawing her with him so the light shone more clearly on her face. He took her mouth again.

Danna gave herself to the second kiss, to the lingering of his mouth on her lips. He caressed her throat and chin gently, as if asking permission to go further, which she quickly gave. She hadn't answered his question, but then, he hadn't really needed an answer. She knew how he'd feel next to her, remembered the last time he'd kissed her, and allowed her body to melt into his, to satisfy the longing.

With a swift, abrupt movement Cullon broke the kiss and swung her into his arms. He smiled lazily as he walked to the control panel and entered two commands. One to activate the door lock and another to reduce the gravity to zero. Within seconds, still cradled in his arms, Danna found herself floating toward the ceiling.

"Hold on to me," he said as he turned, sending them into a slow sideways roll. He kissed her again, igniting the erotic hunger that had existed between them from the start.

Danna arched her hips, searching for and finding the hard proof of his arousal, pushing herself into it. She closed her eyes, luxuriating in the weightlessness and in the arms that held her firmly. She could feel his body exuding controlled power, tension, desire.

"How are we going to manage this?" she asked, as they drifted upward in a sensual ballet of kisses and caresses.

He smiled. "Slowly. Very, very slowly."

He put his lips to hers and kissed her roughly, his tongue exploring her mouth. His hands ventured over her body, as they rolled and tumbled like slow-motion acrobats. Danna gloried in the feel of it, in his strength and power. She felt her body awakening with an intensity of passion she hadn't thought possible. His hands cupped her breasts, holding them so tightly they ached. Bending her backward, he found the tab that would unfasten her jumpsuit and pulled it down. The soft garment opened to her navel.

"This is where things get interesting," he said as he worked his hands inside.

Her legs were wrapped around his thighs and she could see the ceiling getting closer. Just when she expected them to go bump, he rolled again, reaching out with one hand to grasp the ceiling's gravity grips. "Grab on."

She did, hanging suspended in air as he moved down her body, taking the jumpsuit with him. In less than a second, she was wearing nothing but a gossamer pair of panties and an impish smile. "My turn."

"Not yet."

He "swam" down to the console that was shoehorned into the far corner of the bay, and touched a panel on its surface. A large viewing iris opened in the bulkhead, showing what the ship's navigational system was seeing; stars glittered like powdered diamonds against the velvet expanse of endless space.

Pushing off from the floor, he joined her at the top of the room. Using her as an anchor, he held her at the waist and kissed her breasts, moving from one to the other, his tongue laving her nipples. Her panties disappeared to be replaced by Cullon's hot hands. He kneaded her buttocks, and she moaned with pure pleasure.

As the sensations cascaded through her, Danna closed her eyes and slipped from a world held together by gravity into one of buoyant sensuality, a place where passion ruled and common sense had no purpose.

She let go of the ceiling grip and they were floating again. Danna could feel the hot, damp core of her rubbing against his erection. Each subtle twist and turn heightened their awareness of each other.

Cullon twisted them around harder and faster, propelling them toward the ceiling again. When the grip came into reach he wrapped his left hand around it. He unfastened his pants. Danna took over from there, dragging them over his hips and down his thighs until she could cast them off to float aimlessly about the room with her jumpsuit. His breath unraveled in a soft groan as she kissed her way up his body.

When she decided he'd had enough, Danna broke loose and sailed slowly pass him, gently somersaulting ninety degrees to look behind her. Cullon followed, and they caromed about—playing, tumbling end over end in the absence of gravity. The circumstances made their nudity all the more intimate and anticipation coursed along Danna's nerve endings, a velvet static electricity of arousal.

"Every day I live holds magic for me," Cullon said, offering an explanation Danna didn't know she needed until he gave it. "Every place I go possesses its own energy. I like the excitement of my life, the unpredictability, the challenges and the danger. I need them to feel alive. Can you accept that?"

"Yes."

There was no other answer she could give. She'd accepted him for what he was from the very beginning—a man who lived in the moment. If she wanted him, she'd have to live in that moment as well, expecting no guarantees, having no regrets.

Wanting as much from their time together as possible, Danna covered his chest and shoulders with feverish kisses, testing his reaction to her. Her hands explored at will, measuring the heat and length of his arousal. Smiling, she let her mouth do some exploring, too.

The taste and scent of him was elementally male. With simple gratitude that she was female, Danna ran her hands up the inside of his thighs in erotic torture for all the nights he'd kept her awake thinking about this very moment.

Cullon let go of her completely, holding onto the ceiling grips with both hands. "Wrap your legs around my waist."

Tentatively, Danna gazed into his eyes, soft gold with glints of emerald green. Then she kissed him, very gently as her fingers curled into his hair. She did as he asked, wrapping her legs around him, opening herself to the inevitable mating of male and female. His arousal, smooth and hard and hot, nuzzled against damp, sensitive folds. Danna shuddered with anticipation.

His passionate assault was like a slow-moving storm. If they had been lying on the exercise mat, which was wisely adhesived to the floor along with everything else in the bay, his entry would have been almost brutal. But zero gravity turned his first deep thrust into a marveling flood of warmth.

Danna felt herself being stretched and filled by hot, inching degrees as the first consuming tremor rippled through her body. Holding her in place, Cullon began a slow, precise roll of his hips that settled into a long series of deep thrusts.

He kissed her throat, then nibbled at her earlobe. "I knew you'd feel good," he whispered.

Danna reveled in the way Cullon lavished her with

displays of affection, stroking her, caressing her, worshipping her body as if he was a supplicant.

The brush of his lips grew more heated as he continued to move slowly—very slowly—in and out of her. The slower he moved, the higher she burned. The yearning between her legs intensified, until she was clinging to his shoulders and using what little leverage their weightless state allowed to hasten the pace.

She moved in rhythm to him, over and around him, taking his length, until the excitement spiraled and pleasure grew. Danna buried her face in the hollow of his neck to muffle her cries of need, while her body quivered and pulsed and burned and finally convulsed.

They floated in air, midway between the ceiling and floor, somewhere between magic and reality.

Overcome by sensation, Danna went limp in his arms, as they continued to float. Slowly, everything came into focus—sensations, thoughts, a sense of her own identity, like a landscape emerging with the light of day. Still wrapped in Cullon's arms, feelings rolled through her like breakers onto a beach.

"How are we going to get down?" she asked, not really caring. She could stay adrift like this forever, completely satisfied, thoroughly content with the moment.

Cullon smiled. There was a curious, golden gleam to his eyes that made Danna feel warm all over. He swung out his arms in long strokes, swimming them back to the floor. They glided the length of the bay until Cullon could touch the environmental panel.

"Ready?" he asked.

"Not if we're going to hit the floor like a ton of bricks," she said, holding on to him with both hands.

"Nice and easy," he told her as he initiated the gravity control then pushed away from the bulkhead.

The momentum took them back to the exercise mat. They hovered over it a few seconds. Danna could feel the weighted pressure of air as gravity began to return to the bay. "I feel like a deflating balloon," she said laughingly.

Cullon rolled just in time to absorb the shock of their landing. Still wedged deep inside her, Danna felt a piercing slash of sensation as they came to rest. Cocooned in satisfaction, and anticipating more of the same, she pressed her cheek against the warm, steely texture of his chest and breathed in his scent.

"That was wonderful," she sighed dreamily. "Absolutely wonderful."

"I'm glad," Cullon whispered into her ear. "Now, let's see if we can do better than wonderful."

He rolled again, bringing her under him. He used his weight this time to keep her in place, to keep her legs spread achingly wide and her hands captured above her head, as he took her in deep, demanding strokes.

Though she should have been too sated to respond, Danna discovered that her body had a mind of its own, that it trembled and stiffened, hardened and softened, sizzled and pulsed according to how and where he touched her.

Cullon possessed her, and she yielded in reply, feeling him enter her, feeling her own body close around his erection. She arched her hips and they ground together, sliding, pumping, pressing into each until their hips bruised, but the sweetness obliterated the pain.

Beyond the viewing portal, stars still gleamed and comets streaked across the inky void. Minutes passed . . . or was it eons. Danna couldn't be sure. The pleasure Cullon was forcing upon her was a shield from reality, even as her thoughts warned her that she was falling into an emotional tempest that could easily end up being a one-way street.

She shuddered as he drove into her, going deep, then deeper still, forcing her body to respond, forcing her mind to go blank until instinct and the primal need to mate overcame everything else. His expression was almost feral as he conquered her. And it was a conquering, a claiming that went beyond physical.

Danna could barely breathe by the time she climaxed. Her body was damp with sweat, her eyes too heavy to open. Cullon tensed, then joined her. He buried his face in the hollow between her throat and collarbone, biting her gently as he thrust deep one last time and poured himself into her.

It was a long time before either of them spoke. Blissfully content, Danna lay wrapped in his arms. Her fingers stroked the sweaty planes of his chest and the golden tangles of his hair. He still hadn't withdrawn from her; instead, he rolled to put her on top of him again.

Danna glanced around the bay. Her jumpsuit had floated down to drape itself over a piece of weight-lifting equipment, Cullon's leggings hung limply from one of the ceiling grips, and her panties adorned the console screen. Just as she was thinking she'd have to retrieve them soon, a sensor on the console chimed three, short, consecutive peeps.

"Time to go," Cullon said, easing away from her. Beautifully naked, he laughed when he saw where his leggings had landed.

"Let me get dressed before you go floating up to the ceiling," Danna said. She stepped into her panties and jumpsuit before turning to face her lover again.

Her lover.

The idea had plagued her for days, but now that she had given herself to the Korcian, Danna wasn't sure what to say. Despite the sated lethargy that filled her, she was still on a physical high and very much aware that having sex with a man didn't constitute more than that—sex. Fantastic sex. Hot sex. The best sex ever. But still just sex.

As if Cullon sensed her doubts, his fingers tugged at her dark hair, gently reeling her back into his arms again. The kiss he gave her was a hot siege and totally possessive. She belonged to him now, and he meant for her to know it.

"Meet me in command," he glanced at the time display on the console, "in fifty-four minutes, and I'll introduce you to Marasona."

She accepted another kiss, this one quick and hard, then left him to retrieve his clothing while she went to her quarters, stripped out of her clothes a second time, and treated herself to a pulsating shower.

She stepped into the command module exactly fifty-two minutes later. Cullon was already there, seated at the main control panel. Gilfo, wearing a pea-green jacket and black leggings was strapped into an auxiliary seat. Danna wondered if the dwarf had any idea what had happened below deck only a short time ago. If he did, it didn't show.

"Where do you want me?" Danna asked when Cullon finally turned his head to look at her. She didn't mind the wait considering the danger a miscalculation from interstellar speed to cruising speed could create.

"Here." He pulled a second auxiliary seat into place. "Strap yourself in."

Danna followed his instructions, surprised by the telemetry showing on the control screens. "So that's how it works," she said. "You plot an injection point for cruising power and an exit point for interstellar speed simultaneously."

"That's the simple mechanics of it," Cullon said. "The fine science is plotting the time differential." He pointed toward a small G-type star on the telemetry screen. "If I don't get this right, we'll end up eating that star."

"Then get it right," she said.

"I'll do my best." The look he gave her was more lover than ship captain's and it set Danna's blood to pumping. It also told her that their relationship was only beginning.

Danna took a moment to study the lines of his face. They were handsome and rugged—clean, hard lines, but his smile softened the contours. She knew that he had had a number of lovers. He was too expert a sexual sorcerer not to be well experienced. But the past didn't bother her, perhaps because she'd agreed to live in the moment. And this moment was enough for her. She had a handsome Korcian as a lover. And there would be more moments—future moments to be anticipated and finally enjoyed.

Whatever complications arose from their Tribunal duties would have to be dealt with when the time came. Until then, she was going to enjoy the ride.

"Ready?" Cullon asked.

Gilfo and Danna both acknowledged the question with a simple yes.

The next second Danna felt as if she were in zero gravity again, in free fall, dropping endlessly toward the bottom of a black abyss. Suddenly, a great actinic burst defaced the darkness, diffused and white around its periphery, tinged a hard red-violet in the opaque core. For a microsecond, the screens blurred as navigational tracking was shifted from one space buoy to another.

Then, just as suddenly, the descent, if it could be called that, took on the qualities of a dreamscape. Even the darkness of space had a light to it, stretching the reality of what had been into the reality of what would be. Colors, bold and bright, congealed, then drained away, like water spilled from a glass. Stars, asteroids, and planets all looked distorted, as if they were being seen from a great distance, elongated and strangely silhouetted against an unknown light source that was growing brighter.

Then, in less time than it took the human eye to blink, all was as it had been. The glaring light had disappeared and all Danna could see was the black-on-black horizons of space.

"Where are we?" she asked, not recognizing anything on the star chart that now showed benignly on the monitoring screen.

"That's Megaera," Cullon said, indicating a G6 star. "And that is Marasona."

Danna looked at the information pouring in from the scanning sensors. Marasona wasn't much of a planet. It fact, it just barely qualified as a habitable world. Its oxygen level was scanty. It sat far enough back from Megaera, its G6 sun, that it had only two kinds of weather, tolerantly cold and freezing. Its axis stood almost straight up, which meant its inhabitants didn't go south for the winter because the winter came to them wherever they were. The only thing that made it useful to anyone were the rich deposits of minerals below its surface.

"How long before we can land?" Danna asked, unbuckling herself from the auxiliary seat now that the speed change had been made.

"Another six hours," Cullon told her. He called up a high-mag view of the planet. The holograph superimposed itself over the viewing screen. "I'll put the ship into high orbit and take the shuttle down."

"I'll be ready," Danna said. "What kind of docking information are you going to give the Marasonan authorities?"

The sensors had indicated a security net around the planet. It was a customary array that alerted the ground authorities to approaching ships. Shuttles couldn't pass through the net without a clearance code, not unless they wanted to dodge hostile fire.

"The usual," Cullon said nonchalantly.

When he didn't elaborate, Danna got suspicious. "You've been here before."

"A time or two."

"And . . ." she prompted. "No more secrets, Commander."

Cullon didn't say anything. He simply waited for Danna to realize that secrets were his livelihood.

Motionless, Danna waited, praying that none of the rioting emotions beneath her professional veneer showed through. A second later, she couldn't help but think that Gilfo's interruption was deliberate. If she could feel the tension seething between herself and the Cullon, the dwarf most certainly picked up on it. His tone was solicitous.

"I suspect Cullon wants to make a preliminary reconnaissance before the Tribunal begins its official investigation," Gilfo said. "Marasona isn't the most hospitable world."

"You're not going down there without me," she told Cullon. She stepped in front of him as he moved to exit the command room. "And don't even think about pulling that big, bad Korcian act on me. I'm not going to sit here staring at stars while you turn the Tribunal into a one-man show."

For an instant, Cullon's eyes went from glimmering gold to a dark, forbidding brown, but Danna stood her ground. They both knew this wasn't about subjugating his command privileges. It was about trust. It was about every other moment they would share.

Cullon looked at her for a moment, as though considering whether or not to throw her in the brig. But in the end, he said. "If you show yourself on Marasona looking like a League diplomat, we won't find out anything. Colonists don't like governments sticking their nose in where they're not wanted."

Danna looked down at her neat emerald-green slacks and embroidered overshirt. "Okay," she said casually. "What should I wear?"

Cullon smiled with the first hint of warmth she'd seen since she'd stepped in front of him, blocking his path. His eyes pinned her as if he were trying to dissect her soul. "Something ultra sexy. If you're going with me, you have to make everyone who sees us together think you *belong* to me."

An involuntary ripple of excitement laced through

Danna. Cullon wasn't going to let her forget that she had given herself to him, and in that giving, at least to his way of thinking, she'd surrendered all. For the time being, Danna decided to let him have his way.

"Okay. Six hours should give me enough time to come up with something sexy and provocative. But no navel jewelry. It makes me itch."

Ten

The world that turned slowly below the shuttle was a sea of low-walled craters, a vast marsh of ancient, partially healed wounds created by the seismic shock of thousands of meteors.

Danna watched from the shuttle window as the chunk of carbonaceous material, 260 kilometers in diameter, loomed closer. Marasona was a colony on the edge of Terrestrial influence, sparsely inhabited and basically lawless. It had been claimed by the Imperium for mining operations eighty years ago.

The planet's terrain had a deadly sameness about it that disturbed Danna. Was this all there was? Mountains showed like brownish-gray wrinkles on the cold surface. The land was an even duller brown, desert dry and unwelcoming. Coarse sand shifted on the surface like streamers of dirty lace.

As if to answer her unspoken question, she noticed a bulge creeping over the northeastern quadrant. Cullon dipped the *Star Hawk* into an orbital approach and the image enhancers presented a sharp representation of what Danna had originally thought was a settlement dome. The formation was gargantuan, a mind-staggering matrix of metal girders and poly-steel framework. The man-made monolith jutted thousands of feet above the crater-scarred surface of the planet.

"Mother Imperium," Cullon said.

"That's a mine!" Danna couldn't believe her eyes.

Cullon's answer was a mirthless chuckle. "Want a closer look?"

He didn't wait for a reply, but aimed the shuttle nose down at the planet and accelerated speed. They raced through the atmosphere like a bullet hurled from the barrel of a gun. Danna held her breath as the control panel momentarily blurred with a squall of glowing pixels before assimilating the information being fed to it by the shuttle's exterior sensors.

She stared awestruck as Cullon brought the shuttle over the massive mining shaft. Lights shone intermittently on the tunnel wall, small drops of illumination that did little to alleviate the deeper shadows of the vertical shaft that dug deep into the planet's belly. She could make out rings of excavation, and what appeared to be a catacomb of tunnels, jutting off from the main shaft in a horizontal invasion of the planet's mantle.

"Look," Cullon said, pointing toward one of the shuttle's interior sensor arrays.

Danna noticed a speckling of small dots, as if the monitor had a bad case of the measles. "What are they?"

"Miners. We're picking up the signal from their subcutaneous transponders."

Danna watched as the tiny dots moved around the monitor screen like bees inside a hive. Nanotechnology reduced the size of an electronic component to one-millionth of a meter, roughly ten times the size of an atom. With a minute implant injected under their skin each miner's location could be monitored. In case of an accident, the victims could be located and hopefully rescued before their air tanks emptied.

"What about landing clearance?" she asked as Cullon directed the shuttle toward a clutter of structures that Danna soon realized was the actual settlement. The colony, populated by sixty thousand people at last census, was a ragtag of mismatched buildings, bright lights, and narrow streets.

"The only clearance you need here is money," Cullon said succinctly. "Greed fuels this world."

Danna remained silent until the shuttle was resting on a concrete tarmac with weeds protruding from the cracks that criss-crossed its surface. It wasn't a main landing port, but a deserted fueling station on the outskirts of town. A precautionary frequency scan had turned up only the normal pattern of corporate and personal transmissions.

"You're just going to leave it here?" she asked, appalled by the idea of someone stumbling onto the shuttle and investigating its Korcian technology.

"Gilfo's on board the *Star Hawk* monitoring us. If the proximity sensors alert him to anyone's presence but ours, he has the retrieval codes."

"So that's why he didn't come down with us."

Cullon smiled as he unbuckled himself from the pilot seat. "Once you get to know me better, you'll learn I never block myself into a corner. If Gilfo has to retrieve the shuttle, we'll rendezvous at another set of coordinates."

"How is he going to know the difference between intruders and us?"

"My commlink frequency."

The answer given, there was nothing left to do but leave the shuttle. Reaching the hatchway, Cullon stopped to look at Danna, his gaze direct and appraising, like a commander viewing a raw recruit for the first time.

For several torturous moments, all was silent. His expression was a mixture of approval and disapproval and something Danna couldn't quite put a name to. Resignation, she supposed, because he knew she wasn't going to stay behind, safe and snug in the shuttle.

Danna almost smiled. He was so fiercely male, her Korcian lover, bristling with ingrained protective instincts that were even stronger now that she'd become his woman. What she'd taken for arrogance at their first meeting was simply his true nature.

He'd asked her to accept him for what he was, and she had. Now it was time for him to accept her. To accept the fact that by submitting to him, she hadn't become subservient, but an equal.

"That isn't going to keep you warm," he said, surveying the costume she'd created from bits and pieces of her wardrobe.

"I didn't think comfort was a priority." She pivoted around so he could see all of her. "You said sexy. This was the best I could do."

Impatiently, Danna ran her hands over her hips, then forced herself to stand still for Cullon's inspection.

Her top was a one-sleeved halter of soft silk that ended just below her breasts. The bottom half of her transformation started a good two inches below her navel; yellow silk, tight and snug across the hips and butt, and flaring into loose-fitting trousers around her legs. Beaded sandals finished off the outfit.

Rather than wear a mixture of conservative jewelry, Danna had chosen only a pair of dangling gold earrings that she'd bought on a whim and an assortment of gold and gemstone bracelets she'd inherited from her grandmother. The bracelets were old-fashioned enough to be unusual.

She'd programmed her makeup mask to a theatrical setting that had darkened her brows, tinted her eyelids a glimmering aqua blue, and painted her mouth a beckoning kiss-me red. The final flourish was a blue satin cloak with a crimson lining.

"You're going to need something else," Cullon said, turning away from her, but not before Danna saw the flash of desire in his tawny eyes.

"What?"

"This." He was holding a small syringe in his hand. "The air is thinner here. This will help you breathe."

"What are the side effects?" Danna asked, unclasping the gold interlocking buttons that held her cloak in place.

"You'll get sleepy when it wears off. Nothing serious."

She flinched at the pinprick. "What about you?"

"My physiology is different than yours," he replied before he drew her into his arms and kissed her until her knees went weak. "Let's go."

He stopped on the way to the exit hatch to collect his laser pistol. Danna didn't comment on the small weapon that looked incapable of the violence it could inflict. The pistol was standard operating equipment for an Enforcer.

At twilight, the area Cullon had selected to land was deserted. The buildings surrounding the old landing port were dark and dismal, blending in with the faded metal structures behind them. The dim evening light caused the streetlamps to glow a stark white against the mauve-gray sky.

With her cloak drawn snugly around her, Danna walked by Cullon's side. The wind lifted, and dust rose thick about them. It swirled and billowed, forming reddish-gold dust devils that danced at their feet. The debris littering the street was hidden by a kindly darkness. There were strange smells and sounds, and faint lights showing in a few windows of the neighboring buildings. In the distance, a mining freighter, driven by a primitive heavy-ion motor, belched exhaust fumes, leaving a shivering tail behind the ship that distorted the night sky.

Danna looked to Cullon. His eyes picked up a reflection from the moonlight and seemed to flash with emotion.

"I warned you," he said.

Danna accepted the "I told you so," with a slight shrug of her cloaked shoulders. She looked overhead. The only beautiful thing Marasona had to offer was its three small moons, Aello, Podarge, and Ocypete, named after the mythological rainbow goddess and her sisters, the harpies.

"Where exactly are we going?" she asked as they turned the corner only to find more mottled buildings in front of them.

"There."

Danna's gaze followed the direction of his hand and saw what appeared to be a nightclub—a very seedy club with a haphazard sign over the metal door and no visible windows.

"Stay close," Cullon said, claiming her arm as he led her inside.

The interior was as shabby as the exterior: low-hanging glow tubes created more shadow than light. The evening crowd constituted men and women dressed in drab colors, mostly work uniforms with the Imperium insignia stitched on the right upper sleeve. Toward the back of the rectangular room, where the shadows were the deepest, customers were engaged in various games of chance.

Terrans and Korcians were in the minority on Marasona, but Cullon handled the disparity by focusing his feral eyes on anyone who stared their way.

Danna tried to remain calm in the face of adversity, but it was difficult to stay focused on unfriendly faces when Cullon was touching her. His hand was warm, very warm, and it was wrapped around her upper arm like a human manacle.

Danna had her wish—wherever the Korcian went, she was going, whether she liked it or not.

They approached the bar that was nothing more than a scarred, metallic counter. The bartender stared at Danna, then rubbed a beefy finger across his thick lips. "Nice. Very nice."

Danna looked at him in return, at the curly, dirty, reddish-blond hair, the acrid green eyes almost hidden in deep, dark sockets beneath shaggy brows, at the broad face and flattened nose, and said a silent prayer of thanks that she'd come to Marasona with a well-armed Enforcer as her escort.

"Is the Colonel around?" Cullon asked.

The bartender's eyes simmered with mistrust. He filled a smudgy glass with dark ale, then sat it down in front of Cullon. "Who's asking?"

Cullon reached into the front pocket of his flight jacket and pulled out a coin, a gold currency credit that could pay for a hundred glasses of ale. "I am."

The bartender narrowed his expression, letting it roll into a blank look that said he was thinking, before picking up the coin and tucking it into his own pocket. "He's upstairs. Last door on the right."

His hand at her back, pressing her gently forward, Cullon led Danna up a flight of dimly lit steps and into an even darker corridor.

"Who's the Colonel?" she asked as they approached a metal door that looked a bit too ominous for her liking.

"Colonel Zeindar. He was discharged from the Korcian Guard a few years back."

"Honorably or dishonorably?"

Cullon smiled a predator's smile. "There is no dishonorable discharge from the Korcian Guard. If you're found guilty of a crime while you're wearing the uniform, you're executed."

"Isn't that a little extreme?"

"Not from a Korcian perspective," Cullon answered dryly. "Zeindar was exiled because the courts didn't have enough proof to find him guilty."

Danna stopped in her tracks. "Are you telling me that Korcian justice assumes guilt until innocence is proven?"

Cullon reclaimed her arm and started her walking again. "In Zeindar's case it did. He had access to certain information that found its way into some unsavory hands. Unfortunately the key witness against him died unexpectedly. The Military Council offered Zeindar a choice, exile or life on Iris Five. Zeindar opted for exile."

"Do you think Zeindar can tell us what Namid was doing here on Marasona?"

"Maybe. Either way, it never hurts to know the neighborhood."

When they reached the door, the surveillance sensors flashed for several seconds. Then, as if the door was reluctant to open, it creaked noisily and slid into a wall pocket.

Cullon stepped inside.

Danna followed.

"Ahhh, Gavriel, the archangel of the High Council, I wondered if our paths would ever cross again," the man sitting beside the unadorned desk announced. "Please, do come in."

Danna watched as Zeindar came to his feet. Here in the dimly lit room his bulky body seemed to struggle to stand erect. Yet erect he stood, as if refusing to give into the infirmities of old age. His thin lips stretched into a smile beneath a well-trimmed moustache. He looked to be in his late sixties, but was probably younger.

Danna noticed a sharpness to his gaze, not anger, but inquisitiveness; the gaze of a man who questioned whatever he saw—perhaps because he hadn't questioned sufficiently in the past.

"A Terran," he remarked approvingly as his gaze swept Danna from head to toe. "Unexpected, but very beautiful. I commend your taste in females." He straightened his jacket, a garment of dark leather that fit a bit too snugly over his belly. "Please, sit. I'll pour us some wine. It isn't every day that I get to enjoy the company of a fellow Korcian."

"I need information."

"What else could I possibly offer," Zeindar replied jovially. "As an exile I have nothing but my eyes and ears to offer the Empire."

"For a price," Cullon said calmly.

"But of course," the ex-colonel acknowledged with a sly smile. He stood at a small bar, pouring their drinks, his age-twisted hands moving deftly in spite of their appearance. Then he turned, raised his own glass high, and said, "To the Empire."

Cullon repeated the toast, then drained his glass. Danna held hers, untouched, as she watched the drama unfold between the two men, one an Enforcer of the Empire's stringent laws, the other an exile and assumed traitor.

"Now, my young friend, what can I do for you?" Zeindar asked once he'd resumed his seat behind the desk.

"Tell me about a young Korcian who visited Marasona about six months ago."

The colonel's expression said he knew exactly who Cullon was taking about. A slow smile creased his face. "Might that be the one who kept company with our illustrious governor? I don't care for LuFarr myself, then again, my tastes don't run to politicians. Can't be trusted."

"And traitors can?"

Zeindar laughed, genuinely and loud. His stocky body shook with pleasure as he reached for the glass he'd refilled before returning to his desk. "Excellent reply, my young friend. Really quite fine. But if you can't trust me, then why ask me for information," he said more disagreeably. He waved Cullon toward the door. "Go ask the governor."

"What's your price?" Cullon asked.

Zeindar placed his glass on the desktop and brought his hands together, peaking his fingers under his chin.

Cullon continued to stare at him. It was several moments before the older Korcian spoke.

"A travel pass."

Cullon laughed. "Even I don't have enough influence to get you back on Korcia, no matter how limited the time."

"No, I don't suppose you do. However, I do suspect you're here on High Council business. If I'm right, then you have enough influence to get me *inside* the Empire. I'll settle for a few days on Benatorr." He paused to take a drink of wine. "I have a son. I want to see him one last time before destiny condemns me to death on this forsaken lump of rock."

"A travel pass had better get me information I can use," Cullon said with a cold threat to his voice.

Zeindar smiled condescendingly. "You inquired about a Korcian. A civilian who visited our little colony."

"How do you know he was a civilian?"

Zeindar lowered his glass. "I spent most of my life in the Guard. I know a soldier when I see one."

Cullon didn't argue. "Do you know his name?"

"Namid. An awkward youth with no fire in his eyes. Doomed to insignificance by his own insignificance. I'm surprised you're interested in him. What did he do to offend the Empire?"

"You mentioned the governor?" Danna inserted the question.

Cullon looked her way, his eyes a piercing gold. The quick stare was enough to let her know she was supposed to play the role of a good-little female and keep her mouth shut. Danna ignored it and looked directly at Zeindar. "Tell me about LuFarr."

"Curious as well as beautiful," Zeindar remarked.

"Answer the question," Cullon directed.

"Which question?" Zeindar asked with a mild

chuckle. "What is it you really want to know, my young friend?"

Danna watched as Cullon calculated the risk of telling an assumed traitor what only a choice few in the galaxy knew to date. When he made his decision, his expression silently warned Zeindar that if the conversation went beyond the grimy walls that surrounded them the exiled colonel wouldn't live to use his extorted travel pass.

"The young Korcian, Governor LuFarr, and the Imperium," Cullon said. "Is there a connection?"

"Interesting question," Zeindar conceded. He leaned back in his chair. "Very interesting. Shall we start with the Imperium?"

"Start anywhere you like, just get something said."

Danna quickly found herself mesmerized by Zeindar's narrative. He might have been a professor of political science lecturing on the blurred complexities of the galactic economics, patiently clarifying each twist and turn of the diplomatic wheel. He supplied conjecture where knowledge failed, making certain they understood he was merely guessing at some things.

The Imperium was not simply an industrial complex, it was the corporate head of a very long, very dangerous serpent, an organization of intergalactic financiers dedicated to building industrial cartels beyond the interference and control of either the League or the Empire.

"Tell me something I don't know," Cullon replied when Zeindar paused to take a drink of wine.

"LuFarr's connections reach into the hierarchy of both governments. He may be new to Marasona, but his family isn't new to the Conglomerate. LuFarr is the avatar of a new order of corporate governors," Zeindar replied matter-of-factly. "The Imperium funds endeavors throughout the galaxy. It blackmails those who can't be bought, and bribes those you'd least expect. Very successfully, I might add."

"Meaning what?"

"Meaning LuFarr didn't invite Namid into his home unless it benefited him to do so . . . one way or the other."

"He stayed at the governor's palace?" Again, the question came from Danna, and again Cullon glared at her.

Zeindar's grin was nothing short of crafty when he nodded. "He was *entertained* for several days."

"Entertained or detained?" Cullon asked briskly.

"Oh, entertained, I'm sure," the exiled colonel replied. "LuFarr leads an extravagant life. He enjoys flaunting both his power and his wealth. But don't be misled. His magnetic presence can mesmerize, but it's a mask. A brilliantly conceived, ingeniously programmed mask. So is his mind."

Cullon stood up, thanked Zeindar for his time and promised to see a travel pass delivered as soon as possible. "Three days, no more."

"Three days," Zeindar agreed, then added. "If you want to meet LuFarr personally, he frequents a club near the Imperium Headquarters. It won't be hard to recognize him, he's Sultanian by birth."

Cullon said his farewell in the Korcian tongue. Danna expected he did more than wish the colonel long life and prosperity, but she had no way of telling. Both men were too well versed in keeping secrets to reveal anything to her watchful eye.

Her head was reeling with possibilities as Cullon led her out of the room, down the stairs, and then outside where a cold blast of wind made her shiver. The files she'd studied on Marasona had mentioned little about its newest governor. Zeindar had called him an "avatar" of a new order. It didn't sound promising.

"The club Zeindar mentioned. Do you think it's the same one I saw in the dreamscape?"

Cullon took her arm and started walking. "There's only one way to find out."

Eleven

As they walked along its streets, Danna couldn't help but compare Marasona to an exhilarating nightmare, a ghostly dream of dark shadows and unexplored crevices. Cold. Dusty. Smelly. Isolated from the rest of the galaxy by more than distance, it seemed to exist only within itself. There was an eerie calmness on its narrow streets, walled in by tall buildings with sooty windows that made Danna feel as if she were being watched by unseen eyes.

She could see the Imperium Headquarters long before they reached it. The sprawled wings that gleamed on its sixty-story summit acted like a gold-coated beacon, drawing them forward.

When they reached the governmental square the city changed abruptly. A phalanx of glistening skyscrapers towered on all four sides, their impressive architecture promising all the accoutrements of luxury and high tech combined. The streets boiled with people, the buildings glowed with illumination tubes that spelled out the names of restaurants and nightclubs, pleasure palaces and gambling casinos. Nothing was disallowed or forbidden to the city's residents.

"There," Danna said, pointing toward a club with an entry door that opened directly opposite the Imperium building. "It seems to be in the right place. Shall we start there?"

Relatively quiet since leaving Zeindar's office, Cullon pulled her to the side, away from a group of mine workers intent on having a good time to erase the day's hard labor. His voice was a deep whisper as he said, "LuFarr's Sultanian birth may make him stand out in a crowd, but he's not to be trusted. Stay with me, and—"

"Keep my mouth shut," Danna said with a smile. She made a murmuring sound as she stood on her tiptoes, kissed the side of his neck, and whispered back, "Sorry, big guy, but that's not my style."

In retaliation, Cullon's big hand smoothed inside her cloak and over her hip. He gave her butt a gentle but firm squeeze. "I knew I was going to regret bringing you along."

Still on tiptoe, and pressed against his thigh, Danna used her tongue this time, tracing the small patch of bronzed skin she had just kissed. Getting even was more fun than she'd expected. "I'll make it up to you."

Cullon muttered one of his favorite curses, then took Danna by the arm and headed for the door of the nightclub.

The instantaneous, hysterical cacophony of the music caused Danna's eardrums to throb as she walked by Cullon's side toward a circular, glass-polymer bar. Her eyes were attacked next, by the tear-provoking heavy perfume worn by the waitress, a near-naked Gasparian with large breasts and jeweled nipples. She had no name for the other pungencies that filled the air except too many bodies squeezed into too small a space.

The club was at its undulating peak. A rainbow of psychedelic lights exploded against the walls and ceiling in rhythmic crescendos while several groups of holographic dancers, projected inside glittering gold cages, mimicked ancient mating rituals. The lifelike, naked images formed a violent writhing wall at the rear of the flashing dance floor.

Danna reminded herself that diplomacy often required its practitioners to enter a world far removed from the perfection it strived to obtain. Nevertheless, she found herself moving closer to Cullon.

As if reading her thoughts, Cullon put his arm around her waist, drawing her even closer. He ordered two drinks, then directed Danna to a table that was at the back of the club, next to a black metal exit door. They had both spotted LuFarr the moment they'd entered the boisterous nightspot. He was seated in a semi-circular booth with three others: one man and two women. Danna paused, concealed by drinkers and dancers, to look at the Marasonan governor.

His Sultanian heritage made him stand out in the crowd. The albino pallor of his skin, the translucent ice-blue eyes, and the platinum paleness of his hair contracted sharply with the dark, exotic beauty of the woman pressed against his side. He was younger than Danna had expected, with a precise coldness to his appearance that made her think of a corpse. The remaining male and females were a mixture of races, each lavishly clothed and bejeweled. The picture they presented was instantly recognizable: people of power indulging themselves by mixing with the masses.

"Take off your cloak," Cullon instructed her as he placed their drinks on the polymer table. "I want him to see you."

Danna bristled, not liking the implication of the words, but removing the satin-lined cloak anyway. She'd never been one to flaunt her sexuality, but if the club was any indication of LuFarr's personal tastes, she was going to have to do more than sit quietly in the corner to get his attention.

"He's already looking at you," Cullon said, his eyes gleaming gold and green, as only his eyes could. "No. Don't look around. You belong to me, remember."

"Vividly."

"Good," he said in the throaty whisper that made Danna want to reach across the table and touch him. "Just keep concentrating on me. I'll watch the governor and his lovers."

"Both of them."

"All three of them."

Danna didn't comment, she was too busy absorbing the feel of Cullon's warm hand as it traveled up the length of her arm. "Drink your wine," he whispered as he moved his chair closer. "I'll need a reason to return to the bar soon."

Danna lifted her glass and took a sip of wine. Not used to expressing physical affection in public, she tried to look as if it were perfectly natural for her to be fondled by Cullon's strong hands no matter the time or place. In reality, it wasn't entirely an act. The thought of how they'd made love, and how they would make love again, made her heartbeat quicken.

"What else do you know about LuFarr?" she asked, mentally reviewing the limited files she'd read on the Marasona governor while onboard the *Star Hawk*. None of them has mentioned his sexual preferences.

"He's new to the corporate scheme of things, but a fast learner," Cullon replied, nestling his mouth against her throat as his hand explored her naked back above the line of her silk trousers. "Whatever his background was on Sultana has been cleverly erased from permanent records. There are rumors that he killed his father and his brother. The Sultana government refuses to admit he was ever born."

Danna shivered at the thought of how many crimes

the illustrious governor of Marasona had or had not committed. The brief look she'd gotten of him told her that his blood was as ice cold as his eyes. Her expression darkened.

"What's wrong?" Cullon asked.

"Circles within circles," she told him with a light shrug. "Betrayals, secret loyalties, and who knows what else."

"Welcome to my world," he crooned into her ear.

Danna's nerves tingled with the uneasy sensation of being watched by unfriendly eyes. She knew LuFarr was looking in their direction. She could feel the coldness radiating across the crowded room.

"I'm going to get up from the table." Cullon's voice was low pitched but it cut easily through the surrounding chatter. "Give me time to reach the bar before you turn around and look at the crowd. Don't single LuFarr out, but don't avoid eye contact either."

"Please don't tell me that you want me to flirt with him," Danna said. "I don't think my acting abilities are that good."

"You don't have to flirt. Just let him get a good look at you. That's all it will take."

"Take for what?"

"For him to want what I have."

He left the table before Danna could comment. She waited, giving Cullon time to weave his way through the growing crowd and reach the bar that was now being hosted by two nearly-naked Gasparian females—twins no less.

Casually, she turned in her chair until she was facing the room. In the sea of faces, Danna saw a minimum of guarded, hostile looks. She let her eyes wander aimlessly over the club's populace: mine workers in clean uniforms, some in civilian clothes, but all gaunt-faced and pale from long hours spent underground; women in various forms of dress and undress, all smiling and laughing and having a rousing good time while psychedelic oranges and yellows and sickening greens played a visual tattoo on their faces.

Finally, her gaze settled on the booth where LuFarr sat. In the mist of the maddening music, deep shadows, and wild, blinking lights, the governor seemed totally relaxed. His face was narrow in the brow, high in the cheekbones, tapering to a pointed chin, but his mouth was full and lush. He smiled at her, then licked his lips.

The sexual connotation was crude and blatant. As if to make sure she understood his meaning, LuFarr reached over and licked the half-exposed breast of one of his lovers. The woman smiled, then lowered her hand below the table to return the caress.

Danna forced herself to smile back, not an inviting smile, but a sarcastic one, as if the sexual exchange was nothing more than amusing. Cullon's remark before leaving the table had forced her to draw the obvious conclusion: LuFarr was the prey and she was the lure.

As if the silent exchange with LuFarr had meant nothing, Danna glanced around the room a second time. She looked up as Cullon headed back to the table, giving him a genuine smile, one she was confident LuFarr observed and noted.

"What next?" she asked as Cullon placed a fresh glass of wine in front of her.

"We finish our drinks, then leave."

"That's all."

"LuFarr has seen you. That's enough for now. I'll let him stew over the fact that you'll be in my bed tonight, not his. If I know his type, and I do, he'll find a way to contact you tomorrow."

"On board the *Star Hawk*?"

"No. We'll stay in the city overnight," Cullon said. He resumed the attention he'd lavished on her before leaving the table, but this time his hand came to rest on her knee. A few seconds later, it was gliding up the inside of her thigh. "If LuFarr is half as informed as I think he is, he already knows that a Korcian shuttle

landed this evening. In fact, I'd wager my dagger that
he knows our names."

"That can't be good."

"On the contrary, it's exactly what I hoped for." He
picked up his glass and took a drink before meeting
Danna's gaze. "Don't worry. I'm very good at covering my tracks. The only thing the governor is going to
find out about us is what I want him to find out."

"What about Zeindar?"

"He knows better than to say anything. Not if he
wants to see the sunrise."

Danna shivered at the conviction in Cullon's voice,
but she didn't question it. She'd known from the start
that he lived by a different set of rules.

"If we have new identities shouldn't I know them,"
she asked.

"We're lovers on a holiday," he whispered into her ear.

"I can think of better places to play lover's games."

He looked at her, offering a convincing smile. "We
like our games with a bit of danger attached. Just like
LuFarr."

"I'm flattered, but do you really think he's going to
make the effort to find me?"

"Yes. He won't be able to resist you any more than I
could," Cullon breathed the words into her ear, before
biting down on the lobe. "Kiss, me, then let's get out
of here. I'm getting hard. The sooner I have you in
bed, the better."

"I didn't expect this," Danna said, surveying the room
Cullon had rented at a hotel only two blocks from Imperium Headquarters. It was large and tastefully furnished with a huge bed and a lavish bath.

There wasn't a balcony, but the holographic window
designs made it just as interesting. Danna walked to
the control panel and browsed through the selections.
Once the large panes of polymer-enforced glass re-

flected the allusion of mist-covered mountains and a moonlit river, she turned to smile at Cullon.

"Very nice."

The room was dim, illuminated by a single light centered over the bed and the holographic moonlight that bullied its way into the room, past the sheer drapes that Danna had drawn closed. The pale green coverlet on the bed had been folded down by a hotel servant, exposing crisp white linens. Across from the bed, a fragrant candle burned on top of a white marble stand, its floral scent perfuming the air. A bottle of wine and two glasses sat on a nearby table, waiting Cullon's attention. But his attention was elsewhere. His eyes were riveted on the woman who was slowly undressing in front of him.

With other females, Cullon had always adopted the role of the aggressor, the conductor who orchestrated the way they made love, the pace, the intricacy, the mood, when it began, when it ended. Some had remarked that it was as if he didn't trust them to appreciate the lyricism of the sexual act or to reach the proper crescendo without his explicit direction. But with Danna, Cullon was going to allow himself to be a player, not just a leader. He was going to succumb to temptation, to be seduced as well as to practice seduction because he could tell she wanted it that way.

The difference, he supposed, was that with other females, even at the height of his ardor, he was conscious of what he was more than who he was, an Enforcer, always on alert, always suspicious. But not with Danna. She wasn't a paid companion, or an asset he was working for information. She was different.

Without taking her eyes from his, Danna walked naked to where he stood and began to unbutton his shirt, her fingers moving leisurely, deliberately. Cullon bent forward and traced the line of her mouth with his tongue as her hands removed his clothing. He feasted on the warm flesh of her neck. Her arms dropped to her sides and she tossed her head back, lifting her chest, broadening the canvas on which his mouth painted abstract bolts of lightning, stripes of heat that seared her skin and left her trembling with desire.

Her body was perfect for lovemaking, full breasts that responded to his laving tongue, slender hips that moved in tantalizing rhythm to his probing fingers. Her legs, long and sleek, moved against him in an unconscious attempt to get closer. Her mouth was on his neck, breathing on him, biting him, teasing him with swift snakelike swipes of her tongue.

Cullon grimaced with a pleasure that bordered on pain. His sex pulsed with the need to get inside her.

The dresser was closer than the bed. Backing her up to it, Cullon was able, by arching backward, to enter her and take a swelling nipple into his mouth at the same time. The synchronous movements, one thrusting, one drawing, enraptured Danna within seconds. She leaned back, gripping the edge of the dresser with both hands.

He took her fast and hard. There was no foreplay, but then they didn't need it. They had both been ready for this, both wanting it since they'd stood face to face in the shuttle. They performed like finely tuned instruments; pushing and pulling in concert, creating a harmony that was uniquely their own.

Cullon felt Danna tense, drawing him deeper into her just before she quaked in climax. He erupted, too, releasing the molten liquid of passion. Filling her, emptying himself.

They supported each other, both laboring to breathe. It was several minutes before either one of them could speak.

"Ummm, not bad for starters," Cullon said as he carried her to the bed. He stepped back once he'd deposited her in the center of it and smiled. "Don't move."

"The hypo must be wearing off," she murmured lazily. "I'm getting sleepy."

"Not yet. Keep those beautiful eyes open a while longer."

He filled the glasses with sparkling wine and carried them to the small table beside the bed, pausing long enough to give a voice command to the sound system. In immediate response, the unit sent the lilting notes of an unknown composer into the air. The music, combined with the aromatic scent of the candle, and the earthy tang of arousal blended to produce a tantalizing atmospheric aphrodisiac.

Cullon looked at the soft, deep valley between her breasts, remembering the taste and texture of her skin when he'd kissed her there. It was all he could do to keep from pulling her to him to repeat the process. Sexy. She was more than that. She was vibrantly female. Intelligent, independent . . . and his.

He put a damper on his libido long enough to remind himself that when a man set things in motion, he couldn't always be sure what direction they'd go, or stop them in time. That's how he was feeling now, as if he'd unleashed something that was certain to spin out of control.

Neither of them spoke. Each drank wine while drinking in the sight of the other's nakedness, sating their thirst while their hunger grew. When the glasses were empty, Danna put hers aside and pressed her lips against his with an urgency Cullon recognized as matching his own, yet still he pulled back.

"Not yet," he whispered.

He pulled a flower from the vase near the bed, then gently deplumed the yellow blossoms and rubbed the soft petals against the pink aureoles that tipped her breasts, then lower, slowly charting the length of her body. When her back arched and she moaned, Cullon pulled away, wanting to prolong their lovemaking, but she grabbed at him.

"Oh, no, you don't, big guy. Now," she said. "Right now."

Cullon laughed. "You like it, don't you?"

"Too much." She rolled her hips upward at the same time that she dug her nails into his shoulders. "Do it!"

Cullon entered her and together they stripped away time and captured eternity. There was no one else, it was just them, just now, just the exquisite pleasure of their bodies linked in a symphony of movement, rising higher and higher, culminating in an incredible release followed by delicious contentment.

"You always surprise me," Danna murmured sleepily.

"Is that bad?"

"No. Just surprising." She tilted her head so she could look into his eyes. "This could get complicated."

"It's already complicated."

Twelve

Cullon woke just before sunrise. Danna was sleeping contently at his side. He left the bed, knowing she'd sleep for hours more if left undisturbed.

He dressed, entered a note on the console just in case she woke up before he got back, then left the room. Exiting the hotel, he walked across the square, in the direction where he'd left the shuttle, his pace unhurried. The wind picked up, and Cullon let it massage his face into full wakefulness as he turned down a narrow alley and continued south, annoyed by the questions that still needed answers.

Then he heard the sound. It wasn't the result of wind and sand against buildings; it had nothing to do with the early morning cold or the unfriendly weather of Marasona. It was the sound of a human footstep. His ears were the ears of a trained professional; distances were judged quickly. The sound did not come from ahead of him, but from behind him.

Cullon continued walking, the rhythm of his footsteps unbroken. He turned down another alley, this one taking him away from the shuttle instead of nearer.

He heard the sound again. Faint, barely audible when mixed with the sound of the wind and the awakening city, but definitely a footstep. Whoever was following him had moved back, and that told Cullon two things: They would wait until he was away from an occupied building, and whoever was following him was either careless or inexperienced or both.

Cullon's left hand remained at his side; his right had unfastened his jacket and was now gripped around the hilt of his dagger, strapped in a sheath around his waist. He stepped into another alleyway, this one more shadow than light and flattened himself against the cold metal of the building, melting into the shadows. He stayed against the wall, the dagger drawn and ready.

The sound of footsteps preceded the rushing figure as it raced to make the same turn.

"Press yourself against the wall! Your hands in front of you. High! Get them high and keep them there. *Now!*"

"Please!" The man spun halfway around, but Cullon was on him, throwing him back against the wall. He was young, barely in his teens. His age was obvious from his face; it was pale, the eyes wide and clear and frightened.

"Slowly," Cullon cautioned. "Turn around, but keep your hands where I can see them."

The young man moved, turning, but keeping his back to the wall, his hands still high. "I didn't do anything wrong," he said, his voice crackling with fear. "I don't mean any harm."

"Who are you?"

"Megar. I work for Colonel Zeindar."

"Doing what?"

"Cleaning up mostly, and errands." The boy took a quick gulp of air, gathering courage. "He sent me to deliver a message."

Cullon stepped back, sheathing his dagger as he moved. "So deliver it."

The youth gasped another deep breath, then straightened his shoulders. "He said if you wanted to know more about your friend you should go to the refinery. Ask for a pilot by the name of Kydukov."

"Is that all?"

"The refinery and Kydukov's name. That's all, I swear."

"Away with you," Cullon said, motioning for the young man to retrace his steps. When Megar hesitated, he asked, "Is there a second message?"

The youth rubbed his hand across his chin. "Colonel Zeindar said if you find what you're looking for he wants five days, not three. He said you'd understand."

"I understand," Cullon said. He looked straight into Megar's frightened eyes. "You can tell Zeindar that if I get what I came for, he'll get what's due him."

With that, the young man was gone, racing back the way he'd come.

Cullon waited until the boy was out of sight before resuming his journey. When he reached the shuttle, he contacted Gilfo.

"Is all well?" the dwarf asked.

"So far," Cullon said. "It appears that Namid became friends with Governor LuFarr."

"What kind of friend?" asked Gilfo. "Not the treasonous kind, I hope."

"Maybe," Cullon replied. He didn't like the words "maybe" or "perhaps." They were too equivocal. Words that concealed, rather than revealed. But at this point in time, they were the only words that applied. So far, all the Tribunal had was rumor, circumstantial evidence, and innuendo, but it was piling up at an impressive rate.

"How is Officer MacFadyen?" Gilfo asked.

"Still sleeping," Cullon said, knowing the dwarf

could hear the smile in his voice. "She drew the governor's eye last night."

"I do not like to think that you would use her for bait," Gilfo said. "She is not accustomed to dangerous games such as the ones you play."

"Don't worry. I'll keep her safe. In the meantime, keep monitoring the colony transmissions. If LuFarr communicates with any of his corporate friends off world, I want to know about it."

Cullon ended the transmission, then resumed his walk. He retraced his steps, heading back toward the square. He didn't stop until he reached an eatery owned by a Gasparian named Lospa. Cullon knew the proprietor from previous visits. Lospa ran his business with the keen eye of a thief and an ear to anything that might be useful to a prospective "buyer."

Beyond the glass latticework that was the entrance to the café, Lospa was all teeth and obsequiousness to his customers. When he saw Cullon he was obviously startled; for a split second his expression turned serious, then he recovered and approached the Korcian with a wide smile.

"Welcome, my old friend," he said, motioning Cullon toward a small table in the corner. The square was easily seen from an adjacent window.

Cullon was served, his breakfast come and gone, before Lospa joined him again. The pleasantries they shared were brief.

"What do you know about a freighter pilot called Kydukov?"

Lospa arched his brows, shrugging slowly. "What is there to know? He delivers ore from the mine to the refinery."

"Nothing more?"

"There is always more on Marasona," Lospa answered.

"What?"

The restaurateur gave another shrug. "I can't say."

"How much?"

Lospa looked around, then leaned over the table, putting his round face closer to Cullon's ear. He named his price, waited for Cullon's acknowledgement, then said. "It is rumored that he pilots a transport for the Imperium. A very private transport. One that can take a man with one name away from Marasona and deliver him—with a new name and travel papers—to anywhere he wants to go. For a price, of course."

"How close is Kydukov to LuFarr?"

Lospa helped himself to a cup of coffee from the carafe the service drone had yet to remove from the table. "Close enough. He will not betray the governor easily."

Cullon smiled as he paid for his meal (a great deal more than the food was worth). "I don't expect him to."

There was activity everywhere as freighters were unloaded and made ready for a return trip to the mine. Giant cranes swung cables cradling metal crates of raw ore over the side of the hovering ships and into the larger, deeper holding bays of the transport trailers that would deliver the ore to the guts of the refinery.

Amid the squeals and rasps of metal rubbing against metal, giant floodlights glared down on the catwalks where sweating crane operators and refinery employees worked fast and silent, but not fast enough for the overweight supervisor who stood on the observation deck above them.

He bellowed for the men to work faster: "We're behind schedule. Get your asses moving!"

The workers responded with groans and grunts as they did what the boss ordered.

Security guards milled about as the freighters were unloaded, weapons slung casually over their shoulders. The officer at the gate stopped Cullon with an arrogant tone. "The refinery is off limits unless you have a pass."

"I'm looking for a man called Kydukov," Cullon replied. "One of your freighter pilots."

"What for?" The guard's tone was somewhat less hostile when Cullon stepped out of the shadows and into the morning light. He offered a politely hesitant smile; he was no fool when it came to Korcians.

"Nothing that's important to anyone but me," Cullon said, reaching into his pocket for the expected bribe.

The guard took it, then added. "That's Kydukov's freighter being unloaded now."

He opened the gate and Cullon stepped into the melee of machinery and dock workers. He threaded his way along a wire-mesh catwalk to the landing platform. A few minutes later, he was looking at Kydukov, a man whose heritage was a mixture of galactic races.

The pilot had the cocky expression of someone well connected with the Imperium. His gaze swept over Cullon, conveying mild surprise and blatant disapproval. "What do you want?"

"A few answers," Cullon replied passively. "We have a mutual friend. Chimera Namid."

"I don't know anyone by that name." The pilot straightened his perennial slouch and whisked his hand to the side. "Sorry, but I'm due back at the mine."

"Wrong answer," Cullon said, holding him in place with a stare.

"Get out of my way!"

Cullon's strong fingers gripped the loose cloth of Kydukov's flight suit, crunching into the flesh of his lower rib cage and pushing him back against the hull of the freighter. Out of sight of anyone else on the docks, words were whispered harshly into his ear.

"Chimera Namid. A young Korcian you flew from Marasona to a transport station that made connections to Ramora," Cullon said. "I advise you to remember him quickly. I'm not a patient man."

"I pilot a mining freighter, not a transport," Kydukov said through his teeth. His voice was a taut whisper.

"Another wrong answer." Cullon pushed the barrel of his pistol into the man's chest. He was in the element he knew best, a two-legged primeval cat who hunted its prey without mercy. "If I don't get the right answer, I'm going to burn your heart out. The laser is set on low. You'll live until I slice through the last artery."

"LuFarr will kill me."

"That's a possibility. I'm a definite," Cullon said, lessening his hold on the pilot's flightsuit, but keeping the laser pistol close to his heart. "Who arranges the change in identification papers?"

"I don't know," Kydukov told him, flinching when he thought Cullon might strike him. "I don't know! All I do is pilot the transport."

"Did you take a young Korcian away from here a few months ago?"

Kydukov winced at the question. "Yes. But I don't know his name. I flew him to Sarisbernia. Where he went from there was his business, not mine."

"He stayed at the governor's palace. Is that normal?"

Kydukov took a deep breath. "Not always. If LuFarr likes someone he invites them to the palace, then he makes them pay a token for his permission to leave."

"What kind of token? Money? Information?"

"He gets the money for providing new identities and transport. The token has to be something personal." The pilot gulped down another quick breath of cold air. His words created a dissonant counterpoint to the clacking sounds of cranes and ion motors. "He keeps the stuff at the palace. In his trophy room."

Cullon studied Kydukov's face for a long moment, then tucked the laser pistol away. "Don't worry, I have no intention of telling the governor that you and I had this little chat. Keep your mouth shut and you won't have any problems."

Cullon left Kydukov standing on the catwalk and returned to the hotel. If the pilot was right, something of Namid's had been left behind on Marasona, something Danna might be able to use for an imprint. As he entered the hotel, Cullon accepted LuFarr's bizarre habits and shifted his thoughts to a more immediate purpose . . . getting inside the governor's trophy room.

Thirteen

The magnificence of the governor's residence wasn't lost on either Cullon or Danna. The Imperium administrator had created an expensive haven for himself; part castle, part fortress, part functioning home with an incredible view of the city and the northern mountains. The private quarters, contained within the gothic monolith of the Imperium Headquarters, were off-limits to anyone lacking a personal invitation; only the most elite of Marasona's citizens were given that privilege.

Tonight's invitations had been ostensibly issued to celebrate the governor's new term of office, but Cullon had the distinct impression that there was a secondary motive; to provide an evening where LuFarr could flaunt his wealth while he enjoyed his perverted idiosyncrasies.

"Stay close," he said, cautioning Danna.

She linked her arm through his and smiled. "Don't worry, big boy, LuFarr gives me the creeps. I can hardly wait to see his trophy room."

"As soon as I've located it, I'll give you the signal. When we leave I want it to be quietly and quickly."

"Are you going to tell me how you found out about it in the first place?"

"Later. Right now all I want you to think about is catching LuFarr's eye. I'll do the rest."

"That shouldn't be hard in this dress."

Cullon paused to look her over from head to toe and not for the first time. She was carved ivory packaged in topaz silk. Floor-length, tight, and strapless, her dress was the ideal wrapping for a precious gift. She was as lovely as any female in the room, lovelier because her beauty was understated and would grow with each second of observation by the beholder's eye.

It was one of the things Cullon was counting on. He needed LuFarr's attention focused on Danna while he found the trophy room.

Giving her an encouraging smile, Cullon led her to where security guards waited to scan their ID badges. Cullon's badge was one he had used before, on another corporate colony in Sector Six. The identity search would show that his occupation was that of a discreet, freelance pilot. Danna's credentials would show her to be the spoiled granddaughter of a Terran industrialist. If LuFarr had been curious enough to check, and Cullon was certain that he had, the records would reveal that Cullon and Danna had met a few weeks ago on Pryratia where her grandfather, Randolph Bickmore, had attended an economic conference.

Outside the gold inlaid doors where they had entered, there were another set of guards. Four more guards occupied each corner of the massive reception area, the chevron of Marasonan Security stenciled on the breast pocket of their gray uniforms.

Entering the residence, Cullon felt that instead of walking into a private sanctuary he'd somehow stepped into a carefully painted portrait. The intricately inlaid murals of multi-colored tiles, the lights focused on LuFarr and LuFarr alone, the throne-back chair, the gold encrusted jewels that adorned the governor's hands and neck, the scepter-straight posture of his body—the Sultanian was a king at court.

"What do we do now?" Danna asked as Cullon escorted her across the room, away from where LuFarr was sitting on his dais.

"Nothing. Unless I'm mistaken, LuFarr has been waiting for you to arrive." He gestured her toward a buffet table. "Let's walk over and sample the delicacies. We'll wait for the governor to make the first move."

"What makes you so sure that he will?"

"We got an invitation, didn't we?"

It took less than a minute before they heard a mellifluous voice behind them at the buffet table. "It's unusual to see a Terran matched with a Korcian."

Cullon turned to see the governor's lips spreading apart in what was suppose to be a smile, but in truth was nothing more than a baring of teeth.

"What brings you to Marasona?" LuFarr asked.

"Nothing of importance," Danna replied before Cullon had the chance. "We wanted to get away from . . . shall we say, the more structured aspects of life. I've always wanted to visit the outer regions." She linked her arm through Cullon's, moving until she was plastered to his side. "The big guy's indulging me."

"I can't imagine any man not indulging you." LuFarr's lips moved again, in that odd curl designed to convey amity and goodwill. "So tell me, Miss Bickmore, what do you think of Marasona?"

"It's intriguing."

"Yes, intriguing." LuFarr's voice dropped an octave, underlining the word "intriguing," making it clear that he didn't consider Cullon an obstacle, and that he liked what he saw. There would be no discussion, no argument, no changing his mind. The governor wanted Danna, and he always got what he wanted. "Please, make yourself at home. Enjoy the food and drink. You will find none better anywhere in the galaxy. I must attend to my other guests, but I will return."

"Thank you for your hospitality," Danna said. She disengaged herself from Cullon's arm, allowing LuFarr to think that she'd momentarily forgotten her current lover. "I look forward to seeing your art collection. Rumors label it spectacular."

"Rumors are often correct," LuFarr replied, smiling in self-appreciation. He inclined his head to Cullon, before lifting Danna's hand to his mouth and applying a courtly kiss. "Later, when my other guests are occupied with their own interests, I shall show you the gallery. It is indeed spectacular."

"What gallery?" Cullon asked as soon as LuFarr had moved beyond hearing distance.

"The one filled with black market art," Danna told him. "There was a reference in his file, so I did some cross checking. LuFarr likes to think of himself as cultured. He collects art. Stolen art. He has some of the finest pieces in the galaxy, including a Scozzi sculpture that mysteriously disappeared from a Terran museum twenty years ago."

Cullon had read the reference in LuFarr's file, but he hadn't taken the time to dig deeper. None of the three True Bloods who had been murdered had ties to the arts, Korcian or otherwise. The possibility that the gallery and the trophy room were one and the same rolled through his mind, but he dismissed the idea. LuFarr might flaunt ill-gained works of art to appear sophisticated, but the tokens he collected from his victims would be set aside for moments of private gloating.

"Who are these people?" Danna asked, her gaze sweeping the room. The women were adorned in varying stages of fashionable undress, some with their breasts completely exposed, while the men were attired in everything from monkish robes to jewel-studded leather.

"Misfits and scavengers, petty thieves and criminals," Cullon told her. "They're here because they can't function in a structured society. If I had an extradition warrant in my pocket, I could haul most of them off to prison."

To keep with the mood of the evening, Cullon introduced Danna as the rather mysterious Miss Bickmore, his friend from Earth. He did his job well, providing just enough information to intrigue a number of LuFarr's guests. Those who might wish to learn more about the lovely Terran were told the least while others, too imbued with themselves to care, were told the most, so they could relate the gossip to others.

LuFarr had returned to his throne chair. There was a zone of empty space around him, an invisible margin his guests didn't cross. The servant who sat food and drink on a low table by his chair pulled back even as he reached forward to place a wine glass at the governor's disposal; the two sentries standing on opposite sides of the dais leaned away rather than toward him to address his requests. Nearby, his three lovers waited, their eyes roving the room as if deciding upon partners for the evening's scheduled entertainment.

By habit, Cullon scanned the crowd for signs of danger and found the threat possibilities low. The only hot spot was a guard who'd found Danna particularly interesting. If she left the room, chances were the guard would follow.

Cullon didn't like the idea of leaving Danna alone, but he couldn't afford to arouse LuFarr's suspicions. Assuming the governor judged other men by his own low standards, the idea that Cullon might enjoy some private philandering wouldn't be excessively shocking. That meant Danna had to carry the show.

"It's time to be a diplomat," Cullon told her. "I've

got to find the trophy room, which means I've got to get out of this one without drawing unnecessary attention."

"What do you want me to do?"

"Mix and mingle your way across the room, but not so close to LuFarr that he reads it as an open invitation. And don't get jealous when I take one of the ladies out of the room with me."

Danna gave him the expected glare, then smiled convincingly because she knew others were watching. "What lady did you have in mind?"

"It doesn't matter," Cullon said, glancing around at several of the females who had been giving him inviting smiles since he'd arrived. "One's as good as another."

"You want me to keep LuFarr on a leash while you indulge your fantasies elsewhere."

Cullon couldn't tell if she was angry or not. Her voice had slipped into diplomatic mode. He countered with a smile and a kiss that was normally reserved for private moments. "You'll need several leashes. In case you haven't noticed, you're the center of attention."

"Not because you didn't do everything possible to put me there," she said accusingly.

Cullon kissed her on the cheek this time. "If they toast the governor, take a glass, but don't drink the champagne."

"Why not?"

"It's spiked with an aphrodisiac."

"You're kidding me, right?"

"Money can buy almost anything here. Especially information.

"So, who did you bribe?" she asked, looking amused.

"One of the guards at the main entry, downstairs," Cullon told her. What he didn't tell her was that he'd also purchased a nifty little master key that would get him into any room in the building. It duplicated the bio-scan imprint of the governor's personal assistant.

He waited until Danna had made her way halfway

across the grand salon, where she began a conversation with a man who looked to be more interested in the male guests than the female ones. Amused by her choice, Cullon cast a quick glance toward a woman dressed in a black-sequined kimono that was split to her hip then held together with leather lacings that eventually formed a collar around her neck, Cullon gave her a surreptitious smile.

She smile backed, the look in her eyes pure invitation.

Less than a minute later, they were strolling out of the grand salon and into one of the outer rooms where small groups of guests had gathered to engage in various stages of foreplay, preparing themselves for the sexual orgy that would conclude the evening.

Cullon guided the woman into one of the adjacent rooms. He'd barely gotten the door closed when she untied the leather lacing around her neck and stripped out of the sequined kimono. Cullon watched, faking interest. When she walked toward him, he put his hands on her shoulders and squeezed just the right tendons and nerves. She slumped toward the floor. He caught her, carried her to a nearby sofa and stretched her out, posing her as if she were simply sleeping off a bout of exhausting sex.

On his left wrist, concealed under the sleeve of his tunic, was a tiny syringe. He'd taken a risk bringing it. If the guards had done a body scan, they would have found it. But the governor's invitation had gotten them inside with nothing more than a flash of their ID badges and the hefty bribe he'd paid the guard whose name has been supplied by Lospa.

Cullon injected a minute amount of the sleeping agent into the underside of the woman's right arm, then left the room. The drug would keep her immobile for several hours.

As expected, the guests in the outer salon were too preoccupied with one another to notice Cullon. He kept to the shadows as much as possible, slowing to a stop as he emerged into a second hallway, one that led away from the party. Somewhere in the maze of the heavily decorated residence, he would find LuFarr's trophy room. But where?

He found a large room that appeared to be an office: in seconds a guard in a gray uniform stepped out to greet him.

Cullon looked around as if he'd accidentally lost his way. "Sorry, I seem to have misplaced the party."

The guard didn't hesitate. He pulled a short-barreled pistol, leveling it at Cullon's chest.

Cullon's right hand shot up and out, clasping his fingers around the barrel of the guard's pistol, twisting hand and weapon violently in a counterclockwise motion. When the guard would have shouted for help, Cullon gripped the man's throat with his left hand, choking off all sound and propelling the guard deeper into the room. As the man fell, Cullon ripped the weapon away from his twisted wrist, and brought the handle down sharply on the guard's skull. The man went limp; Cullon tucked him behind a sofa.

Once again, Cullon pulled the syringe out of its concealed pocket and injected the guard. By the time he regained consciousness, two of the governor's guests would be long gone.

Cullon began searching the room, the guard's pistol now concealed under his tunic. Finding nothing, he moved into the next room, a private suite with mirrors and colored illumination globes hanging from the ceiling.

It didn't take for him long to find it . . . not a trophy room, but a trophy case.

Cullon put his training to work and concentrated on disarming the sensors that protected the safe. It took him a full hour.

What he saw when he swung the metal door wide made him angry. Namid's token was easily found among the collection. All too recognizable, and all too dangerous.

Cullon ignored the Sumaese rubies and a sapphire as big as Gilfo's fist. He retrieved the small object Namid had forfeited to the governor of Marasona, closed the safe, and reset the sensors.

Making his way back to the party, he paused at every corner, listening for voices. All he heard was the drunken laughter of LuFarr's guests. There was no time to think of what he had found, he had to reach Danna and get them away from Marasona. The colony didn't have a penal system, it had hard labor in the mines or death. Both were cheaper than housing and feeding prisoners.

Entering the grand salon, Cullon threaded his way through a jagged line of drug-induced dancers who were peeling off their clothes to the rhythm of percussive music. The party was getting out of hand; Danna could dissuade her many admirers for a few minutes, but no longer.

Cullon pressed his way through a frenzied gathering of LuFarr's favorite lovers. The governor was watching with a smile on his face as two male guests lustfully worshiped the body of a young Gasparian female, naked and spread-eagled on the banquet table.

Cullon saw Danna in the corner, her eyes wide with shock and disgust. He walked rapidly to her side, pushing aside several admirers. He diverted their attention by pulling Danna into his arms and kissing her fiercely. He ran his hands roughly over her hips, pushing her against his erection. Several guests applauded, thinking they would soon have another coupling to watch.

"Don't fight me," he whispered into Danna's ear as he fondled her breasts. "Act like you're enjoying it. I'm going to carry you out of the room."

"I don't care how you do it, just get me the hell out

of here," she whispered back as she leaned into his embrace, then kissed him as fiercely as he'd kissed her.

Cullon swept her up into his arms and headed for the nearest door.

LuFarr materialized in their path.

"Bring her this way," he said, assuming that both Cullon and Danna were under the influence of the aphrodisiac he'd added to the champagne.

Cullon felt Danna stiffen in his arms, but he shut off her protest with a quick glance. He followed the governor from the room, down a short corridor, and into a private pleasure suite. The holograms were already activated, showing men and women in various stages of sexual activity.

"Put her on the bed," LuFarr commanded as he began stripping out of his clothes. His translucent eyes were alight with lust. "You can watch."

Cullon set Danna on her feet instead.

"*She* can watch," he said. The next second, his hand clamped around the governor's throat.

LuFarr struggled; it was useless and he knew it. Cullon surged his right hand along the edge of the governor's waist and dug his fingers into the base of the rib cage, yanking back with such force that LuFarr almost blacked out.

"Keep quiet," Cullon warned as he pulled LuFarr to the bed and spun him around, forcing him down onto the mattress. He put his knee in the small of the governor's back and his lips next to the man's ear. "I'd enjoy nothing as much as I'd enjoy killing you," he whispered. "Tell me about Namid Chimera."

"Who *are* you?" asked LuFarr, his eyes almost bulging from their sockets.

"A man who wants an answer." Cullon tightened his grip on the governor's throat. "Tell me about Namid Chimera."

"He was nothing, a nobody," LuFarr gasped.

"Yet you brought him here, to your penthouse palace. Why?"

"He can't talk when you're strangling him," Danna pointed out.

She put her hand on Cullon's wrist. His grip relaxed instantly. LuFarr breathed easier, but only for a moment. The pistol Cullon had taken from the guard suddenly appeared. It pressed coldly against the governor's left temple.

"Namid," Cullon reminded him in a lethal tone. "Why did he leave the Empire?"

"I don't know," LuFarr answered. "I didn't ask why. He was willing to pay the price. That's all that mattered."

"And the token?" Cullon commanded. The barrel of the pistol pushed harder against LuFarr's temple, indenting the skin while the albino governor turned even paler.

"A fancy that caught my eye," LuFarr grunted and gasped at the same time. "That's all, I swear. A token of the Korcian's appreciation, nothing more."

"I don't believe you." Cullon's voice was sharp, his hand steady on the trigger of the pistol. "Was Namid a messenger? Who is your contact in the Empire? Give me a name. Now!"

"There is no name," LuFarr swore. "Namid was nothing, I tell you. A pleasant distraction. Nothing more!"

"You've got someone inside the Empire," Cullon insisted. "Was Namid a courier?"

"No."

"Try again."

In the wan light, LuFarr's pale blue eyes washed to a watery gray. He made a grab for Cullon's hand, the one tightening around his throat. Cullon twisted the barrel of the laser pistol harder against his temple, tearing the skin.

"What plot is the Conglomerate conspiring against the Empire? he asked impatiently.

"There is no plot," LuFarr insisted. Helpless as he was, the governor's will was still prodigious. "We have no need of plots and spies. Time will prove us the victor."

"He's dodging the question," Danna said. "Saying one thing to avoid another."

Beyond the closed door, a woman called the governor's name, insisting that LuFarr return to the party and the sexual games. Cullon shouted out that LuFarr would be along as soon as they finished with the Terran female.

"Call for help and you're a dead man," Cullon said. He handed the pistol to Danna. "Keep that aimed at his heartless chest."

"What are you going to do?"

"Just something to guarantee we won't have a security patrol on our tail for a few hours." Cullon removed the syringe, ejected the empty vial, and inserted a new one.

"What . . . What is that?" LuFarr's pupils were dilated with fear. He was trembling and there was drool leaking from the side of his mouth onto the silken coverlet.

Cullon injected the drug into the pulsing vein in the governor's neck. By the time he'd returned the syringe to its hiding place, a half-naked LuFarr was lying limp on the bed. His once aroused penis now flaccid and pale. "Let's get out of here."

Fourteen

"You think the freighter pilot, Lufarr, was the second person in the dreamscape? The man Namid met outside the club," Danna asked. They had returned to the *Sky Hawk* over an hour ago. Gilfo sat on a nearby stool, waiting along with Danna for Cullon to explain why he had immediately charted course for Korcia.

"You've met LuFarr. Does he strike you as someone Namid would meet on a dark street corner?"

Danna recalled the triumphant look on LuFarr's face when he'd told Cullon to carry her into the private suite. The Conglomerate was all about money to a point, and when its members had enough money, power became the only thing that mattered. The power to manipulate and deceive. The power to dominate. The power to give and take, and the exhilaration of thinking yourself invincible. Cullon was right, LuFarr wouldn't have met Namid in the dark, he would have demanded that the young Korcian come to him.

"I agree," Danna said, "but that doesn't explain why we're headed for Korcia."

"No, but this does." Cullon pulled an object from his pocket and laid it on the galley table.

Danna looked at what had to be a military insignia.

"A general's medallion," Gilfo said, reaching for the token LuFarr had thought valuable enough to lock in a safe. Lying in the palm of the dwarf's hand, the gold caught the light and shone like a small ray of sunshine captured in a circle of black stone.

"Not just any general's," Cullon said. "The men who wear that medallion sit on the High Council."

Gilfo returned the medallion to the table, then climbed down from the stool and went to work making a midnight snack. He glanced back long enough to ask, "Are any of the current High Generals from the house of A'vla Namid?"

"No," Cullon answered.

Danna looked at the medallion, but she didn't touch it. "Maybe it belonged to someone in Namid's family. A family heirloom that he brought with him for sentimental reasons."

"Not likely. The cross-bar design at the top means the badge wasn't awarded until after the Trava Conflict," Cullon said. "That was less than fifty years ago."

"You asked LuFarr if Namid was a courier. Have you changed your mind about True Bloods committing treason?" Danna asked, perhaps too bluntly.

The expression on Cullon's face was rooted in doubt as he pushed the medallion toward her. "I have to know."

The meaning behind his words was unmistakable. Danna could feel the effort it cost him. Until he'd found the medallion, he'd been certain that no True Blood could betray the Empire.

Danna hesitated for a moment, not sure if this was the right time and place to submerge herself in a dreamscape. She wanted to talk to Cullon, to reassure him that one man's sin, if that was what she was about to see, didn't stain another man's soul. But Cullon's gaze was centered on the medallion and the clues he was waiting for it to reveal.

The moment Danna cupped her hand around the medallion, she felt a feather-light pressure within her mind—an indefinable sense of *someone*. As she closed her eyes a smear of leaping, coruscating light glowed beneath her eyelids.

The dreamscape arrived without preamble, tugging at her with invisible fingers. The sense of crossing from the present into the past became a feeling of weightlessness, a sense of heat, a spinning of mind and heartbeat.

Shapes came out of the emptiness around her—a towering structure of gold, shivering shadows, a black vortex shot through with red sparks, like a whirlpool of smoke and fire. Danna felt herself drawn toward the fire. She sensed danger in the spiraling smoke—death or something worse.

She managed a deep breath and forced herself to remember that this was a dreamscape. Someone else's past. In the present, she was sitting across the table from Cullon. The thought gave her strength as she was pulled deeper into the boiling shadows of the tower.

Not a tower . . . a huge domed chamber. The sparks were flickering specks of light from a thousand candles, the smoke a thick mist covering the outer gardens that would burst with color in the sunlight. The chamber could have housed a palace within its walls. It was built of pale marble, great blocks joined seamlessly together. Tiers of backless benches girdled its circumference, rising like stairsteps to a third of its height. A series of stained-glass windows, depicting scenes of ancient battles, ran like a circlet of colored jewels below the point where the walls and ceiling met.

A young man sat curled against the wall of an upper balcony, his knees drawn to his chest. Danna sensed the conflict radiating from him—a compound emotion that encompassed fear and hope.

He sat, concealed from those below him, listening to their words. They spoke of generations past when kings had ruled the Empire, and how they had been forced to unseat those kings in order to protect what others would steal from them. But those days were gone and the great generals would see the Empire protected for future generations. It was an oath they swore aloud, then confirmed with their own blood as a dagger was passed around the table.

"It's a farce; these generals and their code of honor. They'd do anything to preserve their precious Empire," the young man mumbled under his breath. *"It's all a game."*

Danna felt an odd suspension of her own thoughts as she absorbed those of the young man. The dreamscape shifted again, taking on the contours of a dream inside a dream. The colors blurred at the same time they intensified, driven by the young man's thoughts. It was as if she were examining his life from some isolated perch in time.

He sat in a tiny room without windows. There was a leather leash around his neck that anchored him so he couldn't move more than a few feet from the chair. He was naked, bloodied and bruised from the discipline his father had inflicted. The physical pain was secondary to the hunger that fed his mind. There had been beatings, meant to kill the hunger, but the hunger hadn't been expelled. It lived within him, stronger than ever.

The door opened and a man walked into the room. He was tall and slender with a solemn expression. Even the summers, the sacred summers when his father called him home, didn't exclude the servant. He was the boy's guardian, the one assigned to see that the disciplines of becoming a man weren't forgotten.

"It's an important day," the guardian said. *"Your behavior must be impeccable."*

The boy nodded. "What must I do?"

"It's a test. A test of your manhood."

The boy shriveled back into the chair, but the man ignored his reluctance. He removed the collar and leash and helped the boy into a dark robe that hid his bruises.

They walked side by side, down a long corridor that led to a small auditorium. At the far end of the center aisle a man stood waiting, his eyes held a coldness and strength that said he expected total obedience.

The boy hesitated as his father stepped aside to reveal the test. Lying before him, stretched out on a table draped in red silk and bound by ropes, was a young woman. She was naked. Her eyes were glassy, as if she'd been drugged, but inside their depths was a stark terror the boy recognized all too easily.

Danna mentally staggered under the impact of the young man's memories. The dreamscape shifted again, and the boy was back on the balcony, older now but still filled with anger.

She could feel the struggle within him, an abrupt desire to shout his hatred out loud, to be heard above the oaths of fidelity being pledged in the great chamber. He pressed himself back into the darkness of the balcony, trembling with fear that he might be seen, and yet courageous enough to have invaded the sanctuary.

Before Danna could grasp a full image of the young man, the colors began to recede, like a sun sinking into a black ocean. When she opened her eyes they filled with tears.

"What?" Cullon asked.

Danna uncurled her hand and let the medallion fall to the tabletop. She reached for the wine glass Gilfo put in front of her and took a drink. The dreamscape was gone, but the dark, unsettling sensations remained. When she sat her glass back on the table, its crystal base chimed against the polished metal, like a small bell tolling time.

Slowly, choosing her words with as much precision as the dreamscape allowed, she told Cullon what she had seen. And what she had felt—the inner rage of a son who knew he would never meet his father's expectations.

"Describe the chamber to me. In detail."

Danna closed her eyes and called up the images she'd seen. "It was circular with a domed ceiling. The balcony formed a semi-circle above it. There were shadows, but I could see banner tapestries and small alcoves filled with life-size sculptures."

"The High Council," Cullon said numbly. "The father, did you see him clearly enough to identify him if you saw him again?"

"No. His face was shadows and distorted lines."

"The young man on the balcony, was it Namid?" Cullon asked in a low voice.

"No," Danna said. "I'm certain of that."

"Then who?" The question came from Gilfo who had climbed back upon his stool. Across the table, his amber eyes widened. "Was it Ackernar or Eyriaki?"

Danna thought back to the imprints she had gotten from the two men's belongings and shook her head. "No."

Cullon made an exasperated sound deep in his throat. Danna saw the struggle in him, the imbalance between his trust in her ability as an psychometric, and his instinctive need to believe only what he could see with his own eyes.

"Then we have another player. Whoever gave this medallion to Namid is the son of a High General," Cullon said.

"That's circular logic," Danna objected. "Namid could have bought the medallion at a trade fair or novelty shop. LuFarr coveted it because he recognized it as a symbol of power in the Empire. We don't know who this medallion belonged to."

"No general who has ever worn that badge would abandon it to a merchant," Cullon said. The bright light of the galley cast his features into sharp relief. To make his point even stronger, he added, "Namid left his life behind, his heritage, but he took this medallion with him. It has to mean something."

"Until I can identify someone, all we have are pitiful theories about a dysfunctional father and son."

"No," Cullon said, his voice dead sober. "We have ten High Generals."

"How many of them are True Bloods?"

"Three. Tutunjan, Caliphn, and Tscharka."

The unspoken assumption lay heavily in the silence that followed, but the acknowledgment was in Cullon's eyes. If True Bloods were being systematically assassinated by the military, the stability of the Empire was at risk.

Danna stepped out of the shower in Cullon's quarters to find him waiting. He knew she'd intentionally come to his room rather than her own to prove a point. They'd started this investigation together, and they were going to finish it together. He hadn't said a word to her when she'd left the galley. He didn't say one now. He simply picked her up and carried her to the bed, then undressed and stretched out beside her.

"Cullon—"

He placed a finger on her lips. "Ssssh."

His hands moved soothingly over her damp hair and down her back in long, slow sweeps that molded her against his body. Gently he caressed her, tracing the contours of her face and throat, her breasts and belly.

She lay like a contented cat under his touch, her eyes closed. She half dozed until his touch changed. No longer soothing, his hands and mouth moved to arouse her.

There was an urgency to his desire, a need to lose himself in her. To master her. To take control of her because everything else seemed out of control. It was in the drumming of his heartbeat, in the harshness of his breathing, and in the sweat that gleamed on his shoulders and chest. Yet he held back, afraid of what might happen if he let go.

The very possibility that a High General was responsible for the murders of innocent men was enough to make Cullon furious, but he didn't want to unleash that fury on Danna.

"Make love to me," she whispered.

"I'm not feeling gentle," he warned her.

"Neither am I."

Starved for the oblivion only sexual completion could offer, Cullon satisfied his hunger. He felt her body tremble. She wanted him as much as he wanted her. He could feel it in her legs as they stretched out beneath him, digging into the bed and becoming rigid. Her hips began to move, undulating and shifting, enticing him to follow. He joined her, thrusting himself inside her, using his physical strength to hold her captive as he lost himself in the warmth of her, the wet of her.

He buried himself as deep as possible, grasping at her flesh with the fury of a man who fears loss. She welcomed him with a deep contented sigh. The deeper he went, the more she welcomed him.

Their fierce coupling left the imprint of his teeth on her neck and scratches from her nails across his shoulders and lower back. Physical proof of a furious desire.

His flesh in her, hers enclosing his, the intoxication of feeling totally alive; the spinning, reeling mosaic of space through the viewing port. They were all the same. A single rhythm, a single energy, a single purpose—to live in that moment and nothing more.

He remained on her, in her, holding her even when their bodies had nothing more to give.

Fifteen

Some ten hours and eight million kilometers out of Marasona orbit, the *Star Hawk* ceased acceleration to assume its approach to Aquitaine Station. Cullon peered out into the depths of space at the churning colors of the Cygnus Nebula, the station's nearest neighbor. They had made good time. According to the scanners, they would be within docking range in a matter of minutes. Cullon didn't anticipate any problems—except the one sleeping in his bed.

"You look like a man with serious thoughts on his mind," Gilfo said as he entered the command module. He climbed into the co-pilot's seat, then wiggled down into the soft leather to make himself comfortable. "Aquitaine Station," he said, casting a glance at the control panel. "Is this a routine refueling stop, or do you have something else in mind?"

"It's time for you to return to Ramora," Cullon said. "I've come full circle. Whoever killed Namid is still on Korcia."

"What about Danna?"

Cullon stared at the dwarf, taking time to frame his

answer. His original assignment had been to find a
killer. It wasn't a task outside his skills. He was good at
his job; he'd proven it time and time again, both inside
the Empire and out. He knew the inner workings of the
High Council and the Korcian Guard. He knew patriots
and traitors, information dealers and arms merchants,
the good and the bad of a hundred worlds. But Danna,
a woman he'd never meant to be more than an assistant
in his search, had unexpectedly become more.

Would he leave her behind?

The question beat in his mind, insistent as a clock
ticking off time.

"Namid's murder is only part of it," Cullon said at
last. "If I find his killer, I'll be closer to finding out if
the Conglomerate has infiltrated the Empire."

Gilfo's face tightened. "Speaking in the singular
leads me to believe that you intend to send Danna back
with me."

Cullon declined answering. It was becoming in-
creasingly difficult to disguise his feelings, but necessity drove him to complete his mission. His first
obligation had to be to the Empire. If the puzzle had an
answer, it was sixty thousand kilometers away on Korcia. Once there, he'd start with the established facts.

Fact one: The fundamentalist movement was gaining support within the Empire. In its view, the collapse
of the High Council would aid a king's ascension to
the throne. Fact two: The military would do whatever
was necessary to preserve the status quo. Fact three:
The Conglomerate existed to manipulate any political
situation to its own advantage.

In this case, the facts were connected, intricately entwined in a conspiracy whose players were unnamed.
But Danna had proven that the names and faces of the
past could lead to the names and faces of the present.

Accepting that, Cullon was forced to accept another
fact. Danna would travel to Korcia with him.

"Don't even think about dumping me on a transport station."

Both men turned to find Danna standing in the doorway between the command module and Cullon's private quarters. She was dressed in her usual onboard attire, a loose-fitting jumpsuit and soft-soled shoes. Her hair was still mussed from sleep, but her eyes were bright, her expression determined.

"Until I'm relieved of duty by a *League* superior, I'm part of the Tribunal."

"We'll discuss it later." Cullon said as he transmitted the ship's registry code to the docking master on Aquitaine. "I've got to get this bird into a cage."

Danna gave him a delicately twisted smile. "We'll discuss it now."

"Later."

Gilfo climbed out of the co-pilots' seat and motioned for Danna to take his place. Then, being a seasoned diplomat in his own right, he made himself scarce, heading for the galley and a quick snack before they docked.

"You didn't tell me that you planned on making a stop at Aquitaine," Danna said as she fastened the chair's safety harness. "Do we need to refuel?"

"That and a systems diagnostic," Cullon said. He disengaged the auto-controls and took command of the ship. The humming frequency of the engines changed in pitch as the *Star Hawk* slowed to begin its final approach.

Before Danna could say more, which Cullon knew she intended to do, the voice of the docking master came over the commlink. "Welcome to Aquitaine. Docking Ring Four, Bay Two. Confirm coordinates and registry, if you please."

Cullon confirmed the transmitted coordinates and the ship's registry code, then manually switched their trajectory. His gaze was drawn toward the command module's panoramic viewing screen as the space station loomed larger and larger.

Aquitaine was a full-service facility. Its construction had been a joint venture on the part of the League and the Korcian Empire, a gesture of collaboration that had followed the signing of the Vuldarr Treaty.

Like most deep-space stations, it was a lumpy, ungainly structure encased by twelve docking rings. Inside was an amalgamation of fabrication and repair shops, computerized diagnostic laboratories, and living quarters for the thousands of workers it employed. The smallest of the twelve rings, occupying either the lowest or the highest rung on the circular ladder, depending on one's point of view, housed a transport terminal.

The sixth docking ring caught Cullon's attention. Floating within the horseshoe shaped tractor slip was a Korcian patrol cruiser. Floodlights glared down on its metallic hull as workers replaced hatches over the hollow throats of three missile tubes. His face was admirably grave as he maneuvered the *Star Hawk* toward its own docking berth, but a twinkle of recognition lurked in his eyes.

"Do you know that ship?" Danna asked, their confrontation postponed until the docking sequence was complete.

"It's the *Thirl*, a class three cruiser out of Beleth."

It took another fifteen minutes to get the *Star Hawk* nestled safely within its own docking bay. Leaving the ship to the maintenance crew, Cullon escorted Danna down a flight of stairs and into a wide corridor that snaked through gray metal walls. The odor of maintenance oils and the acrid sting of welding smoke filled the air as they passed by one of the fabrication shops.

The main section of the station was a structure of balconies, each a little narrower than the one below it. The main floor was crammed with shops and eating establishments, all of them flashing bright signs to distract from the bland gray metal of their construction.

Escalators moved sluggishly from the four corners of the pavilion, transporting their passengers to and from the tiered balcony sections.

"Where's Gilfo?" Danna asked as they passed a small café that specialized in pastries, the dwarf's favorite snack.

"He's packing," Cullon said. "There's a transport leaving for Ramora in six hours."

"You aren't wasting any time, are you?"

"There isn't time to waste. Gilfo will report to Ambassador Synon, then return to Japola."

"So where are we going?" Danna asked.

"To pay our respects to the caption of the *Thirl*."

"An old friend?"

"You could say that."

They took the escalator at the far end of the pavilion to the second tier, then headed for a hatchway labeled Docking Bays Four and Five. They passed more maintenance shops, a section dedicated to worker dormitories, and a large refueling bay before reaching the sixth docking ring. A Korcian sentry, immaculate in his black-on-black uniform, came to attention as they approached.

"Please inform Captain Jaseera that Cullon Gavriel requests permission to come aboard."

The sentry relayed the message through the commlink strapped to his right wrist.

"Permission granted," he said a moment later.

The clear, sharp chime of an entry sensor sounded as the hatchway irised away to reveal a flexible entry tube that had been fastened to the main hatch of the *Thirl*. The cruiser was too large to be sheltered within a bay.

Once they'd reached the other side, they were greeted by an officer, who scrutinized their station passes briefly, but closely, then escorted them up-ship to the captain's quarters.

"It's good to see you again, Cullon," the *Thirl*'s female captain said, stepping forward to—not extend her hand, but place an affectionate kiss on his cheek.

"It's good to see you, too, Tasiq. May I present—"

"Danna MacFadyen," Danna interrupted, extending her hand.

Cullon hid his amusement. It was apparent Danna didn't want him labeling her until she could personally decipher just where the *Thirl*'s beautiful captain fit into the scheme of things.

"Tasiq Jaseera. Please, sit down." Tasiq moved around the console, easing into a high-backed swivel chair with a loose-limbed grace. "Cullon, pour us something to drink."

Cullon poured and served glasses of wine to Danna and Tasiq, before helping himself to a stein of dark ale. He sat down near Danna, facing the console. "Before I forget to mention it, Tasiq, I have to say a captain's uniform becomes you."

"Gives me respectability, you mean," Tasiq replied wryly.

Cullon raised his glass. "You've always been respectable."

"Tell the High Council that. A class three cruiser assigned to patrol Sector Eight is their version of disciplinary action."

"I'm not the one who told Admiral Gahiri to mind his own business," Cullon replied laughingly. "What did you expect, a flagship?"

"Want to tell me what you're doing on Aquitaine?"

No," Cullon answered, "but I wouldn't mind exchanging a little homeworld gossip. How are things on Korcia?"

"What sort of gossip are we talking about?"

"Fundamentalists. Do you know any? Someone worth knowing, that is."

"One or two. Why? Are you thinking about joining the movement?"

"I might need a discreet introduction."

"You're a True Blood. That's all the introduction you need."

"Where would I introduce myself?"

Tasiq leaned back and smiled. "Any cocktail party or public assembly you choose to attend, I would think. Let your politics be known. Someone's sure to notice."

Whether that someone would be friend or foe wasn't mentioned.

"I didn't think the movement was that widespread." Cullon said.

"More so in the cities than the rural areas. If you run into an aging socialite by the name of Valura Ulgart, you might introduce yourself. It's said he's a jealous guardian of the king's rights," Tasiq answered as she reached for her wine. She took a sip, then paused, as if inviting comment. When there was none, she continued. "I can't say the movement is well organized, but it does have an underground network of supporters, many of them prominent True Bloods like yourself."

"What about military supporters?"

"A few, but the basic difference in philosophy prevents too many from making the commitment to a proposed monarchy. It's a long shot, and they know it."

"Idealists have a way of hanging on to the impossible until it becomes possible," Cullon said.

"Don't look at me," Tasiq laughed. "I haven't been an idealist since I lost my virginity. Speaking of which, why don't you join me for dinner."

Cullon noticed that Danna kept her diplomatic tranquility intact when he accepted the invitation.

"Excellent. I've got to check in with the bridge crew, so make yourselves comfortable," Tasiq said. "I hope you enjoy Korcian fare, Miss MacFadyen, the ship's chef enjoys impressing visitors."

"I look forward to it," Danna replied.

She waited until Tasiq left the room before dropping the smile. Cullon expected some jealous words, what he got was a cold glare and a stern, "I know what you're thinking."

"I didn't think you could read minds."

"I can't, but I can read the writing on the wall. An introduction to your friendly, neighborhood fundamentalist isn't going to accomplish anything but pissing off whoever's killing True Bloods. You're going back to Korcia to paint a bull's eye on your chest."

"And you're concerned for my safety."

"Adding your name to an assassination list goes above and beyond the call," Danna argued.

"No, it doesn't."

The beginnings of what was likely to be a long, strenuous debate was cut short when a sensor's soft chime announced the arrival of the ship's chef. Ensign Eshsol entered the room with brisk enthusiasm. Danna and Cullon were shown menus, which only Cullon could read. He ordered for both of them with no argument from Danna.

She plunged back into conversation the moment the door slid shut behind the *Thirl's* chef. "I know you're a danger-jockey, and things aren't happening fast enough to keep your adrenaline pumping non-stop, but—"

"I'm an Enforcer," Cullon said, cutting off whatever logic she was about to deliver.

Danna gave him a look that said he was also impossibly stubborn. "Won't your family and friends think it odd if you suddenly abandon your Enforcer loyalties and start spouting fundamentalist rhetoric?"

"I don't have to spout rhetoric. The house of A'vla Gavriel follows Namid's in the line of succession. If the fundamentalists succeed in reinstating the monarchy, my father will sit on the throne."

Danna absorbed what he was saying immediately. If a Gavriel was next in line to the throne, then it stood to reason that Cullon's father could be the next True Blood to be murdered.

"Have you notified him?" She asked, her voice softening.

"My father is retired," Cullon said. "He's no longer privy to classified information. I voiced my concerns to Viceroy Surazheia. He's arranged for a discreet bodyguard."

Cullon returned to the serving bar to pour another ale. There were moments of his life that demanded total privacy, classified moments that couldn't be shared with anyone but a select few within the Enforcement Bureau. And there were moments like this . . . moments that he *could* share.

He looked at Danna. She was sitting quietly, waiting for him to voice his concern over his father.

He didn't.

Danna's recent dreamscape of a father and a son had triggered private memories, and, this time, Cullon hadn't been able to push them back. His brother's death had been an accident, but Marok Gavriel had never forgiven his oldest son for the death of his youngest.

Reluctantly, Cullon allowed the memory to take hold of him. Two boys, two brothers, playing energetically where children had no business playing. They had fooled the sensors and gained entry to his father's weapons locker. Even now, Cullon could see the blood gushing from Serran's chest. He closed his eyes for a moment, knowing the image would soon dissolve into the subconscious blackness where it was permanently stored.

It had been agonizing for him to face death the first time, but the misery had eased as the days passed, until he'd walked smiling into a room without knocking and heard his father telling his mother that they had lost their *most* beloved son.

Cullon didn't like admitting how savagely his father's words had hurt him. Not just the betrayal of knowing the youngest Gavriel son had been loved more, but the terrible, cutting blow of realizing his father blamed him for Serran's death.

Yet in a way, he couldn't help but be grateful for his father's callousness. Since that day, Cullon had learned to hide more than his feelings. He'd learned to conceal his thoughts, to camouflage his motives, to be whatever the circumstances demanded him to be. . . . He was an Enforcer, trained to act without guilt or regret, totally untouched by those around him.

Until now.

There was no great, singular moment of revelation that Cullon could name, yet the time had come to admit that *something* irreversible had happened to him. Something totally unexpected. Something that ran deeper and stronger than the need to keep himself separate and apart. He wasn't certain if he said Danna's name or simply beckoned her with his gaze. He only knew that she was there, standing by his side, reaching out to touch him, banishing the memories.

"Cullon . . ."

He pulled her into his arms and kissed her. Not passionately, but tenderly. Her warmth pressed against him and he held her close, like a talisman against unnamed devils. "We'll leave as soon as Gilfo's onboard the transport. At maximum speed the *Star Hawk* will reach Korcia in less than ten Earth days."

"Is this an apology?"

"Should it be?"

"You just introduced me to a former lover. If that doesn't deserve an apology, I don't know what does."

A quick smile jerked at Cullon's mouth. "Subtlety isn't one of Tasiq's strong suits."

"What are her strong suits?" Danna asked, then shook her head. "No, forgot it. I don't want to know."

"We were lovers once. Now, we're only friends."

He kissed her again, but his time Cullon could feel the uncertainty within her. When she kissed him back, it had the tentativeness of a cease-fire.

* * *

"**We were lovers once.** *Now, we're only friends.*"

The words stayed with Danna as Tasiq held her glass high and proposed a toast to the Empire. As they began eating, Danna gave Cullon an ambiguous look that mingled worry and hope. Worry, because she knew he had every intention of protecting the Empire with his very life if necessary, and hope because she wanted to believe that one day she wouldn't be listed among his "friends."

"Where to from here?" Tasiq asked of Cullon as a yeoman served up steaming plates of something Danna couldn't pronounce.

"Home. We're leaving for Korcia as soon as we've seen a friend of ours off on the next transport."

"Home. To Korcia with a Terran in tow!" Tasiq said with amusement in her voice. "No, offense, Miss MacFadyen."

"None taken," Danna said, exchanging a conspiratorial smile with Cullon. "I'm looking forward to seeing your homeworld. I've heard it's beautiful."

"Yes, it is. I'm afraid it's also extremely prejudiced when it comes to Terrans. We find them unnaturally arrogant." Again, the remark was made with a sense of humor attached to it.

Danna replied in kind. "We *have* managed to assemble the majority of the galaxy into a humane democracy that allows freedom of speech."

Tasiq laughed out loud. "Oh, I like her Cullon. I sincerely do. She's got fire."

"And a temper," he said with obvious pride that he managed to rouse that temper on a regular basis. "Meklina's going to like her."

"Meklina?" Danna asked, looking up from her plate. She had no idea what she was eating, but it was delicious.

"My mother," Cullon said. "She has a formidable temper of her own."

"Gavriel males are notoriously tyrannical," Tasiq said.

"Really? I never would have guessed." Danna grinned, liking Tasiq Jaseera despite herself. "How many Gavriel males are there?"

"Two," Cullon answered. "My father and I. The rest of the family are trivial, troublesome females."

Another laugh from Tasiq. "He's talking about his sisters. Both of which he utterly adores."

"Speaking of people we adore," Cullon said, taking charge of the conversation before it could be completely diverted from the purpose he had in mind. "How is General Arius?"

Tasiq continued smiling, but her eyes darkened. "Commanding the Tenth Fighter Squadron, for reasons only the Great Creator and Viceroy Surazheia understand."

"Arius is an excellent strategist," Cullon said. "With the Conglomerate sniffing at our borders, we need commanders who know what they're doing."

"Don't bother with the military rhetoric," Tasiq countered. "I'm not impressed by General Arius or his credentials. He's a self-centered opportunist."

"You didn't think that when you were his aide-de-camp."

"That was then, this is now."

"But you do agree that the Conglomerate poses a threat to the Empire?"

"Of course, I agree. I've spent the last six months chasing pirate ships out of Sector Eight. You'd think with the exploding economy of their colonies, they wouldn't need to sneak across our borders, but they do. I blasted one to stardust on our last run. The idiot captain actually fired at a Korcian cruiser! He must have been carrying a bellyful of pods because his ship exploded like a supernova."

"Did you report it to the Council?"

Danna knew Cullon received a daily *précis* from the Bureau which summarized anything of note occurring within his assignment perimeters, but data reports didn't include the raised eyebrow or the shift in voice tones that signaled true importance from a sentient source. She knew Cullon was picking up one of those signals now: Korcian cruisers had been alerted to actively seek out unauthorized vessels along the borders.

"I was given orders to capture the next ship—if possible," Tasiq said. "The Viceroy wants origination codes and serial numbers. Once we have them, we'll have a traitor to execute."

Danna wasn't a military expert, but she knew what a pod was, and the damage it could do. Robotic pods were routinely used to blockade suspicious ships until they could be boarded and inspected. Small, but extremely lethal, the pods were linked so that a saturating salvo of fire power could be delivered with a single command. Once, several decades ago, when the Empire had countered an invasion from the Belzoni Alliance, pods had been used to blockade entire planets.

If the Conglomerate was storing munitions, it was gearing up to cause trouble.

The ironic thing was, if Namid had been the link between the Conglomerate and the Empire, he had helped himself to an early death. Whoever had orchestrated Namid's murder knew what he was doing. Contrary to popular thought, most criminals weren't that accomplished in hiding their tracks. Amateur killers didn't have friends inside the Conglomerate. If she hadn't been able to imprint on the objects Namid had left behind, the Tribunal wouldn't have gone to Marasona. Without the token from LuFarr's safe, the link to a general on the High Council couldn't have been established.

Sinister theories of conspiracy swirled in Danna's head. The abyss of corruption that was the Conglomerate reached into the hierarchical corners of the galaxy. The inhabitants of those corners knew who they were, but no one else did. The Conglomerate spinmasters never revealed their true agenda. Profiles were kept low because the stakes were high.

Had the Conglomerate taken on the creed of terrorists, fueled by an intoxicating greed for power? If Cullon was right, someone on the High Council was systematically murdering True Bloods until the heir to the throne was the one the Conglomerate wanted reinstated as monarch. In the calculus of politics that meant a king who could, with a single command, turn the might of the Korcian Empire against the League.

"Now that's a name I haven't heard in a long time," Cullon said, invading Danna's thoughts. "It's good to know that Commander Oudhia hasn't abandoned his ambition."

"*Chief* Commander Oudhia was promoted and assigned the Seventh Tactical Brigade," Tasiq replied. "Some say he's finally getting the recognition he deserves."

"What are the others saying?" Cullon prompted.

"That Oudhia can't be trusted with any agenda but his own."

"Excuse me, did you say Oudhia?" Danna asked. "There was a former ambassador to the League named Oudhia."

"A distant uncle of the commander's," Tasiq told her. "I won't bore you with the eccentricities of their relationship. Suffice it to say, they don't consider themselves family." At such close range it was difficult for the *Thirl's* captain to hide her surprise at Danna's sudden curiosity. "I didn't think Korcian politics interested anyone but Korcians."

"I majored in political science at the University. Politics have always intrigued me," Danna said. "I doubt the Treaty of Vuldarr would have been signed if it weren't for Ambassador Oudhia's powers of persuasion. His speech to the Planetary Assembly is legendary."

The soft beeping of Cullon's wrist communicator interrupted the conversation. Cullon answered the call, then stood. "I'm sorry, Tasiq, but it's time to say goodbye."

"I'm glad we had time for dinner," she said, turning her gaze from Cullon to Danna. "And I'm very pleased to have met you, Miss MacFadyen. When you get to Korcia make sure Cullon shows you the ruins at Sinshoumedir. They're magnificent in the moonlight."

Sixteen

Gilfo was waiting for them in the transport terminal. The dwarf's casual nonexpression changed into a smile the moment he saw Danna.

"I was hoping you would come to say goodbye," he said. "I wanted to tell you how very much I've enjoyed getting to know you."

"Likewise," Danna said, bending down to place a kiss on his chubby cheek. She couldn't be certain, but Gilfo's leathered face seemed to take on a blush. "I'm sure we'll meet again."

"I will endeavor to make sure we do," the dwarf said. "And I shall assure Ambassador Synon that if the truth can be found, you and Cullon will reveal it."

Danna wished she could share his confidence. At the moment, all she could think about was making the necessary connection between Namid's dreamscapes and the one that belonged to a general's medallion. Without the connection, there was little hope she'd be able to puzzle out anything of importance.

The short blast of a loading siren alerted the transport's passengers to finish their farewells. Workers bound for assignments on the colonized worlds of Ezbon and Ahura picked up their flight bags and hurried toward the boarding gate, while several young couples, eager for a sensual honeymoon on the world of Gasfar, waved an enthusiastic goodbye to their families.

"May the Great Creator bless your endeavors," Gilfo said, shaking Cullon's hand. "You have found an extraordinary woman, my friend. Take good care of her."

"I will." Cullon promised.

Danna waited until Gilfo was about to disappear into the belly of the transport ship to wave a final farewell. When she turned to Cullon, he was studying her with an expression she'd never seen on his face before.

"Are you ready?" he asked.

"Yes." It was all she could say. Expounding on the details of what they were about to undertake wasn't necessary. She and Cullon both knew that she was going to have to imprint with the general's medallion again. And the cartouche ring. The strength of their dreamscapes meant there was more to learn.

They returned to the *Star Hawk* and began preparations for the trip to Korcia. Food provisions were stored, the ship's systems personally rechecked by Cullon after a final diagnostic by the station's maintenance crew, and a course set into the computer. Danna sat in the co-pilot's seat as Cullon initiated the delicate maneuvers necessary to exit the docking bay. Once they moved beyond the tractor slip, the sleek space bird pivoted to follow the specified trajectory, then quickly accelerated to maximum speed.

Cullon stayed at the command console for another ten minutes before transferring control to the computer. "Next stop, Korcia," he said as he punched in the final transfer sequence.

"Just the two of us," Danna said.

She looked out the viewing port as stars began to blue-streak. In space, a ship was everything, a fragile home in the perpetual winter darkness of the galaxy. She knew Cullon considered this one his home away from home.

"Yes, just the two of us."

He held out his hand as Danna stood up. She took it, and they went into his private quarters. Cullon poured them a drink.

"I want to do another reading on Namid's ring," Danna said.

"Now?"

"There's so much we still don't understand. I couldn't get a clear imprint the first time, but I know the ring has something to tell me. I could sense its secrets."

Cullon put down his glass and tugged her into his arms. "Korcia is days away, you've got plenty of time to discover the ring's secrets."

Danna drew in a quivering breath as Cullon pulled her close and buried his face in the curve of her neck. The softness of his kiss made her shiver again. "You're distracting me."

"Good. That's exactly what I had in mind." He took the wine glass from her hand and set it aside. "I want you."

She had to laugh at his devilish expression. "I suppose I could wait a few hours."

With each piece of clothing Cullon removed, he lingered: kissing her breasts, stroking her nipples erect with his tongue. He laid her on the bed and continued to touch her slowly, rhythmically. When she was completely naked, his tongue flicked its way up her body until he lay on top of her.

"Your clothes," she said, wanting to touch him as thoroughly as she was being touched.

He left her just long to get rid of them. When he returned to the bed, he pulled her on top of him. She rose to her knees, facing him as he gently bit her nipples. His hands kneaded her buttocks, guiding her to him. She began to move up and down, slowly taking him, then holding him inside before gliding up, only to move down and take him again. Deeper this time.

She made love to him with a passion that was meant to make memories, anything he wanted, any way he wanted it. She clung to him, milking him with her body, moving with him, making soft purring sounds deep in her throat. When it was over, they lay spent, breathing heavily.

Much later, Danna wasn't entirely sure how much time had passed because she'd dozed contently in Cullon's arms, she awoke to conspiracy theories running through her mind. As if alerted by her mental unrest, Cullon awoke beside her.

"What are you thinking?" he asked as he smoothed his hand over her shoulder.

"The ring."

"And the medallion," he added. He caressed the side of her face, his fingertips delving into the tousled curls of her hair. "You're not sure they're connected."

"And you are?"

His tawny eyes studied her somberly. She sighed and rolled away from him slightly, but he was having none of it. He pulled her back where she'd been and held her there. "Tell me about the dreamscapes," he said. "The colors."

Danna told him succinctly, describing the vivid reds and blues, and how, in both dreamscapes, she'd been overcome by an intense feeling of vertigo, a harrowing sense that she had somehow overstepped the perimeters of the dreamscape into some forbidden realm.

"You didn't see anyone in the ring dreamscape," he said, still holding her close. "What makes you so sure that the boy you saw in the medallion dreamscape wasn't Namid?"

"I can't explain why, I just know."

"But you want to know more?"

"Don't you?"

"Yes."

He left the bed and walked naked to the cabinet where he'd placed the belongings of three dead men. He carried the metal box to the table and opened it. "Do you want to take a shower and get dressed first?"

"Yes." Her mind would be naked enough once she began the imprint.

They showered together, then dressed. While Cullon went to the galley, Danna stared at the cartouche ring bearing the symbol of A'vla Namid and a general's medallion embedded with the bitter memories of an abused child.

She remembered the dreamscapes she'd entered before, seeing the colors of anger and despair, feeling the humiliation and loneliness felt by others. At times like this, she felt more a prisoner of her skills than a gifted diplomat.

And like a prisoner, she had few choices. The ring and the medallion were the keys to the truth, and that truth was the name of a murderer. Impatiently, she prowled the room, sourly cataloging facts and assumptions. Too many assumptions.

"Are you ready?" Cullon asked from the doorway.

Danna managed a smile. "As ready as I'll ever be."

She took time to sip the tea he'd brought, letting its warmth lessen the chill that had taken hold of her. Then, composing herself, she closed her eyes and took several deep breaths. Wordlessly, she held out her hand.

Cullon dropped the ring into her open palm.

Almost instantly a crescendo of silence descended over her mind, a blurring of thoughts . . . nothing made sense, nothing was real. The sensation felt both deeply familiar and profoundly strange. The next second, she was in a cloud of red vapor, all senses dormant. Numb and unfeeling.

As the crimson cloud swirled around her, Danna's memory ceased to be her own. Her head filled with visual doggerel, images that came from other places and times. There was a crash of thunder, followed by a blaze of lightning, but they were inside her head; real and unreal at the same time.

As the storm raged in streaks of blood-red vapor threaded with flashes of iridescent silver, emotions coalesced around Danna until she was drowning in a sea of feelings. They formed a patchwork of color inside her head, a mosaic of love and hate, and every emotion in between. Danna tried to keep her own mind detached from the dreamscape, but it was impossible.

Impressions began to come at last, unfolding out of the past like two-dimensional figures on a stage. The interplay of light, color, and shadow shifted delicately, mirroring the soft cadence of her own breathing, taking her back through time . . .

A moment of nothingness gripped her just before the dreamscape opened up like a great multicolored flower, beckoning and beautiful.

Lovers

They lay wrapped in each other's arms, resting contently as sunlight drained through the trees and dappled their bodies in golden light. Beyond the trees, a pond lay flat as polished glass, reflecting the soft enamel blue of the sky. The lovers exchanged a kiss, then spoke, but their words were whispered and private.

Suddenly, the colors changed. The sunlight was replaced with a crimson so dark it bordered on black. Lightning kindled fire in the clouds, turning them a blazing gold.

"Get up!" someone shouted. "Put your clothes on and get back to your quarters."

The lovers came to their feet, as their accuser rushed forward, shouting curses. He was dressed in a black military uniform. He lashed out, knocking Namid to the ground.

"You bastard!" the man shouted. Namid tried to get to his feet, but the big man rushed him again, bellowing an incoherent curse. His heavy fist caught Namid on the temple just as he was rising and sent him to his

knees. Another wild kick caught him on the shoulder and slammed him into the ground.

Danna felt herself flinch with each blow of the man's fists. The colors broke, scattering like splintered glass, and a rush of pain washed over her. One of the lovers cried out and Danna heard the sorrow in his voice.

The sounds and colors slowly turned into soft echoes as the walls of Danna's mind gave way, unable to hold the dreamscape inside any longer.

Several deep breaths later, she opened her eyes to the dimness of the room and Cullon's concerned face. Feeling the cool weight of the ring in her hand, she dropped it onto the coverlet.

"Are you all right? For a moment, you looked as if you were in pain. What did you see?"

Danna looked into the feral glint of Cullon's eyes and knew he was angry because he was helpless to protect her whenever she stepped into a dreamscape. She answered the compulsion to touch him, to smooth the furrow from his brow, to push back the unruly hair that fell over his forehead.

I'm fine," she told him. "I want to try the medallion."

"Why not wait until you've had some sleep?"

"I have to know."

"What did you see?"

Danna shook her head. "Not yet."

Cullon gave her the medallion.

Danna drew a calming breath before closing her right hand around it. She barely had time to draw a second breath before a black void opened up before her, as if space itself had flown apart and pitched her into a bottomless abyss. All sensation left her as she was sucked down until a bolt of invisible energy slammed her up again, propelling her toward a finite brightness.

Mentally stunned, Danna struggled not to get lost in the light. She was in a state of exalted awareness, her every sense tuned to the dreamscape unfolding around her. It was like passing through a secret doorway into a place of emotional power. Throbbing blues and greens, streaked with orange and gold, shimmered like the notes of a monstrous orchestra.

Danna's mind swam through the colors until she found the finite brightness again. It pierced through the veil of darker colors like a rising sun.

They walked hand in hand near a reflecting pool bordered by gaily colored flowers. It was a lovely sight, but it wasn't enough to quell the dread that haunted him. "You can leave. He holds you here only because you let him."

"To leave would be to let him win."

"I thought you wanted to be with me?"

"I do."

Color whipped and danced like torchlight, enveloping the two lovers, but the dream of loss, of disinheritance, of being driven from one's home stayed with Danna. The fearful images of the ring dreamscape superimposed themselves over the swirling colors as Danna struggled to be free.

Cullon's voice came to her, and she clung to it, letting it rescue her from the tangled madness. Slowly the pressure in her mind and body eased, and she began to breathe normally again. The colors loosened around her, like a cut noose; she could see the room again, and Cullon's face.

"What?" he demanded. "What did you see?"

"Namid," Danna said, her voice low and shaky. She opened her hand and dropped the medallion. She'd been holding it so tightly it had left an imprint. She rubbed her palm a moment before lifting her eyes to meet Cullon's intense gaze. "And his lover."

"Who?"

"A man. Namid's lover was a man. The same young man I saw hiding in the gallery of the Council Chamber."

"I suspected as much," Cullon said.

Danna's eyes widened in surprise.

"I visited several of the clubs when I was on Ramora, looking for someone who might have known

Namid," he explained. "One of the licensed companions told me that she'd entertained Namid several times. She also said he preferred sleep to sex."

"The Empire isn't intolerant of sexual preferences," Danna said.

"The Empire is a military entity, ruled by men," Cullon said. "We support sentient rights, in theory, but the High Council isn't as liberal as the League. It's entrenched in tradition. Fifty years ago Tasiq would never have progressed beyond the rank of lieutenant."

"So where does the Conglomerate fit in?"

"I'm not sure," Cullon said. "If Namid's lover is the son of a High General, then we're looking for a man who's masking one loyalty while professing another."

"You mean a military man who actually wants to see the Empire revert to its original monarchy."

"One of those little coincidences that add flavor to life," Cullon said with a humorless smile. "A High General would be privy to any action the military takes against the Fundamentalists. How better to serve two masters than to alert one to the other's thoughts."

"You think Namid found out and fled Korcia because he feared for his life? I see your point, but I didn't sense that sort of fear in him."

"Maybe his fear was for someone else."

"The general's son?"

"It's a possibility," Cullon said.

Danna knew the frustration in his voice came from the circumstances he was being forced to accept. The more they knew, the more unanswered questions arose. "It could also mean that the traitor Viceroy Surazheia is looking for is among his most trusted advisors."

The very possibility of an alliance between the Korcian Empire and the Conglomerate could easily mean war.

A war, Danna knew, the League would have little chance of winning.

Seventeen

As they approached Korcia, Danna could distinguish the huge land mass that circled its middle. North and south of the equatorial continent lay deep blue oceans, crowned on opposing poles by pristine ice caps.

The trip from Aquitaine Station had been filled with pleasures and disappointments. As time passed, Danna felt more and more as if she existed in two realities. First, the pleasant reality of being Cullon's lover. No matter how many times he touched her, she still felt the first exhilaration of love, the excitement, the energy. And then there was the second reality, the uncertainty of not knowing what the future held.

She'd tried several more imprints, but neither the ring nor the medallion had revealed any new secrets. It was as if she'd exhausted the total sum of their knowledge.

"What are you thinking?" Cullon asked as he disengaged the computer controls and took command of the ship.

"Something I learned during my student days," Danna replied a bit sadly. "An old French phrase. *Plus ça change, plus c'est la même chose*. The more things change, the more they stay the same. No matter how many lessons history teaches us, there are always those who refuse to heed them. The galaxy's past is riveted with games of wealth and war, one political holocaust after another."

"Are you talking about history in general or Fundamentalists in particular?"

"Both," she said. "The man we're looking for is committed to a cause—his cause. Rightfully committed from his point of view, even if others see it as murder."

"I'll start the Registry working on the backgrounds of the High Generals currently sitting on the Council. If he's not there, we'll look at the previous Council. It rotates every five years. In the meantime, enjoy your first view of Korcia."

Danna did just that. The land, covered in tropical greenery, fell in gullies and precipitous ravines toward the sea. Waterfalls cascaded from the summits of volcanically formed mountains. The jungle had a quality of savage grandeur. Flowers bloomed so brightly they dotted the landscape as if colored confetti had been tossed to earth by the hand of God. Lying in the splendor of the sun, the solemnity of narrow valleys and dark foliage created the illusion of an untouched Eden.

"It's beautiful," she said, whispering because the sight demanded reverence.

"It's always had the ability to take my breath away," Cullon said with pride. "Look there."

Danna's gaze turned westward to where a mountain range mingled its summits with the clouds. On the uppermost heights, rocky upheavals shaped themselves to mimic battlements and stone castles, outlined by shafts of golden sunlight.

"Korcia," Cullon announced, as they passed over the capital city that took its name from the planet.

"It looks like something out of Greek mythology," Danna said, staring at a building that resembled the Parthenon. From her point of view, several thousand kilometers above the surface, Korcia looked like an un-spoiled Paradise.

A silver river threaded its way through terraced meadows, past modern temples of pale stone and polished glass on its way to the sea. Built on a dormant volcanic cone, the majority of the buildings were embedded into the rocky cliffs that plummeted to meet the tumbling, windswept waves of the northern ocean. In the middle of it all sat the impressive tower of the High Council, its domed roof glistening like liquid gold in the sunlight.

"Where do you live?" Danna asked, eager to get her feet on the ground and begin exploring.

"Just north of the city. My house overlooks the ocean." He aimed the *Star Hawk* for the clouds. "We'll have to dock the ship first."

The docking station Cullon chose was filled with efficient, uniformed Korcian technicians who greeted the *Star Hawk* like a long lost friend. But all of them, no matter how they tried to hide it (and some didn't bother), were shocked to see the ship's Terran passenger.

Standing on the main docking platform where several rows of shuttles were lined up like soldiers at attention, Danna wondered if Cullon's family would greet her with the same shock.

"I'm nervous," she admitted as Cullon emerged from the airlock and took her hand. He led her toward a small shuttle designed to carry only two passengers.

"Don't be. Despite our reputation we're actually a very friendly people."

Cullon flew the shuttle with his usual expertise, skimming the treetops so she could see the intricate play of jungle and mountains as they made a second approach to the capital city.

Cullon's house, as he called it, was actually an alabaster villa sprawled across the edge of a cliff like some great slumbering cat. It was long and low, with a pillared veranda that circled an inner courtyard. Beyond the house, the setting sun painted the landscape in soft colors—golden yellow, warm orange, dusky red. One hue followed another until they were all swallowed by the indigo of twilight. It was like stepping into a dreamscape, except this time, Danna knew it was real.

The warm ambience of the evening surrounded her like a cocoon, but the chirping of birds and the rumbling sounds of the ocean couldn't override the silent message transmitted by Cullon's questioning gaze.

This was his home. Did she like it?

"If I had a house like this, I'd never leave it," she said, taking his arm and tugging him toward the villa. "I can't wait to see what it looks like on the inside."

They were halfway to the door when it opened to reveal a man who stepped out onto the front portico. He was of average height, lean and sharp featured. His age was impossible to gauge by the energetic way he moved, but his hair had whitened at the temples.

"Welcome home," he called out to Cullon.

"Danna, this is Ellua. He and his wife, Niska, have been with me for years" Cullon said by way of introduction. "Ellua, this is Danna MacFadyen."

Danna smiled at the servant who was in turn giving her a thorough once over with eyes that shone maple brown streaked with honey gold. When a gradual smile came to his otherwise stiff lips, Danna knew she'd passed muster.

"Your family will be pleased that you've returned, Master Gavriel," Ellua said, motioning them toward the house. "It has been nearly a year since you last slept in your own bed."

"I look forward to sleeping in it tonight," Cullon said, giving Danna a sideways glance she knew the servant didn't miss. "But first, a hot bath and a good meal."

When they entered the house, Danna had to stop and stare at the elegant simplicity of its furnishings; low benches covered in boldly colored fabrics, tables and chairs made from gleaming dark wood, white tile floors, and tall vases filled with fragrant jungle flowers.

"This way," Ellua said, stepping in front of them.

Danna followed, glancing right, then left on her way to what she knew upon sight was the master bedchamber. A cooling ocean breeze ruffled the sheer curtains covering the windows.

"Welcome to Korcia, Miss MacFadyen," Ellua said after pouring two glasses of wine, then leaving them on a tray near the door that opened onto the center courtyard. "I will tell Niska to prepare the evening meal."

With that, he was gone, disappearing behind an inlaid door that he closed with a soft click of the latch.

Inexplicably, standing there, in the middle of Cullon's bedroom, on a world that few Terrans had ever seen, Danna began to think that the gulf between a League diplomat and a Korcian Enforcer was unbridgeable. How could she possibly fit into Cullon's life, into his world?

It was the first time she'd openly admitted to herself that she wanted more than an affair with this man.

"You'll want to notify the Viceroy of your return," Danna said, forcing herself to think practical thoughts. The longevity of their relationship was still in question.

Keeping that in mind, she didn't have to *fit* into Cullon's world. She was just a visitor, a temporary lover who would eventually have to return to her own life, her own world.

"Not yet," Cullon said. He walked to where she was standing and pulled her into his arms. "I've never brought a woman home before. Ellua probably ran to the kitchen to tell Niska. Want to bet how long it will take her to find a reason to knock on the door?"

Danna's smile was like her body, warm and inviting, as she wrapped her arms around his neck. "Does that mean we can't take a bath together?"

"I'll lock the door," Cullon said, lifting her into his arms and heading for the bath.

Danna told herself to take whatever pleasure Cullon could give without complaint, and this was one of those times. She could no more resist the passion in his touch than she could stop breathing.

Within minutes, steam was rising from a sunken tub. Cullon stripped out of his clothes and was waist deep in the water before Danna finished undressing. He held out his hand, and she stepped down into the tub that was a technical marvel of white marble, black and gold mosaic tiles, and bubbling water jets.

Danna could feel the sexual anticipation building already. Sex with Cullon. Heady. Staggering—a rush of heat, a flurry of fantasies freed and running through her mind. Intimate. More intimate the she'd ever had with any other man.

He drew her to him, then kissed her, searching the textures of her mouth with his tongue, slowly building her desire.

His hands were as attentive as his mouth, running slowly over her body, touching her the way he knew would arouse her the most, caressing her until she was trembling with response.

Her nipples tingled as the hard wall of his chest pressed against them. She could feel the flexing of his muscles every time he moved. Unable to help herself, she gave in to the urge and pressed her pelvis against his muscled thigh.

She kissed him gently, her lips molding his with tender care, her head titled to one side, her hands moving lightly on the wide expanse of his steam-dampened shoulders.

Danna thought she would melt from the searing heat of the kiss. Her arms wrapped around his neck. She needed to be closer to him. She could feel the size and hardness of him pressing against the part of her that ached and wept for his touch. His big hands squeezed her bare bottom, kneading, pulling her even closer. But not close enough.

Unexpectedly, Cullon turned her around and pressed her down over the rim of bath. The coolness of the tile sent a shiver through Danna, but the steamy warmth of the water and Cullon's hands chased it away. When his fingers tangled in the web of dark curls between her thighs, she moaned.

"Spread your legs."

Danna did as he asked and felt the gentle probing of his fingers as he traced the soft, hot folds of her sex.

He'd never taken her this way before, and she gasped as he caressed her until she melted around him. He dipped his head to scour her throat with voracious kisses and small bites that sent shivers all the way to her toes.

She breathed his name when he nudged up against her, letting her know that he was hard and ready. He penetrated her with one long stroke. Her name came to his lips as he sank into her wet, silken center.

"Slow and easy," he whispered. He held the flushed weight of her breasts in the palms of his hands and rolled her nipples between his fingers. "I've thought about this for a long time. You, here on Korcia."

A streak of sensual lightning ran the length of Danna's body as he continued to make love to her—slow and easy. She moaned as nimble fingers massaged, stroked, and tugged at the small, sensitive nub that controlled her passion. Cullon rocked his hips against her, pushing deeper. Wanting to please him, Danna moved reflexively, tightening around him, needing the feel of his body buried within her own. Needing the completion she knew he was intentionally withholding.

His whispered words were a soft wind over her body, telling her how much pleasure she gave him, and how much he would give in return. He held her anchored against him with one arm while he drove deeper and deeper in slow, measured strokes meant to keep her hanging on the brink of ecstasy. The anticipation of completion intensified their hunger for each other, but even Cullon couldn't contain the whirlwind forever, and finally it grew into a tempest neither could resist.

It was a long time before they had the strength to separate their bodies and get on with their bath, which turned into a sensual treat all its own.

By the time they were dressed, Niska was tapping on the door, issuing an invitation to come sit at the table she'd just set on the terrace.

Danna, dressed in a wide-legged red silk jumpsuit, walked onto the terrace ready for inspection. Like her husband, Niska studied Cullon's unexpected house guest with a thorough eye, then extended her hand.

"It's a pleasure, Miss MacFadyen."

"Please, call me Danna."

"Sit. Eat. Enjoy," Niska said, moving ahead of them to a table that was set with crystal goblets. "I've prepared Cullon's favorite meal."

"Anything you cook is my favorite meal," Cullon said.

Once they were alone, dining under a Korcian moon that bathed them in pale light, Danna took a sip of wine to wash down the best food she'd ever eaten. "I don't know what it was, but it was absolutely delicious."

Cullon reached for a second helping of the flaky, almost transparent meat. "On Earth you'd call it shellfish."

"Korcian lobster!" Danna laughed. "My father used to steam lobsters and crabs on the beach, then we'd sit around a bonfire and lick our fingers clean."

"My father—" Before Cullon could finish the sentence, Ellua came rushing out onto the terrace.

"Forgive the intrusion, Master Gavriel, but the Viceroy requests your presence immediately."

"Very well," Cullon said, pushing away from the table. "Inform him that I'm on my way."

"He keeps calling you Master Gavriel," Danna said, following Cullon into the house. "I didn't realize True Bloods were addressed as royalty."

"We're not," Cullon said. "Ellua is just old-fashioned."

"He's been with you a long time, hasn't he?"

"He insisted on coming with me when I left my father's house."

"You make it sound so formal. So final," Danna said, hearing something in his voice she hadn't heard before—the ring of a disagreement never settled.

"It was formal," Cullon told her. "On Korcia, when a young man leaves his family to enter the military, there's a formal celebration."

"You told me you weren't military."

"Every boy who reaches the age of consent is military, at least for a time. I served in the Seventh Tactical Brigade for three years before I requested a transfer to Enforcement."

"The Seventh Tactical. Isn't that the unit Commander Oudhia was just promoted to command?"

"*Chief* Commander Oudhia," Cullon corrected her. "If you're going to mingle with Korcian society, you'll have to get the ranking right."

"Am I going to mingle with Korcian society?"

"Yes. Starting with the Viceroy."

"He didn't invite me."

"Viceroy's don't invite, they command."

"Then, he didn't *command* me." She hadn't been all that thrilled about meeting Viceroy Surazheia the first time, via a deep-space holographic transmission.

"He'll want a full report," Cullon said. "You can describe your dreamscapes better than I can. That means you're coming with me."

Eighteen

Danna's expectations to see the High Council Chamber from within were postponed when Cullon pointed the shuttle away from the city. The sky was a blanket of low-lying clouds, the air steamy with the dispelled heat of the jungle, the moon hanging full just above the horizon. As they approached the Viceroy's residence, Danna's expression was carefully unreadable.

When the shuttle landed, she stood on the circular tarmac and looked out at the long sweep of lawn, the fountains that sent sparkling sprays of water high into the night sky, and the arbors of blooming vines, augmented by motion sensors and bio-scanners.

"He's waiting," Cullon said, taking her arm to reassure her that they were in this together.

The long path from the landing tarmac to the house was paved, submerged lamps lighting the way at night. The Viceroy's mansion (it couldn't be described as anything less) was a large Athenian-style structure with wide marble steps leading up to thick double doors carved in relief. Along the front were pillars spanning a veranda the width of the building.

Nearing the house, they were met by uniformed guards who greeted them solemnly. They were both scanned inside and out before being ushered up the marble steps. Inside, another guard greeted Cullon by name. As requested, they followed him to a large door where he entered a clearance code, before stepping aside.

"Ready?" Cullon asked, looking at Danna.

"No, but I don't think it matters," she answered, trying to summon up her normal diplomatic serenity and failing. The number of League citizens who had actually meet a Korcian viceroy face to face could be numbered on one hand.

The door opened to reveal a large office and a circular console table. For a personal residence, the room was as ascetic as a penal cell. Viceroy Surazheia stood at the head of the console table. Standing to either side of him were the officers of his personal staff, stalwart men with vigilant eyes and ears who had been with him for years. Quiet conversation halted the moment Danna appeared at Cullon's side.

The Viceroy gave a sharp order and the officers exited the room, nodding to Cullon as they passed and staring at Danna as if they'd never seen a Terran female before. Perhaps they hadn't she thought, managing a smile for courtesy's sake.

When they were alone and the door had been sealed against unwanted intrusions, Viceroy Surazheia moved away from the table with a swift, agile stride that belied his age. He stood erect, his patrician features blank, his black uniform immaculate, his eyes clear and calculating. Schooled in the intricacies of battle strategies, his enemies called him an emotionless war machine, while his officers and troops bragged that he possessed one of the shrewdest intellects the Korcian military had ever produced—an uncompromising warrior who successfully ruled a roost of warriors.

Whatever the opinion, he was a man who demanded respect.

"Lord Viceroy," Cullon said, snapping his heels to attention as the highest ranking officer in the Empire stepped forward in greeting.

"Gavriel."

Surazheia's face looked pale under the dim lights, but his eyes were not to be dismissed. They burned bright and steady, centering briefly on Cullon before shifting to settle upon Danna.

"Officer MacFadyen," he said, his voice an odd mixture of ice and heat. "I trust your journey to Korcia was without incident."

"Yes. Thank you."

The Viceroy's gaze moved back to Cullon. "You have something more to report."

Cullon had already spoken with the Viceroy, at least long enough to convince him to provide protection for Marok Gavriel. This conversation was meant to fill in the blanks.

"A great deal," said Cullon. He went on to describe, in detail, what they had learned on Marasona. When he reached the point where Danna had imprinted with the ring and medallion back to back, he turned the conversation over to her.

The room fell into momentary silence.

"What did you see?" Surazheia asked when Danna didn't immediately offer the information.

Unsure how to begin explaining what most would consider ambiguous evidence at best, Danna turned her thoughts to sights and sounds found nowhere but in her own mind. When she began speaking, it was in a low, controlled voice meant to convey theory, not emotion.

Finishing with her "sense" that there was a linkage between Namid and the son of a High General, Danna met the Viceroy's unwavering gaze. "I haven't been able to imprint with the ring or the medallion again," she admitted. "I realize that most of what I've told you can be interpreted as emotional assumption, but I assure you that such a *link* does exist."

"You are basing this assumption on what?" Surazheia asked coldly. Before Danna could answer, he continued by saying, "I find it hard to believe that your *psychic acquaintance* with Namid was of an extent to presume what his motives may or may not have been when it came to the Empire. As for the unidentified individuals you have described, they serve no purpose until they are given names."

Cullon stepped forward in Danna's defense, but the Viceroy stopped him before he could speak.

"On the other hand, there might well be a degree of substance to your hypothesis," Surazheia said in a deceptively quiet voice. "It is on that possibility that I've ordered Cullon's father to be guarded. As for the Conglomerate, even the theoretical potential to shift the balance of power across the galaxy is enough to warrant strong action. However, I must make it clear that the Council cannot move on assumption, psychic or otherwise. I need facts."

"I'll get the facts," Cullon said.

Danna read his face, thought by thought. He seldom let his emotions show, which was why they affected her so deeply when he did. At the moment, his face was set, his voice firm, and his mind made up. Whatever the Empire needed, Cullon was ready to give.

Viceroy Surazheia returned to his desk, where he sat and spoke calmly. He could have been a military instructor, explaining the tedious but necessary mathematics of a new weapon. "You can start with the facts of a fourth murder."

Danna thought him dryly dispassionate as he announced the death of yet another Korcian citizen.

"Another True Blood?" Cullon's voice was dry, as well, whatever emotion he felt carefully controlled.

"Yes. Shamron Rakosi."

"When?"

"Six hours ago, in Molnar. He was a second lieutenant assigned to the Communication Consulate."

"How was he killed?"

"His throat was cut."

Danna grimaced. The deaths were getting bloody.

"I've notified the Consulate Commander that you will be investigating the murder," Surazheia said. "He's expecting you."

"We'll leave first thing in the morning," Cullon said.

Surazheia considered the reply for a moment. His hesitation brought a tart response to Danna's lips in readiness to defend her abilities as an investigator, but a glance from Cullon said she couldn't afford to alienate the Viceroy at this point. Accepting his direction, she waited.

"I can't provide protection for every True Blood in the Empire," the Viceroy said, looking to Cullon. "But I can protect the eldest of each of the families."

"Discreetly," Cullon advised. "Whoever is doing this is well-versed in our security methods. We can't afford to tip our hand."

"Find whoever's responsible and put an end to this," Surazheia said. It was a pronouncement, not a request.

Molnar was located four hundred and fifty kilometers north of the capital city in a jungle valley where the gnarled roots of trees writhed down into rich volcanic soil while their tops stretched tall into an indigo-blue sky. A film of mist hung over the river that bisected the valley. Except for an occasional burst of jungle flowers and narrow intervals of bottle-green water bordered by high cliffs, the jungle lay uninterrupted.

"How many ranks are there?" Danna asked as Cullon guided the shuttle past a rock-faced mountain at the eastern end of the valley. Along the mountain wall were seeps and springs that fed the river, each with its own clinging garden of moss and ferns.

"What?"

"You said I'd need to learn military rankings so I don't offend anyone. How many are there?"

"One hundred and forty."

"What!"

He smiled for the first time since leaving the capital. "The Korcian Guard is divided into three branches. The Fleet is commanded by the Admiralty and is commissioned with the protection of the Empire's main defenses. Before being appointed to the High Council, Tutunjan was High Admiral of the Korcian Fleet."

"Now he's a High General."

"High General is a courtesy title that applies to anyone who sits on the High Council, regardless of their actual service ranking," Cullon explained.

"What rank did Viceroy Surazheia hold before joining the High Council?"

"High Admiral of the Korcian Fleet."

"The same rank Tutunjan held before becoming a member of the High Council."

"The rank he still holds," Cullon said. "He may be addressed as High General, but he still commands the Fleet."

"So he's a High General and a High Admiral."

"The best of both worlds," Cullon said. "The only thing better is being elected Viceroy of the Council."

"The only thing better is calling everyone 'sir' and being done with it," Danna told him.

The morning sunshine streaming through the shuttle's portals made Cullon's tawny hair shine like sunlight itself. Danna's chest hurt with the pain of having to leave him one day. Although she prayed for a speedy conclusion to the murders, there was part of her that didn't want the Tribunal assignment to end. When it did, her relationship with Cullon would cease to exist as well.

Beside her, his gaze shifting between the instrument panel and the soft shimmering hues of morning sunlight warming the dark, night-kissed jungle, Cullon continued with the lesson. "The second branch is Strategic Command. Their forces are trained to defend Korcia itself, should the homeworld come under attack. In the event of war, the entire Guard falls under the jurisdiction of Fleet Command."

"Which section does Captain Jaseera belong to?" Danna asked. She'd gotten past the hurt of thinking about Cullon with another woman. It was bad enough thinking about the future pain she was going to have to face when they went their separate ways.

"Strategic Command. Tasiq reports to a squadron commander, who reports to the Senior Commander for Sector Eight, who reports to Chief Commander Arius of the Tenth Fighter Squadron, who reports to General Manoba, who reports to—"

"Okay, I get the picture. How about ground forces?" Danna asked, although she couldn't image anyone getting past the Fleet. To date, no one ever had.

"The Tactical Brigades. There are ten of them. Their command structure is similar to the Fighter Squadrons."

"So how do I address an officer of the Korcian Guard without mistaking a lieutenant in the Strategic Command for a captain in the Tactical Brigade? Everyone I've seen so far wears the same uniform— black on black."

"You don't," Cullon chuckled. "You wait for me to address him. If I'm not with you, protocol demands that he introduce himself, using his full rank. Of course, that doesn't mean you'll be able to tell which branch of the Guard he serves. The only way you'll know that is to memorize the different insignia on Guard uniforms."

"I suppose there are as many insignia as there are ranks."

"Officers above the rank of lieutenant wear a combination of markings. In the Tactical Brigades, rank is shown on the shoulders of a uniform as well as the chest. In Strategic Command, it's displayed on the cuffs of an officer's uniform until they reach the rank of captain. After that, you have to look at the shoulders again. Unless you're talking to a protocol officer. They wear their rank on their right sleeve."

"What's a protocol officer?"

Cullon gave her a crooked smile. "A Korcian diplomat."

"Then they're not military."

"Yes, they are."

Danna looked as confused as she was. "How can a military officer be a diplomat? Diplomacy is about concession and compromise, about listening when everyone else is shouting. I can't imagine a Korcian soldier compromising on anything but where he shoots you—in the heart or in the head."

Cullon laughed out loud. "When I said a diplomat, I meant an interior one. Protocol officers are the liaison mechanism between the three branches of the Guard. It's not an easy job. The branches are very competitive, especially when it comes to promoting one of their own up the ladder to the High Council. The more seats they fill, the more—"

"The more clout they have," Danna finished for him.

Cullon's shoulders lifted in a slight shrug. "You didn't expect us to be any less human than the rest of the galaxy, did you?"

"Okay," Danna said with a puff of breath. "Forget the military for a moment. Tell me about Enforcement. You have a preference for black, but your flightsuit doesn't match the ones I've seen other Korcians wearing. When Ambassador Synon introduced you, he called you Commander Gavriel."

"Security Enforcement doesn't wear uniforms or insignia for obvious reasons."

"What about rank? Are you a commander?"

"Yes."

"So what's the structure for Enforcement?" she asked. Learning about the infrastructure of Korcian society was one way to distract herself from what she'd be expected to do once they reached the Consulate. Cullon would need her to imprint with one or more of Lieutenant Rakosi's belongings. Danna wasn't looking forward to it.

Cullon aimed the shuttle for a gap between two mist-covered mountains and Molnar came into view. It was a cluster of pale buildings, tiled roofs, and jungle foliage that had been cut away to make room for civilization.

"Enforcement has two divisions," Cullon said as he reduced speed, then transmitted the shuttle's call sign for landing clearance. "One for municipal law enforcement and another for Empire security. Municipal agents report to the provincial governors. Essentially, they're local police, complete with uniforms and badges. Security agents report directly to the Council."

"I don't have to ask which division you work for."

Cullon diverted his attention away from planting the shuttle on Molnar's tarmac just long enough to give her a quick, hard kiss. "Don't worry. I'm very good at what I do."

"I've noticed," Danna murmured under her breath. She unhooked her safety harness and came to her feet. It was time to meet more of the Korcian Guard.

The Communication Consulate was one of hundreds positioned throughout the continent to supervise communications, both military and civilian. The Consulate Commander was a middle-aged officer named Mataress. Having reviewed his records, Cullon knew he'd graduated from the Academy an ambitious second lieutenant with a supercilious attitude that he'd mistakenly thought would gain him ground. It hadn't. Commanding a Communication Consulate was an assignment given to those who had failed the test of battle command.

Mataress's dark hair was graying at the temples, but he still stood tall and erect, his shoulders stiffly squared. Cullon introduced Danna, drawing no expression from Mataress. He invited them to his office, but pragmatism ruled the moment; there was no time for polite chatter. Cullon declined the invitation. "I'd like to see the body."

"This way," Mataress replied with crisp curtness. It was obvious that he disliked the idea of a man under his command being murdered, and just as obvious that he somehow felt the deed tainted his own career.

"You don't have to come," Cullon said, leaning down to speak so only Danna could hear the words.

She shook her head. "I'll be fine."

They followed Mataress down a long hallway, bordered on both sides by offices with closed doors. When they reached the end of the corridor, Mataress led them down a set of stairs, into an underground level that served as a storage area for the Consulate. They continued through a series of bland hallways until they reached a door guarded by an anonymous-looking ensign, who snapped to attention the moment they rounded the corner.

"I had the body contained immediately," Mataress told them.

"Open it," Cullon told the guard.

The ensign punched the necessary code into the keypad and stepped aside. The door opened to reveal a room empty of all but the polymer, vacuumed-sealed casket of Lieutenant Shamron Rakosi.

Cullon walked to the casket. It was sealed with an electronic latch. He pressed a button and the small dial changed from red to pale blue. A hiss of frigid air accompanied the opening of the casket's translucent lid.

Death had set Rakosi's features, eyes gazing blankly into nothingness, mouth slightly open in a last attempt to suck air into his lungs, hands clenched into fists. Cullon studied the face for a long moment, then forced his gaze lower.

The skin was taut and clean with no signs of bruising. The stomach and chest were lean, the shoulders and upper arms well-muscled. The blood had been cleaned away, but the open gash that ran across the throat was bluish and swollen. The knife had cut deep and clean, severing the jugular vein and the vocal cords in a quick, professionally executed slash.

Cullon closed the casket before looking at Danna. She had been standing by his side, close enough to see the body. He tried to gauge its effect on her, but nothing showed on her face. Turning to Mataress, he asked. "Did you find the weapon?"

"No."

"Where was Rakosi found?"

"In his quarters. He didn't report for duty as scheduled. The shift officer found him slumped over his console. An alert was sounded, and the Consulate was locked down."

"Was the room scanned?"

"The entire Consulate was scanned," Mataress assured him.

"We'll inspect his quarters now," Cullon said, knowing there was nothing he could do for Lieutenant Rakosi but release his body for ceremonial cremation. *And find the man responsible for his death.*

It took less than five minutes to reach the barracks that housed the junior officers of the Consulate. They were in the rear of the compound, a row of unimpressive, impersonal buildings symbolic of military life no matter the homeworld.

Mataress disengaged the security sensor attached to the door, then stepped aside.

"You may return to your duties," Cullon told him. "I'll find you if I need you."

Mataress hesitated. He didn't like being dismissed.

The murder *had* taken place in his Consulate. His reluctance lasted a moment before he accepted that there was nothing the Enforcer wanted or needed from him.

"You could have been more diplomatic," Danna said once they were alone and inside Rakosi's quarters.

"You're the diplomat," Cullon replied. "You could have said something."

"What, and spoil the illusion that I'm invisible?"

Cullon ignored the remark and began searching Rakosi's room. It was neatly kept, except for the over-turned items on the console desk and the dark stain of blood that hadn't yet been cleaned off the floor.

Cullon disregarded the blood, pulled out the console chair, and sat down. He entered his private code into the system. A micro-second later he was given full access to Consulate personnel files.

"What are you looking for?" Danna asked.

"I want to see the last entry in Rakosi's daily log," Cullon told her. "I checked his Registry file while you were having breakfast. He had the makings of a good officer."

"What about his personal life? Did he know Namid?"

"Nothing in the Registry indicated that they'd ever crossed paths. His family lives in Abreact. That's in the southwestern province. His father retired from the Guard ten years ago."

"That didn't come from his father," Danna said, pointing to a small crystalline ball resting on the desk a few inches from the console controls. "It's too feminine."

Cullon had to agree. The clear globe contained a perfectly formed, wild jungle orchid. The amethyst petals were tipped in white, the cradling leaves a vibrant green. The only flaw was a tiny crack running along the globe's flattened base.

"A lover's memento," Cullon suggested. "I doubt it can tell us anything about Rakosi's death."

"No, but it may be able to tell us something about the man," Danna said, reaching for it.

Cullon stayed her hand. "Seeing the body upset you."

"Of course it upset me. Imprinting with any of Rakosi's belongings is going to upset me, but that doesn't mean it isn't necessary. His throat was cut. It was a violent, ugly death."

Cullon continued reviewing the log. "Nothing," he said, not bothering to hide his disappointment. "The log was accessed, but there's no entry." He disengaged the console. "The man who murdered Rakosi isn't here at the Consulate. Not now."

"How can you be so sure?"

"The way he was killed. It isn't the kind of wound that would be inflicted if two men were fighting. Rakosi was a trained soldier, he wouldn't have turned his back on an opponent with a knife in his hand. That means the man was waiting for him. Waiting for Rakosi to sit down and do what any officer does before assuming his shift."

"Log in," Danna said. "Rakosi logged in, but he didn't complete the entry because—"

"Because his throat was cut."

Danna looked around the room. "It's not very big. Where would someone hide?"

"He wouldn't have to hide. The medical scan put the time of Rakosi's death within minutes of the evening shift change. The barracks would have been filled with officers coming and going, anyone wearing the right insignia with a forged ID badge could get in or out."

"Are you going to interview the men who served with Rakosi?"

"That depends."

"On what?"

"On what you see when I put these in your hands," Cullon said. He picked up the globe, then went around the room to collect some other items. "Do you want to

try the imprints here, or would you rather go somewhere else?"

He waited while Danna looked around the room, at
the bed that hadn't been slept in, at the crisp black uniform hanging on the outside of the closet door, at the
row of books on a low shelf, within easy reach of a
man who liked to read before falling asleep. Glancing
toward the window, that had been sealed to keep the
crime scene secure, she said, "I'd rather be outside."

It was simple enough to find the rear exit to the barracks. Taking her hand, Cullon led her toward the jungle, where streams of silky mist rose in lacy currents
toward the treetops. The morning sun barely penetrated the heavy canopy overhead, and for a moment
Danna felt as if she'd stepped into some strange primordial world.

"I did a scan of the area before we landed," Cullon
said, wading through waist-high ferns to clear a path
for her. He lifted a flowering vine that had wrapped itself around two trees to form a bridge of red flowers.
"There should be a small glade just ahead."

True to his word, they reached the glade in a matter
of minutes. Birds chattered and chirped above them,
protesting the invasion of their privacy. A small animal
darted into the shadows, near a bubbling spring. To
their left was a pile of rocks, rising a hundred feet tall,
but it was little more than a molehill compared to the
mountains cresting on the horizon.

They found a slab of stone, smoothed by centuries
of torrid, tropical rains.

"What do you want first?" Cullon asked.

Danna looked at the items Cullon had selected: the
crystal globe, what she assumed was a lieutenant's
badge, since he'd removed it from Rakosi's uniform,
and a wrist commlink.

"Let's start with the badge."

Cullon handed her the gold bar with a diagonal slash of silver running though it. His eyes widened fractionally, silently asking if she was ready to step into another dreamscape. Danna gave him a reassuring smile before closing her eyes.

It took several seconds for the dreamscape to come to her. It's colors tinted her mind with a soft light that blurred before it clarified.

A tavern of some sort with music and rough, manly laughter. Rakosi stood as someone proposed a toast. He smiled, then drained a glass of dark ale.

The image faded back into a blurred swirl of colors.

Danna opened her eyes and smiled weakly. "'He was celebrating his promotion with friends . . . and thinking about the future." She handed the badge back to Cullon. "I didn't sense anything but personal satisfaction."

He handed her the commlink.

Once again Danna closed her eyes and cleared her mind. After several minutes, she shook her head. "Nothing," she told Cullon. "I can't get an imprint, not even a vague one."

"Isn't that unusual?"

"No. Not if an object doesn't hold an attachment for its owner."

"That leaves the globe?"

Danna could feel the jungle heating up around her as Cullon gave her the globe. Perspiration beaded on her forehead as she freed her mind of the stress and burden of finding a murderer. She focused on the heavy perfume of the tropical air, the birdsong in the surrounding trees, the rustling of leaves above and around her.

The dreamscape flowed into her, like the heat of the sun, golden and invigorating. Color ignited in swirling flashes of blue and gold. Infinitesimal cracks flashed like lightning, as if the colors were fighting to escape—to become real once again. Fractured images began to appear, a shadowing half-dream that closed out the present to recreate the past.

The face was slender, the eyes dark, the smile soft and feminine. She laughed as she ran through the jungle, playing hide and seek with her lover. When he caught her, they kissed.

Walking arm in arm, he stopped to pluck a purple flower from its green mooring. He drew it over her cheek, then anchored it in her chestnut hair. They kissed again.

Danna watched, every sense tuned to the lovers, her body awash with the same energy, the same elated feeling of being alive, of being in love. Unconscious of the tears that were wetting her face, she willed the dreamscape to last. For an instant the warmth of it flowed over her skin, fitting itself to every pore; then without warning—it turned cold. The vibrant colors congealed into shifting, shapeless shadows.

The room was dark, the halls beyond the door echoing with voices, but he willed them away as he looked at the globe—remembering. He smiled.

A figure emerged from the shadows like some dark djinn. Rakosi gasped as a hand covered his mouth and nose, jerking his head back. The knife blade moved like a living thing, a steel predator thirsty for a taste of blood.

One last gurgling gasp. The globe rolled from Rakosi's limp hand and onto the floor. His attacker disappeared, fading back into the back shadows that had created him.

The shadows grew, pouring into Danna. Dream and reality became interwoven, a world of whispering ghosts and never-changing darkness. She fought it— fought the feeling of dying, like Rakosi had died, but the darkness clung to her, pulling her down.

"Danna!" Cullon had to pry her fingers apart to get the globe out of her hand. He tossed it to the grass. "Danna! Open your eyes. It's only a dream."

It was a struggle to breath. Danna's throat closed and the back of her eyes burned with tears. Helpless against the things that welled up inside her, she couldn't look at Cullon, so she looked at the jungle instead, and thought of what it would be like to play hide-and-seek in its steamy depths—right now—this very moment, because life, no matter how strong and capable you were, didn't come with any guarantees.

"Danna?" Cullon's voice was low. Concerned. His hands smoothed over her arms, warming her against an invisible chill.

"You were right," she said, her voice shaky. "It was a lover's memento. She was beautiful. *They* were beautiful."

Cullon didn't have to ask what else she had seen. The answer was in her eyes—deep and dark and fearful.

"He was holding the globe, staring at it and thinking of the day she'd given it to him as a keepsake." Danna struggled with the words, but she got them said. "Then I saw . . . I saw the knife."

"Did you see the killer?"

"No," she said wearily, feeling suddenly exhausted. "Just shadows."

Nineteen

"I thought cocktail parties were a diplomat's specialty," Cullon said as he took Danna's arm and guided her to a quiet corner of the veranda where they could observe the Viceroy's guests.

"This isn't a party, it's a trap," Danna said. She knew tonight was the night he intended to publicly announce his conversion to fundamentalist thinking.

"Only if properly sprung," Cullon said. He searched the sea of black uniforms that was crowding onto the terrace. He was looking for Valura Ulgart, the defender of "king's rights" that Tasiq Jaseera had mentioned, the man he'd made certain was at the top of the Viceroy's guest list.

Danna was right, the party was a ruse—bait for whomever wanted another True Blood dead.

It had been three days since they'd returned from Molnar. After Danna's imprint, Cullon had questioned Rakosi's fellow officers and friends, with no substantial results. Rakosi had been respected by his peers, all of whom appeared genuinely shocked by his death. His personnel file had described him as competent and responsible. When he made a mistake, he corrected it as efficiently as possible, never attempting to lay blame elsewhere. In short, if he had lived, he could have looked forward to a long and prosperous military career.

If he had lived.

"They were beautiful."

The sound of Danna's voice when she'd described Rakosi and his lover still echoed inside Cullon's head. Looking at Danna now, dressed in glistening white, it was impossible for him to characterize his feelings in a single word. She had shared his investigation, his life, and his bed for several weeks, and yet she maintained her individuality. Not so much as a Korcian slang word had rubbed off on her. She was thoroughly and uniquely herself. Thoroughly and uniquely female. The most intriguing, most addicting, woman he'd ever met.

There was no "getting enough of her."

He joined in with every man on the terrace in admiring her beauty, indulging himself in the sight of her. Being an analytical animal, he had tried to step back, to categorize his feelings for her, but the sensations were too potent to deny. He was falling in love with her, and if he was truthful with himself, he wasn't sure he wanted to deny it any longer.

For years, he had lived an emotionally celibate life, keeping his heart in an impersonal prison that permitted no visitors, no escape. He had satisfied his physical needs, at the same time that he had consistently and deliberately avoided entanglements. He'd used Enforcement as an excuse. That, and the fact that no one had come into his life who affected him the way Danna did. No one had ever burrowed her way inside his soul the way she had. From that first night on Ramora, he had known she was an unusual woman, had known that her uniqueness went beyond her paranormal skills. Nothing she had said or done since then had dissuaded him from that point of view.

If anything, she continued to impress him. She wasn't cynical or blasé. She was open, and honest, and sincere.

"I'm surprised you brought me," Danna said, breaking into his private thoughts.

"Why?"

"You're a True Blood about to make his intentions publicly known. What if your Mr. Ulgart doesn't approve of a loyal True Blood mingling with a Terran?"

"Once he sees you, he'll understand that I'm helpless when it comes to your charms."

Danna laughed. "I'm as much of a sucker for flattery as the next woman, but I'm sure Korcia has lots of *charming* ladies. And I'm also certain that Ulgart would prefer to see you matched up with one of them. Terrans are notorious for contaminating bloodlines. All that open-minded thinking, you know."

"You're notoriously beautiful," Cullon said, leaning down to give her a quick kiss.

He stopped his thoughts at that point. He knew where he wanted his relationship with Danna to go, but he also knew it wasn't the right time. Not yet, not until they had both fulfilled their obligations to the Tribunal.

With that admitted, the honesty of the situation crept over Cullon like a sunrise. Danna had claimed ownership to a part of him he hadn't realized existed, and now that part was alive and wanting—needing *her* to be complete.

Together, *they* were beautiful.

It was a strange admission, coming from a man who had chosen a life of solitary confinement, a life that offered few friends and a galaxy of potential enemies, but Cullon knew it was true.

"What is it?" she asked.

He smiled down at her, realizing that sometimes the most significant things in a man's life happened when he least expected them. "I was just thinking about the ruins at Sinshoumedir. They are lovely in the moonlight. I'll take you there, if you like?"

"Not if it's a repeat performance," Danna told him with a dark glare that said she hadn't forgotten Jaseera Tasiq.

Cullon laughed. "I never took Tasiq there. Whoever she *enjoyed* them with, it wasn't me."

"Then it's a date," she said, linking her arm through his. "But first, get me through this evening. I still can't tell a captain from a general."

An hour later, Danna noticed a young blond woman slipping through the crowd. Her gaze was glued to Cullon, her face brightened by a smile. She was dressed in a gauzy dark blue sarong with a jeweled neckline, the customary evening attire for Korcian ladies of quality, or so it seemed from those attending the party. Considering the tropical climate, the apparel made perfect sense.

"Ellua told us that you were home," the young woman said, snaking her arm through Cullon's as her lips brushed his cheek with a sisterly kiss that helped Danna to identify her. She was one of the "adored" siblings Tasiq had mentioned. "Father and Mother are still inside, but I couldn't wait to find you." She looked directly at Danna. "Everyone's talking about her."

Cullon grimaced, but Danna smiled. She liked Cullon's sister immediately. Her personality was unguarded and effervescent, a refreshing change from the stares Danna had been receiving all evening.

So far, Cullon had introduced her to three captains of the Korcian Guard, along with six lieutenants, four commanders, and one stout general who hadn't bothered to hide his shock at finding a Terran female among the Viceroy's prestigious guests.

"Jalyn, this is Danna MacFadyen. Danna, this is my youngest sister, Jalyn."

Jalyn's catlike eyes sparkled as she extended her hand in greeting. "Welcome to Korcia."

"Thank you," Danna said, hoping the introduction to Cullon's parents went as smoothly.

"I didn't mean to be rude," Jalyn said. "It's just that Cullon comes home so rarely these days, and he's never brought a woman with him. And you're Terran."

"Yes, she is, and a very beautiful one at that."

The remark came from slightly behind them. Cullon, with Danna on one arm and Jalyn on the other, turned them in unison to face the man. Danna recognized him from the data files she and Cullon had been studying for the last three days. He was Valura Ulgart, an assumed Fundamentalist leader.

Cullon made the necessary introductions.

"The Empire should encourage more Terrans to visit," Ulgart declared. He was a tall, stalky man with thinning brown hair. Because his face was long and his skin loosened by age, he presented a jowly look that belied the intelligent gleam in his blue-green eyes. "I for one would enjoy seeing some of the League planets. Earth, in particular."

"We would welcome you," Danna said, surprised by his cordiality. She'd expected a stuffy old man.

Ulgart looked at her in contemplative silence for a moment before replying, "I have studied your history, and found it littered with moderates and radicals alike. Which are you, may I ask?"

"It depends on the circumstances," she replied.

Ulgart laughed. There was nothing unkind or mocking about his laughter; he'd simply found her reply amusing. He looked to Cullon. "Beautiful and witty. Pity she isn't Korcian. I'd encourage the match."

Danna lifted her gaze to Cullon. An I-told-you-so look gleamed in their dark depths.

"Are you a scholar of Terran history, Mr. Ulgart?" she asked, knowing Cullon would want her to prolong the conversation. He'd planned tonight with exactly that in mind.

"I am a scholar of all things historical, Miss Mac-Fadyen, but I find Korcian history as thrilling, and as diverse, as any the galaxy has to offer. It is hard to imagine such a thing, as we stand here among the loyal members of the Korcian Guard, drinking wine from the Viceroy's personal cellar, but once, centuries ago, this great Empire of ours was ruled by kings more powerful than any monarch your history has ever recorded. One of them founded the House of A'vla Gavriel."

"Cullon told me," Danna said. "I'm impressed."

"As you should be. The House of A'vla Gavriel was the most successful dynasty in galactic history." He transferred his gaze to Cullon. "A dynasty that is still very much alive."

"Yes, it is," Cullon said, his tone subdued yet resonant.

Ulgart's eyes literally sparkled with excitement. "It's good to know that you haven't abandoned your family's history."

"I wouldn't think of it," Cullon replied, continuing to bait the trap. He let the remark hang in the air for a moment while its significance was absorbed by the older man.

"There's Father and Mother," Jalyn said, eagerly changing the subject. It was obvious she cared little for history or politics.

"Welcome home," Meklina Gavriel said, kissing her son on both cheeks. She was a graceful woman, ivory-skinned and fair-haired. When Cullon whispered something in her ear, she laughed. It was a delightful laugh, low and throaty and infectious. Just like her daughter's.

"Cullon," Marok Gavriel said as he joined them.

"Sir," Cullon replied.

Meklina, Cullon's mother, greeted Danna with the same exuberant smile Jalyn had displayed earlier. His father, Marok Gavriel, gave her a reserved nod.

"We were just discussing the A'vla Gavriel dynasty," Ulgart said, his tone modulated and relaxed. "You've always been an opinionated man, Marok, do you think a rekindling of our grand past would enlighten our future?"

"I think what is in the past is there because its time has come and gone," Marok said, looking squarely at his son. When he raised his drink to his mouth it was impossible not to notice the cartouche ring on his right hand. The ring that proclaimed him a True Blood. "Meklina, why don't you and Jalyn show Miss Mac-Fadyen the buffet table. I'm sure she will find some Korcian delicacy to interest her. I want a word with Cullon."

"Of course," Cullon's mother said.

Cullon watched as Danna allowed herself to be pulled away and into the crowd.

"If you'll excuse us, Valura," Marok Gavriel said to the supposed leader of the Fundamentalism movement.

"Of course." Ulgart looked to Cullon. "Perhaps we can talk again later."

"I look forward to it," Cullon said.

The crowd on the terrace was thinning. Small groups mingled on the wide marble stairs leading into the main house, while others huddled in private groups near the buffet table, awaiting the appearance of the Viceroy.

"What did you want to talk to me about?" Cullon asked.

"A Terran?" his father said, arching a brow.

"Yes."

"She *is* very lovely."

"She's many things. The least of which is outspoken, stubborn, and independent."

"A fault of Terran females, or so I've heard." His father paused to take a sip of wine. When he met Cullon's gaze again, his expression softened. "It's good to have you home."

"It's good to be home," Cullon said, surprised by his father's show of sentiment. He studied the face that was so much like his own and wondered if the past was really past.

Having retired from the Registry, Marok Gavriel knew full well the sort of assignments his son drew as an Enforcer. They had never discussed Cullon's chosen career, but Cullon had always sensed that his father approved of what he did. It was the one thing that had kept them bound together over the years.

Before Cullon could suggest that father and son spend some time together, perhaps sailing on the Gesba Sea (something they had done frequently before Serran's death) the Viceroy made his appearance. He was immediately followed by the members of the High Council.

"You should rejoin your companion," his father said. "She is certain to draw the Viceroy's attention."

Cullon agreed. He trusted Danna, but he couldn't be certain how she'd respond if she associated one of the guests with the unidentified men she'd seen in her dreamscapes.

Danna welcomed Cullon's steadfast presence as General Tutunjan publicly scrutinized her from head to toe. She was determined to deny the general the satisfaction of a transparent reaction, but on the inside she couldn't help but be apprehensive. The longer she looked at him, the more she felt herself growing cold, as if an arctic wind had suddenly displaced the tropical breeze.

Tutunjan was tall and broad, his shape exaggerated by the silver epaulets on the shoulders of his uniform. The features of his face were firm and precisely molded. There was an air of stringent control about him coupled with an edge of danger. His eyes were a penetrating cobalt blue, specked with silver. Intelligent eyes. All-seeing eyes. The eyes of a genius. Or a madman.

Danna couldn't help but think of the dreamscape, of the man standing in the shadows while his son raped an innocent young girl. Was this the same man? The same demented father?

Her sixth sense was sending tingles up and down her spine. The wondering. The suspicion. Sooner or later it had to end. Cullon placed his hand casually against the small of her back, as if he knew exactly how she felt.

"Welcome to Korcia," Tutunjan said, his thin lips spreading into a brief, almost illusory smile.

"Thank you," Danna replied. Cullon had cautioned her that addressing a High General was akin to addressing royalty on old Earth; one didn't speak until one was spoken to, and only then in direct response.

"May I ask what purpose brings you to Korcia?" Tutunjan asked, unafraid that his bluntness might be misconstrued as rudeness. This was the man who had ordered the Korcian Fleet to alert following the explosion onboard the *Llyndar*. That order had since been rescinded, but tensions between the Empire and the League were still high—the very reason Danna's presence in the Korcian capital was causing such a stir.

"No purpose really." She feigned a sincere smile. "I've always wanted to visit the Empire. Cullon was gracious enough to give me the opportunity."

Danna waited, along with everyone who was listening, while Tutunjan evaluated her answer. She'd met men like him before, powerful men who strained everything through a filter that was their own narrowmindedness. Tutunjan's expression was openly skeptical. It was apparent he didn't believe her. It was also apparent that this was the Viceroy's home and that Danna was one of his guests.

"Saved by the bell" took on a new meaning as a series of chimes announced the Viceroy's formal greeting to his guests. Strict protocol demanded that the members of the High Council stand with him. With a commendable display of manners, Tutunjan excused himself to do just that.

"I admire the ease with which you handled that introduction, Miss MacFadyen. I've been told that Terrans are dangerously honest when it comes to speaking their minds," Marok Gavriel said, rejoining his family near the buffet table. "General Tutunjan isn't known to be the League's enemy, but neither is he reputed to be its friend."

"If you mean that Korcians wouldn't recognize subtlety if they stepped on it, then I agree," Danna responded, hoping Cullon's father had a sense of humor. "Your son is the least subtle person I've ever met."

Marok grinned like the proud father he was. Cullon arched one eyebrow. Danna flashed him a wily smile and a sassy wink before she turned to look over the crowd again. She was admiring the dress of one of the officer's wives when she recognized a guest—Commander Mataress from the Molnar Consulate. He was speaking to a younger man, one she had seen step onto the terrace with General Tutunjan, an aide perhaps.

She looked to Cullon, hoping to ask if he had deliberately requested the Viceroy to add Mataress's name to the guest list, or if the Consulate Commander was here because Korcian etiquette demanded it. Unfortunately, Cullon was engaged in conversation with his parents. Forced to wait for a more opportune moment, Danna tried to look innocuous.

Her innocent act lasted all of two minutes—until the young officer speaking with Mataress turned to address another guest.

It was Namid's lover!

Suddenly breathless, Danna stepped closer to Cullon.

"What is it?" Cullon asked, leaning down as if they were sharing a personal intimacy in a public place.

"The man standing next to Commander Mataress,"

Danna whispered. "The young lieutenant. He's the man from the dreamscape. The one I saw with Namid."

For a moment, Cullon looked as if he didn't believe her. "Are you certain?"

"I'm certain. Who is he?"

"Excuse us," Cullon said to his parents as he took Danna by the arm and steered her to a less populated corner of the terrace. He turned, putting his back to the other guests.

"Who is he?" Danna asked again.

Cullon's eyes blazed gold before darkening to a foreboding brown. "His name is Khaled. He's General Tutunjan's son."

Twenty

Danna was restless. It had been three days since the Viceroy's party, and she'd learned nothing more about Tutunjan's son, Khaled, other than the fact that he was assigned to the Seventh Tactical Brigade, acting as aide to Captain Pheyell.

"What do you plan to do?" Cullon asked, as he dressed to meet with Valura and his Fundamentalist friends. "Walk up to Khaled and ask him if the scars from his father's abuse have healed?"

"I'm a trained diplomat," she said. "I know how to be discreet."

"There's no being discreet when you put a High General under suspicion," Cullon retorted, his tone impatient because they'd been arguing for the last hour.

"What he did to his son was a crime." Danna raised her voice in frustration. "The Empire has laws."

"Yes, we have laws." He walked to where she was standing near the windows that overlooked the ocean and wrapped his arms around her. "The only evidence we have of Tutunjan's abuse is a dreamscape. Our courts won't allow a psychometric image that can't be confirmed to be entered as evidence, and Khaled never reported the abuse."

Danna pulled back to look at him. "What about the servant? The guardian? The man who made sure Khaled didn't step out of line when he was away at school."

"I had the Registry do a search. His name was Rihan. He died eight years ago."

Danna wasn't ready to give up. "Tutunjan forced his son to rape innocent young girls. I saw one in the dreamscape. I know he drugged them, but what if one of them remembers something?"

"You're reaching," Cullon said.

"Of course, I'm reaching," Danna replied more angrily than she intended. She pulled away from him, too angry to be contained, even by his arms. "It's not just a matter of law, it's a matter of justice."

"I'm not disagreeing with you, but the only way Tutunjan can be held accountable for his actions is for his son to step forward and file an official complaint. I don't see Khaled doing that at this point, not unless we can link Tutunjan to the murders. And for that, we need facts."

"I know," Danna conceded. "It's just so frustrating."

"I have to go," Cullon said, pulling her back into his arms for a quick kiss. "Valura is expecting me."

Another reason for Danna to be frustrated. Cullon was actually doing something, while all she could do was sit around and think about what should be done.

She needed to know more about General Tutunjan and his son, but there wasn't anyone she could ask but Cullon. She didn't have access to the Registry files, and she'd learned yesterday when she'd had lunch with Cullon's mother and Jalyn that Korcian woman didn't gossip, or rather, they didn't gossip when their luncheon companion was a Terran.

She had learned that Cullon's other sister, Danica, was married to a Fleet captain. They lived in the central province of Moloduvena. The couple was expecting their first child.

The only other tidbit she had gleaned was actually an observation. Cullon's family wasn't pleased that he'd joined Valura's little band of rebels. When she'd mentioned that Cullon was with the older gentleman, his mother had frowned. Jalyn had remarked that her father didn't care for Valura and his foolish notions.

Danna watched Cullon leave, wondering how she could get the information she needed without approaching Khaled directly. The League didn't maintain an embassy on Korcia. When the answer came a moment later, Danna did a little jig around the room, then hurried to the console in Cullon's office.

She accessed a directory of the city. When she found the name and communication code, she entered her request.

An hour later, she was entering the office of Brice McDermott, League Trade Attaché to the Korcian Empire.

McDermott's office was near the Korcian Trade Bureau, the same agency that had once employed Chimera Namid. The building was constructed of pale stone, fitting into the theme of the city. McDermott was waiting for her in the front office, his eyes alight with excitement.

He was a small man with age-rounded shoulders and thinning brown hair, but his deep, sonorous voice called attention to his Terran heritage.

He took her hand, clasping it in both of his, as if she were a lost-long friend. "I can't tell you what a pleasure it is to meet you, Miss MacFadyen. I heard, of course, that the city was recently blessed with a Terran visitor. We get so few, you know. Actually, I was contemplating how to introduce myself, when I received your message. Please, do come in. I've taken the liberty of ordering some refreshment."

Danna smiled. She'd finally found someone who

liked to talk. McDermott had been the League's Trade
Attaché for three years. She wasn't sure what kind of
information she was going to get out of him, but with
three years of Korcian residency under his belt, he had
to know more than she did about the Empire and its
residents.

"I understand you met Cullon Gavriel on Ramora,"
McDermott said, repeating the story Cullon had circu-
lated among his friends and family. No one, except the
Viceroy, knew of her diplomatic connection to the
League.

"Yes. I work there, but I'm on sabbatical."

"You couldn't have picked a better vacation spot,"
McDermott told her. "Korcia is a lovely planet."

They spoke of Earth-bound things for over an hour,
until Danna tactfully steered the conversation to the
capital city and her amazing delight at its beauty.

"Yes, I felt the same way the first time I saw it," Mc-
Dermott said. He poured more tea, his actions almost
birdlike in their animation. "It's a city of towering
spires and sweeping bridges. I still stare in awe at the
gold-encrusted domes and the glittering mosaics. It's
hard to image that a city such as this is the home of the
most technologically advanced fighting machine in the
galaxy."

"It is a controversial beauty," Danna agreed. "And I
met some of the personal components of that fighting
machine a few days ago. Cullon and I attended a party
hosted by Viceroy Surazheia. Talk about testosterone."

McDermott laughed. "The High Council is an impressive lot, I'll give you that."

"General Tutunjan didn't seemed all that pleased to
see me," Danna said, beginning her fishing expedition.
"I suppose it had something to do with the recent
alert."

"The alert was a bit exhilarating," McDermott
replied with an impish smile. "The most excitement
I've had in quite some time. They shut down my com-

munication module and put me under house arrest. It
was a precautionary tactic, but I have to say, it was a
compliment to think anyone in the Guard imagined me
a threat."

"Have you ever met General Tutunjan?" Danna
asked, wanting to keep McDermott focused.

"No, but I've studied his career. I'm a military en-
thusiast, and General Tutunjan is a walking encyclope-
dia of Korcian military tactics."

"Really?" Danna said, her tone oozing interest.

McDermott took the bait. "General Tutunjan, or
more correctly, High General Tutunjan." He paused to
take a sip of tea, then jumped back into the conversation. "Tutunjan is the archetypical Korcian imperial
officer. Austere, distant, and uncompromising. I've
dubbed him "the last Teutonic Knight.""

"Why?" was all Danna had to ask.

McDermott settled back in his chair to tell her. "He's a
collection of contradictions. Did you know that he's
never traveled beyond the Empire's boundaries? He can't
abide the idea of other humanoid races cluttering up the
galaxy with their inferior ways. One has only to look at
his military career to know how devoted he is to the cause
of Korcian superiority. It is on Tutunjan's escutcheon
that the names of some of the Korcian Guard's greatest
victories are emblazoned. He was responsible for the defeat of the Travaians during the Great Conflict in the
outer regions. It was a bloody campaign, but one Tutunjan relished. After the Travaian threat was eliminated, he
was promoted to High Admiral of the Korcian Fleet."

"That makes him sound a little too enthusiastic for
my tastes," Danna replied. Underneath her cordial expression she was putting two and two together. If Tutunjan wanted war, he'd come damn close to getting it
with the explosion onboard the *Llyndar*. If she allowed
her imagination to stretch, she could see him eliminating Khaled's lover and putting the galaxy on edge all
in one cleverly planned maneuver.

Unaware of her thoughts, McDermott continued talking. "I daresay, if General Tutunjan could roll back time and undo the signing of the Treaty of Vuldarr, he would leap at the opportunity, convinced in his heart of hearts that he was serving the majesty of the Empire."

"Isn't Tutunjan a True Blood?" Danna asked, wondering how much McDermott knew about the Fundamentalist movement.

"Yes, but I doubt it holds the same significance for him that it does for other True Bloods. A passion for war runs in the Tutunjan family. Being a True Blood is secondary to being a solider. I'm making an assumption, of course, but everything I know about the general leads me to think that I'm correct."

Danna decided to test the waters with an assumption that had been rolling around inside her own head for the last few days. "I'm no expert on Korcian politics, but isn't Tutunjan in line to take over as Viceroy?"

McDermott's thin chin brushed against the high collar of his jacket as he shook his head. "Untangling the skeins of the Korcian political web is a challenge, I'll give you that. However, there is no direct line of succession. The Viceroy has to be elected by a unanimous vote of the High Council. Tutunjan has a very good chance of filling the seat when Surazheia's term is finished, but, I, for one, hope he isn't elected. Even with the Treaty of Vuldarr intact, I fear Tutunjan would ignore its mandate for peaceful coexistence and cooperative trade. After all, the zenith of any soldier's career is the last great battle, the one that turns his name into a legend. And Tutunjan is a soldier to the marrow of his bones."

"What about his son?" Danna asked. "I saw him at the Viceroy's party, but I didn't have an opportunity to talk to him. He looked pleasant enough."

"Yes. I've heard that young Khaled doesn't share his father's blind devotion to the Empire." McDermott looked around the room before leaning forward in a conspiratorially manner. "I've also heard that his lack of enthusiasm comes with a price."

Danna wondered if McDermott knew about Khaled's sexual preferences. Since Namid had worked only a few blocks from the League Trade office and there were several open air cafés where he might have met Khaled for a drink, she assumed their relationship wasn't a total secret.

"In what way?" she asked, keeping what she knew to herself.

"I'm gossiping," McDermott said, "but keep in mind that my duties here are mundane and more automatic than challenging. Once trade treaties are established, they pretty much take care of themselves. To fill the time, I watch and listen. I've often thought about recording my observations, a social study of the Korcian race, you might call it."

"I'm sure it would make interesting reading," Danna said. She imagined McDermott was a lonely man, the only Terran in a city populated by millions of Korcians.

"Normally, the son of a prominent general would have no trouble being assigned to the capital. It is, after all, the center of military influence," McDermott continued. "But Khaled has never served here. In fact, his entire military career has been spent in obscurity. Captain Pheyell heads a small fighter group of the Seventh Tactical Brigade, stationed out of Omarura, which is about as far from the Korcian capital as you can get and still remain on the planet. Omarura is also known as a disciplinary outpost. When a young member of the Guard steps out of line, it isn't unheard of for him to be sent to Omarura for a refresher course in how to be a good little soldier."

Danna looked surprised, even though she wasn't.

McDermott kept talking. "Keep in mind that the Tutunjan family has produced generation after generation of warriors willing to sacrifice their lives for the

Empire. It's the foundation of their family honor, not unlike the medieval ideology of Earth's ancient history. I'm sure the general expects his son to follow in his footsteps."

"I'm sure he does," Danna commented, before directing the conversation back to Earthly things. She didn't want McDermott to get suspicious of her interest in the Tutunjan family.

Half an hour later, Danna thanked the trade attaché for an enjoyable afternoon.

"You talked to the League's trade attaché about General Tutunjan." It was obvious from Cullon's tone that he wasn't happy she'd gone investigating without him.

Danna kicked off her shoes and walked to the bedroom window that overlooked the ocean. The seaward approach to the city was dominated by rugged cliffs above a vivid blue-green sea. When she turned back around, Cullon didn't look any happier than he had a moment before.

"Don't glare at me. I didn't tell McDermott that I was a member of the Diplomatic Corps, and I didn't talk to him about Tutunjan. He talked to me."

Cullon kept glaring.

"McDermott's a sweet little man. A bit on the nervous side, but you'd be nervous too if you were the only Terran in the neighborhood." She turned the conversation around by asking, "How was your day? Did you make any progress with Valura?"

"Some. I'm beginning to think the Fundamentalist movement is just a bunch of old men reliving the past. Valura believes a restoration of the monarchy will improve the Empire's image. He thinks our galactic neighbors will be less frightened of a king and more willing to trust us as we expand into the outer regions."

"What about the military? Do Valura and his friends

think a king is going to wave his royal hand and turn the Fleet into a trading armada?"

"I'm not sure they've thought beyond the coronation," Cullon told her. He'd been sitting at his console when she entered, snacking on fruit and sipping a glass of wine while he worked. "At least not the group Valura leads. They're too academic."

"Does that mean there's a militant group?"

"If there isn't, the theory that the Fundamentalists are behind the murders goes out the window. I can't imagine Valura ordering an assassination."

"What if someone is using the movement to mask the real motive?" Danna said. "What if someone out there just hates True Bloods?"

Cullon arched a brow. "Are you talking about a personal vendetta?"

"I'm not sure what I'm talking about, I'm just theorizing."

"Stop pacing and come here," Cullon said when she circled the room for the second time. "What did McDermott say about Tutunjan?"

Danna edged her way between the chair and the console desk and straddled Cullon's legs. She wrapped her arms around his neck and looked him straight in the eyes. "McDermott said Tutunjan doesn't like anyone who isn't Korcian."

"How would he know? A League trade attaché doesn't have any association with the High Council."

Danna smiled. "He's a watcher, an observer of people and their habits. And a listener," she added, recalling how many times McDermott had used the phrase, "I've heard."

"What else did he say?"

"That Tutunjan's loyalty is to the Empire first, and his True Blood heritage second, that he wants to be Viceroy, and if he's elected, he'll make war his legacy."

"That's one big assumption."

"The point I'm getting at is that Tutunjan is an ambitious man, a man with very stringent ideas about what is right and wrong for the Empire. And his son is a disappointment."

"Are you saying that Tutunjan had Namid killed to teach Khaled a lesson?"

"It's a possibility. No, hear me out. I know you think I'm obsessing about Tutunjan because I see him through Khaled's eyes, and maybe you're right. But I know what I saw. Tutunjan isn't a normal man. He's a monster. Why wouldn't he think like a monster. He can't keep Khaled chained to a chair, so he does the next best thing. He kills his lover to prove that he's still in control, and hides the murder in a series of True Blood assassinations, casting the blame on the Fundamentalists. And there's a bonus. If he wants to go down in history as the greatest general in the Korcian empire, he sets the stage for distrust between the League and the Empire by blowing the *Llyndar* into a gazillion pieces in League territory."

Cullon put his hands on her hips to hold her in place. "Aren't you forgetting the Conglomerate? I smell their hand in this somewhere."

"Maybe they are in it. Who's to say Tutunjan isn't using them to spread a little chaos on the side. If he is itching for a war, he could use the Conglomerate against the League."

Cullon looked skeptical. "You're reaching again. I can't take a far-fetched assumption like that to Viceroy Surazheia, he'd laugh me out of the Council Chamber. We need facts."

Danna smiled. "I think I may have one."

"What?"

"Omarura, Khaled's current residence, is known as a disciplinary outpost." She cocked her head to the side. "Know what I think? I think the High and Mighty General Tutunjan has a new guardian for his son."

"Captain Pheyell?"

"In a manner of speaking. Suppose Khaled stepped out of line by continuing to see Namid and got himself transferred to Omarura." Danna wiggled her way up Cullon's thighs until she was close enough to whisper in his ear. "I bet you a full body massage, wine and candles included, that Khaled's transfer to Omarura and Namid's sudden departure from Korcia happened within a few days of each other."

Cullon accessed the Registry files, then asked if Danna wanted her massage before or after dinner.

Cullon stood on the eastern terrace that overlooked the ocean and stared out at the tumultuous waves. He'd soothed Danna with a massage, then made love to her until she had fallen asleep from exhaustion. But his gut wouldn't let him rest.

Every instinct he had, instincts developed over the years to the point that he trusted them implicitly, told him that the pieces of the puzzle he and Danna had uncovered weren't being put together properly.

Assumptions and contradictions and dead men. That's all he had. He thought about Danna's theory, that Tutunjan was at the core of the murders; a perverted mind carrying out a perverted agenda. Maybe she was right. Maybe he was being blinded by his own loyalty to the Empire, but his gut didn't agree.

He tossed the contents of his wine glass over the banister, intending to return to bed. As he turned, he heard the sounds—sounds he was familiar with—the soft scratch of fabric as a man crouched low, the subtle click of a laser cartridge being shifted into the firing cylinder.

The next thing he heard was the almost inaudible spit of the cartridge being fired. Cullon spun, but not in time. The next second, he felt a razorlike burn against the side of his neck. He dropped the wine glass and lunged to the right, doubling low into a ball and rolling, then springing back up and onto his feet. A second shot was fired. The missile imbedded itself in the wall beside his head, sizzling as it burned into the stone.

Cullon remained in a crouched position, inching forward, eyes scanning left and right. He started to circle to the left when something hit him full force in the ribs, finding its mark with the force of a battering ram. An explosion of pain sent him flying backwards, but years of physical and hand-to-hand combat training immediately came into play. With an almost unconscious effort, his body accepted the impact and rolled, allowing him to regain his footing.

He lashed out with a spiral kick, catching his assailant in the upper thigh with enough force to send him staggering backwards. The black-clad figure swayed for a second, and in that instant, Cullon charged, head down, legs pumping against the terrace floor to give him momentum. His head rammed into the man's shoulders, hammering him into the wall.

The man swallowed a breathless grunt as the laser pistol dropped to the ground. He bent forward, gasping for air. Cullon raised his hands over his head and brought them down as a single, solid fist into the man's upper back, slamming him forward onto his hands and knees.

He picked up the weapon, then grabbed the bent-over man by the hair, yanking his head back. "Who sent you?"

The man said nothing.

"Who sent you?" Cullon asked again, his voice low and throaty.

Then from some obscure pocket in his clothing, the man pulled a knife—a thin stiletto blade with a hollow injection tube. Cullon stepped back, knowing the blade was loaded with poison. He had used the same sort of knife himself. A single scratch, the lightest of punctures, and paralysis began in seconds, death moments later.

The man came to his feet, the thin blade thrusting forward, the most difficult thrust to parry, a move used by only the most experienced killers.

Cullon leaped backward as the lethal blade criss-crossed through the air in slashing diagonals. He lashed his right foot out catching the man in the armpit, staggering him for an instant, but not long enough. Cullon kicked out a second time; his assailant whipped the blade back, then slashed laterally, missing Cullon's kneecap by a fraction of an inch.

Cullon watched for the next move, the next swing of the man's arm. When it happened, he kicked out again, catching the man's shoulder with his right foot. He fell, grabbing at thin air as he crumbled to the terrace. Cullon kicked at the hand holding the stiletto. The man's wrist bent as he tried to hold onto the blade and the point of the poisoned knife pierced his skin.

He lay speechless, the blade still clutched in his hand, and stared up at Cullon in a kind of ethereal disbelief. He'd failed. His fate was sealed.

"Who sent you?" Cullon asked one last time, hoping the man would answer.

He couldn't. The poison was already in his bloodstream.

His body jerked spastically, then went rigid. His eyes were still open, staring at nothing, his lips parted in death. The process had taken less than thirty seconds.

Cullon leaned over and lifted the man's hand, carefully separating the fingers so he could remove the still lethal blade. He stood up and turned, surprised to find Danna standing in the doorway. She was clutching the front of her robe to keep it closed against the wind blowing in from the ocean. Eulla and Niska stood just behind her, their face frozen in shock.

How long had they been there?

"You're bleeding!" Danna rushed toward him, her dark eyes wide with fear—for him.

It took him a second to remember that he'd been hit

with the first blast from the laser—a searing cut on the right side of his neck. He'd felt only a twinge of pain before adrenaline and his survival instincts had taken over.

"I'm fine," he said, making sure she didn't come in contact with the blade.

Niska and Eulla had disappeared into the house—Niska to get something to treat his wound, Eulla to pour him a drink.

Danna looked past him for a moment, her eyes fixed on the dead man. Cullon lifted her chin, forcing her to meet his gaze instead. He smiled. "Well, at least we're making progress."

"Progress!" Her voice was high, still laced with fear. "Only you would call nearly being murdered progress."

Cullon guided her into the house. Once she was seated with a drink in her hand, he walked to his console and entered an alarm code that would bring an Enforcement team. Only then did he accept the drink Eulla had poured. Only then, did he allow Niska to clean his wound and apply a regenerating gel.

"Who was he?" Danna asked.

"I don't know," he said. "But I intend to find out."

He walked to where she was sitting, pulling her up and into his arms. His world immediately narrowed to a pair of soulful brown eyes and a smile that made his heart beat erratically.

"Don't worry. I told you I'm very good at what I do."

"I saw that for myself, but it doesn't keep me from worrying about you."

"Then maybe this will." He clasped their hands, palm to palm, fingers entwined, then took her mouth in a slow, deep, kiss that was intimately fusing; he was a part of her, just as she was a part of him.

The hum of a shuttle landing on the rear lawn brought them apart.

"My fellow agents," Cullon said. "You'd better get dressed. We have work to do."

* * *

The assassin was dead. The only link to who had sent him were the weapons he'd used against Cullon. Danna knew she would be imprinting with those weapons very soon.

She returned to the bedroom, unable to shake the fear that had gripped her when she'd seen Cullon dodging laser fire.

Something had awakened her, and she'd gone looking for him, not wanting to sleep again until he was by her side. When she'd stepped out onto the terrace and seen him fighting for his life, her heart had jumped into her throat. She still wasn't sure if she had screamed, bringing Eulla and Niska from their beds, or if they had heard the same noise and come out to investigate on their own.

She had never doubted his ability to take care of himself, tonight being a perfect example, but she'd be a fool to underestimate that same capability in the men who had already murdered four True Bloods and forty-five innocent *Llyndar* crewmen.

What if Cullon hadn't been awake and standing on the terrace? What if he hadn't heard the assassin in time to defend himself? What if he'd been sound asleep? His physical skills and instincts were obvious, but would they have been enough to save his life if the assassin had gotten close enough to plunge the poisoned stiletto into a sleeping man's skin?

Before she'd fallen asleep, lying in Cullon's arms, Danna had felt unusually vulnerable. Despite the intensity of their lovemaking, doubts had entered her mind. Doubts about whether Cullon's passion for her was sexual or emotional, about whether their moments together were meaningful to him or an, albeit pleasant, passing of time. Doubts about whether there could ever be more between them than their current affair.

She still had those doubts, but the assassination attempt had cemented one thing into her heart and mind. You loved who you loved, it was as simple as that. And she loved Cullon. He had become the most important thing in her life.

Twenty-one

"I thought the Registry was the Korcian version of a census bureau," Danna said as they approached a large building in the northeastern sector of the city.

She was still recovering from the raw emotions that had gripped her all morning. Every time she looked at Cullon, she imagined him lying dead in the assassin's place.

The stats Cullon had pulled from the Registry files hadn't given them anything more than facts and figures. According to the DNA sample the Enforcement team had processed when they'd removed the body, the assassin was Lieutenant Shol Maleha, recently discharged from the Seventh Tactical Brigade after ten years of military service.

"The Registry serves more than one purpose," Cullon told her, as he glided the shuttle onto the landing platform on the north lawn adjacent to the Registry Complex. "The Registry you're referring to maintains DNA samples of the entire population, records births and marriages and deaths, and keeps an index of all military personnel. But that isn't all it does."

"Let me guess, it oversees the Enforcement Bureau."

"Registry oversees *everything* connected to the Empire," Cullon said, as they walked up the front steps and into the atrium-style entrance of the Registry Building. "You should be flattered. You're the first Terran to ever pass through these doors."

"I'll be sure to act impressed," Danna said, already awed by the architecture. Beyond the customary guards and scanning station lay a rotunda with a domed ceiling that rose at least a hundred feet above the marble floor. Alcoves had been cut into the rotunda wall to hold life-size statues of past Korcian Viceroys. The ceiling was one large stained-glass painting, depicting scenes from Korcian history.

Morning sunlight flowed through the stained-glass home in rainbow streams, coloring the pale marble floor and bringing the entire rotunda to life.

"Will General Tutunjan be here?" Danna asked once she'd been cleared by the security guards, who had tripled-checked her authorization before allowing her inside. Cullon had simply waited with a smile on his face.

"No. General Caliphn acts as Director of the Registry."

Danna walked by Cullon's side as they crossed the rotunda to one of three transport tubes. "Caliphn is a High General, isn't he? One of the three True Bloods on the High Council."

"Yes." Cullon paused to look at her, his gaze sharp and probing. "You know why you're here, don't you?"

"You need me to imprint with the assassin's weapons," Danna said. "No problem. The sooner we bag the bastards responsible for all this, the better."

"Are you sure?" Cullon asked. "If Maleha killed before, this dreamscape could be very emotional."

Danna smiled, wondering if he realized just how emotionally involved she'd become with everything, especially him. The first time she'd looked at him, she hadn't been able to get past his eyes: those incredible, ever-changing Korcian eyes that spoke more in a single glance that any five men could say with their voices. "You'll be with me, right?"

"Yes."

"Then I'll be fine."

They stepped into the elevator. Cullon entered his clearance code into a sensor panel, and the door closed. He added one last word of caution before the tube swished them to wherever in the complex they were going.

"Whatever you see in the dreamscape, you see. Don't worry about the consequences."

Danna had to laugh. "Easy for you to say. You're not the one who may end up accusing a High General of treason."

When they exited the transport tube, Danna was surprised to discover that instead of making an upper or lateral move through the complex the tube had actually taken them underground. The long, illuminated corridor that faced them as they stepped out of the tube had rock walls reinforced with circular metal beams that arched overhead like metallic ribs.

The corridor was empty, but Danna could see at least three clearance-code consoles from where she stood.

"Why here?" she asked, as Cullon stopped to enter his clearance code into the first monitoring console. "I can imprint almost anywhere."

"The Viceroy let General Caliphn in on our little secret this morning," Cullon said. "Needless to say, he isn't happy about being kept in the dark. He wants you monitored during the dreamscape."

"Monitored how?"

Cullon guided her beyond the first checkpoint and started walking toward the second. "You'll be in an interrogation cell."

"Strapped to a sensory chair," Danna said, familiar with the equipment used when interrogating a prisoner. She knew that some psychics registered unusual brain wave patterns when they were monitored. She'd been tested as a child, but she had no idea what her synaptic profile looked like when she was imprinting. With any luck, it would be strong enough to convince General Caliphn that she wasn't faking it.

"Okay, I've faced doubting Thomases before."

"Good," Cullon said.

Two more checkpoints and a hundred yards of rock-encased corridor later, they arrived at a large blast door. Cullon pressed his palm to the sensor screen. It glowed red, then blue, then white. Seconds later, Danna heard the hiss of powerful hydraulic gears as the door irised open.

They stepped into a small anteroom, where a full-body scan was done before another door opened with a pneumatic sigh. Danna was beginning to understand the "other purposes" Cullon had mentioned. If she was right, the *real* Registry was actually the central brain of the Korcian Empire.

The League had a similar organization, known as PSA, Planetary Security Agency. Danna had never been inside the PSA's main facility on Earth, but she imagined it had just as many underground tunnels and checkpoints.

They passed through the second anteroom with a simple palm scan, then on to another where the Viceroy and General Caliphn were waiting.

The moment her introduction was complete, General Caliphn stepped forward. He was a big man, tall and thick-boned with a jutting nose and eyes that were more green than blue under dark, highly-arched brows that gave him a batlike appearance. "Lord Viceroy, I ask you to reconsider your decision. This breach of security is unthinkable."

"The decision has been made," Viceroy Surazheia replied in the tone of absolute authority.

"Yes, Lord Viceroy." The general stepped back with a formal bow of subordination. "As you wish."

Cullon had something to say after that. "Officer

MacFadyen, I shouldn't have to tell you that anything you see or hear in the Registry is not to be discussed or revealed to any of your League associates."

"I understand," Danna replied, knowing they had nothing but her word, which meant the Viceroy was more trusting of her abilities than she'd first assumed.

"This way," General Caliphn said, heading for yet another sensor panel. A second blast door opened to reveal the *Inner Sanctum* of the Korcian Registry.

It was a cavernous room with a low ceiling. Actually, it was a room within a room, double-walled, resting on and surrounded by titanium alloy plates. The outer perimeter walls were solid rock. The inner facility, where the internal and external security of the Empire was constantly monitored, was lined with consoles and holographic maps.

Danna recognized some of the equipment—satellite receivers and transmitters, voice and data scramblers, encryption and decryption stations, and navigational sensors that allowed operators to see the exact location of every ship in the Korcian fleet.

The consoles were manned by technicians, male and female, whose faces were bathed in the eerie glow emanating from the screens and holographic displays in front of them.

Danna followed Cullon along a metal catwalk that circled the inner facility, knowing every eye in the Registry was focused on her. She didn't have to act impressed. She was.

They made their way to another room within a room. The outer area was benign—a table and chairs and a computer console. The inner room was the interrogation cell with a sensory chair bolted intimidatingly into the floor.

"It's painless," Cullon said, as he opened the door to the cell and motioned her inside. "Just pretend you're sitting in the co-pilot seat onboard the *Star Hawk*. I'll be right outside the door."

"Who will be monitoring me?" Danna asked.

"General Caliphn."

Danna stepped up and into the chair before she allowed herself any second thoughts. She didn't like it, but she'd come too far to turn back now.

The sensors built into the chair's back and arms would monitor her cardiac and respiratory responses, as well as any unusual muscular activity, such as excessive blinking of her eyelids. The sensory helmet would register the synaptic activity within her brain.

"We're not using restraints," Cullon said. He strapped on wrist and ankle monitors instead.

Danna could tell by the look in his eyes that he wanted to kiss her before he attached the sensory helmet. She winked at him, knowing it was the best either one of them could do with an audience.

"Don't worry. I'll be right outside the door," he said again.

From his tone of voice Danna decided he was more nervous than she was. She caught a glimpse of a skeptical-faced General Caliphn, standing at the console, and a solemn Viceroy Surazheia just before Cullon lowered the helmet's opaque visor. She knew the sensors registered a rise in her respiration and heart rate the moment she was shut off from the rest of the world.

"Can you hear me?" Cullon asked.

"Yes," Danna answered. She could feel his leg brushing hers, but he sounded miles away.

"The first thing I'm going to put in your hands is the laser pistol Maleha used."

Danna closed her eyes beneath the visor and began taking slow, deep breaths, inhaling through her nose and exhaling through her mouth. She put the idea of being in an interrogation cell behind her, focusing instead on the last thing she'd seen before entering the Registry—a peaceful blue sky dominated by a morning-fresh sun.

A few moments after her fingers closed around the weapon, Danna felt the dreamscape nudge its way into her consciousness.

A formless void, a sea of nothingness, estrangement from the world as she knew it. Black on black slowly gave way to a boiling cauldron of color, streaks of phosphorescent red slicing through a golden aura.

Then, a surreal clarity.

A flash of white moonlight tunneled through low-lying clouds. The canyon was deep and narrow, a mile-long gorge with a river running through it. The water shone like hammered lead.

The dreamscape changed, and Danna found herself in a place of shadows and secrets.

Men. A dozen, maybe more. All dressed in black, all huddled around a scarred metal table. Dust and cobwebs. The musky scent of a room long closed against the outside world. Whispers, and low grunts of acknowledgment.

"One by one," a voice called out. "One by one, we will achieve our victory. One by one, we will purge those who would undermine the Empire."

The scrape of weapons being pulled free of holsters and checked into readiness. Fingertips running along the edge of polished blades to test their sharpness. Cheers of support for their unnamed leader.

"One by one," the voice echoed again. "No more bending our knee to True Bloods. No more giving way to their arrogance. No more watching them gain what by right should be ours. No more!"

Cheers, long and loud. Fisted hands raised in tribute. The man stepped out of the shadows to receive the adoration of his followers. He was tall, his face scarred, his eyes blazing in their green intensity. He motioned for another man to join him. The younger officer stepped forward, his dark hair blending into the shadows that circled the room.

Danna trembled with the sensation of having her

mind and body invaded by the dreamscape just before it bled away into an array of colors that shimmered like oil on water. She could still sense the dark presence as she spread her hands wide and let the pistol fall to the floor.

She was gasping for breath as Cullon lifted the sensory helmet off her head.

"Are you all right?"

Danna looked through the transparent walls to find both General Caliphn and Viceroy Surazheia staring at her. She didn't know what the sensors had recorded, but General Caliphn looked considerably less doubtful than he had before.

"Mataress," Danna said, as Cullon removed the wrist sensors and began massaging her hands.

"The Consulate Commander?"

"Yes," she gulped out the word. "I saw him. He's one of them."

"Them?" Cullon helped her out of the chair and into the outer room where she sat down at the table. A glass of water was waiting for her.

Danna sipped it before finishing her explanation. The aftermath of the dreamscape was still with her. She took several minutes to compose herself, then looked at Cullon. "I saw a group of men. They meet in an abandoned building, or maybe a warehouse. I'm not certain. It was dark and dirty. Their leader is an older man with a scarred face."

"You said you saw Commander Mataress. Are you sure it was him?" Cullon asked.

"Yes." She described what she saw. "The leader called him to the front of the room. I can't be certain, the dreamscape began to fade, but I think he was giving him an assignment."

"All this from holding a laser pistol in her hand," General Caliphn said belligerently. "Does the weapon belong to Commander Mataress, is that what she's telling us?"

Danna shifted her gaze from Cullon to the general. After such an emotional dreamscape, she wasn't inclined to be on the defensive, which is where the general's remark had put her, so she came right back at him. "An imprint can take me anywhere the object has been. The assassin was in that room. I could sense him. He cheered right along with the rest of them. He hated right along with the rest of them."

"Tell us again." It was the Viceroy speaking this time. "Tell us everything you saw, everything you heard. Take your time, Miss MacFadyen. I'm listening. *We're* all listening."

Danna closed her eyes in an effort to regain the images of the dreamscape that were still racing around inside her mind. She described the mountains and the narrow river that ran at the bottom of the deep gorge. Yes, the room could have been inside the mountain, like the one they were in now. She couldn't be certain. The only walls she had seen had been masked by shadows.

"And you're certain that Commander Mataress was the man you saw step to the front of the room?" Cullon asked, reaffirming what she'd said the first time.

"Yes."

He looked to the Viceroy and General Caliphn. "Mataress is the Commander of the Consulate. He was also in charge of the security scans after Rakosi's murder. If he didn't kill Rakosi himself, he could have easily arranged for someone to enter and exit the compound without detection."

"A possibility to be considered," the Viceroy replied. He looked to Danna. "Are you able to imprint again?"

Danna nodded, wanting it over and done with it, needing to know if she'd misjudged General Tutunjan after all.

When Cullon reached out to help her stand, she shook her head. "No sensory chair. Either they believe me or they don't."

The room went silent for several moments, each man digesting what she'd just told them, reassessing the situation.

"Very well," the Viceroy said.

"All traces of the poison have been removed," Cullon assured her as he opened a sealed container and removed the hollow stiletto. He placed it her hands.

Danna looked down at the deadly knife, at its long needlelike blade, and shivered. She closed her eyes, but she didn't need to clear her mind. The dreamscape took over with a vengeance. She was instantly surrounded by a brittle luminance, like the crystalline pattern of ice on a windowpane. As it dissolved, making way for a sculpture of random colors, she found herself in a place without length or breadth or height, as if infinity's many dimensions had welded themselves into one obscure landscape.

Everything around her was revealed in astonishing clarity; she felt as if she could see through the very eons of time. Then the clarity faded, to be replaced by a dark haze that slowly gave way to another image.

The mountains were thick slabs of raw rock jutting above the jungle floor. The sun was a blood-red disk, leeching color from the sky. But there was another light . . . coming from deep within the mountain.

Danna's mind glided down the tunnel as effortlessly as a bird sailing on the wind. The deeper she went, the colder it got. So cold. So dark. Then a blaze of light.

Segregated groups of men, talking among themselves. Their leader stood in the middle of the light, his scarred face grim, determined.

A young man joined him, accepted his orders, then sheathed the poison-filled knife in a pocket on the leg of his uniform. He looked to the leader one last time, then gathered his other belongings and left.

Danna felt him pass her in the tunnel, his body, her mind, a momentary contact only she recognized.

She dropped the knife, then rubbed her hands

against her clothing to clean them of its memory. When she opened her eyes, Cullon was kneeling at her side.

"What did you see?"

Danna looked into his eyes, saw the warmth and concern there, and let it vanquish the chill of the dreamscape.

"Ambition and hatred," she told him.

"What?" General Caliphn demanded. "What is she talking about? The assassin? The man with the scarred face?"

"Enough!" Viceroy Surazheia commanded. "We will give her time to organize her thoughts."

It was several minutes before Danna could look at the Viceroy and General Caliphn with any real composure. When she did, their expressions were a mixture of doubt and curiosity.

"The mountains again, and a tunnel," she told them. "It's where they meet. The scar-faced man was there, he's definitely their leader. He ordered Cullon's assassination."

"The mountains are full of caves," General Caliphn pointed out antagonistically.

"Not a cave. A tunnel. The walls were smooth. It was manmade," Danna replied, ignoring his rudeness.

"Would you recognize the scar-faced man again, if you saw him?" Cullon asked.

"Yes."

Cullon looked to his superiors. "She needs to rest."

He took Danna to a room furnished like a standard military barracks, with a cot and a table and chairs. "Try and get some sleep."

"They don't believe me," Danna said as she stretched out on the bunk. The dreamscapes had exhausted her.

"Yes, they do." Cullon leaned down to kiss her. "They don't want to believe, but they do."

"What happens next?"

"You sleep, while I go hunting."

She sat up and reached for his hand. "Not without me."

He smiled, then kissed her again. "I meant searching the database. There are several places that fit the description you gave us. I need to narrow down the possibilities."

When she woke, Danna had no idea how long she'd been sleeping. She sat up, stretched her arms high over her head, and yawned. She was washing her face with cold water when Cullon entered the room.

"I brought you hot tea and some food," he said, putting the tray on the table.

"What did you find out?" She poured herself a cup of the strong Korcian tea she'd become addicted to since arriving on Cullon's homeworld.

"I think it's one of two places," Cullon said, helping himself to one of the sandwiches. "There's a munitions dump in the western province of Jayuguan. It hasn't been used for over a hundred years. The second possibility is an abandoned military base near Argalant, about six hundred kilometers from here. We're scanning both areas for any suspicious activity."

"And the scar-faced man?"

Cullon voice-activated a holographic wall unit. "I've reduced the search parameters to military personnel with facial disfigurements and scars. If we don't find him here, we'll move on to the civilian files."

Danna made herself as comfortable as the room's straight-backed chair would allow. Considering the size of the Korcian military, she and Cullon could be here for days.

As the faces appeared, minus any personal demographics, Danna eliminated them one by one. Two hours passed before the right scar-faced man showed himself.

"That's him!"

"Are you sure?" Cullon rotated the image a full three hundred and sixty degrees.

Danna stared at the wide, whitish scar that began at the corner of the man's right eye and ran down his face and neck to disappear under the collar of his uniform. Malicious eyes stared back at her, dark and green with only the slightest trace of amber hidden in their cold depths. "Yes, I'm sure. Who is he?"

Cullon disengaged the screen before turning to face her. "Chief Commander Oudhia, Seventh Tactical Brigade."

"The same Oudhia whose uncle was Ambassador Oudhia? The same Commander Oudhia you and Captain Jaseera discussed the evening we had dinner with her onboard the *Thirl*?"

"One and the same," Cullon said unhappily. "It's probably a good thing that Ambassador Oudhia is dead. I doubt he'd be happy about having a traitor perched on his family tree."

Danna's thoughts retreated to the conversation she and Cullon and Captain Tasiq Jaseera had had onboard the *Thirl* during their stopover at Aquitaine Station.

Tasiq's exact words had been, *"Some say Oudhia can't be trusted with any agenda but his own."*

Twenty-two

"Okay, let's start with what we *do* know," Cullon said a short time later. They had moved into another room, this one with numerous consoles and a holographic map of the Korcian continent. General Caliphn was seated at the head of a rectangular table, with Cullon to his right and Danna on his left. The Viceroy wasn't joining them, confident that the Enforcement Bureau could handle the situation from this point forward.

"Lieutenant Mataress, now Commander Mataress, served under Oudhia seven years ago," Cullon continued. "Rakosi served under Mataress at the time of his murder. Maleha, who tried to kill me, served in the Seventh Tactical Brigade for five years. Oudhia was his commanding officer."

"Go on," General Caliphn said, putting the burden of proof on Cullon's shoulders.

"Oudhia has a long history of being uncooperative. A man his age, with his experience, should have made Chief Commander ten years ago. Mataress has a similar history. He's arrogant and self-serving. Maleha was discharged for insubordination. All three men could be labeled discontents. When I did a thorough search of their military records, I discovered that each of them was passed over for promotion."

"In favor of a True Blood," Danna prompted.

"Yes. But there's more." Cullon looked to General Caliphn. "Chief Commander Oudhia is High General Tutunjan's half-brother."

So Tutunjan did fit into the equation.

"Then Oudhia is a True Blood, too." Danna said.

"Not exactly," Cullon replied. "Oudhia's mother never married Tutunjan's father. The old general was already married. Because there was no legal union, the Registry doesn't recognize Oudhia's right to claim True Blood heritage."

"That's the most ridiculous thing I've ever heard," Danna retorted, momentarily forgetting her diplomatic skills. "It punishes the child for the parents' indiscretion. It's stupid, malicious, and antiquated."

"It's Korcian law," General Caliphn said in a firm voice. He looked to Cullon with a warning. "Be careful where you take this. High General Tutunjan is very highly respected."

"Yes, he is," Cullon replied. "The point I was going to make is that Tutunjan's son, Khaled, serves in the Seventh Tactical. He's aide to Captain Pheyell."

"Has Pheyell been passed over for a promotion?" Danna asked, certain they were on the right track.

"Yes."

"So they hate True Bloods," Danna said. "It fits with what I heard Oudhia say in the dreamscape. Even more, it fits with Oudhia's hatred. Imagine having to sit back and watch while your half-brother, a *registered* True Blood, skyrockets to a seat on the High Council. Why not kill off a few and blame it on the Fundamentalists?"

What Danna didn't say was that she still wasn't sure where Tutunjan fit into the final scheme of things. It was possible that Oudhia was using Khaled's twisted childhood as a weapon against his half-brother. How better to humiliate a High General of the Council than count his son among rebels. Another possibility was that Khaled was using Oudhia's hatred for True Bloods to serve his own purpose, to finally be rid of the father who had abused him for years.

"What do you recommend, Commander Gavriel?" Caliphn asked.

"I think Oudhia, Mataress, and Pheyell should be put under immediate surveillance. We should also filter any communications channeled through the Molnar Consulate. They could be using it as their own private comm center. If that's the case, it explains why the Registry hasn't picked up any private messages between Oudhia and his men. We don't have much time. I'm sure they expect Maleha to return with news of my death. As soon as they know I'm still alive, they'll take evasive action. It could take months to get close to them again."

"I'll authorize the surveillance," Caliphn said. He left the table, only to pause before exiting the room. Turning to look at them, he said, "Treason to the Empire isn't to be taken lightly. Until we have irrefutable proof, we have nothing."

"He's a real charmer," Danna said once she and Cullon were alone.

"I don't think he cared for your evaluation of Korcian law."

"It's a stupid law," Danna said. "If Oudhia's DNA can be traced back to one of your precious kings, then he's as much of a True Blood as Tutunjan. No wonder he's pissed off."

"I'm a True Blood, and I admit pride in being able to say that," Cullon replied. He shut down the desk console he'd been using and stood up. "I also admit that the Empire isn't as progressive in its thinking as it should be. But let's solve one problem at a time, okay?"

"What about General Tutunjan? As much as I dislike the man, I'd hate to see him murdered. At this point it could be Oudhia or Khaled, or anyone in between."

"The Viceroy is one step ahead of you. He's already made arrangements for the general's protection."

The door opened to reveal a sober-looking young officer, who announced, "We've got activity at Jayuguan."

"What kind of activity?" Cullon asked.

"Two transports. The scanner is showing fourteen men entering the tunnel that leads to the old munitions depot."

Cullon headed for the door. "We've got them!"

"No," Cullon said a few minutes later. "This isn't a diplomatic mission. We're going in armed."

"I'll stay in the transport," Danna promised. "I want to be with you."

"Not this time." They were alone again. Danna was sitting on the bunk where she'd slept earlier in the day while Cullon checked his gear. "It's too dangerous."

"You owe me," she said stubbornly. "You wouldn't be gearing up to capture a band of rebels if I hadn't identified their location. You wouldn't know that Oudhia is their leader, or that Commander Mataress is involved. You'd still be sifting through debris on Ramora if I hadn't linked Namid to Marasona and the Conglomerate. You owe me for that information, and I mean to collect on the debt. I'm coming with you."

"I could lock you in this room."

"You won't," she said, daring him the same way she'd challenged him that first day on Ramora. They'd started this investigation together, and they'd finished it together.

Cullon glared at her, apparently displeased that she was calling in her debt. It took some time, but he finally agreed.

"You can't go in those clothes." He looked down at the green silk dress she'd put on that morning. "And you stay in the shuttle. No argument. It's the only way you're going anywhere besides a locked room."

Danna didn't like it, but it was better than pacing the floor, wondering and waiting, fearful that Cullon might be hurt. She'd come too close to losing him. Beyond that was the knowledge that once this was over, she'd have no reason to remain on Korcia. Soon, all too soon, she'd lose him in another way. Until then, every second counted.

"Okay, I'll stay in the shuttle, but you'd better be as good as this as you think you are, because if you get hurt, I'm going to be really pissed."

"I'm good at everything I do," he said, pulling her into his arms to prove it.

He deliberately took his time with the kiss, and as always, Danna was filled with the driving need to be as close to him as possible. It drummed through her veins like liquid thunder.

When he was done proving that he could kiss her into mindless oblivion, he held her away from him, and said, "I'll get you something to wear."

When he returned, Danna stripped out of her silky dress and into a snug-fitting black uniform.

"You might need this," he said, handing her a compact pistol. "It's loaded with stun cartridges. All you have to do is aim and press the trigger."

Danna holstered the weapon in the belt at her waist. Like all League diplomats, she'd gone through a training course that included self-defense and weapons handling, but she'd never been in a situation like this before. Given all the unknowns they were facing, the stun gun might come in handy.

"I'm ready," she told him once she'd added a slender commlink unit to her right wrist.

Instead of a shuttle, Danna boarded a twelve-man transport. Since Cullon had opted to pilot it, she sat

next to him in the co-pilot seat while ten grim-faced
Enforcers sat behind them, weapons loaded and ready.
A second transport, carrying another team of twelve
Enforcers, awaited take-off clearance.

They lifted off in unison, their course due west of
the capital city. Within seconds the two ships were absorbed into the blue-steel night, their engines humming almost inaudible, their shape nearly invisible as
they cruised mere feet above the ominous night-kissed
jungle.

Danna watched as they traveled deeper into the interior of the continent. Below she could see the landscape open into a wide alluvial plain that followed the
jade-green waters of the Tavoring River. Diffused
moonlight outlined the pinnacles of volcanic rock to
the north.

In the intense quiet of the transport, Danna's mind
began to relive the last few weeks. The excitement, the
tension, the questions and answers that they had
painstakingly weeded their way through to get to this
point. And through it all, Cullon had been at her side.

"Commander Gavriel," the voice came over the
transport's commlink. "Acknowledge."

"Acknowledge, this is Gavriel," Cullon replied.

"Registry Station Six," the emotionless monotone
came again. "Captain Pheyell is in his quarters. He's
received no outside communications in the last hour.
Commander Mataress signed out of the consulate. Our
tracers show him onboard a small shuttle. If he contin-
ues on course, he should arrive at Jayuguan minutes before you do."

"What about Chief Commander Oudhia?" Cullon
asked.

"Unable to locate," Station Six reported flatly. "He
logged off duty six hours ago."

"Acknowledged," Cullon said, ending the transmission.

"Do you think Oudhia is one of the fourteen men already at Jayuguan?" Danna asked.

"Time will tell," Cullon said, changing course to bring the transports in from the north.

A short time later, Danna could see the weatherworn cliffs and volcanic spires of the mountains against the midnight sky. The transports flew through the blue-gray mist rising from the narrow river that ran south to join the Tavoring, before making its way to the sea. The landscape looked familiar, just as she knew it would.

Cullon sent a coded message to the second transport, then landed a few kilometers northeast of the munitions depot. As expected, he ordered Danna to remain onboard. "Keep your commlink open. I'll let you know as soon as we have the situation under control."

Cullon checked his weapon again. Behind him, ten silent Enforcers neatly executed the same move. Danna had never seen a more deadly looking group. Dressed in black, with skull caps and night visors, they would blend into the surrounding jungle like prowling black panthers.

"Be careful," she told Cullon.

He reached out to touch her cheek. "I'm always careful."

The long steady gaze they shared, the complicit recognition that they were in this exciting adventure together, wasn't enough for Danna. She looked deeper into the catlike eyes she had come to know so well and saw what she was looking for. A deeper acknowledgment—they had unfinished business.

Cullon left one man behind to guard the transports and sent the group of men from the second transport ahead to secure the perimeter. He and the remaining men started toward the tunnel entrance in a standard two on two formation.

In Cullon's experience, there was no such thing as a simple victory, no matter how many men you had under your command. Staying alive was the result of being smarter than your enemy. Unfortunately, the enemy he was facing tonight had received the best training the Korcian Guard had to offer. It wasn't the most auspicious start to a mission, but Cullon didn't allow it to worry him.

Enforcers thrived on adversity; it brought out the best in them. To a man, they functioned better when the odds were stacked against them and the wall was at their backs. Each knew that every mission he participated in might be his last. A man who refused to acknowledge his human frailty was a menace to the men who fought by his side. Cullon had personally chosen the men with him tonight, knowing he could trust each and every one.

As he made his way toward the depot entrance, the ground beneath his feet was spongy and moist. The air was humid, rich with the smells of decaying vegetation and luxuriant blooms. Shafts of moonlight lanced down through the canopy to reveal thick vines wound around tree trunks. All around, the ever-present background noise of the jungle hummed and buzzed. In the shadows of the thick undergrowth, unseen creatures crawled and slithered away from his footsteps.

A hundred yards from the tunnel entrance, he crouched low and entered a pre-designated code into his commlink. Minutes later, the leader of the second team, a veteran Enforcer named Mohn, materialized out of the darkness.

"Buttoned up tighter than an admiral's sphincter," Mohn said, his voice a low whisper that was easily absorbed by the night. "Nothing in, nothing out. Not since the scanners went active."

"What about exterior guards?" Cullon asked.

"Negative. If they have guards posted, they're close to the nest and too deep underground for the scanners to register their body heat."

command. In the short second that it took the door's mechanism to respond, Mohn lobbed the grenade into the sealed chamber.

The blast door protected the Enforcement team from the ensuing high-frequency vibrations that would radiate from the exploding grenade in an invisible shockwave.

Cullon counted under his breath, then activated the blast door again. As expected, he and his men walked into a rock-walled room occupied by unconscious traitors.

"Secure them," Cullon said, looking around at the splintered tables and chairs that had been hurled against the walls right along with the men. The floor was cluttered with small pieces of rock that had been dislodged by the sonic impact of the contained explosion.

Mohn and the rest of the men started gathering up stunned traitors and dragging them to the center of the room. Cullon recognized Mataress, his dark hair filled with rock dust. There was a cut over his left eye that leaked blood down his face.

Chief Commander Oudhia was in the group. He began to stir, his eyes shifting beneath his closed lids. He groaned slightly, and then his eyes came open, unfocused at first. When he realized what had happened he cursed long and hard, his face taking on the pugnacious look of a drunk hoping to pick a fight. Only, he'd lost this fight before it had had a chance to begin.

"Get this scum out of here and into the transport. Then secure the area."

It only took a few moments and a quick head count for Cullon to realize they had a problem. The Registry scan had picked up fourteen men arriving in a single transport, followed by Mataress in a private shuttle. They should have fifteen men in custody, but three decommissioned guards in the tunnel, and eleven traitors in the fourth level chamber totaled fourteen, not fifteen. They were short one man.

"Check for an exit hatch," Cullon shouted. "Someone got out before the grenade went off."

As his men scattered, Cullon contacted the Enforcer he'd left behind at the transport. There was no reply. Fearing the worst, he tried to raise Danna. Again, no reply.

Danna sat in the co-pilot seat, forced to watch as Khaled casually wiped a bloodied knife against the leg of his uniform. She knew the guard Cullon had left behind was either dead or dying.

"I'm surprised Gavriel brought his Terran whore along," Khaled said, his voice hostile and defiant. His expression was a mask. None of the vulnerability she'd seen in the dreamscapes was exposed to the human eye.

Danna wasn't a trained psychologist, but she knew enough about human nature to know that Khaled was a multi-layered personality. She doubted logic or reason would work on him at this stage. He'd killed, and he would kill again.

The only thing she could do was keep him talking and hope that Cullon would return to the transport before Khaled decided to either kill her or use her as a hostage. Once they were airborne, Danna knew they couldn't bring the transport down without killing both her and Khaled.

She looked at the stun gun he'd knocked out of her hand because he'd been the last person she'd expected to come through the hatch. It lay on the floor, but too far out of reach for her to think she could retrieve it before Khaled pounced. Her commlink had been disabled, as well. The only weapon she had was her wits.

"I know you and Namid were lovers," she said, hoping a change in tactics from frightened female to confidante might buy her some time.

Khaled gave a harsh laugh. "You know nothing," he spit at her. "Nothing."

Danna met his gaze, seeing trouble in his eyes now instead of triumph. "I know you're torn between hating your father and loving him. Is that why you joined forces with your uncle? Were you going to kill your father yourself, or was Mataress going to do it for you?"

Khaled didn't move a muscle. He stood staring at her, his breathing heavy, his eyes beginning to dilate with hatred once again. "Mataress is a coward."

Danna knew then that Khaled had been the dark figure hidden by shadows, the one who had cut Lieutenant Rakosi's throat. Had he poisoned Ackernar and Eyriaki, as well? No, she decided, that would have been Mataress, the coward.

"You weren't sent to kill Cullon because your uncle was afraid that someone might see you, that you'd be recognized," Danna said, pushing the envelope because every word she said, every response she drew from Khaled bought her precious time.

Khaled's mask was back in place. Nothing betrayed his reaction, no twitch of muscles, no flexing of his fingers, no accelerated breathing. He lowered his gaze to the knife in his hand, his expression sharpening to a hard edge that was as deadly as the blade.

"My uncle thought Maleha needed the experience. He was stupid. You don't come at an Enforcer in a frontal attack, you wait until he's sleeping, or looking the other way, then you catch him from behind."

Khaled's cold smile turned into a sneer. He held the bloodstained knife up so Danna could see it. "I'm a better soldier than my father realizes. He doesn't think I have the guts for battle, but he's wrong."

"Is that why you took his general's medallion and gave it to Namid as a keepsake? Did you want to impress him with how powerful you'd become one day?"

Khaled simply stared at her, coldly dispassionate once again.

"I know Namid cared for you. He didn't want to leave you."

"What do you know about anything?" he shouted. "You think you know, but you don't. You can't know what it's like to be hated because you can't feel like other men, act like other men. Namid knew. His family shunned him, too. But he was afraid to fight back. So he hid. He hid what he was. We had to meet in secret. I hate secrets!"

Danna searched Khaled's face for the young man she'd met in a dreamscape, the frightened young man who had sat naked in a chair, chained to the wall, but he was gone. She was looking at the man his father had twisted and manipulated into being.

"It's over," she told him. "The Registry knows about Oudhia, and Mataress, and you. I told them. I told them everything."

Khaled laughed as he pushed himself away from the console, his composure suddenly replaced by the menacing memories that shaped his life. "Father thinks I'm weak. I'm not. He calls me stupid, but I'm smart. I'm smart enough to kill you and get away with it. I'm smart enough to kill my father, if I want."

Danna sensed his suffering the same way she'd sensed it in the dreamscape, as if it were her own. Worse still was knowing that by now Khaled had to realize that by not denouncing his father to the authorities he had betrayed something infinitely greater than a son's love for his father. He'd betrayed himself.

Khaled's voice quieted to a whisper when he spoke again. "You don't understand. No one understands. Namid loved me. He was the only one who's ever loved me."

"And you loved him," Danna whispered back, hoping she could reach a small portion of that love, reach the compassion that came with it, the need she knew was buried somewhere deep within Khaled's heart.

"He was leaving me!" he shouted. Without warning, he slapped Danna across the face. "Do you know how many beatings I suffered because of him? But I never gave in. I joined the military, but I refused to marry some officer's daughter and beget children so my father's precious True Blood heritage could continue for another generation."

"I'm sorry," Danna said, realizing Khaled's troubled mind didn't differentiate between love and hate. They were one and the same to him.

Khaled stared at her with a puzzled expression. When he finally spoke, his voice was emotionless. "Namid was leaving me. He deserved to die."

Cullon sprinted through the jungle, mindless of the prickly leaves and thorny vines that snagged and cut at his clothing and skin. He nearly stumbled over the body lying in his path. His eyes turned to golden flames as he recognized Barnikel, the Enforcer he'd left behind to protect Danna.

His throat had been cut.

Somehow, someone had gotten out of the depot. Maybe he'd never been inside. Maybe he'd been left to guard the transport the same way Barnikel had been left behind.

Accessing his scanner, Cullon read the images of two life forms still inside the transport. He forced his heartbeat to slow, pushing aside the panic that had been lodged in his chest since he'd been unable to raise Danna on the commlink. He summoned all his warrior instincts, focusing on what had to be done to get her out unharmed.

Around him, the sounds of the night intensified. Golden eyes swept the area, identifying every creature

huddled in the darkness, every vine and flower. He
could smell every scent the jungle had to offer, feel the
heaviness of the humid air as he breathed it into his
lungs.

Cullon knew Mohn and a team of men were behind
him, but he didn't have time to wait. He had to get into
the transport while there was still time. Once the engines were activated, the hatchways would automatically seal.

Crawling on his belly, Cullon made his way toward
the rear hatch. Knowing there was only one way to
take the fifteenth man by surprise, he pulled the sonic
grenade from his weapons pack, set it to minimal impact, lifted the hatch high enough to get his arm inside,
and tossed the grenade.

Five seconds later, Cullon rolled through the hatch
himself. He located Danna instantly, slumped in the
co-pilot's chair, her expression dazed by the sudden
surge of sound waves that had struck interior of the
transport.

The man struggling to his feet, with a knife in his
hand, was taken out by a well-aimed burst of laser fire.
The sapphire bolt sliced through the air and into the
man's left shoulder.

Before pain had time to register on his face, Khaled
Tutunjan slumped to the floor, only to come up again,
the knife in his right hand this time. He rushed forward, his eyes ablaze with a berserk fury that only a
second blast of laser fire could stop.

Twenty-three

It had been three days since the Jayuguan depot had been cleansed of Oudhia and his band of traitors. Three days since Cullon had been forced to kill Khaled Tutunjan in self-defense. Three days since the High Council had met in secret session.

Danna had given her statement to the Viceroy and General Caliphn, repeating what Khaled had told her. That he'd been personally responsible for the deaths of Chimera Namid and Lieutenant Shamron Rakosi, plus the forty-five innocent men onboard the *Llyndar*.

Her final act as a member of the Tribunal was to send an encrypted report to Ambassador Synon on Ramora, which would be forwarded to Gideon at the League Diplomatic Headquarters on Earth. The report had included the sincere and heartfelt regrets of Viceroy Surazheia and the Empire.

Danna knew the message would prompt a reply: she'd be expected to return to Ramora as soon as she could arrange transport.

Watching the message disappear into cyberspace had aroused a jumble of feelings inside her. Relief that the puzzle had finally been solved, remorse over Khaled's tragic life and death, and an unbelievable sadness all her own. How was she going to go on without Cullon in her life?

"Sorry, I'm late."

Danna turned around. She had no idea how long she'd been lost in thought. Cullon was standing a few yards behind her, his dark clothes blending into the shadows that had overtaken the veranda since sunset. She smiled and walked toward him. "Not that late. Niska hasn't set the table yet."

She slipped her hand into his, then raised on tiptoes to kiss him on the cheek. "How are the interrogations going?"

"First things first," Cullon replied, pulling her into his arms and giving her the kiss she'd been waiting for. They walked into the house, hand in hand.

"I spent the afternoon with my father," he told her as they shared a before-dinner drink.

"Is everything all right?" Danna asked, still sensing that there was unsettled business between the two men.

"It will be," Cullon said with a cryptic smile.

"Why do I get the impression that I've missed something," she said.

When Cullon didn't reply she realized that the family part of his personal life was off limits. Considering how close she was to leaving Korcia, Danna didn't press the issue. She steered the conversation back to the interrogations that had been going on at Registry for the last three days.

She might have been a principal player in the investigation, but now that it was over the High Council wasn't about to air their dirty linen in front of a Terran diplomat. Cullon was her only link to what was happening inside the Registry and the High Council. As they sat down to dinner, she asked. "Have you questioned Captain Pheyell yet?"

"First thing this morning," Cullon said. "As far as we

can tell, he wasn't a part of Oudhia's group. For the record, he stated that he hadn't asked for Khaled to be made his aide, but there wasn't any way he could refuse General Tutunjan's request to have his son transferred."

"So Khaled was sent there by his father."

"Yes," Cullon said, not elaborating on Pheyell's reputation as a hard taskmaster.

Danna continued asking questions. "Will the Fundamentalists be left alone with their dreams of a Korcian king reclaiming the throne, or will Oudhia's using them as a front for murder force them underground for good?"

"Since they weren't involved in the murders, I think the High Council is content to let them dream," Cullon said. "Sooner or later, every hierarchy is replaced by another. Who knows, one day the Empire may find itself in need of a king."

"What about the men Oudhia recruited, the ones you found in the depot with him?" she asked.

"If they're found guilty of treason, which they will be, they'll be sentenced to death."

Danna flinched. "Along with Oudhia and Mataress."

"Yes. Mataress is the one who arranged for Ackernar and Eyriaki to be poisoned. Oudhia gave the order for all the deaths, with the exception of Namid."

"I suppose we'll never know what actually prompted Namid to leave Korcia," Danna said. "Maybe he knew Khaled was getting in over his head with Oudhia, or maybe he simply couldn't abide the idea of loving someone who was willing to betray the Empire."

"Maybe he saw what Khaled was becoming and feared for his own life," Cullon suggested. "Not that it did him much good."

"Maybe. The remorse I felt from Namid in the first dreamscape, as if he were mourning someone, could have been his reaction to Khaled growing more and more bitter, until he became obsessed with proving his worthiness," Danna said.

Khaled had murdered, true, and if he had lived he would have had to stand accountable for his crimes, but Danna couldn't find it in her heart to condemn him unequivocally. She had *felt* the torrents of pain and anger he'd had to bear, and the desire for revenge that had fuelled him.

Cullon sat back, waiting a moment before replying. "We may never know. That's the tragic part."

Danna couldn't agree more. She sipped her wine, growing restless again at the thought of how soon she'd be leaving a world she was only beginning to understand. "What about the munitions you found? Was Oudhia selling them on the black market?"

"He denies having a connection to any corporate colony, but he wasn't stockpiling weapons like the ones we found without good reason. He was selling them off to the highest bidder to finance his own private war, and the Conglomerate is always the highest bidder when it comes to illegal arms. It may take an interrogation chair and a dose of psychotropic drugs, but we'll eventually get the name of his contact. In the meantime, he and Mataress are enjoying their penal cells."

"What about General Tutunjan?"

Amid all the flurry of the last few days, there had been one discordant note: There would be no criminal inquiry against General Tutunjan. He'd be left to mourn his son, if indeed he did mourn him, and to live with his own conscience, if he had a conscience, which Danna doubted.

"General Tutunjan has resigned his commission and forfeited his seat on the High Council," Cullon told her.

"At the Viceroy's request?"

"No. Voluntarily. Your dreamscapes may not be admissible in a court of law, but Tutunjan's secret is out, and he knows it. He's lost his credibility with the Council, along with any hope of becoming Viceroy."

"Men like Tutunjan don't just vanish into retirement," Danna said, wishing in this case that it were true. She paused to choose her next words carefully.

There had been a lot said in the last three days, but none of it had centered around her and Cullon and their questionable future. He hadn't said a word about her leaving Korcia, or a word about her remaining with him. She had no idea how deep his feelings ran, although she was certain he felt something for her.

"I'm having lunch with McDermott tomorrow. I want to say goodbye to him before I return to Ramora. Maybe I should introduce him to General Tutunjan, they could collaborate on a volume dedicated to Korcian military history."

Cullon stared at her, but Danna was concentrating too hard on keeping her composure for her to notice the golden glint that had taken over his gaze. He left his chair and came to where she was seated, bending down to kiss her on the side of the neck. "Enough talk. I've got something else in mind."

Danna watched wine-dark waves rush onto the shore of the northern coast. The moonlight cast an argentous glow across the pounding surf as Cullon landed the shuttle near the gateway to the ancient city of Sinshoumedir. Moonlight and shadows blended to create a magical landscape.

"City of Kings," Cullon announced as Danna stared in awe at the alabaster ruins. "There are eight temples, one to honor each of the original monarchs."

"Temples? Then they were worshipped like gods," Danna said, her gaze roaming from one work of art to the next. The ruins were an open-air museum of intricate scroll work, delicate arches, and regal statues. Time hadn't diminished their beauty.

"Not exactly," Cullon told her. "The temples were built to honor individual kings, a place where the citizens could come to offer prayers to the Great Creator for the monarch's protection and prosperity."

Like the current capital city, the ancient buildings

seemed to sprout directly out of the cliffs. Even after thousands of years, the delicacy and fluidity of their architecture was unlike anything Danna had ever seen.

"It's beautiful," she whispered reverently. She could almost hear the whisper of ghosts among the ruins, the phantoms of kings and queens long dead.

"So are you," Cullon said. His gaze elicited a rush of sexual adrenaline that set Danna's body on fire.

Words that should come easily to them dried up as they stood close enough to touch.

Danna couldn't look up to meet his gaze, unsure what she might find. If this was their last night together, then she'd grasp it with all the love in her heart.

There would be plenty of time for tears later.

Cullon drew her alongside him as they walked down the marble-paved road that led into the inner city. In a walled piazza just west of the temple dedicated to A'vla Gavriel, a jungle spring bubbled to the surface, filling a huge basin that had once been the gathering place for the city's women and children.

Just beyond the fountain, in an alcove sheltered by slender palms and exotic vines, Cullon knelt on the grass. Danna knelt with him. Their faces were so close they could taste each other's breath. From her knees up, Danna pressed against the length of him.

His fingers gently traced the lines of her face, as if to imprint a tactile memory of her. Danna inclined her head, curving her face into his warm, callused palm. She wanted to tell him how much she loved, but she was afraid the words would ruin the spell woven by the ancient ruins.

His mouth closed over hers. For all the hungry urgency of his kiss, it was nectar sweet. She wanted to melt into him, to let this final night of mutual possession spin into eternity.

Their mounting desire was more then sexual, it was an overflowing need for completion, to fill the aching hollow at the center of their beings.

For Danna, it was as if this were the first time, the only time she'd ever been with a man. Cullon made her quiver and tremble. He made her ache. He made her feel as if every cell, every corpuscle, every pore was a center of delight, a sleeping sensation that required only his touch to be awakened and aroused to extraordinary heights. He made her want to crawl inside his skin, to be so close, so intimate that one heartbeat would be indistinguishable from the next.

A web of moonlight created an aura of magic, and all around them, the earth and sky sang; night birds calling to their mates, insects humming and chirping, the ocean churning violently onto the shore. A breeze wafted through the leaves, swirling drops of dew into a silver mist and intensifying the pungent scent of exotic flowers.

"What do you want?" he whispered hoarsely.

"You."

"How?"

"In me."

Fighting for control, wanting the night to last forever, Danna turned her body so she could lie down and pull him down beside him. She held him in her arms and studied his face with quiet wonderment. Then, slowly, she began to celebrate his body like an ancient priestess celebrating the renewal of the sun.

"Touch me," she whispered, wanting the pleasure returned.

Answering her need, his mouth found the slope of her breast and closed hotly over her nipple. He sucked strongly, creating waves of burning pleasure that swept from her breast to her toes. "Cullon," she moaned, her voice a whimpering plea.

"Gently," he said, coming over her. "Slowly."

Despite his words, their lovemaking became a passionate struggle. More than the simple joining and appeasing of sexual hunger, they met as equal physical entities, neither asking nor giving quarter.

Direct. Demanding. At times intimately ruthless, they fitted their bodies together, recess and curve, hardness and softness. He sank deeper into the wet, luscious core of her only to have her muscles grip him, drawing him even deeper.

They mated in a rising and falling tumult, felt the mounting ecstasy of it vibrating through their bodies. Dynamic and elemental. Together they moved, reaching for and finding the steady primordial rhythm their surroundings demanded.

Danna wished time would stop at exactly this moment—the moment just before passion accelerated to its maximum, cresting to a point where there could be no more feeling—the moment just before the whirlwind ended.

The inner tightening and trembling of Danna's body precipitated Cullon's climax. Danna looked into his eyes—those incredible eyes—amazed by the compelling feelings that gripped her heart, but it wasn't the time to weigh and measure meanings. Soon they were trapped in a violent, throbbing vortex, and there was no meaning beyond pleasure.

Later, Cullon lay breathing deeply and quietly at Danna's side. She lay quietly, too, her intelligence slowly stirring to life through her body's physical contentment. She stretched like a cat, lazy and sated. But at the same time, she felt sulky and annoyed, more at herself than at Cullon. She'd known from the start that their affair might end with one last night of passion.

She had promised herself that she'd keep her pride intact. She'd already arranged to take a transport to Aquitaine Station, and from there, on to Ramora. Her career was waiting. She'd find a way to say goodbye—without tears.

Looking up at the stars, Danna wondered where they were leading her. More importantly, she wondered if she'd be content once she got there.

Her heart said no.

Cullon turned on his side. Danna started to speak, but he kissed her. "Ssshhh," he whispered. "We'll talk in the morning."

Danna relaxed in his embrace, letting her body speak more eloquently than any words.

Slowly, subtly, the rhythm began again.

Danna packed her things, moving about the room with calm determination. Cullon was at the Registry again. Part of her wanted to sneak away from the villa without having to bear the excruciating ritual of a formal goodbye. The other part wanted to see him one more time, look into those tawny jungle eyes one more time, kiss him one more time.

One last time.

It was unlikely that they'd meet again. His life as an Enforcer would keep him on the edge of danger, taking him to wherever that danger presented itself. Her life, her chosen career, would take her back to Ramora, then on to . . . where?

"What are you doing?"

Danna paused in the act of placing the Korcian souvenirs she'd collected into her open travel bag. She turned to look at Cullon, knowing the time had come, and dreading it with every fiber of her being.

"Packing," she said as casually as possible.

"For what?"

"To return to Ramora."

He didn't say anything, he just glared at her.

"The investigation is over," she said, using the same logic she'd used on herself. "The Tribunal's work is done. Ambassador Synon is expecting me back."

Wordlessly, Cullon marched across the room, took her by the wrist, and dragged her down the hall and out of the villa.

"What are you doing?" Danna demanded, struggling against his inescapable grasp.

"Trying not to strangle you," he grumbled as he lifted her into the shuttle.

"Where are we going?"

"The Viceroy wants to see you."

Danna didn't say anything. She'd said enough. She'd done enough. Cullon was a grown man. If he had something to say, he was capable of saying it.

He didn't speak a word.

When they reached the Viceroy's personal residence, he helped her out of the shuttle. Once they were processed through the sentry checkpoints and inside the house, Danna wondered what the Viceroy wanted. He'd already voiced a formal thank-you for her help in the investigation.

Danna was shocked to see Matthew Gideon sitting comfortably in the Viceroy's office.

"What . . ." she stammered as Matthew strolled across the sparsely-furnished room to embrace her like the old friend that he was. "What are you doing here?"

"Negotiating," he said with a smile.

Danna looked to Cullon, then to the Viceroy, then back at Gideon. "I don't understand."

"Sit down," Gideon said, "and I'll explain."

Danna sat, but her mind was still accommodating itself to seeing the senior League diplomat on Korcia. "How long have you been here? Why didn't you tell me you were coming?"

"One thing at a time," Gideon told her. He was a lean greyhound of a man in his late fifties, with sandy-silver hair, and a permanent gleam of intelligence in his blue eyes.

"I think some refreshments are in order," Cullon said. "This is going to be a long conversation."

As soon as Cullon handed Danna a cup of tea, Gideon began speaking without preface. "Before the *Llyndar* incident, Viceroy Surazheia and I were engaged in a lengthy conversation regarding the Conglomerate and the expanding influence of the corporate colonies."

"Engaged where?" Danna interrupted. "Here? On Korcia?"

"Yes."

"You were here, have been here, the entire time?" Danna took a measured breath. "But you contacted me from Earth, I saw the transmission code."

"You saw a code disguised to *appear* as if it came from Earth, as did Ambassador Synon each time he contacted me," Gideon clarified. "No one, but a select few in the League government, and the Viceroy's most trusted staff officers, know that I'm on Korcia. It's imperative that my presence remain a well-kept secret."

"Why?" Danna shook her head, hoping some logic might appear out of the puzzling comments Gideon had made so far. "If you were here when the *Llyndar* exploded, why form a Tribunal? Why put the Fleet on alert?"

She looked to the Viceroy, but he seemed content to let Gideon do the talking.

"Because that's what would have happened if I *hadn't* been here," Gideon explained. "Actions had to follow the expected course."

He paused to take a sip of his own tea, then smiled. "Maybe the best way to explain this is to go back a few years. One hundred and two years, to be exact."

"The signing of the Treaty of Vuldarr," Danna said. She glanced at Cullon who had made himself comfortable in an oversized chair near the Viceroy's desk. He was smiling, as if he was enjoying her confusion.

"Before you give me a history lesson, I want to know how long Commander Gavriel has known about your presence on Korcia?"

Cullon answered for himself. "I was introduced to Ambassador Gideon yesterday morning."

"Again, no one could know until we were ready for them to know," Gideon said. He leaned back, settling in for the lengthy explanation Danna required. "The Treaty of Vuldarr was a milestone in galactic history.

For the first time in over five hundred years the Empire and the League weren't at odds. However, as eloquently phrased as the treaty might be, it accomplished little, short of ending the hostilities between our governments. Since then, the League and Empire have become tolerant neighbors, going their separate ways as they served heir own interests."

"Political friendships are routinely tested by differences in opinion," the Viceroy said, finally joining the conversation. "But tolerance all too often results in diplomatic quagmire."

"That, in a nutshell, is the ethos of Conglomerate philosophy, and the reason they're getting the best of us," Gideon said, stepping in again. "For the last twenty years, the League has been playing a dangerous diplomatic ballet with the corporate governors. We send out Liaison Officers, the governors wine and dine them, then continue on their predetermined course. Which is doing exactly what they want, whenever and however they want it."

"We don't have jurisdiction in the outer regions," Danna said. "Neither does the Empire."

"Correct, but we do have an obligation to the billons of League and Empire citizens who depend on us to maintain the peace," Gideon replied. "It's that obligation that brought me to Korcia. It's time for the League and the Empire to do more than tolerate one another. We've always had conspirators and conspiracies, but it wasn't until the first corporate colony was founded that the conspirators of this time, our time, formed a single ideology. The Caesars the Conglomerate have put into power have only one goal—to rule everyone and everything. With that idea in mind, the League and the Empire have decided to focus on their commonalities."

"Focus how?" Danna asked, still unsure what she had to do with the political agenda Gideon was outlining.

"I trained you to be a diplomat," Gideon said, "but there are times when diplomacy is an ally, and there are times when it isn't. What I'm proposing, what Viceroy Surazheia is proposing with me, is to take affirmative action against the Conglomerate. Chief Commander Oudhia's involvement in selling illegal weapons is only the tip of the iceberg. The problem is that we can't see what's below the water because we've mucked it up with our own politics. Neither of our governments has faced the problems the Conglomerate represents because, until now, we didn't have a solution short of galactic war."

"What exactly are you talking about?" Danna asked, wanting to make sure she was grasping the picture that was forming in her mind.

"The most daring espionage game of the century," Gideon answered. "If we want to know what the Conglomerate is thinking, what they're planning, we have to get *inside*. We have to know who's pulling the strings and use that knowledge against them. Precious research and technologies from both the League and the Empire are being siphoned off. Stolen by those who pretend to be a part of us. We have to find those people—our masked enemy—and expose them. Watching you and Colonel Gavriel during the course of this investigation—"

"Colonel Gavriel!" Danna interrupted.

"I've been promoted," Cullon said, all smiles. "They want me to run the . . . I'm not sure what we're calling it."

"For now, I think the label Directorate is sufficient, Gideon said. "And Gavriel isn't the only one who's earned a promotion." He looked at Danna. "An official ceremony will take place next month, until then I'm afraid you'll have to celebrate privately, Ambassador MacFadyen."

Danna was dumb-struck. All she could do was stare at Gideon.

"Don't act so surprised, you've earned it. And more." It was several long seconds before she found her voice. What she'd dreamed of was coming true, and yet, all she could think about was Cullon, never seeing him again, never touching him again. Finally, she asked. "An ambassadorship to what posting?"

"To Korcia." Cullon delivered the news with a light laugh and a look that said, "Did you think I was going to let you get away?"

All Danna could think to say, given her audience, was, "Korcia doesn't have a League ambassador."

"It does now," Viceroy Surazheia announced, sounding surprisingly pleased with himself. He left his seat behind his desk to help himself to a glass of ale from the serving unit. When he turned to look at the three people gathered in the room, he seemed part pensive, part eager for the challenges ahead. A minute of silence passed, then another, before he spoke.

"As Ambassador Gideon and I see it, the Directorate will be a small, highly active group of individuals. A covert agency known only to the upper echelons of our respective governments. Colonel Gavriel will select and supervise the agents from a base here on Korcia. You, Ambassador MacFadyen, will be his link to the League, representing its needs and helping to map out the Directorate's agenda. The two of you work well together. Ambassador Gideon and I anticipate the Directorate reflecting that same level of cooperation."

Danna was elated. She didn't have to leave Cullon or Korcia behind. What more could a girl ask, except maybe for the man she loved to finally get around to telling her that he loved her too.

"The Directorate will have complete access to all Registry data, as well as information gathered by the League's Security Agency, but it will operate independently," the Viceroy said. He looked directly at Cullon. "Pinpointing the men and women whose qualities will allow them to function effectively as deep-cover agents isn't a precise science. It isn't easy to predict how a person will react to the stress of a hostile environment, and the corporate colonies are hostile worlds."

"We'll need people who are trained to look for the tiny errors that can be turned into gaping holes of opportunity," Cullon said. "They'll have to go deep, and stay deep, if we expect to get the sort of information you're looking for. It may take years before we see a difference in how the corporate colonies operate."

"We're prepared to wait decades," Gideon said. "The Conglomerate represents the single most dangerous threat to galactic peace. We can't afford to ignore it any longer."

"We can discuss the finer details later," the Viceroy said, bringing the meeting to an end. "In the meantime, the two of you have data to analyze, potential agents to screen, and an ambassadorship to finalize."

"You knew!" Danna said. "You knew before you took me to the ruins."

"Yes," Cullon said, pulling her back into his arms where she belonged. They'd been behind closed doors since returning to the villa. "Until then, my plan was pretty basic. I was going to kidnap you and keep you onboard the *Star Hawk* for the next fifty or sixty years."

"Say it again."

"I love you," Cullon said.

Danna snuggled close, unwilling to leave the comfort of Cullon's arms. "Just think, an ambassadorship for me, a promotion for you, *and* the Directorate. Our lives certainly won't be boring."

Cullon's catlike eyes gleamed as he rolled to put Danna beneath him. "Boredom, Madame Ambassador, will be the least of our worries."

Twenty-four

Danna and Cullon spent the next few weeks on a grand tour of the Korcian continent. Cullon insisted that if she wanted to be an ambassador to his people, she needed to know more about Korcia than the size of its military. They visited Goamada, where gigantic jungle orchids scented the air, and Kelghazi, in the south, where people still made their living from the sea.

They walked on the beaches, waded in the ocean, hiked through the jungle, and made love in the moonlight. But most of all, they talked. About themselves and the future. Nothing was said about marriage—that time hadn't as yet arrived.

It was time to be lovers and friends, to speak of normal things: the state of galactic politics, the colony of artists that thrived on the outskirts of the Korcian capital, even food they liked and disliked. But beneath their words, emotions simmered that would one day be fulfilled.

When they returned to the capital, the first thing on their list was finding and procuring a building that could be turned into a League Embassy. They chose a large residence near the Registry Complex that could be easily converted to meet Danna's needs. The first floor of the structure would be turned into offices and guest quarters. The second floor, with a rear balcony that overlooked a small courtyard, would become the new ambassador's private quarters.

The renovations were done by a Registry team who paid special attention to making sure the embassy would be technologically secure, including an encrypted communications system, bio-scanners, and motion sensors that would trigger a silent alarm if anyone went into a secured area without clearance. The changes they made to the building also included a private entrance, accessed by an underground tunnel that connected directly to the Registry complex.

Danna's induction ceremony was held in the High Council Chambers. As expected, the tiers of seats that circled the main platform were filled to overflowing. The audience was packed with galactic dignitaries, ambassadors from League and Empire planets, members of the planetary economic and trade guilds, scientists and scholars, and military representatives from both governments. Cullon was seated with his family, near the front of the chamber.

Senior Ambassador Gideon sent his personal congratulations, along with a small congregation of League diplomatic officers, headed by Ambassador Synon of Ramora. Danna was a pleasantly surprised when she saw Magistrate Gilfo seated alongside Cullon and his family.

The dwarf flashed her a bright smile as she neared the podium where Viceroy Surazheia was waiting.

The entire High Council was in attendance, including High General Ninoy, Tutunjan's replacement. The news of Oudhia's treason had reached the public frequencies, but there had been no mention of Khaled

Tutunjan's affiliation with the band of traitors. The
general's resignation from the High Council and his
formal retirement from the Korcian Guard had been
explained away by health issues. He was currently re-
siding at his ancestral home in Saymaah, the largest of
the central provinces.

Dressed in a formal full-length robe, blue with
cloned-gold inlaid thread and a stiff, standup collar,
Danna walked down the center aisle of the Council
Chamber toward a serious-looking Viceroy Surazheia.
The gold amulet of a League Ambassador shone
clearly against the royal blue of her robe. For the first
time since getting up that morning, she was grateful
for the ceremonial garment. It hid the fact that her
knees were shaking.

After presenting her credentials to Viceroy
Surazheia, Danna stated her name, then bowed and
stepped back. The Viceroy accepted her letter of intro-
duction, proclaiming her an *ambassador extraordinaire*
with full diplomatic privileges and welcoming her to
Korcia. He presented her to the assembly as Madame
Ambassador MacFadyen of the League of Planets.
Everyone came to their feet in a burst of applause.

The following morning, Danna began her official
duties. She and Cullon decided that any assignment
the Directorate undertook would be mutually agreed
upon. There would be no favoritism shown to either
the League or the Empire. Whatever the Directorate
did, it would do to the benefit of both governments.

After reviewing a list of possible *projects,* they
decided that their first attempt at infiltrating the
Conglomerate would be on the corporate colony of
Hachyn.

It was known to be a primary supply point for illegal
arms. Oudhia had confirmed, under drug interrogation,
that the arms dealers he had supplied with Korcian
weapons used it as a base of operations.

Hachyn was also a colony undergoing change. According to Registry and PSA intelligence, the newest generation of Hachynites wanted independence from the Conglomerate cloak that had covered their home-world for more than a hundred years. There had even been an attempt on the corporate governor's life.

"We need to get someone inside their underground," Cullon said. "Helping them achieve independence will be a blow to the Conglomerate that could have reper-cussions throughout the galaxy."

Danna agreed. "Do you have someone in mind?"

Cullon smiled. "I've got the perfect man for the job."

It didn't take long for Danna to understand why Cul-lon had selected Aedon Rawn for recruitment. He was the best pilot in the Korcian fleet, and if there was one thing illegal arm dealers coveted it was a pilot who could outmaneuver a Korcian patrol cruiser. Aedon Rawn was that man.

"Do you think he'll agree?" she asked. "We're not talking about a short assignment. It could take him months, even years, to gain the trust of an arms dealer."

"Oh, he'll agree," Cullon said confidentially. "In fact, he'll probably volunteer. He hates the Conglom-erate more than most."

"Why?"

"He was married once. They had a child—a daugh-ter who was killed along with her mother when a trans-port ship was attacked by Conglomerate pirates. Gun runners. There wasn't enough proof for the Empire to intervene militarily on Hachyn, so the incident was of-ficially labeled an accident, but Rawn knows the truth. Trust me, he'll jump at the chance to make things right."

"Revenge," Danna said sadly. "There's an old quote, something about 'doing the right deed for the wrong reason.' "

"Not revenge. Justice. We need someone we can trust to get the job done. Rawn will. He doesn't think of himself as a hero, but he's one hell of a soldier. General Caliphn has been trying to recruit him for Enforcement, but Rawn likes flying too much to give up the Fleet. It's all he's got left."

"What about his emotional stability?" Danna had to ask. "Can he be trusted to keep things in perspective if he gets close to the people who caused the death of his wife and child?"

"Aedon Rawn is a professional soldier, and the best pilot in the Fleet. He'll keep his cool when things get tight."

"Okay. I trust your opinion. Let's introduce ourselves."

"I'll make the arrangements," Cullon said.

With their initial Directorate assignment chosen and their first agent selected, Danna told Cullon that she'd also hired the first member of her embassy staff. He was surprised to find out that it was his sister, Jalyn.

"I need a personal assistant, someone who speaks the language and who's familiar with Korcian customs." Danna told him. "Jalyn's well-educated, enthusiastic, and her smile is perfect for the diplomatic circuit. Best of all, she won't be suspicious when a certain Korcian colonel spends the night in the bed of the League's newest ambassador."

Cullon smiled as he pulled her into his arms. "When you put it that way . . ."

Since she was being kissed, Danna had to smile on the inside. Once, when she'd first met Cullon, she'd thought that their chosen careers and differing cultures would keep them apart. She'd been wrong. They were a perfect match.